SUFFR... ...SALLY

	DATE DUE		

For Sarah Nairn Lee Redekop

SUFFRAGETTE SALLY

Gertrude Colmore

edited by Alison Lee

broadview editions

Library and Archives Canada Cataloguing in Publication

Colmore, G. (Gertrude), d. 1926
    Suffragette Sally / Gertrude Colmore ; edited by Alison Lee.

(Broadview editions)
Includes bibliographical references.
ISBN 978-1-55111-474-3

    1. Women—Suffrage—Great Britain—Fiction. I. Lee, Alison, 1957-
II. Title. III. Series.

PR6005.O368S9 2007   823'.912   C2007-902172-7

Broadview Editions

The Broadview Editions series represents the ever-changing canon of literature in English by bringing together texts long regarded as classics with valuable lesser-known works.

Advisory editor for this volume: Jennie Rubio

Broadview Press is an independent, international publishing house, incorporated in 1985. Broadview believes in shared ownership, both with its employees and with the general public; since the year 2000 Broadview shares have traded publicly on the Toronto Venture Exchange under the symbol BDP.

We welcome comments and suggestions regarding any aspect of our publications—please feel free to contact us at the addresses below or at broadview@broadviewpress.com.

North America	Post Office Box 1243, Peterborough, Ontario, Canada K9J 7H5 3576 California Road, Post Office Box 1015, Orchard Park, NY, USA 14127 Tel: (705) 743-8990; Fax: (705) 743-8353 email: customerservice@broadviewpress.com
UK, Ireland, and continental Europe	NBN International, Estover Road, Plymouth, UK PL6 7PY Tel: 44 (0) 1752 202300; Fax: 44 (0) 1752 202330 email: enquiries@nbninternational.com
Australia and New Zealand	UNIREPS, University of New South Wales Sydney, NSW, 2052 Australia Tel: 61 2 9664 0999; Fax: 61 2 9664 5420 email: info.press@unsw.edu.au

www.broadviewpress.com

Broadview Press acknowledges the financial support of the Government of Canada through the Book Publishing Industry Development Program (BPIDP) for our publishing activities.

PRINTED IN CANADA

This book is printed on paper containing 100% post-consumer fibre.

Contents

Acknowledgements

The primary research for this edition could not have been completed without a grant from the Social Sciences and Humanities Research Council of Canada. In the course of that research, I have been privileged to work with helpful and knowledgeable staff at The Women's Library (formerly The Fawcett Library) and the British Library. David Doughan, the now retired Reference Librarian at the Fawcett, was especially generous with his astounding knowledge of Women's Suffrage.

For their editorial and historical assistance, and especially for many hours spent searching microfilms and fiches for arcane references, I am indebted to Leanne Evans, Barb Bruce, and James Purkis. I would particularly like to thank Donald S. Hair for the inspiration to take on this project, and Ernest Redekop and Maria DiCenzo for sage advice throughout. It has been a great pleasure to work with Leonard Conolly (who defines the term perspicacious) and Jennie Rubio at Broadview Press, whose interventions have immeasurably improved the text.

Introduction

Suffrage and History

By the time Gertrude Colmore's novel *Suffragette Sally* was published in 1911, women in England had been actively campaigning for the vote for almost fifty years. In 1918, a select group of women over the age of thirty—who were also were also householders, wives of householders, occupiers of property with a £5 annual value, or university graduates—were granted suffrage; but it was not until 1928 that the full franchise was granted to women on the same terms as men. The debates presented in the novel, like those which raged in the newspapers and on platforms, show how the right to vote extended in significance far beyond marking a ballot. In "The Importance of the Vote," Emmeline Pankhurst, leader of the Women's Social and Political Union (WSPU), describes it as "first of all, a symbol, secondly, a safeguard, and thirdly, an instrument. It is a symbol of freedom, a symbol of citizenship, a symbol of liberty. It is a safeguard of all those liberties which it symbolises. And in the later days it has come to be regarded more than anything else as an instrument, something with which you can get a great many more things than our forefathers who fought for the vote ever realised as possible to get with it" (31).

One of those "many more things" was a challenge to the social conventions governing gender roles, though in terms that may seem surprisingly conservative to latter-day feminists. Suffrage organisations were not asking for the vote for all women, but making an expedient demand that sex should cease to be a disqualification for the franchise, and that women should have the vote on the same terms as it was or might be granted to men. As of 1884, voting rights were extended to those men over the age of twenty-one who owned or occupied land or property with an annual value of not less than £10 (Heaton, 1885, 273). Not all men could vote, and suffragists realised that demanding the vote for all women would meet with even more resistance than did their request for a limited franchise.[1] Nevertheless, the idea that women might in any way encroach on the male preserve of political power roused a sustained opposition that revealed the prejudices and "exacerbat[ed] the sexual divisions upon which Edwardian society was based" (Purvis, 2000, 137). The leader of the National Union of Women's Suffrage Societies (NUWSS), Millicent Garrett Fawcett, writes that the anti-suffrage slogan, "Men are Men and Women are Women," speaks to the anti-suffrage division of the sexes into distinct and separate spheres. They unquestioningly assume, Fawcett argues, that this division is ordained by Nature, "'the first and greatest of anti-suffragists'" (1909, 17). An anti-suffrage speaker in *Suffragette Sally* opposes giving votes to women "because they are not men" (151) and, though it is a simple way of putting a complex issue, this pronouncement underlines many of the anti-suffrage arguments. Writing in the *Anti-Suffrage Review* in 1910, Helen Hester Colvill neatly summarises those attributes that contribute to good government—attributes which are said to be absent in women:

... man will point out that woman cannot reason, and that politics, for example, must be guided by reason; that woman is emotional, and that government by emotion quickly degenerates into injustice; that woman, however excellent as a student, is lacking in genius, in imagination, in initiative, in the power of forming abstract ideas, and—he will add—in judgement, which, after all is but a faculty for putting two and two together. On all these points, I fear, man has only to appeal to history and science to prove his case. He will show easily that ever since the world has been ruled by intellect, woman has taken second place. He will explain that she has not the strength

---

1   It is important to emphasise that the aim of most suffrage societies was "to secure for women the Parliamentary vote as it is or may be granted to men." This demand created some contradictions as, for example, when in March 1909, Geoffrey Howard proposed a Bill to give Manhood and Womanhood Suffrage based on a three-month residential qualification, he was denounced as a traitor to the Cause by all major suffrage organisations. Sylvia Pankhurst writes: "Again was witnessed the strange spectacle of the suffrage societies passionately struggling for the enfranchisement of their sex, but, with equal insistence, limiting the demand to a small minority" (1931, 302). Specifically, the WSPU was asking for a removal of sex disqualification, and wanted the government to "carry into law a special and separate measure for the enfranchisement of those women who possess the qualifications entitling men to vote" (C. Pankhurst, *Votes for Women*, 12 March 1909, 428).

of body or of mind to get to the front place; and that where, in isolated instances, she has got near the front, it has been almost invariably with detriment to her success as a mother and wife. (5)

It is decidedly odd that exactly those deficits which render woman unfit for public service supposedly make her an ideal wife and mother. Indeed, the physiological impact of menstruation, childbearing, and menopause were thought to precipitate psychological effects that were incompatible with voting. Physician Almroth Wright, author of *The Unexpurgated Case against Woman Suffrage* (Appendix B), states emphatically that "no doctor can ever lose sight of the fact that the mind of a woman is always threatened with danger from the reverberations of her physiological emergencies" (320). In the home, however, women are superior to men in their spirituality, morality, and ability "to discern wisdom and truth by some mysterious gift of intuition" (Colvill, 4–5). Admitting women to the vote would not only sully those gifts, but according to Mary Augusta Ward, one of the founders of the National League for Opposing Woman Suffrage, would increase "the violent and excitable element in politics," and arouse a "sex feeling and sex antagonism" which would render "the calm and practical discussion of great questions impossible" (1). Worst of all, women entering politics might neglect those duties as wives and mothers which define the woman's special sphere and, through the exercise of which, women have "an influence more profound than men can ever attain to. In the rearing and education of children, they shape the minds and mould the moral nature of each generation" (*Anti-Suffrage Handbook*, 63).

Both pro- and anti-suffragists focussed many of their arguments on what would happen to the home, woman's place in it, and all of its concomitant parts and values, if women were to focus their attention on the political world. Suffragists did not refuse the essentialism of the anti-suffrage positions, but argued instead that the differences between men and women were precisely *why* women should have the vote. Fawcett does not deny that "the point of view, the experience of life, the sphere of activity of women differ in many important respects from those of men," but she does conclude that "these very facts are among the strongest and most irrefutable of the reasons for urging that no representative system is complete or truly national which entirely leaves out the representation of women"

(1909, 21). According to Emmeline Pankhurst, many politicians argued that "'rearing and training of children ... are the things that interest women. Politics have nothing to do with these things, and therefore politics do not concern women.'" Emmeline Pankhurst responded that laws decide "how women are to live in marriage, how their children are to be trained and educated, and what the future of their children is to be" (33). And in none of these areas of concern to women's domestic sphere, Pankhurst argues, do women have the right to contribute to those laws. For Fawcett, those characteristics which distinguish the domestic sphere are precisely those necessary to reform politics: "Do not give up one jot or tittle of your womanliness, your love of children, your care for the sick, your gentleness, your self-control, your obedience to conscience and duty, for all these things are terribly wanted in politics" (nd., 3). Because the very act of asking for the vote brought women out of the home and into conflict, ideologically and sometimes physically, it became important to maintain the public trappings of a domestic sphere configured in these essential terms.

Women who wanted the vote ran the risk of public ridicule, since it appeared to many who opposed it that they had forsaken those qualities which made them women. Consequently, suffrage activists were represented in anti-suffrage media as women who had either abandoned their femininity or who had forgotten it in their attempts to ape men. In such media, a woman who wanted to vote was caricatured as gaunt and unattractive, dressed in masculine clothing, frequently shrieking and definitely not—as Mr. Bilkes in the novel puts it—"up in the nursery looking after her children, more especially the baby; down in the kitchen, seeing to her husband's dinner" (61). In trying to counter these caricatures, many suffrage organisations adopted a preference for what Cicely Hamilton calls "the conventional feminine": "All suggestion of the masculine was carefully avoided, and the outfit of a militant setting forth to smash windows would probably include a picture hat" (75). In 1910, the Women's Freedom League ran a photographic competition in *The Vote* showing prominent members, some of whom had been jailed recently for suffrage activities, performing such domestic tasks as making jam or cleaning the stove. These were to provide "an object lesson to the male 'anti' who so frequently requests us to 'go home and do the washing,' 'mind the baby,' or 'darn the husband's socks.'" A prize of a guinea was offered "for the best photograph showing Suffragettes doing these and various other domestic duties" (*The Vote*, 26 March 1910, 261). *Suffragette Sally* draws attention to this construction of womanliness in scenes where women who are attractive, feminine, articulate, and logical, to someone's great shock, turn out to be suffrage activists. "It was evidently possible," thinks Edith Carstairs, "to be a Suffragette and yet retain qualities between which and Suffragettes wide gulfs were supposed to yawn" (79). Despite this expedient use of domesticity as reassurance to those both pro- and anti-suffrage, many women hoped the vote would allow them a greater sphere of influence. They argued that the vote would provide the means to improve all of those "domestic" areas with which male politicians seemed, if not unconcerned, then perhaps inexpert: laws concerning marriage, divorce, inheritance, child rearing, and education. In addition, they wished to cure such social ills as trivial sentences for criminal (indecent) assault, the white slave trade, prostitution, poverty and "sweated" labour (the exploitative practice of paying workers meager wages for long hours of work, often from home). Not surprisingly, some thought such idealism hopelessly utopian, and insisted that social ills could be solved by means less radical than, as Mary Augusta Ward put it, "the rash and ruinous experiment of the Parliamentary vote for women" (2). Almost one hundred years after the publication of *Suffragette Sally*, we know that the vote is not the glorious panacea suffragists hoped for, and that the movement's challenge to convention did not erase inequality. In the "Author's Note" at the end of the novel, Colmore writes: "this is a story which cannot be finished now" (290). While the suffrage movement brought the issue of women's rights more vehemently before the public than ever before, the story of women's rights has not yet reached its conclusion.

Suffrage, Words and Deeds

Suffragette Sally represents approximately two years immediately preceding its publication, and includes particularly volatile moments in the suffrage campaign during which increasing numbers of women went to prison for their protests, many of whom began hunger strikes and were, as a result, forcibly fed. The election of the Liberal Party in 1905 had offered a certain degree of hope to the suffrage movement, since the Party included a significant number of members, including Prime Minister Campbell-Bannerman, who professed sympathy with the cause. Nevertheless, after years of meetings, resolutions, and petitions organised by both men and women, the government remained disinclined to amend the Representation of the People Act of 1884 in order to give women the vote. Campbell-Bannerman was succeeded in 1909 by Herbert Henry Asquith who professed no sympathy whatsoever to women's suffrage; indeed, Millicent Garrett Fawcett called him "our greatest enemy" (1924, 201).[1] This sort of recalcitrance lay at the root of one of the divides within the suffrage movement: a split between those who continued to pursue reform through procedural channels—the constitutionalists, or suffrag*ists* (who organised primarily under the banner of the National Union of Women's Suffrage Societies [NUWSS])—and those who would come to be known as the militants, or suffrag*ettes*. The term "suffragette" was coined by the *Daily Mail* in 1906 as a term of derision; however, Sylvia Pankhurst writes that the name was "happily adopted" because it implied not just that women wanted the vote but that "'the Suffrag*ettes* [hardening the 'g'] they mean to get it'" (1931, 63, emphasis added). Historian Sandra Stanley Holton argues that the constitutional/militant division is imprecise since many women belonged to suffrage societies that represented one or the other simultaneously. Holton explains that many suffrage activists did not see these "two approaches to campaigning as either mutually exclusive or at odds with one another" (1986, 4).[2] I have maintained the division here, however, because Colmore represents the militant and constitutionalist approaches as oppositional, if not antagonistic. For the suffragettes, patience and polite arguments were not bringing

---

1 Despite a number of Cabinet ministers who were against enfranchising women on any terms (Asquith among them), pro-suffrage Liberal ministers held a clear majority in the Cabinet (Searle, 110). Searle argues that the pro-suffrage majority could have imposed their will on the antis, "if only they could have agreed on how best to proceed" (110). Some Liberal ministers were afraid that giving votes to women would be giving votes to the Conservative Party. Some, too, were conscious that women were a majority in the populace, and were concerned lest enfranchised women, voting as a block, impose their will on government policies. The 1910 Conciliation Bill (see Appendix D) passed two readings by a majority, but Churchill, for example, voted against it because it was "anti-democratic" (Rosen, 137). Despite professions of support for the principle of women's suffrage, Liberal ministers seemed to find numerous ways of derailing any initiative designed to grant it.

2 See also Mayhall, 1994, 340–71; 2003.

reform fast enough, and, frustrated by the slow progress of constitutional methods, the militants decided to take more radical forms
of public action. They felt, as Martha Vicinus notes, that "The time
had come to present the women's political Cause before the public
with methods that had never previously been exploited by women"
(250).

Founded in 1903 by Christabel and Emmeline Pankhurst, the
Women's Social and Political Union was only one of many suffrage
organisations, but its prominent turn to public protest quickly made
it the most visible. In 1905, Christabel Pankhurst and Annie Kenney
took what was to become known as the first militant action. At a
meeting in the Manchester Free Trade Hall, they put to Sir Edward
Grey the question of whether the Liberal Government, if elected,
would give working women the vote. Receiving no reply, they
continued to demand an answer until they were forcibly removed
from the Hall. Outside, they attempted to address the crowd and
Christabel spat at a policeman. They were arrested for obstruction
and assault. Following this example, suffragettes engaged in a range
of actions which included heckling members of the government
at political meetings and by-elections, sending deputations to the
Prime Minister, and participating in marches and demonstrations.
While none of these methods might now seem disturbing or even
especially unruly, they went well beyond the boundaries of decorous
Edwardian femininity. It is worth pointing out, however, that as the
campaign continued, unruly actions increased. Beginning at the end
of 1911, the protests became more violent, culminating in an organised destruction of property. By 1913, suffragettes were cutting tel-
ephone and telegraph wires, smashing windows, and setting fire to
empty buildings—including a partially completed house being built
for Lloyd George. The "guerillists," as Christabel Pankhurst called
them, set pillar (mail) boxes ablaze, carved slogans such as "No Votes,
No Golf" into golf greens, and slashed works of art, the most famous
of which is the Velasquez *Rokeby Venus* in the National Gallery.[1]
Pursuing an entirely "unfeminine" role in the public sphere, the suffragettes were treated with derision and, as public protests became
more heated, were subject to physical violence and incarceration. In

---

[1]   See Rosen, 189–202, 214–45; C. Pankhurst, 232–41; S. Pankhurst, 1931, 393–415; Tickner,
132–38.

other words, women who dared publicly to manifest their desire for the vote, were understood, according to baldly contradictory logic, as *hysterical, unsexed,* and *unwomanly*—designations that authorised the physical violence to which they became increasingly subject. Author Laurence Housman, who helped to found the Men's League for Women's Suffrage, points out that adjectives such as "screaming," "hysterical," and "unreasonable" were, in the school of thought which applied them to militant action, "regarded as essentially and almost exclusively feminine. Suffragists, therefore, are accused, almost in the same breath, both of deserting and of accentuating the characteristics of their sex" (229).

Epithets such as these were most often hurled at the members of the WSPU, and it is this organisation and the challenges it posed to the normative place of women within the Edwardian public sphere, on which Colmore focuses in this novel. Any novel that deals so approvingly with the militant actions of the WSPU must contend, however, with the apparent paradox of representing the society whose principles are succinctly contained in the motto "Deeds not Words." Indeed, given Colmore's allegiance to the WSPU, it is perhaps telling that the famous motto is reproduced nowhere in the text. If "Deeds Not Words" literally encapsulates the WSPU's rejection of interminable and fruitless parliamentary debate in favour of direct action, the motto also emphatically underlines the failure of language in the public sphere. It also presents an imperative that might give pause to someone like Colmore, for whom language was an indispensable part of her contribution to the militant cause. A prolific novelist, short-story writer, and poet whose writings address a range of social concerns, Colmore was obviously committed to the power of words within a militant context.

Colmore's response to the paradox presented by the WSPU motto presents a useful means of approaching two of the novel's broadest concerns. On the one hand, it suggests the tension between representation and history ("words" and "deeds"), while, on the other, it articulates for Colmore the challenge to overcome that tension by harnessing the rhetorical power of language (words which produce deeds). In reading *Suffragette Sally*, then, we must think about how and why the text seeks to represent the events occurring at a certain moment in the history of the suffrage movement; we must also consider the ways in which Colmore uses a particular range of "words"—the language of fiction—to persuade her readers to support, or even participate in, the movement's militant deeds. Indeed, in approaching the latter half of Colmore's project, we may also wish to consider the different sorts of persuasive deeds this novel performs in relation to different readerships. Does the novel produce different rhetorical effects for readers who are unfamiliar with and uncommitted to the movement than it does for those readers whose sympathy and commitment the movement had already won?

In this sense, *Suffragette Sally* returns to issues that Colmore had raised in her 1910 novel, *The Crimson Gate*. Addressing the dual focus of her fictional project, the narrator suggests that

> horrors never yet converted any man or woman to an attitude of mercy.... Those who are ready to help in the crusade against cruelty will hear a still, small voice which speaks to the inner ear; and, if it speaks not, no storm from without will stir them. Truths may be told, facts brought home to them, but having eyes they see not, and having ears they hear not; nor can, till they reach a certain stage upon the pathway of perception. (128)

While knowledge of the "horrors" of suffrage history is a first step, those facts alone remain inconsequential in the absence of the persuasive force—that "still, small voice"—which allows the objective "storms" of history to produce the subjective transformations necessary to "stir" the individual into action. Clearly, *Suffragette Sally* spoke to those already travelling upon the path, but it equally, and perhaps more importantly, sought to rouse the "still, small voice" of those who were indifferent or antagonistic to the movement's goals.

It would be difficult to overestimate the novel's simple didactic function, given that it expends considerable energy merely in educating the reader about the history of the suffrage movement. Though *Suffragette Sally* is a work of fiction, many of its characters are only slightly disguised or renamed celebrities of the suffrage movement. Many of its scenes depict historical events in great detail, drawing especially—and sometimes very closely—on reports in *Votes for Women*, the newspaper published by the WSPU (see, for example, Appendix C.1). For some contemporary reviewers, the novel produced the shock of familiar events reconfigured. A writer in *The*

Vote comments that certain scenes seem "almost too realistic, and if the reader did not know that they are in every case drawn from actual occurrences, he would be tempted to ask, 'Can these things be?'" (Appendix E.5). A reviewer in *Votes for Women* concurs: "The general public will probably say that this book is exaggerated—that such scenes as are depicted could not have happened in civilised England. But the women in this movement know that the incidents are only too real, that the scenes are only too familiar, and knowing, they thank Miss Colmore for what she has done" (Appendix E.2). At the time the novel was published in 1911, some of the events detailed in it were barely three months past, and the almost documentary aspect of the novel suggests that the deeds of history, to a very large degree, are capable of speaking for themselves. The power of fiction here lies not in its capacity to depart from reality, but in its attention to those aspects of reality which have themselves the power to shock the reader. And as the reviewers suggest, the power of these events lies not merely in their shock value, but in the moral consequences of the shock they deliver: an unavoidable outrage at the disjunction between these events and the moral foundation of a British civilisation in which such events are unthinkable. In this sense, the novel works both to educate the ignorant, and to recontextualise historical events of which many were already aware, but which, perhaps, had been presented in such a way as to obscure the moral imperative they articulated. In this respect, the documentary character of the novel falls within a fairly classic realist model, and seeks to represent a recognisable (though largely unfamiliar) social reality with an eye to producing readerly identifications that can create a new "fellow feeling."

And yet to see the novel primarily as a documentary fiction would be to underestimate its resources. The novel makes a case for the power of fiction as being somehow distinct from the journalistic writing upon which it sometimes draws so heavily. This power, it suggests, lies in the rhetorical effects it can produce within readers who are committed, indifferent, or antagonistic to the suffrage movement—a power that lies in the act of storytelling itself. Consider, for example, Colmore's representation of one of the most emotionally charged of the protests: the hunger strike. In June 1909, Marion Wallace-Dunlop was arrested for stencilling "it is the right of the subject to petition the King, and all commitments and prosecutions for such petitioning are illegal" in the House of Commons on the walls of St. Stephen's Hall. She was sentenced to one month in prison but, having been refused political prisoner status—and many in the WSPU felt they should be treated as political prisoners—became the first suffragette to adopt the hunger strike.[1] She fasted for ninety-one hours after which she was freed and, over the next few months, thirty-seven suffragette prisoners followed her example (Rosen, 123). Their actions gave fuel to opponents' convictions of militant hysteria but, according to Sylvia Pankhurst, gave suffragettes the hope that "the way had been found to the vote itself" (1931, 308). The government responded by instituting a policy of forcible feeding, or "hospital treatment," on the grounds of preventing suicide by starvation (*House of Commons Debates*, 5th series, vol. 11 [27 September 1909], cols. 923–25). The WSPU, appalled by such gross bodily violation, sought the opinions of medical experts on the dangers and the horrors of the procedure, and doctors wrote letters of protest to the mainstream press using phrases such as "revolting torture," "violence and brutality," and "official cruelty" (*Votes for Women*, 1 October 1909, 1–2).

Colmore's account of the procedure in the chapter "Contrasts" is both reassuringly clinical and alarmingly intimate. As opposed to the usual first-person testimony of the kind that appeared in *Votes for Women*, Colmore's version is third-person and impersonal. The woman waiting in prison to be force-fed is not only anonymous, her body parts are not even described with personal pronouns. "The teeth," "the jaws," "the throat," and "the stomach" are the subjects of this operation, possibly because the woman is so depersonalised by those performing the procedure, and perhaps because she is the

---

1   By the Prison Act of 1898, prisoners could be placed in one of three divisions. The first division was for those who had committed contempt of court or sedition. They were allowed the privileges of wearing their own clothes, having access to books and newspapers, continuing to work and draw a salary, having limited rights to visitors, sending and receiving a letter once every two weeks, and buying food and wine to be brought in. These privileges were not extended to second and third division prisoners who had to wear prison clothes and eat prison food, were kept in solitary confinement apart from one hour each day, were required to do prison labour such as sewing, and could receive one letter and have one visit after the first four weeks of their sentence. The distinction between second and third divisions seems to have been made on the basis of the prisoner's character. Those who were considered respectable were allocated to the second division; those who were not, to the third (Crawford, 569).

figure who stands in for all those women who were forced to undergo it. What is so striking about the narrative in this scene is that the reader begins as an observer of the woman but, as the scene continues, the distance between the woman and the reader is diminished. We are told that the hunger strike dims the vision, so the woman listens for the doctors and wardresses approaching the door and then opening it. When they arrive, she can only see their hands. From their hands, we move to her mouth where the steel gag is inserted, and then we follow the feeding tube down her throat, into her stomach and back up again as her stomach resists the food. Reducing the safety of the narrative distance implied by the third-person, Colmore puts the reader in the position of both violator and violated. This disturbing intimacy forces the reader to confront the violence of the force-feeding. The language describing the brutal isolating force of the woman's pain creates an empathic community of readers; out of the victim's humiliating isolation arises a powerful respect for her martyrdom.

Fictive power is thematised throughout the novel, not least of all in relation to Lady Henry Hill (a fictionalisation of prominent suffragette Lady Constance Lytton), whose charismatic leadership seems largely bound up with the kind of narrative fluency that speaks to the "still, small voice" in her audience. An excellent example of Geraldine Hill's persuasive power—at once disarmingly, even typically, feminine and dangerously radical—comes in relation to the sympathetic, though anti-militant suffra*gist*, Edith Carstairs. Edith's faith in the Liberal Party, bolstered by her romantic attachment to the Liberal member of Parliament Cyril Race, has convinced her that militancy has turned men against votes for women, and leads her to insist that "she was a suffra*gist*, and must show the men of England—the men who, as her mother pointed out, had the power to give or withhold the vote, and who must be propitiated therefore, and not incensed or defied—must show them that it was possible to be womanly and at the same time—determined?" (55–56). When Edith meets Geraldine, who is charming, attractive, womanly, *and* militant, she is sufficiently curious to listen to her account of how militancy began. As they walk on the beach in the morning mist, Geraldine tells the story of Christabel Pankhurst ("Christina Amherst") and Annie Kenney ("Annie Carnie") questioning Sir Edward Grey about his Party's policy on votes for working women at the Manchester Free Trade Hall. Geraldine is a narrator so skilled that she can "call up the scenes of which she [speaks]" (80), and Edith's imagination is receptive enough to see them. In narrative terms, the novel's didactic impulse often translates into scenes which purport to show rather than tell. Here, as in the rest of the novel, is a conviction that, if readers only knew the "truth" of the situation, they could not help but be sympathetic. From this point on, Edith becomes the novel's model of a receptive reader who, though initially averse to militant methods, eventually sees enough and learns enough to recognise their necessity. Geraldine's narrative technique allows Edith to hear the many voices contributing to the event, and because the scene is focalised through Edith, we see her become interpellated into the story as she begins to use a discourse she has learned from Geraldine. As the two women walk on the beach, Geraldine's voice fades, and Edith sees and hears the scenes as though they are projected on the mist. The narrator's reverential tone makes clear the immense significance of what is about to happen: it is a moment "cut on the heart of history" (80). In the Free Trade Hall, the Liberal candidates speak in "glowing words" of "fine prospects and great promises, splendid reforms" (81). The tone of the account is rousing, and might easily have appeared in a partisan newspaper. The voice is authoritative and omniscient, moving seamlessly from the whole country's expectations of a new political order, to the platform upon which those expectations are promised. Interestingly, this exalted perspective on the Liberal Party coincides exactly with Edith's, though her trust turns to doubt as the candidates persist in ignoring Annie Carnie's question. Geraldine repeats the speaker's discourse on liberty in order to point out the restrictiveness of those splendid reforms and improved conditions, and Edith picks up on the same words as she comes to observe that Annie Carnie and Christina Amherst are beaten by "the men who had cheered in praise of liberty and progress" (82). Similarly, she adopts Geraldine's metaphor for the suffrage campaign, seeing Annie Carney as "the first wave of the in-coming tide, the first to break, and be broken, on the rocks" (82). Edith's education here is partly historical, but more importantly, it is discursive: she has to hear the voices and internalise the discourse in order to understand the militants.

This first act of militancy has an almost mythic halo surrounding it, and would have been well-known to sympathisers, though

Geraldine's rendition of it differs from many accounts by focussing the action on working-class Annie Carnie rather than on middle-class Christina Amherst. In order to highlight the extent of the violence these two women suffer at the hands of Liberal supporters, Geraldine emphasises that neither women is a threat and that neither behaves hysterically. Carnie is described as "little," "slight," and so "small" that she has to stand on a chair to be seen. She has been a mill hand since the age of ten, and wishes to take back to 96,000 women cotton workers the Liberals' position on giving votes to working women. The question is never answered, and as the women persist in asking it the crowd's jubilation turns to anger and then to violence. The men in the audience strike blows that draw blood, and it takes six men to drag each woman from the Hall. As they do so, the future cabinet ministers "look on and say nothing" (83). Geraldine's rendition of this scene is designed to produce outrage at Liberal hypocrisy, and at the juxtaposition of celebrating liberty for men while denying it to women; this motif will be repeated throughout the novel. Her narrative technique, an intra-textual example of Colmore's own, attempts simultaneously to make familiar to readers those women who had routinely been represented in the Press and elsewhere as dangerously and unnaturally removed from a proper femininity (or simply as "hysterics" and "wild animals"), and to offer a critique of the language of liberty, which is itself deeply embroiled in this demonisation. As Geraldine comments later in the novel: "it is the things that are done to women, and not the things they do, which makes the part they play in this movement seem unwomanly to many people" (182).

Suffrage and Class

This episode is also important for foregrounding another of the central issues to which the novel attends: social class. In her autobiography *Unshackled* (1959), Christabel Pankhurst writes that this protest was a means of gaining publicity, specifically through the notoriety that would come from imprisonment: "now there would be an act the effect of which would remain, a protest not of word but of deed. Prison this time! Prison would mean a fact that could not fade from the record, a proof of women's political discontent" (48). She knew, she writes, that the crowd would become angry, but also that their violence proved "our question was a thrust which had touched the new Government-to-be in a vital spot" (51). Most interesting, in comparison with Geraldine's account of the protest, is Christabel's tactical use of Annie Kenney: "Annie as the working woman—for this should make the strongest appeal to Liberals—rose first" (50). Less calculatingly strategic than Pankhurst, Colmore's focus (via Geraldine) on Annie Carnie (and, by extension, on the 96,000 working women she represents), draws attention to the victimisation of working-class women in a political system that denies them votes.

Historians offer conflicting accounts of the working-class membership of the WSPU, and there is evidence that it was a source of some controversy at the time.[1] A number of factors might have contributed to this. The WSPU had had socialist and labour associations since its inception in Manchester, where it had attracted support largely from working-class women. Ties with both the Independent Labour Party (ILP) and with the working-class, radical suffragists, however, were eroded after the WSPU moved its headquarters to London in 1906 and its militancy increased. While many suffragists disagreed with the Labour advocacy for universal adult suffrage, working-class women rejected the terms upon which the WSPU was asking for the vote—"as it is or may be granted to men"—on the grounds that a property based vote would only enfranchise the wealthy, at least in the first instance. Sylvia Pankhurst, for example, writes of the resulting taunt—"Votes for Ladies"—the influence of which, "militating against real support of the suffrage movement in working class circles[,] was ever a strong undercurrent" (1931, 416). She asserts that "members of the suffrage movement, militant and non-militant, had always been largely of the middle class" (1931, 416), whereas Emmeline Pethick-Lawrence, co-editor with her husband Frederick of *Votes for Women*, describes the suffrage struggle as a moment when "women of the upper middle and working classes realised a new comradeship with each other. Neither class, nor wealth, nor education counted any more, only devotion to the common ideal" (1938, 188). Christabel Pankhurst insists that members

---

1 On the WSPU's labour affiliation and relationship to working-class women see, for example, Liddington and Norris; Rosen, 24–78; Holton, 1986; Purvis, "The Prison Experiences of the Suffragettes in Edwardian Britain," 1995, 103–33; Purvis, 2003, 85–87.

of the WSPU brooked no class distinctions, and were all members of "the aristocracy of the Suffragettes"; but she also concedes that the government is "more impressed by the demonstrations of the female bourgeoisie than of the female proletariat" (66–67). Possibly, the militant agenda of the WSPU demanded sacrifices that the "female proletariat" could not afford to make. Middle- and upper-class women might risk the censure of friends and family if they went to prison, for example, but working women risked their livelihood and that of their families.

Suffragette Sally certainly attempts to present a classless community of women, although the novel does contain moments of discord. For example, Sally first encounters the suffragette movement in a hall on Regent Street in London's West End where she has gone on her afternoon off. Those who are entering the hall are "people of all kinds and classes" (49), from "regular swells, richly dressed" (49), to those like Sally who have come "to have a look at the splendid, fashionable shops" (49). Sally is persuaded into the meeting by someone whose language identifies the speaker's working-class background: "Ain't yer never 'eerd 'er? Come along in along of me" (49)—but though her guide is a member of her own class, Sally recognises that the speakers on the platform are different: "fine ladies and gentlemen," including "the beautiful lady" (50), Lady Henry Hill, whose words awaken "the bird in her breast" (51). Further differences between Sally and the well-dressed speakers are underlined by the geographical spaces they inhabit in the city: Lady Hill in Mayfair and Sally in the Bilkses' north London home, where her window looks not only "on to a space of roofs, grey, smoke-begrimed, and dreary in their sameness" (49), but on to the upper windows of Holloway prison.

In "The Politics of a Moral Crusade," Shirley Peterson argues that the novel "mutes the difference between working-class women and their upper-class sisters" because it wishes to "shape the ideology of the working-class women to that of the middle and upper classes" (109). Both Edith and Geraldine, for example, claim that class distinctions fall away in the movement, but are able to do so only because each one speaks from a position of class privilege. Sally, though she delights in the thought that she and Geraldine, "Lady 'Ennery 'Ill," might stand together in the fight for all women, is acutely aware of the differences between herself and "them ladies" (155), and humbly grateful that they should allow her to stand with them. Sally's Cockney accent is typographically distinct from that of characters from other classes. Whether or not Colmore's representation is accurate or closer to parody, the language difference highlights differences between Sally and other characters, foregrounding her class in every word she utters. As a working-class woman, Sally is treated with brutality while she is in prison, and Colmore represents her abuse at the hands of prison officials in grim detail. Sally loses her life because she has been so abused, but also because she has abided by militant tactics. In this context, Peterson suggests that Colmore's focus on Sally-as-martyr "insinuates the working-class woman's expendability in the larger scheme of women's struggle for political identity" (111). But this is too simple. Sally's death is the emotional high point of the novel because she makes the greatest sacrifice and she becomes, of course, a symbol of all that is wrong with a world in which women have no power. It is also the occasion for Colmore to gesture to the American Civil War as another battle against injustice, and so Sally's death is immediately succeeded by lines from the stirring "Battle Hymn of the Republic." A cynical reading might indeed mention that Sally is the most disposable character because she has the least influence—such a reading might include a gibe about cheap sentimentalism. Sally is not, however, a minor character, and the title would suggest that the novel foregrounds *her* story, not those of Geraldine or Edith. Sally's death is poignant because she has suffered acutely, yet still believes passionately in the aims and the justice of the movement; and it is this movement to which, after all, the novel is trying to persuade its readers—some of whom may have led lives similar to Sally's. Sentiment is a powerful tool, especially when it is roused by events that "really" happened. Most importantly, though, Sally has been treated as she has precisely because she is a working-class woman and, as such, she has no means to combat the injustices she encounters. She gives up her job, her romance, and eventually her life for the cause, but one might wonder to what extent her sacrifice highlights less her expendability than it does the two-fold liabilities of sex and class. In this way the novel highlights how working-class women are victims of greater abuse than are their bourgeois sisters and are therefore even more in need of the vote.

Colmore pursues this interrogation of class issues within the suffrage movement in terms of her representation of the historical figure of Lady Constance Lytton (Appendix C). Of particular significance in this context are Lady Lytton's (and Geraldine's) efforts to bring differential, class-based prison practices to light. In general terms, Colmore has Geraldine herself recognise the extent to which her persuasive power is bound up with her class status. As an educated, titled woman, she is able to articulate the need for reform and "compel a hearing" (124). Lady Geraldine is, like the historical Lady Constance, arrested for throwing a stone at a government minister's car. While other suffragette prisoners are hunger-striking and being forcibly fed, Geraldine is examined by three doctors who determine that her heart is too weak to stand this procedure. She is released after a few days, horrified that her title has accorded her special treatment. In response, she disguises herself as a working-class woman, Anne Heeley, and is again arrested. Unlike Geraldine Hill, Anne Heeley is given no medical examination before she is forcibly-fed; and even when she is so seriously ill that the doctor does examine her heart, the heart he examines is that of a working woman and is pronounced sound. Geraldine's social standing helps to publicise her experiences, though not to convince the authorities that they are true. Ironically, her class does not trump her sex, and officials repudiate her story: "officialdom consisted entirely of men, and was consequently impartial, unprejudiced, infallible; whereas Lady Henry was a woman and necessarily hysterical" (260).

Without dismissing the extent to which the novel may sometimes seem to be confined by the bourgeois ideology that Peterson sees as dominating the suffrage movement, one might also point to a number of important ways in which it chafes against those ideological limits by ensuring that social class is always visible. An interesting addendum to this concern is Colmore's treatment of the figures of Emmeline and Christabel Pankhurst. Given that the Pankhursts were not only central to the WSPU, but were frequently the objects of ecstatic encomia within the literature of the movement (Appendix C.4), it is noticeable that in *Suffragette Sally* they are very much in the background. "Mrs. Amherst" (Emmeline Pankhurst) appears in two chapters—once on a deputation and once in the dock at Bow Street Police Station—but these representations, respectful though they are, are almost verbatim from reports in *Votes for Women* to which Colmore adds little by way of comment. This is remarkable by comparison to the laudatory portrait she paints of Charlotte Despard, president of the Women's Freedom League, whose fictional character addresses Sally in the chapter "A Bundle of Papers."[1] Despard was a wealthy widow who used her money to "embark on a career of practical socialism" (Crawford, 166). She opened a welfare clinic for children, was a Poor-Law guardian, and worked to "improve the social and economic position of ... impoverished women" (166). Like Colmore, she belonged to the Theosophical Society, a spiritual and philosophical movement which claimed to be a revival of an ancient-wisdom religion. Both were supporters of animal welfare through groups such as the anti-vivisectionist National Canine Defence League (Kean, 1998, 138). Despard was also a member of the International Labour Party, with which the Women's Freedom League maintained ties. In the novel, she appears only once, but the portrait is so affectionate and so reverent that we can only assume Colmore's respect for Despard's social activism is pronounced. In both the movement itself and in Colmore's novel, the vote is proclaimed as a means to improve the lives of disadvantaged women. Colmore constantly places this issue before her readers.

Suffrage, Readers and Community

There is little documentary evidence of who read *Suffragette Sally*. The WSPU must have been favourably disposed, however, since the novel was reviewed and advertised in *Votes for Women* and sold—with a cover in the WSPU colours of purple, white, and green—by the WSPU Woman's Press. For those who were opposed to women's suffrage, especially to militancy, the novel counters the stereotype of militant hysteria with rational argument and sympathetic characters. For those already converted, *Suffragette Sally*, like *Votes for Women*, must have created a sense of solidarity, especially among those women who had participated in the most strenuous of militant activities. If one of the novel's aims is to encourage readers to translate words into deeds—that is, to take action in support of the

---

1   Despard had been a member of the WSPU until 1907 when a disagreement over governance of the organisation caused a split. Despard was among those who advocated for a democratic constitution, whereas the Pankhursts were concerned that such a structure would be detrimental to their militant operations (Crawford, 720). Those women who left the WSPU formed the Women's Freedom League (WFL).

movement—then it is worth considering an example of how it creates an activist community that will work for a common cause.

As Martha Vicinus and others have pointed out, the suffrage movement was figured very much as a spiritual crusade.[1] Toward the end of the novel, Sally Simmonds says that being a suffragette is "religion and politics; and women's place-is-the-'ome all in one. For religion's 'elpin' them as is put upon; an' that's wot we do. An politics is fightin' agin the Government an' that's wot we do.... An' women's-place-is-the-'ome, is lookin' after children and widders an' such like; an' that's wot we want to do if they'd only let us 'ave a look in" (276). Colmore uses two different yokings of religion and politics in the novel. First, she aligns the militant movement specifically with Jesus' instructions to His disciples in Matthew 10, as well as linking the martyrdom of suffragettes through hunger-striking and forcible feeding to the Crucifixion. Second, she characterises institutionalised religion as a tool of reactionary politics. Sally's representation of what it is to be a suffragette puts the movement within the context of both militancy and charity, and her recognition that charity is achieved by militancy comes also to Edith and Geraldine. The ethics of violence are widely discussed, and violent actions are graphically described (particularly forcible feeding and other abuses in prison), as well as the violence suffragettes sometimes suffered in the streets while on deputations to the Prime Minister. Only the suggestion that this bodily sacrifice was martyrdom for a higher cause can explain the fervour with which women faced the tortures that were inflicted on them. Colmore constructs martyrdom as a method of justifying the moral rightness and especially the militancy of the Cause, which she represents through images of radical Christianity. Organised, hierarchical religion gets short shrift in the novel in the person of Edith's Uncle Beauchamp Leigh, "one of those clergymen" who "shrink away from anything which is of the essence of the faith which they profess. He thought himself a devoted Christian, but would have been scandalised had he been transported back nineteen hundred years and asked to shake hands with the Nazarene, uncrowned as yet by centuries of recognition. He was for Church and State and an increased Navy" (77). The suffragettes in the novel, however, identify

---

1   See Vicinus, 247–80; Morley and Stanley; Mulvey-Roberts, 159–80; Hartman, 35–50.

precisely with the stigmata and sacrifice of the Nazarene whose actual presence would have horrified Uncle Beauchamp. More specifically, Colmore deliberately and carefully places the suffragette cause within a very specific messianic context—Jesus' instructions to his disciples in Matthew 10—and within the redemptive context of the Crucifixion.

One does not have to travel very far through the pages of *Votes for Women* to encounter religious, even apocalyptic language, and Colmore's biblical imagery echoes the spiritual imperative of the suffrage movement. It is important to note, however, that Colmore was, as many suffrage supporters were, a member of the Theosophical Society, whose philosophical and spiritual underpinnings may not have been as familiar to general readers as were those of Christianity (though the two are not mutually exclusive). Charlotte Despard, indeed, saw Theosophy as "the reconciler of all the religions of the world" (47). The attraction of Theosophy for suffrage activists may have been in its principle of equality, as Despard explains: "our first object is to form a nucleus of the universal brotherhood without distinction of race, creed, sex, caste or colour" (7). Colmore's spirituality, according to Joy Dixon, is articulated in the novel through the character of Rachel Cullen, who describes the suffrage movement as part of an evolutionary force: "the spirit [Colmore] argued, saw more clearly than the physical eye, and in every conflict between women's spirituality and men's materialism ... the material victory might go to the men, but the spiritual victory belonged to the women" (202). Colmore's critique of Uncle Beauchamp's brand of Christianity is echoed by one of the founders of the Theosophical Movement, Helena P. Blavatsky. In a letter to the Archbishop of Canterbury, Blavatsky points out that Theosophists respect all religions, but she makes a distinction between the teachings of Jesus and the doctrines of the churches. These latter, she argues, have made Christianity "a stepping-stone for ambition, a sinecure for wealth, sham, and power; a convenient screen for hypocrisy" (138). This is why, perhaps, Colmore focusses on the teachings of the Nazarene "uncrowned as yet by centuries of recognition."

Whether using Christian or Theosophical language, *Suffragette Sally* is a sustained attempt to see militancy, martyrdom, and social reform as taking place with God's approval. Early in the novel, Edith

Carstairs has decided to work for suffrage in a way that her romantic attachment, the Liberal Cyril Race has declared to be "worthy of women, the way that was void of violence" (109). Having reached this decision, she passes a familiar sign-post, and suddenly sees it as a cross: "An omen was it, or just the outcome of her thoughts? For peace, surely, was the message linked with that sign, peace and goodwill. Nay, but there were other words: 'I come not to bring peace, but a sword'" (110). Colmore obviously sees the biblical passage from which this quotation comes, Matthew 10:34, as anticipating and justifying suffrage militancy, and she uses its language throughout the novel to anticipate what happens in the lives of the three main characters. Matthew 10 is Jesus' instructions to his twelve disciples on how to spread the Word, and His warning that discord is an inevitable first consequence of preaching and accepting "the kingdom of heaven" (10:7).

The themes of persecution, discord, and subsequent Divine Judgement in Jesus' instructions are linked to the fifty-third chapter of *Suffragette Sally*, where Colmore borrows four lines from Julia Ward Howe's emotionally compelling "Battle Hymn of the Republic"; these lines are designed to rouse the reader to look beyond the ending, and to translate the message of the novel into political action. The apocalyptic message of the "Battle Hymn" is that God is a militant who, far from asking us to love our enemies, echoes the prophecy in Genesis that the "Hero, born of woman, [will] crush the serpent with his heel." It is not violence for which the soul must atone "before his judgement seat," but a false peace; or, in the context of the novel, useless constitutional methods. Judgement Day, as the "Battle Hymn" suggests, has now come, and Colmore's choice of the fourth verse for this final chapter brings us back to Matthew: "And whosoever shall not receive you, nor hear your words.... It shall be more tolerable for the land of Sodom and Gomorrha in the day of judgement, than for that city" (10:14 and 15). Written during the American Civil War, and used as an anthem by the Union Army, the "Battle Hymn," as quoted here, places the suffrage cause in a context of a successful battle against oppression.

If strife is one consequence of speaking the word, however, another is cure. Jesus' disciples are given the power to heal "all manner of sickness and all manner of disease" (Matthew 10:1), and part of preaching is to "heal the sick, cleanse the lepers, raise the dead, [and] cast out devils" (10:8). The novel's arguments constantly point out that the vote is but a doorway to social reform; it is an opportunity to speak for the silenced. Although Sally is the character who dies, martyred to the cause, Geraldine is the one who is given redemptive qualities. She is the intercessor through whose personality others are brought to the movement. She takes on the role of healer at Aunt Margaret's Home of Rest and, in prison, she "lay[s] a healing touch" upon an old woman who is "sick in soul" (126). More specifically, she is the means of redemption for those who are not believers.

In the chapter "The Valley of Vision," Geraldine is in prison under the identity of Anne Heeley. Lying on the floor of her cell, and embittered by the pain of the forcible feeding, she looks at the window: "In that window were three panes of clear glass, and on them, as the light fell, there came shadows of the moulding that looked like three crosses. They brought to Geraldine's mind the familiar scene of Calvary, and she thought, 'What did they stand for'? [...] 'One for the Lord Christ who died for sinners, and one for the sinner who was kind, and one for the sinner who had not yet learnt to be kind'" (258, 259). Seeing this vision, Geraldine's hatred fades, and she becomes, through her bodily suffering, the Christ-like means of redemption for those who have abused her, particularly the doctor who, as the narrator says, "knew not that by the forgiveness of the woman, whom, as a working woman, he despised, he was brought a little nearer to the glory that waits, far onward on the upward path of evolution, for every living soul" (259). It is not, perhaps, unusual that a revolutionary movement would see itself as having God on its side. However, suggesting that a woman could identify herself with the crucified Christ, and that her body could bear stigmata of a kind, not as a mark of subjection but of community, places bodily inscription in a particular historical and literary context, and creates a powerful rhetorical precedent for martyrdom and militancy.

In her "Author's Note," Colmore writes that "[t]his is a story which cannot be finished now" (290). For the novel to be finished, her readers must write the ending, and to do so involves speaking the Word. Matthew 10 not only authorises the disciples' speech but exhorts them to "preach ye upon the housetops" (10:27). *Suffragette Sally* suggests that readers go and do likewise, and that only through the words and deeds of the faithful will the novel find its desired conclusion.

Gertrude Colmore (1855–1926)

In her introduction to *Voices and Votes* (1995), Glenda Norquay writes that, as the focus of feminist literary criticism has changed, "we may have lost sight of what it means to write as a direct intervention in public and political debate" (3). Gertrude Colmore could certainly remind us of this, given that her novels, short stories, and poems are extensions of her social activism. Her writings address a range of social concerns, from madness and alcoholism to animal rights. The plight of poor and "fallen" women occupies much of her poetry, and she wrote tracts on education and on trades that traffic in animals. Beyond her activities as a campaigner, little is known about Colmore, and much of what is known is from her obituaries in *The Times* and *The Vote*.[1] In 1988, Ann Morley and Liz Stanley wrote a biography of suffragette martyr Emily Wilding Davison; as part of this, they reprinted Colmore's *The Life of Emily Davison: An Outline*. In the course of their biographical detective work on Davison, they discovered additional details about Colmore, and speculated about the web of friends and associates that might have been common to the two women.

There are few details about which we can be certain. She was born Gertrude Renton in Kensington, the sixth daughter of John Thomson Renton, a stockbroker. In the British Library is a small book, printed on vellum, called "Renton [notes on the family of William Renton of Edinburgh]" published in 1900. It contains a barebones genealogy of her family from the birth of William Renton in 1678; however, it provides little information about Gertrude apart from her date of birth. She was sent to school in Frankfurt, and was, according to her obituary, also taught privately in Paris and London. She married H.A. Colmore Dunn, a barrister, and dedicates to her husband and father *Poems of Love and Life* (1896), "written chiefly in the four years that passed between the death of one and the death of the other." In 1901 she married another barrister, Harold

---

1   Colmore is included (as Gertrude Baillie-Weaver) in the 2004 *Oxford Dictionary of National Biography.*

Baillie-Weaver, who was a member of the Humanitarian League as well as the Men's League for Women's Suffrage. Together, they joined the Theosophical Society in 1906, and continued to work for humanitarianism and animal rights. Colmore was a member of the WSPU, and contributed short stories to *Votes for Women*. She also wrote stories for *The Vote*, and her obituary in that paper gives some indication of her personality, as well as of her involvement in the suffrage movement. She is described as "a very early member of the Women's Freedom League, and always extremely kind and helpful in every way, sharing in demonstrations and meetings, speaking and writing. With a very pleasing, magnetic, gentle personality and high courage, her sincerity was quickly recognised, whilst her clear and logical mind made her a forcible speaker, easily convincing her hearers of the justice of our cause" (10 December 1926, 390). Harold Baillie-Weaver pre-deceased her by only a few months.

Both Harold and Gertrude worked and spoke for the Theosophical Society. For a short while, they hosted Krishnamurti[1] and his brother Nitya at a house in Wimbledon (Lutyens, 77). From Colmore's lecture to the Theosophical Society (Appendix A.3), it is clear that she saw those causes for which she worked—votes for women, spirituality, humane and ethical treatment of animals—as intimately connected. Colmore often includes references to these particular causes as a way of delineating her characters. The unlikeable Uncle Beauchamp in *Suffragette Sally*, for example, is a member of the pro-vivisection Research Defense Society (78). Geraldine, on the other hand, is associated with care of the weak and suffering. When the physical torment of the forcible feeding brings her to despair, she overcomes her desire to let her life slip away by thinking of the sweated women, joyless children and abused animals whose lives she can help by living (255–56). The demonic Donnithorne in *A Brother of the Shadow* (1926) collects cats he wishes to torture as part of an obscure rite, and threatens to harm Billy's wife Jessica for, among other things, the

---

1 Jiddu Krishnamurti (1895–1986) was thought by Theosophists to be the disciple who would serve as a vehicle for the coming of the World Teacher. He had been prepared for this position since childhood by Annie Besant and Charles Leadbeater who virtually adopted him, raised him within the Theosophical Society and had him educated in England. In 1929, Krishnamurti renounced his association with the Theosophical Society. He spent the rest of his life as a philosopher and spiritual teacher, travelling the world, lecturing and writing.

work she does to protect animals. Donnithorne is defeated by John Scott, a member of "The White Brotherhood" which is composed of close approximations of the Theosophical "masters" who mediate between the human and the divine. The novel's title refers to those who, according to Madame Blavatsky, are characterised by "abuse of psychic powers, or of any secret of nature; the fact of applying to selfish and sinful ends the powers of Occultism. A hypnotiser, who, taking advantage of his powers of 'suggestion,' forces a subject to steal or murder" (1889, 293). Theosophical principles are communicated indirectly in the novels by a mystical character, usually a woman, whose calm wisdom brings peace to those around her, such as Rachel Cullen in *Suffragette Sally*, Mrs. West in *The Crimson Gate* (1910), and Judith Home in *Priests of Progress* (1908). Theosophical teachings are most clearly in force in Colmore's last novel, *A Brother of the Shadow*.

Connected to her Theosophical principles is Colmore's campaign for the ethical treatment of animals. In *Trades That Transgress* (1918), she writes about the fur and feather trades, about performing animals, the unmerciful methods of slaughterhouses, as well as fox-hunting and cockfighting. In language which would fit perfectly into *Priests of Progress* or *A Brother of the Shadow* she writes that by using animals in these ways, we are transgressing Love's Law: "The Law of Love is stern as well as gentle, inviolable as well as tender, limitless as well as definite; but it is unyielding because it is true, inviolable because it is perfect, limitless because it is divine" (4). She goes on to say, as do many of her characters, that those who think in this way will face ridicule and disapproval, "the imputation of sentimentalism, crankiness and exaggeration" (5). Because of this, perhaps, the anti-vivisectionist, anti-vaccinationist *Priests of Progress* ends with a "list of authorities for the actual theories and practices" attributed to the characters. Hilda Kean points out that this novel's message was so forceful that it was "condemned by physiologists who discussed how to mount a 'counter attack.'"[1] Harold and Gertrude's work on behalf of animal welfare was commemorated in 1928 by C.L. Hartwell's statue, *Protecting the Defenceless*. Dedicated to "all protectors of the defenceless" and particularly to Gertrude Colmore and Harold Baillie-Weaver, the

---

[1]   Hilda Kean, "Weaver, Gertrude Baillie-" *ODNB*, 2004.

statue stands in the St. John's Lodge Public Gardens of Regent's Park in London (Kean, 1998, 189).

Colmore's novels do have a tract-like quality to them, in the sense that characters will debate, sometimes at great length and occasionally at the expense of credibility, the causes they espouse. Her novels are sometimes sentimental and melodramatic, and not just in the cause of animal welfare. Her hagiographic *Life of Emily Davison* (1913) includes scenes in which the suffragette martyr's mother senses her injured daughter's soul pass by her like a bird, and in which a ragged man waits two hours to throw a ragged rose onto Emily's coffin. Moments like these are not uncommon in her fiction; it could be that emotional engagement was one of the ways in which she hoped to speak to the "still small voice" in her readers. Certainly in the case of anti-vivisection, she is fierce, and novels such as *Priests of Progress* include some graphic scenes of animal abuse. That said, however, she knew how to appeal to readers, and though her characters are sometimes mouthpieces for particular causes, her stories are compelling and engaging. Her unusual novelistic skill is evident in *Suffragette Sally*, which remains a reminder that fiction can make an intervention in public and political debate.

Gertrude Colmore: A Brief Chronology

1855   Gertrude Renton is born on 8 June at 5 Upper Lansdowne Terrace, Kensington, the sixth daughter of John Thompson Renton and Elizabeth Renton, *née* Leishman.

1882   Marries Henry Arthur Colmore Dunn, barrister on 18 July.

1888   Colmore's first novel, *Concerning Oliver Knox* is published. It was re-issued in 1893.

1896   Publishes *Poems of Love and Life*. In the "Dedication," she writes "To my father, who gave me, and my husband, who discerned, developed and educated in me, any good that I may possess of character or talent, I dedicate these poems, written chiefly in the four years that passed between the death of one and the death of another."

1901   On 2 January, marries Harold Baillie-Weaver, barrister.

1906   The Baillie-Weavers join the London branch of the Theosophical Society.

1908   Publishes *Priests of Progress*, an anti-vivisection novel.

1911   Publishes *Suffragette Sally*.

1913   Publishes *Mr. Jones and the Governess*, a collection of suffrage short stories.
Publishes *The Life of Emily Davison*.

1914   The Baillie-Weavers are founders of a Theosophical Society suffrage league.
During WWI, Colmore was a pacifist. She was stoned in 1914 in Saffron Walden for speaking against the imminent war.

1916–21   Harold Baillie-Weaver is the general secretary of the Theosophical Society 1921.

1918   With Beatrice de Normann publishes *Ethics of Education*. Publishes *Trades That Transgress*.

1915   Move from Essex to Wimbledon, Surrey with the intention of acting as guardians to Krishnamurti, hailed by Theosophists as the new messiah (see note 1, p. 33). In *Candles in the Sun*, Emily Lutyens (sister to Constance

Lytton) writes that the arrangement never worked: "The rented house was a hideous villa, with texts all round the walls. The boys [Krishna and his brother Nitya] never felt at home there. They had to mind their p's and q's, to be punctual, to apologise for every small lapse, and all their misdeeds were passed back to Lady De La Ware and through her to Mrs Besant" (78).

1926   Publishes *A Brother of the Shadow*, her last novel.

18 March, Baillie-Weaver dies after a battle with stomach cancer.

26 November Colmore dies of heart failure.

1928   C.L. Hartwell's statue, *Protecting the Defenceless*, is dedicated "To all protectors of the defenceless" and particularly Gertrude Colmore and Harold Baillie Weaver, St John's Lodge, Regent's Park, London.

1984   *Suffragette Sally* is re-published as *Suffragettes: A Story of Three Women*.

A Note on the Text

Suffragette Sally was published in 1911 by Stanley Paul and Co., London. Pandora re-published it in a facsimile edition in 1984 under the title, *Suffragettes: A Story of Three Women*, with an introduction by Dale Spender. The first edition of the novel is hard to find, though there are copies in The British Library and the Women's Library in London; the 1984 edition, though now out of print, is more widely available in libraries. I have checked the two volumes against one another, and they are identical, with one exception: the 1984 edition excludes the first stanza from Cowper's "God Moves in a Mysterious Way," which appears in the 1911 edition just before Chapter I. The copy text for this Broadview edition of *Suffragette Sally* is the 1911 edition. I have not modernised Colmore's spelling.

Original author notes have been retained in the text and are identified by asterisks. Where necessary, editorial explanations of these notes are included in square brackets immediately following the note.

SUFFRAGETTE SALLY

CONTENTS

"God moves in a mysterious way
His wonders to perform;
He plants His footsteps in the sea,
And rides upon the storm."

Cowper.

I desire to express my indebtedness to all those whose printed, written or spoken experiences have helped me in the writing of this book.

CHAPTER I
A DARK EVENING

"A maid whom there were none to praise,
And very few to love."

Wordsworth[1]

Six o'clock and an ink-dark winter's evening. Ink-dark it was out in the quiet country where massed clouds hid the stars, and the waning moon was still some hours from her rising.

Edith stood at the open door and looked out into the blackness. The thin, dim shaft of light which rayed out from the hall seemed but to deepen the darkness beyond. She listened to her friend's retreating footsteps and thought how dreary the walk would be all the way to Pagnell, with only that little bobbing spark, which represented the lantern, to show where to tread. Agatha had her dog, to be sure, for company, and did not mind whether she walked the two and a half miles by day or by night. To her it was nothing to plunge into darkness; to see only black nothingness when she came to the brow of the hill, instead of the valley with fields sloping gently; the tall, bare poplars stripped of their leaves by nature's providence and of their branches by man's inartistic hand; the winding lane which led to the broad main road. Nothing to her it was to turn into that road, where tramps trudged limpingly on their way from town to town, and loneliness was emphasised inasmuch as solitude was less sure. To Agatha all this was nothing; but Edith did not like the darkness. All her life she had been afraid of it; she was glad to turn back into the lighted hall and shut the darkness out.

On and on that darkness stretched, all round the house for lonely miles; unbroken in the quiet fields and silent woods, touched here and there on the solitary roads by village lights; far eastward to the sea, far north and south, and to the west some forty miles, to where London lights defied and conquered it.

A sky, starless and deserted by the moon, mattered little where lamps were frequent and shops poured floods of brightness out on to

---

1   William Wordsworth (1770–1850), "She Dwelt Among the Untrodden Ways" (1800).

the pavements; and Sally Simmonds, hastening along Holloway,[1] did not notice that above the street lamps the night hung densely black. She had had her two hours out and was hurrying home—that is to say, to the home of her employers—to get the master's supper. She was late, and the master did not like to be kept waiting; nevertheless, though her feet hastened, Sally's mind was not occupied with supper, nor with Joe Whittle, though she had seen Joe that afternoon, though he had put his arm round her waist, and though demonstrative affection was pleasant to Sally. Joe was in the background, dimmer even than the dim presentment of the master and his supper which loomed upon the outskirts of her consciousness. The forefront of that consciousness was filled with a medley of impressions, new, stimulating; giving rise to all manner of queer sensations and ideas; absorbing her attention, translating her from the humdrum streets into an extraordinary world, dazzling, undreamed of.

Instinctively she hurried, and instinctively she took the right turns to bring her to Brunton Street; but the real Sally was no more in North London than the moon was in the sky. Sally, indeed, was in a sky of her own, and she came down with a sort of flop to sober sordidness when she reached the area gate.[2] How it creaked! No chance of stealing in unnoticed. Mrs. Bilkes would hear her to a dead certainty, and be down upon her with red face and scolding speech. Well, it was worth while if—

The back door was opened from within; not the mistress, but the master stood on the other side of it. That was worse in one way, though better in another. The mistress scolded, but the master kissed.

"You're late, my gal. Come in, there's nothing to be afraid of. *I* ain't hard on you. You've got to pay for keeping a starved man waiting, though. Here now, don't be nasty over it, and I'll swear all I'm worth that the dining-room clock's ten minutes fast."

---

1   Holloway Road (now the A1 motorway) runs south east from Upper Holloway through Holloway and Lower Holloway, all wards in the Borough of Islington, North London. The area at the time was economically diverse: the north-west end of Holloway Road was populated by clerks and artisans, while the populace became poorer and conditions more overcrowded toward the south-east (Baker, 29–37). Brunton Street, home of the Bilkses, is fictional, but since the house has a view of Holloway Prison, would be further to the north.

2   The area is a "sunken court, shut off from the pavement by railings, and approached by a flight of steps, which gives access to the basement of dwelling-houses" (*OED*).

The master's arm was round her waist and the master's hard, bristly moustache scraped her cheek. She did not want that encircling arm, and she greatly disliked that particular moustache, yet she accepted the embrace almost without resistance. It was in the day's work, so to speak; most men were like that; most masters, at any rate—in Sally's experience; and it was pretty well a foregone conclusion when she undertook the post of "general" at Nine Brunton Street that Mr. Bilkes would kiss her when Mrs. Bilkes was not looking. She had known it from the look on his face, the particular glint in his eye; having to fight the world "on her own" had made her a judge of faces. As for complaining—the mistress always took the master's side and called you a bad name, and you lost your place for nothing. It was best to keep quiet; and she took what she called "jolly good care" that the unsolicited attentions went no further than an occasional embrace.

So she gave a mental shrug of the shoulders, wiped her cheek when she got into the kitchen, and set the supper to heat. It had been prepared before she went out, and while it was getting hot she took off her jacket and hat, put on a crumpled white apron and a grey-white bow of coarse lace, which did duty as a cap, and went upstairs to lay the cloth.

Mr. Bilkes was lying back in the arm-chair by the fire, absorbed, apparently, in the evening paper. Mrs. Bilkes was sitting by a small side-table, making a blouse. She looked up as Sally came into the room.

"You're late, Sarah. It's past seven now, and the cloth not laid."

"Very sorry, mum."

"This clock's ten minutes fast"—from the arm-chair.

"Stuff and nonsense. I put it right to the second yesterday, when I wound it up."

"I'll swear to it. I took the time as I came up from the city."

Sally took no notice of the offered means of excuse; she made no answer to Mrs. Bilkes's accusation, but kept a determined silence as she hastily placed a cruet-stand, knives, forks, plates, and glasses on the table. "I don't want his lies," she was thinking, "nor his takin' of my part. I *am* late and I don't care if I am. It's worth it."

Worth it indeed! What did Mrs. Bilkes's fault-finding matter? All Sally wanted was to get the supper out of her way, and a quiet half-hour to herself before the washing-up; a half-hour in which she could sit down by the fire and think. You could think better looking into the fire; in its red depths there were almost pictures sometimes of what you were thinking about.

It was all on the table now, the steak and onions, the bottled stout, the cheese. Sally, with a couple of dish-covers in her hand, prepared to descend the kitchen stairs and give her whole attention to setting in order the whirling impressions which were rioting within.

But the time was not yet. From above came a sound, a child's voice calling.

"Drat the child!" She nearly said it, but not quite; Sally was tender to children. "It'll be Dorothy wanting a drink," she thought, heaved a sigh, and mounted the stairs to the room she shared with two little Bilkeses.

"Wot is it? a drink? Why didn't you arst yer ma for it afore she come down?"

"No, we's not thirsty. We wanted to know if you'd come back."

"Well, I'm back all right. Be good children and go to sleep."

"Ma put soap in Stanny's eye, an—"

"An' I cwyed," said Stanley.

"An' ma said he was a baby an'—"

"An' I'm not."

"No, he's a big boy, and big boys always go to sleep."

"But, Sally—"

"But please, Sally—"

Alas! when Sally at last reached the kitchen, it was only to hear the dining-room bell ring. Supper was over, and so was the chance of a half-hour before the fire.

Then it was clear away, and wash up, and take down the boots, and put everything ready for the morning. She was weary when at last her time was her own—bed-time; her body craved rest, her head throbbed. Nevertheless, when bed-time came, Sally did not go to bed.

CHAPTER II
A SONG OF FREEDOM

"It takes a soul
To move a body."
E.B. Browning[1]

Sally did not go to bed. She put out the candle, for Mrs. Bilkes had a way of coming to see if any light crept out from under her door; then she sat on the edge of her bed and looked out through the square of window in the sloping roof, out into the darkness. Darkness was the next best thing to a fire; it shut out immediate surroundings.

Sally's window looked on to a space of roofs, grey, smoke-begrimed, and dreary in their sameness, and beyond the roofs could be seen, when it was light enough to see anything, the upper windows of a large, dark-walled building, Holloway prison. It was not a cheerful view; the darkness was better.

It was cold in Sally's room, and Sally's body grew chilled while she left it sitting on the bed, and went away into the new country which had opened out before her that afternoon.

A large hall in the West End of London, and people streaming into it, people of all kinds and classes; ladies, regular swells, richly dressed; "toffs" in overcoats and tall silk hats; girls who might have come, as Sally had come, to this part of London, just to have a look at the splendid, fashionable shops. It was not dark any more, but daylight, the lifeless daylight of a London winter's day.

"'Ave yer got to pay?"

"Pay? Lor' no. Ain't yer never 'eerd 'er? Come along in along of me."

No more dull daylight, but the radiance of electric lamps; crowded benches; a platform with fine ladies and gentlemen upon it. One of them was speaking, one of the gentlemen; he was going to say but a few words, he said, but to Sally it seemed that he said a great many. She could not follow him; it was like preaching, only that there was no mention of God or heaven or hell; she began to fidget

1   Elizabeth Barrett Browning (1806–61), *Aurora Leigh* (1856).

and to wish she had stuck to the shops. And then——. Then came the beautiful lady—whom the gentleman called upon. "I will now call," he had said, "on Lady 'Ennery 'Ill"—or that, at least, is what to Sally's ears he had seemed to say.

She heard him say it again, as she stood far away from that shivering body of hers on the bed, stood in the lighted hall. She had stood most of the time that the lady spoke, for she had been in the last row of all, close up against the wall, so that it had been possible to stand, and all the hats and heads between her and the platform had been more than her interest and her patience could bear. She could listen better when she could see uninterruptedly, and once the tall lady with the brown hair and the clear voice had begun to speak, Sally wanted to listen.

She forgot the shops and forgot the time; she only wanted to hear; to hear, and—how she wanted to ask questions, to understand! To understand it all, just because she understood a part; because the wonder of it and the strangeness of it were not completely strange, entirely unknown; because, in some queer way, some unknown thing in herself seemed to have a dim knowledge of the things the lady said. It seemed to Sally as if there were some bird within her, fluttering, moving its wings, longing to fly towards the platform and join in the song that Lady 'Ennery 'Ill was singing. It was not a song of course, but a speech; she was only speaking; and yet, in some odd way, it seemed to Sally that there was a sort of song in what she said. A song of freedom it was, a song which told that women, however poor, however put upon, had a right to have a say in the things which mattered most to them; that it was unjust that a human being, whether rich or poor, married or not married, should go without the rights that were given to human beings, just because she was a woman; that justice was stronger than any other force, and that justice was bound, in the end, to be given to all. Sally could not remember the leaping sentences, could not recall the words, the meaning of many of which was naught to her. But the general meaning of Lady Henry's speech had, at the time at least, reached her understanding. As she said to herself, "She put it so plain."

The plainness seemed to go out of it when Sally had left the hall, and to give place to a confusion of swarming ideas which were yet stimulating in their force and novelty. And through them all went the song; yes, and the battle-cry. For there had been a call to arms—

was it only in the voice, or in the words too, of the speaker?—a call to all women; to stand together; to be full of courage; to fight for themselves and for each other; most ardently for the poorest, the most oppressed of all. To stand together; she and Lady 'Ennery 'Ill! To stand up for all the women that were put upon! She hardly knew for what she was to fight; what was the liberty, what the rights, of which the speaker spoke. But the bird in her breast knew.

The wings of that bird fluttered all the way from Regent Street to Holloway. She had bound them fast for a while, with steak and onions and cheese; but now they were free again, and wafted her far away from Brunton Street, through dim regions which opened out from that large lighted hall far away to the south-west of her window. Then, at last, the wings quivered and drooped, and Sally was back on her bedside, staring out into the darkness, chilled and tired and hungry, for in her absorption she had found no time for her usual evening meal.

She crept into bed quickly, quietly; her limbs were cold, her head ached, but her heart was aglow.

CHAPTER III
FANTASY AND FACT

"If a new and grand idea appears on the mental horizon, it creates fear in the camp of those that cling to old systems and accepted forms."

Paracelsus[1]

There were phantoms in the lane; there always had been phantoms; ever since Edith had been able to see anything, she had seen their beloved shapes. Beloved, for there was nothing dreadful or terrifying in the fleeting forms that were outlined, even in the daylight, and full-fledged entities in the dusk. Dainty rather were they, and delicate, sometimes quaint, as Edith's fancy was quaint and delicate

---

1   Philipus Theophrastus Bombast of Hohenheim (aka Paracelsus) (1493–1541), "Alchemy and Astrology" (quoted in Franz Hartmann, *The Life and Doctrines of Philippus Theophrastus, Bombast of Hohenheim known by the name of Paracelsus. Extracted and Translated from his Rare and Extensive Works and from some Unpublished Manuscripts*. New York: United States Book Company, 1891).

and dainty; fairies, elves, hobgoblins, sprites; vaporous and few in the sunlight; peeping from summer leaves, hiding behind the boles of summer trees; trooping through the dusk; elusive, silvery, and glittering, in the light of the moon. The emotion that came to her, either in expectation or in vision, had its portion of timidity, but a timidity that was hardly akin to fear diffidence, a shy ecstasy, a delicious sense of trespass into an unknown country, these were rather the ingredients that composed it.

In the daytime, in dusk, and in moonlight, Edith had been used from childhood to follow alone the windings of the lane, and she knew those windings almost inch by inch, and the aspect of them at different hours and in varying weather. There were the grey days, when the little, sad-faced, long-haired "numbkins" (it was the name given by her child's mind) peered forth from colourless hedges; there were the hours of flashing sunshine when fairies leapt in the quivering, heated air; the sunset evenings when the elves hardly dared to show themselves against a sky whose tints killed out the colour from gossamer garments; stormy twilights when phantom folk, swift passing on the wings of the wind, called faintly; breeze-stirred dusks when they whispered as they played; rainy days when they sheltered beneath leaves and shook down showers from the branches. At all times, in all moods, Edith knew the lane and its phantoms; except the time of night, the phase of darkness. From the darkness she shrank; it seemed to her an enemy; and at the time of which I write, she had not yet learned to know it as a friend.

The elves and fairies, the hobgoblins and the sprites, had always been in the lane; from her babyhood, almost, they and Edith had foregathered; but girlhood brought phantoms of a foreign fibre; foreign to the "little people," but innate in girlhood's dreams. Knights, princes, heroes, peopled the hedge in solitude; clad, not in armour, but in the prosaic garb of modern days, yet clothed upon with chivalry, loyalty, honour, courage and romance. In Edith's day-dreams the perfect knight was, like Bayard, *sans peur et sans reproche*;[1] but she was too practical to separate romance from the world as it is, and he presented himself to her vision in the ordinary dress of an ordinary gentleman. He?—they rather, for no solitary defined figure, no one

---

[1] Chevalier de Bayard (Pierre du Terrail) (1475–1524), was a French knight and national hero, renowned for his bravery. He is known as the knight *sans peur et sans reproche* (without fear and without reproach).

type held her fancy, but all the heroes of all the ages, in turn, walked in the lane, gallant, gay, courageous.

It was a terrible day for Edith when they were scattered, scared from their haunts by the advent of a real live lover; terrible and disconcerting, inasmuch as they were all of superfine quality, and the concrete wooer was deplorably commonplace. A young doctor, dapper and self-confident, he was beginning his professional career as assistant to one of the medical men in the neighbouring town, and Edith, as he informed her, was the first woman he had asked to be his wife.

Edith's mother was affronted at the fact that he should dare to lift his eyes to Miss Carstairs of the Pightle (pronounced Pytle, though the Carstairs boys were used to designate their home the Pigtail): Edith herself was distressed because those eyes entirely lacked fire, because the whole personality of the man was unsympathetic to her. She was sorry to hurt him, though she had a hope that the hurt would soon be healed; she was sorry, continuously sorry, for the damage he had wrought in her private world; since a phantom, persistent doctor joined himself to the select company in the lane, and would not be ousted. He was there, not always to be sure, but far too often, thrusting a prosaic form amidst dear shadows; he was there in intermittent intrusion, fouling the pure waters of familiar fancies; he was there, or threatened to be there, till he was driven far afield by a fellow figure, formed like himself of human flesh and blood, but finer, courtlier, subtler; the figure of Cyril Race.

Edith never forgot the setting in which she had first seen Race, a setting which doubled the value and encouragement of his presence.

A market square, with buildings, some old and picturesque, some mean and modern, on all the four sides of it. Under the wide portico of one of these buildings, an old one, the Town Hall of Charters Ambo, Edith stood, in the hateful position of a beggar, a suppliant; soliciting, not alms, but signatures. There was a by-election in the Charters division of the county, and Edith had been called upon to take part in the work of a young and somewhat timid company.

The idea of extending the franchise to women was still new to the inhabitants of Dawnshire, and was attended by the suspicion which in respectable neighbourhoods attaches to all novelty; and those who brought it forward were still few in number and tentative in method. Edith had joined the local society, with the approval of her mother, who, being a widow, was accounted the equal of her male neighbours, in so far as she was called upon to share in the payment of rates and taxes, and who was of opinion that those who paid the piper should have a voice in calling the tune. Not that Mrs. Carstairs expressed her views by means of this metaphor; Mrs. Carstairs and metaphor did not often meet; it was Agatha Brand who made use of it, as it was Agatha Brand who initiated the policy which was carried out on polling day in Charters Ambo and the villages in the constituency; initiated it, that is to say, in Dawnshire.

It was Agatha too, who had insisted that Edith's services to the Society must be of an active kind.

"It's such a respectable policy," she said to Mrs. Carstairs, who demurred to her daughter asking men, ordinary, rough working men, for their signatures. "It's the policy of the National Union,[1] and you know they have never done anything in the least un-*comme il faut.*"[2]

"Men—common men, are so apt to get drunk at elections."

"That may be to our advantage. Most men are apt to be kindlier in their cups."

"Really, Agatha—"

"You'll never get men to go giving votes to a lot of foolish women unless they *are* drunk," broke in Monty Carstairs, who was at home after his first term at Cambridge.

"Monty," said his mother, "do you consider me a fool?"

"No, mater, of course not, but I should if you were to go and bite a policeman."

"My dear boy, pray do not mix me up with those unsexed[3] creatures whose only desire is to make themselves conspicuous."

"And only succeed in making the cause ridiculous—" added Agatha.

"No connection with the man round the corner, eh?" interjected Tommy.

---

1   The National Union of Women's Suffrage Societies (NUWSS) sought to obtain the vote by non-militant means such as demonstrations, meetings, and petitions. Their policy was "to go into by-elections prepared to support the candidate, irrespective of party, who declares himself the best friend to the cause of women" (*The Common Cause* 1.1 [April 15 1909], 5).

2   *Comme-il-faut* translates as "as it should be," and implies that which is according to custom or propriety.

3   "Unsexed" was used as a term of abuse against, in this case, the militant suffragettes. The term suggests that such women have given up the qualities that make them "womanly."

"And putting back the clock," finished Agatha.

"I almost wonder," said Edith, "that they haven't stopped it altogether." She spoke reflectively.

"They have," asserted Monty. "The thing's dying out as fast as it can."

"Nonsense," said Agatha, "you know quite well that if I were to ask you for your signature, you'd give it to me."

"That's where you're so unfair. If a fellow's asked as a favour, what's he to do? A man can't go against women."

"Oh, can't he?" cried Tommy. "You ask the policeman—just after he's had a bite. Ninepins ain't in it with the way they bowl over the suffragettes."

"*We* are suffra*gists*, not suffra*gettes*,"[1] said Agatha, "and it lies with us to show that women can be determined without being unwomanly. So Edith must do her part, Mrs. Carstairs. You see that, don't you?"

Mrs. Carstairs's vision was not identical with that of Agatha Brand; yet the latter went home triumphant; and thus it was that Edith, on the day of the election, found herself standing at the entrance to the Town Hall, a petition in her hand and something akin to panic in her heart.

At first she had much ado to prevent herself from running away; still more ado, when man after man turned from her and her request with rude refusal or coarse gibe, to keep herself from bursting into tears. Oh, for the lane and the chivalrous knights who wandered with her there! Oh, for shelter, alike from rough tongues and cutting winter wind! Oh, for a fire or a brisk trot to set the circulation going in her numbed feet! It would be unwomanly, she supposed, to run round the market-place. A suffragette no doubt would do it if she were cold, in spite of the crowd; but she was a suffra*gist*, and must show the men of England—the men who, as her mother pointed out, had the power to give or withhold the

---

1 The novel makes a distinction, one that is not uncommon in suffrage fiction, between those who wished to pursue the vote by constitutional means (for example, the National Union of Women's Suffrage Societies, NUWSS), and those who were convinced that more radical, or militant, action would be more effective in persuading the government to grant women the vote (for example, the Women's Social and Political Union, WSPU). The distinction may not have been as definite as suggested here. Holton (1986), for example, argues that many women belonged to both sorts of societies simultaneously (4). In *Suffragette Sally*, however, suffragists and suffragettes are represented as opposite and oppositional.

vote, and who must be propitiated, therefore, and not incensed or defied—must show them that it was possible to be womanly and at the same time—determined? Was that the word Agatha Brand had used? Yes, determined.

Poor Edith! She felt far from determined as she stood, tapping now and again a cold foot against the colder pavement, putting out a timid hand, forcing a faltering voice to say, with little gasps between the words: "Please, will you sign—a petition—to give the vote to those women—who pay rates and taxes?"

There were men who grunted, there were men who snarled, there were men who pushed her aside in contemptuous silence; men who told her that her place was the home (could they but know how she wished herself in that place!); men who told her she ought to get married; men who told her—a gentleman one of these, according to his own estimate of himself—that what she and all women wanted was a husband. A perfect nightmare of men, with manners so different from the manners of the drawing-room and the tennis-court!

Beside these, the yokels, brought in in motor loads from outlying districts, seemed comparatively kind; yokels who scratched their heads and had never heard tell of votes for women; who did not rightly understand what was the use of a vote after all; who did not want their "missuses" to get the upper hand; who did not know—dear, generous, open-minded souls!—but what there might be something in it. Couldn't write, some said, but if the lady would put down their names, they'd put a cross, same as inside on the voting paper; and this illiterate support, though hardly establishing the theory of the superiority of the male mind *qua* male mind, was nevertheless encouraging to a girl whose chief desire at the moment was the accumulation of signatures on a petition paper, where finger-marks seemed to gather more quickly than names.

After the first hour, even Mrs. Alick Brand, dainty and indomitable, showed signs that her courage, if not weakened, was put to the strain. Yet she stood firm, though, as she confessed afterwards, had it not been for shame and for the friendly policeman who guarded the entrance to the Town Hall, directing the voters and incidentally keeping a protecting eye on the petitioners, she must have fled.

"It's the beginning that's the worst," she said. "It will get better as the day goes on."

"Yes, I suppose so; oh yes, of course."

"You've got to get used to it. I believe there's a knack about it, somehow."

"I'm afraid I haven't got it."

"Look at Miss Liddon. She's getting on splendidly."

Miss Liddon was the head of a girls' college in Charters Ambo. She had taken an honour degree at Cambridge, and she stood in the street, asking for the signatures of men who could not read or write, a smile on her face, amused rather than embittered by the irony of the situation.

Somehow it did get better. A friendly tradesman with whom Edith had frequently exchanged, across a counter, trite remarks as to the seasonableness or unseasonableness of the weather, signed the petition with alacrity, making her feel that when her next allowance became due, she would betake herself to that same counter, and there spend the whole of it; and after that, names were scrawled on the paper at more frequent intervals. When at one o'clock Edith went to partake of mince-pies and coffee and warm her feet in a room hired for the purpose, she had turned her second page, and felt, compared with the mood of the morning, almost elated.

It was hard to go back. The room with the fire in it was so cosy and so quiet, and, as the day wore on, the streets and the market-place became noisier and more crowded, the voters more boisterous and more beery. Nevertheless, in spite of the beer, it was to the working-class voters that Edith continued to turn with the greater confidence; they were more boorish, but less offensive than the better dressed men.

"How are you getting on? Better isn't it," asked Agatha Brand.

"Yes, much, though lately I've had rather a slack time."

In truth there had been a period during which Edith had secured not a single signature, and discouragement was once again enfolding her.

"I must make more effort," she thought. "I must explain more— argue. The next that comes my side—Oh dear, here come two men in tall hats! They're *sure* to be rude."

But they were not rude; neither were they voters; they sauntered along, observing the crowd, talking together, but did not enter the portico. As they paused, however, by the pillar close to which Edith stood, she felt bound to make her appeal.

"Will you sign—a petition—to give votes to those women—who pay rates and taxes?"

She knew the formula very well now, yet still could not reel it off without little panting pauses.

"I shall be delighted," the elder man said.

He had what Edith called a jolly face; it was round and rubicund, with little close-cut white whiskers halfway down the cheeks.

"Oh, thank you!"

The younger man raised his hat. "May I sign too?"

"Oh please!" Edith looked up with a half-smile. "You don't know what a comfort it is to come across somebody who's in favour."

"I can't conceive of an intelligent being who isn't. The principle is incontrovertible. It's the methods of some of—"

"Oh, we're suffra*gists*, not suffra*gettes*, who are here today."

"I felt sure you couldn't be a suffragette."

"You think they really do harm to the cause?"

"The Amhurst lot?[1] Haven't a doubt of it. They've put up the backs of the whole Liberal party; and who's going to give the vote if we don't? Men who haven't logical minds and can't stick to a principle, get put off from the whole thing by the outrages called militant tactics. It's people of your kind who will win the day."

"You think it will be won?"

"Sooner or later—certainly."

The young man—for he was young; about three-and-thirty, Edith judged him to be—raised his hat again and passed on.

Edith turned to her petition and read the two signatures. Gillingham was the first, without initial. Lord Gillingham, of course; she knew he was staying in the neighbourhood and had been speaking on behalf of Mr. Bradley, the Liberal candidate. The second signature, in a very distinct, straightforward handwriting was Cyril Race; a nice name she thought, like its owner's face, which was keen, with well-cut features and stamped with the easy self-assurance of the man of the world.

The face remained with her, perhaps because she had seen it first at a time when a pleasant face and a kind word were like water in the desert; remained when that time of effort and discomfiture

---

[1] The Pankhursts and, by extension, the Women's Social and Political Union of which they were the leaders.

had been swept into the past; and Cyril Race took intangible form amongst her phantom friends, more definite in feature than the rest, more vague in character. She knew the heroes of history, what they had done, what they would be likely to do; of Race she knew nothing, save that he held a minor office in the Government, had a distinguished presence, and was in favour of giving votes to women. It was the little knowledge she had of him which made him, in her company of shadows, a potent personality, powerful enough to obscure the vision of the intrusive doctor. The other men she knew were not sufficiently interesting to play such a part as this, just because she knew all about them, because they belonged too securely to her daily life to be admitted within the precincts of the lane. There was Robbie Colquhoun, for instance; but she had known Robbie almost as long as she could remember, and there was no mystery about him, nothing to find out, no element of the unexpected to be reckoned with. She knew him through and through; or thought she did, which came to the same thing.

CHAPTER IV
THE BILKES FAMILY

"At this moment she heard a hoarse laugh at her side, and turned to see what was the matter with the white Queen; but, instead of the Queen, there was the leg of mutton sitting in the chair."

Through the Looking Glass[1]

Mr. Bilkes was in the bosom of his family; an ample bosom, since the Bilkeses were a prolific race. It was New Year's Day, and the bosom—or part of it—had come to dinner; the members of his hearth and home were, naturally, on the spot. The dinner was an early dinner, beginning at half-past one o'clock, and consisted of goose, beef, mince-pies and plum-pudding, followed by nuts and apples and glasses of port.

Mr. Bilkes had a partiality for port: he said it was a good old-fashioned English liquor, and for his part he liked things that were old-fashioned and, above all, English. New-fangled ideas and revo-

---

1   Lewis Carroll (1832–98), *Through the Looking-Glass, and What Alice Found There* (1872).

lutionary politics, these he was dead against, such as the Licensing Bill[1] and the suffragettes. Mrs. Bilkes, the elder, agreed with him; so did the three unmarried Miss Bilkeses; so did the sister who was a wife. The sister who was a widow and whose husband had died of the horrors,[2] was inclined to think that something should be done to stop people getting as much drink as they had a craving for; as regarded the suffragettes, she sided with Ben; they were a parcel of hussies. As a matter of fact everybody sided with Ben, except, sometimes, his brother-in-law, Ned White; but his dissent was usually silent until he was alone with his wife. It was the tradition of the family to side with Ben. He was the youngest, and the only boy, and since his father's death, had been, not only the hope, but also the oracle, of all the Bilkeses.

He lay back now in a leather arm-chair, his coat thrown wide, his thumbs in the arm-holes of his waistcoat, pronouncing judgment on the problems of the day; while his mother, in an arm-chair covered in crimson plush, his wife in a rocking-chair, and his sisters and brother-in-law on the straight-backed items of the diningroom suite, gave ear to his utterances. Ned White's ear was ostensibly, but only ostensibly given; the inner man, comforted by port and his pipe, found it more interesting to watch the whispered games (for children must be quiet when Dadda was talking) of Dorothy, Stanley and Maud.

Mr. Bilkes, so he declared, did not know what women were coming to. Time was when they were modest, stay-at-home, not forward—"You know what I mean."

They all knew.

"But now—!"

Hands went up, and shoulders.

"Fancy if any of you gurls was to go masquerading about the streets! Why, I'd—I'd never speak to you again, much less allow you to darken my doors."

"And I wouldn't blame you, Benjie," said mother Mrs. Bilkes.

"Nor I indeed," said wife Mrs. Bilkes; she spoke tartly.

---

1   The Licensing Bill of 1908 sought to reduce the number of pub licenses by approximately one third. The Bill recommended one on-license to every 750 people in towns, and one to every 400 people in the country (see Asquith, 7; Greenaway, 81–86).

2   The "horrors" refers to "a fit of horror or extreme depression such as occurs in *delirium tremens*," induced by excessive indulgence in alcohol (*OED*).

"Lor' ma, as if we should!"

"Of course not. Why, it's an insult to them, Ben," said Mrs. Turner, the widow. "Though, to be sure, the Lord alone knows what the world's coming to."

"That's just what I say, Beaty," said Bilkes. "What *is* it coming to?" And Mrs. Turner repeated that the Lord alone knew. "When I was a young man—"

"You're not going to set up as an old one surely, Ben," from the youngest Miss Bilkes.

"Well, younger than I am now, we'll say; when I was younger than I am now, the place of a woman was her home; up in the nursery looking after her children, more especially the baby; down in the kitchen, seeing to her husband's dinner—"

At this point the door opened and Sally entered with the tea-tray. Festivity in the Bilkes family meant that one meal ran on into the next.

"Please mum, shall I clear away the glasses and the wine?" asked Sally.

It was Bilkes who answered. "No—yes—leave my glass and put the bottle on the mantelpiece. Well, as I was saying, time was when women stuck to their homes, not pushing forward, nor yet—as some of the deep ones do—drawing back or pretending to draw back, setting up to know better than their betters."

He glanced at Sally, who looked, not at him, but at the children playing in the corner.

"When I was a young—younger man, I mean, gurls were glad to be taken notice of, while knowing their place."

"Whatever were you staring so at Sally for?" asked Mrs. Bilkes, when Sally, laden with wine glasses, had gone out of the room. "I couldn't see anything amiss with her."

"She gives herself airs, that gurl, that's what's amiss with her, and I meant my words to go home to her conscience. What do you think now—" Bilkes lowered his voice and spoke with bated breath. "She's been going to those suffragette meetings. What do you think of that?"

"Never! How do you know? Are you sure?"

"Sure as I am that the good, old-fashioned woman sitting over there is my mother. It was like this I found it out. Jones—you know Jones—two doors down—"

"Isn't his first name Theodore?" asked Mrs. Simmonds.[1]

"Yes, that's him, T.F. is his initials; a good sort; and warm too; hires a brougham for his wife when they go to the pantomime. Well, a week or two—or it might be as much as a month back, he says to me, 'Bilkes,' he says, 'I went to one of those meetings, suffragettes, at the Queen's Hall the other day, just for a lark,' he says, 'to hear the old cats mewing together because they can't get married.'"

"That's the way men talk about them kind of women. So you see!" Bilkes nodded at his sisters.

"You hear, girls?" said his mother.

"Yes, ma; shocking!"

"'Well,' he says, says Jones, 'it wasn't such a lark after all. It must have been a kind of an off day,' he says, 'no hysterics or screaming or pulling their hair down; just a lot of jawing, nonsensical, dull stuff that a sensible man couldn't follow. But the point of my remarks,' he says, 'is, who do you think I sat close to?'"

"Not Sally?" interjected Mrs. Bilkes the younger.

"Yes, Sally, sure enough, Sally, sitting there as cool as a cucumber and clapping her hands."

"I never!"

"Jones didn't recognise her at first. 'I knew the face,' he says, 'but I couldn't put a name to it, couldn't think where I'd seen it. Then all at once,' he says, 'like a flash of lightning, I thought of your area gate.'"

"I never!" said the voices again.

"The Lord alone knows what girls are coming to," remarked Mrs. Turner.

"Just what I say," said Bilkes. "Well—"

"Why didn't you mention it before?" asked Mrs. Bilkes. "You've never passed so much as a single remark about it."

"I wanted to see what she was up to. It might have been once in a way, a sort of curiosity, same as Jones going for the lark of the thing, or it might be a settled habit. I wanted to find out, and being a man and able to hold my tongue, I went about it on the quiet. Twice on her afternoon out, I managed to get to one of those meet-

---

1 Since the conversation here involves the Bilkses, the Whites and Mrs. Turner, Simmonds—Sally's name—would seem to be an error. The speaker should, most likely, be Mrs. Bilkes.

ings in time to see the meeting come out, and each time that gurl was there, and I spotted her." Bilkes made a pause. "The last time I spoke to her."

"You should have left that to me, Ben. Seems to me it's more my place than yours." Mrs. Bilkes spoke with some asperity.

"It's my place, as head of the house, to look after the morals of the house; and it's a question of morals. These carryings on, what do they lead to? The streets, that's the end of it."

"The gurls are present, Ben," observed the elder Mrs. Bilkes.

"Then let them be warned. A manufactory for fly-by-nights, that's what those meetings are; and so I told her."

"Did you?"

"I never!"

"What did she say?"

"Took it high and proud, same as she always does."

"What do you mean by 'always'?" asked Mrs. Bilkes.

"I—I—when she's found fault with."

"I can't say I've known her to be impudent."

"Well, *I* have. Anyhow she was then, though I spoke to her like a father, offered to overlook it and say nothing to Mrs. Bilkes if she'd take my advice and turn over a new leaf. Said she'd rather have her old leaves than my new one. There's upstartedness for you, and all because of these meetings! I don't believe she *was* impudent, my dear, before she took up with them. Upon my word—"

"Here she comes. Oh, Benny, do stop!" said the youngest Miss Bilkes.

"Why should I stop?" The port had made Bilkes bold, and just a trifle confused in utterance. "Not ashamed of my opinions; anybody welcome to listen to them; do all women good to listen to them; ladies *and* servants. *And* servants," he repeated with his eyes on Sally.

"Is the children to have their tea here, mum?" Sally asked.

"Yes, put them at the other end of the table, and they'd better have their pinafores on."

"Come along, Miss Dorothy. Had a nice game, Lovey?" This was to little Maud.

"All women are the same," pursued Bilkes, "whether they're my lady or whether they aren't, and hind-legging on a platform don't make them the equal of men and never will." Sally was dispensing bread and butter.

"Yes dear, by an' by, when yer ma's done with you. A real long story, Master Stanny, and the beautiful lady'll be in it all right, never fear."

"What I can't stand," Bilkes went on, "is women setting up to argue, the same as if they could reason like men. Fashionable ladies! What are fashionable ladies? Nothing but women. Dressing up don't make them into men. Nor titles. You don't get brains from titles."

"Don't drink too fast, Miss Dorothy, or you'll choke."

"It's a question of sex, that's what it is, and a question of argument, and what I say is women are no good at argument; never were and never will be. All the arguments with any bottom in them, all the arguments that hold water, if you know what I mean, are arguments that come from men, same as I've been talking to you now. Women! Faugh! Ladies, specially with titles! Faugh again!"

Sally set down Stanley's mug with a thump. "I know a lady wot 'ld take the shine out o' *your* argyments and leave yer lookin' like a fool," she said.

"Sally! Do you know who you're speaking to?" cried Mrs. Bilkes.

"What's got the gurl?" inquired Bilkes, unable wholly to conceal his satisfaction at having "drawn" her.

The rest of the company murmured "I never!" with the exception of the youngest Miss Bilkes, who smiled to herself.

"Who am I speaking to?" asked Sally. "Why, to 'im wot's been talkin' *at* me ever since I come into the room."

"For your good, Sally, for your good," rejoined Bilkes. "To show you the folly of your ways and where they'll lead to. And who pray is the lady who is so clever as to be able to make me look like a fool?"

"Ben's killing, he is, when he gets sarcastic," whispered Mrs. White to Hilda Bilkes.

"I wouldn't name her 'ere, not if you was to pay me," was Sally's reply.

"Oh, come now! Oh, that's good! You wouldn't name her. Perhaps she hasn't got a name, perhaps there isn't such a lady after all."

"Leave the room," said Mrs. Bilkes, "and take the children. It isn't dignified, Ben, to go on bandying words with her."

"No more it is," agreed Mrs. Turner, "but what the world's—"

"All right, but before she goes, I'd like to ask her what her fine lady would say to this argument—a woman's place is her home. Eh, my gurl?"

"Wot she'd say? Same as I say," Sally answered; "that there's a lot more women nor wot there is 'omes for 'em to be placed in.[1] Come along, children! Here Master Stanny, let me wipe your mouth afore you kiss your dadda."

CHAPTER V
GERALDINE

"I will show myself such an one as my age requireth."

2 Maccabees 6:27

"Henry," said Geraldine Hill, "when you go yachting next month, I'm thinking of spending a fortnight at Littlehampton."[2]

"Littlehampton! What in the name of fortune—oh, propaganda, I suppose."

"Not primarily, no. It's that Home of Rest of Aunt Margaret's; they want to give the matron a holiday, and I thought I'd go and look after the girls. It would amuse me, I think."

"All right. Anything to get you away from that infernal speechifying. You'll be worn out altogether, if it goes on much longer."

"Not I."

"When is it going to stop?"

"When the Government plays cricket."

Lord Henry shrugged his shoulders. He stood for a minute looking out of the window, then came and sat down by his wife and put his arm across her shoulder.

---

1   The greater number of women than men in the population led to what was called the "surplus," "redundant" or "superfluous" woman problem. Specifically, the reference was to those middle-class women over thirty who had not married and who were therefore, according to journalist W.R. Greg, leading an "incomplete existence" (Vicinus, 4). See Yeo, 66; Vicinus, 1–45.

2   Littlehampton is a seaside resort on the south coast of England in the county of West Sussex. Lily Montague and Emmeline Pethick-Lawrence bought the Green Lady Hostel in Littlehampton as a retreat for female factory workers. In *Prisons and Prisoners*, Constance Lytton writes that it was at the Green Lady Hostel, "the holiday house of the Esperance Girls' Club, that I met Mrs. Pethick Lawrence and Miss Annie Kenney. I was two or three days in the house with them without discovering that they were Suffragettes or that there was anything unusual about their lives. But I realised at once that I was face to face with women of strong personality, and I felt, though at first vaguely, that they represented something more than themselves, a force greater than their own seemed behind them" (9).

"You know I never interfere with you, Jerry."

"No, you're a darling, always."

"I leave you a free hand, but I'm bothered about you. I'm sure you do too much."

"Not half as much as the others, the people who really bear the brunt, because I promised you that as long as ever I could, I'd stand aside from the active work."

"But I—you gave me to understand that you didn't approve of it, the aggressive part, any more than I do, interrupting meetings, and so on."

"N—no, I don't—or didn't; it's very difficult. Anyhow I often feel like a coward or a broken reed and it's just because of that, that I feel bound to do what I can do with all my might."

"You won't be able to do anything at all if you go and knock yourself up."

"No fear; the meetings are coming to an end, and next month, as I tell you, if you don't mind going with the Palmers without me (it's you they want, so they'll easily let me off), I'm going to have a fortnight at the sea."

"Yachting always makes you ill if it's the least rough, so honestly I'd rather go without you. And you will take a quiet time?"

"Yes, darling, absolutely. I don't suppose I can help myself, I don't suppose there's any place to speak, even if I were bursting with speeches, at Littlehampton. It's quite primitive, I believe."

"Goodness knows! I half see you holding a meeting on the beach."

When her husband had gone, Geraldine went to her desk and wrote half a dozen letters, very rapidly; she who had been used to dawdle through life, taking even her amusements in leisurely fashion, had learned to be careful of time, had learned, too, to fix her mind on the work of the moment and to put her ideas quickly into words. Then she went over to the window, sat down in an easy chair and took up the paper that was lying on a table beside her. She read it through, skimming a page here and there, reading other pages with close attention. When she had finished it, she let it lie in her lap and looked out into the street.

It was summer, a brilliant day, with the brilliance which is accredited to June and too seldom attends it. The street was gay with passers-by, noisy with motors, bright with sunlight, and through one of the sides of the bay window she could see the trees of the park. But Geraldine's mind was nowhere near her material vision.

She was thinking of Littlehampton, of the Home of Rest, of the girls and women who were sent there. Aunt Margaret, who had started the Home and whose energy kept it going, was what she herself called a practical philanthropist. She knew that there were tired women in the world and she took steps to give them a spell of rest; but she did not, or so it seemed to Geraldine, perceive, in her survey of life, facts in any condition other than that of isolation. All her twos, so to speak, stood separate and apart; she never put them together and noted that the addition made four; in her mind they were not correlated, and her observation of them led to no conclusions.

Aunt Margaret was good and so was her Home of Rest; but after all, a fortnight's leisure to a few women, even if the few ran into hundreds, had no bearing upon the lives, wrought no change in the fate, of the thousands who worked week in week out, from year's end to year's end, with no other aim, no other possibility of aim, than to keep body and soul together; that and no more. The men were badly enough off in the spreading centres where poverty verges upon destitution; but the women!—the women who had to keep themselves, and often both themselves and their children, on wages half and less than half, the wages accorded to men, how were they to be helped, how heartened, how urged to struggle on their own behalf? Not by the philanthropy of Aunt Margaret and her kindly kind; not certainly by soup kitchens or district-visiting or pounds of tea or clubs. They must be individualised, turned from toiling animals, working like animals, just for food and shelter, into women. How? By the raising of wages; yes; by improved conditions; yes; but the "how" was still there, a lock to which a key had to be fitted. How were the raising of wages and the improved conditions to be brought about?

Geraldine Hill had become interested in the women's movement through her heart; she had decided to take part in it through her head. Thinking, studying, setting herself diligently to learn about and to understand the social conditions of her day, she had come to the conclusion, to which so many acute thinkers, not of her own sex only, have come; that only by women will the conditions of the mass of women be bettered, and that the few cannot work for the emancipation of the many, cannot work, that is to say, with full effectiveness, till they are recognised as entities in the State, given a political existence.

Because of this conclusion it was that she had faced the banter of friends, the reproachful solicitude of anxious relations. A vote? What did she want with a vote? Why, nothing, of course. The possession of it was of no importance either to her happiness or her dignity. The woman who was her husband's wife had all a woman could want in the way of consideration, happiness, freedom and, if she would, influence. But she belonged to the ranks of the privileged few: the mass of women had little freedom, scant consideration, an influence limited to that of sex or charm or personality. As for happiness, it was a relative word; there were women whose lives and surroundings permitted no conception of happiness beyond the gratification of the senses. It was of these she had thought when she had braved the ridicule of her "set" and the disapproval of her family, by allying herself with the most strenuous and aggressive of the women's suffrage societies: it was the presence of these in her consciousness, the call of them in her heart, which gave force to her words, the ring of conviction to her voice, and which enabled her to hold the interest, not only of educated audiences but to reach and rouse hearers of the type of Sally Simmonds.

Sally, eagerly making preparations for what she called a thorough change, little dreamed of the rapturous surprise that lay in wait for her a few weeks hence. She had not been dismissed from the Bilkes household. Mrs. Bilkes, hasty and suspicious, knew a good servant when she got her, and Sally, cheerful, good-tempered, and clean, as cleanliness was estimated in Brunton Street, was not easily to be replaced. So she was disposed to overlook the outburst on New Year's Day, especially as Bilkes, emerging next morning from the influence of port, admitted that he had been a bit too sarcastic with the "gurl." Bilkes, indeed, was uneasy as to whether, in the expansiveness of his mood, he had betrayed to the family circle more interest in Sally than was discreet; was uneasy as to whether Sally, reprimanded, would not retaliate by betraying more than was at all to the credit and comfort of Bilkes. He pronounced therefore, that it was none of their business what she did on her day out, and implied that he had taken her merely as the text on which to preach a sermon to his sisters.

It was very soon after this that little Maud developed measles, and then there was no more question of parting with Sally. Sally, indeed, had been more than half inclined to—as she expressed it—make a change; it was her fondness for the children which caused her to hesitate, and when, one after the other, they were taken ill, there was no more possibility of leaving them. Extra work, broken nights, a constant ascent and descent of stairs from kitchen to attic; all this, which might have spelt to many of her kind the necessity for departure, meant to Sally that she must stay on.

"There's some wouldn't give them drinks in the night, but tell them to be quiet and go to sleep. As if they could, pore mites, all dotted over as thick as currants in a pie."

So she stayed and did her best. Her best meant that when Stanny, the last of the children to be attacked, was convalescent, she was worn out, and herself became a prey to illness; not measles, but a virulent influenza, which laid a long and heavy toll upon her vitality.

She struggled through her work with difficulty, and when she managed to get to a meeting, the way seemed a very long one. The dispensary doctor prescribed change and rest, just the two things which it was impossible for Sally to have. She went on as long as she could without them, but at last informed Mrs. Bilkes that change, and a thorough change, she must have; she "couldn't go on no longer."

It was then that Mrs. Bilkes roused herself to do a little in return for Sally's much: she went to the vicar of the parish and asked him if he had any letters for a convalescent home.

There was waiting, uncertainty, delay, correspondence between the vicar's wife and the Honourable Mrs. Carleton; questions, a paper to fill in; and at last—at last—the coveted letter and the date of departure fixed.

Sally left Brunton Street with much kissing of hands and waving of handkerchiefs from the little Bilkeses. She arrived at Mrs. Carleton's Home of Rest for Working Women and Girls the day after Lady Henry Hill had taken the matron's place.

When Sally realised what had befallen her, that she was actually and indubitably under the same roof as "Lady 'Ill," and positively under the care of that admired divinity, her knees gave way—that was how she herself described her symptoms—and she sat down on the bundle she had brought with her; a considerable descent, as it was a small one.

"I never did!" was all she could find to say—"Never!"

CHAPTER VI
SALLY HAS A THOROUGH CHANGE

"The future sometimes seems to sob a low warning of the events it is bringing us, like some gathering, though yet remote storm."

Charlotte Brontë[1]

The sands at Littlehampton are broad and smooth and rockless. Every day when the tide was low, Geraldine walked across their shining silver-brown expanse, sometimes close up against the beach where the sand was hard and firm, sometimes close down by the sea, where her footprints made a sinking solitary line till the in-coming waves washed over them.

Towards evening she took a second walk, shorter, slower and companioned, for some of the inmates of the Home liked a stroll after tea, and Geraldine found that she got nearer to them, to the real individual woman in each one of them, when out walking, than she was able to do within four walls. There was one who never missed the evening walks. Wherever Lady Henry went, there Sally Simmonds was eager to go, and Geraldine soon became aware of the interest, the dawning devotion which she and the cause she represented had aroused in the heart and mind of the maid-of-all-work.

Sally was shy at first, awed; she had never before spoken to a "real lady," and the gentleness and simplicity of the real lady's speech and manner were almost disconcerting. But timidity and self-consciousness were not amongst Sally's failings, and when the first shock of surprise, the first blush of diffidence were over, her tongue was soon wagging as confidentially as though she were in the company of Joe Whittle. It was not long before Lady Henry made the acquaintance of Joe, as drawn by his betrothed. He wasn't half a fool, she learned. He couldn't get to the meetings, being as he worked late, but he

---

1 Charlotte Brontë (1816–55), *Shirley* (1849).

listened to what Sally told him, and though he carried on with a lot of nonsense—Joe was always one for getting at you—she could see as it sunk in. And when she went back, she would be able to answer all his questions, some of which, as she confessed, had stumped her; but Lady 'Ill knew everything, and from the stores of her knowledge Sally would carry away enough information to confound and convince a dozen Joes.

Sally was not the only convert to the cause; there were others, made, as are so many converts to all causes, primarily by the personality of the cause's advocate. Geraldine, if she did not, as her husband had prophesied, hold meetings on the beach, certainly ended by holding several in the dining-room of the Home; and she began to wonder what Aunt Margaret would say; Aunt Margaret who was an anti. To be sure it was Aunt Margaret who had invited the wolf into the fold, and the wolf had made no pretext, even, of donning the clothing of the sheep; nevertheless Geraldine felt in honour bound to tell the shepherd of the ravages she had wrought.

"Dearest Aunt Margaret," she wrote, "I hope you won't be shocked or vexed, but I have converted five of your protégées; three others are wobbly, and all but two interested."

The answer was reassuring as far as Geraldine's conscience was concerned. "Darling Geraldine, I don't mind at all. They'll forget all about it as soon as they get back to their work and their homes."

"Would they?" Geraldine asked herself the question as she walked across the glistening sands; quickly, as was her wont when alone. It was delightful to be alone; for all her propaganda and her interest in making it, the morning, solitary walk was the dearest part of what she called her holiday; dear because it was so different from the stress and hurry of the last strenuous months; because of the quiet, the peace; because of the loneliness. No, not loneliness; aloneness were a better word; she could not be lonely when the sea smiled, the sun blessed, and the wind caressed her. Loneliness, real loneliness meant disapproving faces and alien crowds.

Would they forget, those women? Would they sink back into the rut of drudgery, and quench, in the daily drag and sordidness of their lives, the little fire that she had lighted? There was one would not forget; of that she felt quite sure. The fire burnt steadily in Sally Simmonds's heart, leaped in her mind, glowed in her eyes; those wide, intent eyes, which were the servant girl's only good feature.

The tide was turning and it was time for Geraldine to turn too; she faced round and set out westwards, homewards. She loved the grey-brown expanse with the sunlight on it, the sparkling sea, the soft sound of the tiny waves as they fell gently; baby waves, she thought, making their first efforts to be breakers. This morning the space was not all her own; a figure was following the path she had trod, and drew towards her now that she had turned; a woman's figure she saw while it was yet far off; a girl's as it drew nearer. Passing close, two solitary beings on the wide wet sand, they glanced at each other as they passed. Geraldine liked the face she saw, with its pallor, that was a healthy pallor, tanned faintly by the sun, its blue-grey eyes and dark soft hair; a taking face and a sensitive one.

Turning her eyes westward again from this glimpse of a face, Geraldine perceived ahead of her, lying on the sand, a small white object, a handkerchief she saw, as she came close to it. Perhaps—had she dropped it, that girl? Probably. Geraldine picked it up, turned, and pursued the retreating figure.

The girl was sauntering and it was not difficult to overtake her.

"I beg your pardon; I thought—is this your handkerchief?"

"Oh, thank you! How kind of you! Yes, it's mine. So stupid of me. I hope you haven't come back far?"

"Oh no, not far." Then, because she liked the face, Geraldine continued to stand and look at it. "It's a lovely place to walk, isn't it?" she said with easy friendliness, "so wide and open."

"Yes, yes it is. But I walk mostly in a lane—when I'm at home, that is—and the width of this and the flatness, makes me feel as if—as if I were naked."

Geraldine laughed. "I think I know what you mean. This isn't your home then? You don't live here?"

"Oh no, I came yesterday to stay a week with an uncle and aunt—at the Beach Hotel, I suppose—" The girl looked at a watch on her wrist—"I suppose I ought to be going back to them."

"Let's walk together then, if you're really turning back. I'm on a visit also," Geraldine went on, as the two set out side by side, "and I come here every morning; sometimes heavenly early when it seems as if there wasn't a living thing on land or sea, sometimes later. It depends of course, upon the tide."

"Do you like loneliness so much?"

"Not loneliness, but wide lonely places—for a time, for a change. I feel as if the width and the solitariness of a space like this, for instance—well, as if it sort of washed out my soul and made it fresh again."

The girl glanced at the face beside and above her. "You hardly look—" she began, then paused and smiled.

"Oh, but I do, I assure you. One gets horribly besmudged and begrimed at the work I do, even though it's a labour of love and love is supposed to keep you clean."

"Is it amongst the poor—in the slums, your work?"

"Yes, and the rich. My work is for all women, and it brings me into conflict with all—no, not all, but most, men."

"The suffrage, is it? I work for that too; oh, only in a small insignificant sort of way, but still—Some of it's *hateful*." The girl spoke with emphasis; in her mind was the picture of a portico before a Town Hall, and a throng of contemptuous men. "Men are horrid to deal with," she went on; then added: "At least, not all."

"No, not all."

"It's the militants who turn them against us."

"You think so?"

"Certain of it. That's why I'm a suffra*gist* and not a suffra*gette*. I've been told, by a member of Parliament, that the Government will never do anything for us so long as they behave as they do."

"I've been told that too—by members of both Houses."

"It seems such a pity. Doesn't it?"

"Have you ever watched the tide come in?" asked Geraldine. "When it's far out, a long way from the shore, it ripples along gently, as the woman's movement did for fifty years; a very lady-like tide; and nobody heeds it—nobody on the shore, I mean. But when it gets to the beach, and the slope is steep and there are stones and rocks which stem the force, the irresistible force of it, then the smooth waves change to breakers, and the nearer it comes to its destined goal, the fiercer the conflict."

"But—" Edith said, and stopped.

"But it comes in all the same."

"It was coming in just as fast, wasn't it, when it moved quietly?"

"Because there was nothing to stem it. The rocks—if I may credit the rocks with intelligence—or the lack of it—the rocks, seeing it so far away, so unobtrusive, so patient, imagined in complacency that it would never reach them, or that, if it ventured near, it would be easy to beat it back."

"Then you—do you approve of the militants?"

"If I didn't, I should still stand up for them, since it is they, undoubtedly who have brought on the movement to where it stands to-day."

"But in the fifty years you spoke of—"

"Oh yes, I know, women, splendid, patient, persevering women gave their strength and time and intelligence to dragging it through the initial stage, the stage when the tide was creeping over the level sands; and men like John Stuart Mill[1] gave their brains and influence to speeding it on. With what result? The men were disregarded, the women ridiculed—that was all in those first days. It was as it is with all causes that have life in them. They begin almost tentatively; the waves are just ripples; and are disregarded, laughed at, by those who represent the rocks—the rocks that the tide is going to overtake. It is only when it begins to rouse antagonism, anger, bitterness, that you may be sure a cause is gaining ground."

"Do you think then that nothing is to be done without aggression?"

"Almost, I am inclined to think so. But what makes the thing that is called aggression? Not the steady unfolding of a new phase of the world's development—and all movements of progress are just that—but the opposition which is offered to the unfolding. It is the rocks which make the breakers, it is the rocks round which the in-coming tide eddies and swirls. You cannot blame the sea, which inevitably follows the law laid down for it."

"The rocks make the breakers, you say. Yes—perhaps," said the girl slowly; "but it is the waves that are broken."

"Individual waves: but the tide comes in. And individual women have been and will be broken: but woman will reach her destined place."

---

1 John Stuart Mill (1806–73), English philosopher and political economist, was an advocate of women's suffrage and author of *The Subjection of Women* (1869). He was a Liberal MP for Westminster from 1865–68, and in 1866 he presented a petition to the House of Commons to support an amendment to the Reform Act that would give votes to women. The amendment was defeated by 196 votes to 73.

"It may be—" The words came haltingly and after a pause—"it may be that you are right—in theory. You argue better than I do. But in practice—"

"I argue better than you do because I have thought more precisely and have got my ideas into clearer form; for that reason and no other. As for practice—do you remember how all this began?"

"Hardly. It—there was some trouble at a meeting, wasn't there?"

Geraldine smiled. "Some trouble; that's rather vague. Who and what caused it is the question."

"There were women—who interrupted—surely? I remember hearing about it at the time."

Lady Henry turned and looked at the girl beside her, the girl whose colour had risen, whose eyes had a doubtful look.

"It's evident that you don't know what actually happened. Do you care to know? Shall we turn back a little, or sit a few minutes on this breakwater? Or—must you go?"

"I'm afraid I must; Aunt Bessie—and my uncle is rather particular. But I *should* like to hear what you were going to tell me."

"Although I'm a *gette* and not a *gist?*" The eyes that looked at Edith had laughter in them.

"You really are then, a militant?"

"I forgot to put my badge on this morning, or you would have been warned at once. Yes, I belong to the WSPU. Well, is it all over between us, or are we to meet again?"

"Please let us meet again! I should so like it, and to hear— To-morrow, about the same time.—Are you likely to be here?"

"Most likely—or a little later, because of the tide you know, and looking out for you. Au revoir then."

"Au revoir."

"Oh, I'd better tell you my name, perhaps; Lady Henry Hill."

"And I am Edith Carstairs."

"I'm going to sit here a minute before I go on. Till to-morrow!"

Edith walked away, but before she turned the bend of the beach, she stopped for a moment and glanced back. Lady Henry had not moved from the breakwater; she sat, a still figure, slender and tall, with a blue motor scarf fluttering in the breeze: a militant suffragette.

CHAPTER VII
UNCLE BEAUCHAMP'S BISCUITS

"He hears no more
Than Rocks, when Winds and Waters roar."

Creech[1]

Aunt Elinor and Uncle Beauchamp thought that Edith had been out a very long time. Was her watch a little slow, perhaps? Aunt Elinor suggested. Edith could not say it was. Uncle Beauchamp hoped she had not tired herself, but if she was fatigued he would not, of course, ask her to go out again. Not at all tired? Very well then; they would walk into the town and see if they could get some breakfast biscuits; Uncle Beauchamp did not fancy the toast at the hotel. Aunt Elinor had still some letters to write; it was extraordinary how parish matters pursued you, even if you were ordered complete rest and an absence of all worry.

"You are sure you don't think I ought to write myself, my dear?" asked Uncle Beauchamp.

"Yes, quite unnecessary; I will tell Mr. Saunders what you say."

"Very well, then we'll start, Edith, if you're quite ready."

"Quite, Uncle Beauchamp, thank you."

They set out, the tall, handsome man, and the girl who had something of his beauty of feature, and nothing at all of his rigidity of expression. Uncle Beauchamp discussed the leading article in the day's *Times* and the chances of a general election. It was bound to be soon, he thought; the Government—such an unprincipled Government—couldn't possibly hold long together.

Edith made appropriate and monosyllabic replies; it was never worth while to say what you really thought to Uncle Beauchamp. Her father had been a strong Liberal, and almost from her nursery days she had been used to listen with interest to his political opinions and arguments; questioning him when she and he were alone; sitting, a silent pupil, when he talked with sympathisers, or argued with opponents. To Edith, her father seemed always to get the best of it.

Mrs. Carstairs had conformed to her husband's opinions on the simple ground that everything that dear Richard thought, must be

---

1   Thomas Creech (1659–1700), "To Asteria" (1684).

right; but since dear Richard had become poor Richard, and she was no longer sealed with the seal of his personality, she had veered round to the traditions of her girlhood. They were the traditions of the neighbourhood, and it was so much more comfortable to be in agreement with Beauchamp and Elinor at the vicarage. That Edith should follow in her father's footsteps, though awkward at times, was, on the whole, fitting; and "My daughter is very advanced, just like my poor husband," was expressive of mingled regret and satisfaction.

To Edith, indeed, the Liberal party, as such, was surrounded with a sort of halo. Gladstone, Cobden, and John Bright[1] had met her, phantom-formed, in the lane, discoursed to her of their ideals, fired her with their ambitions, and she believed that their mantle had fallen upon the present Ministry. But it was no use saying what you really thought to Uncle Beauchamp, whether it was a question of politics or church ritual or parish relief. A discreet neutrality was the policy adopted at the Pightle; it saved a lot of bother and it didn't really matter what Uncle B. (only in his absence was his name cut down to its first letter) thought; except, sometimes, in the matter of parish relief.

The Reverend Beauchamp Leigh was one of those clergymen who shrink away from anything which is of the essence of the faith which they profess. He thought himself a devoted Christian, but would have been scandalised had he been transported back nineteen hundred years and asked to shake hands with the Nazarene, un-crowned as yet by centuries of recognition. He was for Church and State and an increased Navy, because religion and the Empire must stand or fall together, and patriotism was amongst the vir-

---

1   Edith's romantic notion of the Liberal Party suggests that the Gladstone referred to here is William Ewart Gladstone (1809–98) who served as Liberal Prime Minister four times (1868–74, 1880–85, 1886, and 1892–94). Called "the grand old man" of British politics, he enacted educational and parliamentary reforms, supported Irish Home Rule, and implemented changes in areas such as the justice system, the military and the civil service. His son, Herbert John Gladstone (1854–1930), was Home Secretary from 1905–10, in which period are included the turbulent events in *Suffragette Sally*. As Home Secretary, Gladstone was responsible for prisons and public order, and these responsibilities brought him into conflict with the suffragettes, particularly after he announced the government's policy of forcibly feeding hunger strikers.

Like the elder Gladstone, John Bright (1811–89) and Richard Cobden (1804–65), MPs for Durham and Stockport, respectively, were known as reformers, particularly for their campaign supporting repeal of the Corn Laws (1838–46).

tues: but he was open-minded and advanced, so that when travelling down from town he bought and read *The Westminster*; besides which, he maintained an interest in science and its achievements. The extent of his scientific acumen may be judged by the fact that he was a member of the Research Defence Society,[1] and believed all that he was told by the honorary secretary. An excellent man, excellent in intention, conscientious in the performance of the duties which he considered to be his, and with literary bias which enabled him to derive real pleasure from the contents of a carefully selected library. It may be mentioned incidentally that he preferred Pope to Swinburne and that he pronounced the finest of George Eliot's novels to be *Daniel Deronda*. The modern novelists he did not read.

In daily life punctuality was the virtue which he most esteemed, or, it would be truer perhaps to say, the absence of which most discomposed him, and the fact that Edith had kept him waiting for a full five minutes had given a slight acerbity to a tongue which he rarely allowed to stray from the path of politeness. Edith had not failed to recognise the familiar note; it would soon die out, but in the meantime it was an additional reason for not saying anything in the nature of contradiction of Uncle B.'s pronouncements; and she restricted herself to the occasional, "Do you think so?" "Really?" and "Indeed," which sufficed to keep the conversation going. The great advantage of a deferential attitude, sparingly expressed, apart from the fact that it smoothed down Uncle B., was that it called for only a tithe of her attention. The greater part of her mind was at liberty to go back to the sands and the breakwater, on which, blue-scarved and tranquil, sat a militant suffragette.

She was very pretty with her brown hair and fair skin. The wind and the sea had kissed a pink glow into her cheeks, and made her brown eyes bright as well as soft. But a militant! and not recognised as such! The latter reflection carried a twinge of discomfiture. For Edith had been convinced that she would indubitably know a militant at sight; there would be a something—a subtle touch—an atmosphere, evident to her intuition if not immediately apparent to her eyes. And intuition had failed as fully as eyesight. Edith—she confessed it to herself while Uncle Beauchamp deplored the devi-

---

1   The Research Defence Society was founded in 1908, "specifically to counter the impact of the anti-vivisectionists" (Kean, 143).

ous ways of the Prime Minister—would have wagered her faith in the sincerity of the Liberal Government that Lady Henry was a suffragist and not a suffragette.

It was a shock to realise her mistake; disconcerting, inasmuch as it is always disconcerting to find that pernicious ideas can be harboured in an attractive personality; pleasant, in that Edith was generous enough to be pleased at the discovery that her opponents were better than her conception of them. Not the rank and file, probably ("Yes, Uncle Beauchamp, I see what you mean"), but it was evidently possible to be a Suffragette and yet retain qualities between which and Suffragettes wide gulfs were supposed to yawn.

"No, I don't think this is the shop where we got them last year. I think Webber was the name, and I'm almost sure it's a little farther on, on the other side."

"I believe you're right. I came in the afternoon and there was an awning out."

Webber proved to be the name over the shop which the Leighs had patronised the year before, and the biscuits were forthcoming. Uncle Beauchamp paid for them, and Edith carried them home. The Reverend Beauchamp Leigh did not like to be seen carrying a paper bag, while a burden of the kind was quite congruous to the dignity of the young woman who was his niece.

CHAPTER VIII
RED IN THE MIST

"Far and near
The grey mist floated, like a shadow-mere,
Beyond hope's bounds; and in the lapsing ways,
Pale phantoms flitted, seeming to my gaze
The portents of the coming hope and fear."

John Payne[1]

The next morning was overcast; a sea mist hid the sun and damped the atmosphere. Would Lady Henry Hill keep the tryst, or did she perhaps only care to walk when the weather was clear and bright?

---

1   John Payne (1842–1916), "Life Unlived" (1902).

"It's next door to raining, child. You're surely not going out in such an atmosphere."

"Why yes, Aunt Elinor, it's just the day one wants exercise, and you know I go out in all weathers at home."

"Which is one of the things I should not allow if *I* were your mother."

"I daresay it will clear. In any case I shall be back in plenty of time to go out with Uncle Beauchamp."

"I doubt whether your uncle will go out on such a day. I shall be very vexed if you catch cold and have to be nursed."

"I never catch cold, at least it's the rarest of rare things, and I promise you I won't to-day. Good-bye, Aunt Elinor."

"Humph!" said Aunt Elinor.

"Would she be there?" Edith hastened, searching amongst figures in the foreground for a little bit of blue. She was there, beyond where the visitors congregated, standing by the breakwater where yesterday Edith had left her. But there was no blue scarf to-day. She was all in brown, with a close-fitting cap that made the brown of her hair look golden.

"It's too damp to sit," she said, "and chilly. Besides, I always walk to begin with, and should miss the exercise. You like walking, don't you?"

"Yes, I walk a good deal."

They moved on; the mist was like a screen about them, shutting them into a space of wet brown sand, with grey intangible walls that shifted as they advanced. Always afterwards, when Edith thought of the militant movement, she saw it take its rise with just such a mist about it, and heard faintly, beyond the voice beside her, beyond the many voices, the plash of tiny waves. Many voices; for Geraldine Hill had the gift, in narration, of calling up the scenes of which she spoke; and Edith Carstairs had the faculty which can see intangible forms, and hear speech independently of actual utterance: and so it came to pass that on the solitary sands that day, where, as it seemed, only two women walked, there was enacted a drama which had been played for the first time nearly three years before; had been cut on the heart of history; and in history's repertoire must ever find a place while the world remains the stage of human action.

The 13th of October, 1905, and the Free Trade Hall at Manchester filled to overflowing.

All through the country there had been a stir; a thrill of unrest and expectation: the power of one party was on the ebb; change and a new order showed, full of hope to some, and to others darkly, on the verge of the political horizon. The Liberals were marshalling their forces, rousing their followers, and in the great Hall of Manchester, one of the Liberal leaders told in glowing words what his party was prepared to do if the people would put it into power. Fine prospects and great promises, splendid reforms; the speaker spoke magnificently of the improved conditions, the fuller liberty to come; and, as he ended, applause broke out; cheers, and the clapping of a multitude of hands.

Far away from that Hall and from that hour, Edith yet heard the applause ring out, and through and beyond it, the plash of tiny waves.

Then, in the body of the Hall—or out of the mist, was it, in the way that those phantom friends of hers came to her in the lane?—a form arose, slight and small enough almost to be that of a child, but a woman's nevertheless; the form of Annie Carnie, the mill hand, who had worked since she was ten years old, had come to the meeting to ask what the Liberal Government would do for working women, and who stood now, holding up a little white cotton banner with black letters on it, spelling "Votes for Women." Standing there, but little taller on her feet than the seated figures around her, she put her question, and hardly was it out of her mouth when around her there were other questions; questions from men; questions to which were given immediate replies. But the woman's question remained unanswered.

Again she rose, but there were men beside her; Edith was no more conscious of the sands or of the sea, as she saw them pull the woman down and force her into her seat, while one of them, a steward, pressed his hat over her face.

"Sit down!"

"What's the matter?"

"Let the lady speak!"

Cries and counter-cries.

Geraldine paused, and two women stood on a still morning, far away from crowds and the cries of crowds. For a minute they walked on, side by side in that grey silence: the cheeks of the one were flushed; the other had grown paler.

"And then—did they answer her?"

"Then Christina got up and asked the question that Annie Carnie had asked; and the men shouted as before, some in favour of giving her a hearing, some trying to shout her down. The Chief Constable of Manchester came down from the platform and made his way to her and promised that if the question was written down, he would see that it was answered."

"That was fair."

"Oh, quite fair. Well, it was written down, and Annie Carnie wrote in addition, that she was one of ninety-six thousand organised women cotton workers, and for their sakes earnestly begged for an answer.

"The Chief Constable took it back with him to the platform and gave it to the principal speaker—the one who had spoken so splendidly of liberty and the relief of the oppressed. He took the paper, read it, and smiled; then passed it on; and it went from hand to hand till it had gone the round of the platform."

"And then—"

"Then?" Lady Henry shrugged her shoulders. "Oh, then it was laid on the table and no more notice was taken of it."

"But that wasn't the end?" said Edith, after a moment's waiting.

"No, it was the beginning—of the militant movement."

The mist had lifted a little; Edith could see now the tiny advancing waves, and dimly, the smooth bosom of the sea.

"There were votes of thanks, of course, praise of the speaker, and applause, and his reply. The meeting was pretty well over, the chairman thanking for his vote of thanks, and people beginning to go ..."

Through the voice beside her, Edith heard again the mill hand's voice, the woman who had worked since she was ten years old and who wanted an answer to take back to the ninety-six thousand other women who were waiting for what she had to tell them. A small woman not easily to be seen in the crowd; but she can stand upon a chair.

"Will the Liberal Government give working women the vote?"

She was the first wave of the in-coming tide, the first to break, and to be broken, on the rocks.

At once and all around her the men who had cheered in praise of liberty and progress were shouting, gesticulating, crying out upon the woman who had dared to speak. The girl beside her—the girl whom Lady Henry had called Christina—put her arm round the little woman's waist, her one arm round her waist to strengthen and support her as she stood; with the other arm, she parried, or tried to parry, the blows that the men were striking, striking at them both.

There is red now in the mist; no, not in the mist, but in the great historic Hall which stands on the site where Peterloo[1] was won. Blood was there on that day, and blood is there again; blood that runs down from Christina's torn hands on to the hat that Annie Carnie had taken off and laid on the chair by her side.

But the girl's voice is calling still: "The question, the question. Answer the question!"

Six men to seize and drag out one girl. But there are so many men! No need to stint in numbers, either with one woman or the other. Christina goes first, and then the mill hand, the spokeswoman of thousands of working women like herself.

The people at the back of the Hall cry "Shame!" but the ticket-holders are shouting "Throw them out!" and on the platform the future ministers look on and say nothing.

Silence. In the Hall? No, the Hall has gone, with the cessation of Geraldine's voice. Silence of the sea and sand, broken only by the in-coming waves.

"Shall we turn?" Geraldine asked.

"I—I didn't know."

"No; most people don't. The Press boycotts us, or puts in garbled versions of our doings, versions which we are given no opportunity to contradict."

---

1   On 16 August 1819, between 60,000 and 80,000 people gathered at St. Peter's Fields, Manchester to listen to speeches advocating parliamentary reform and changes to voting practices. Although the gathering was peaceful—many had come with their families to enjoy what was, by all accounts, a beautiful summer day—the Manchester magistrates became increasingly nervous as the crowd grew. Claiming a threat to law and order, the magistrates dispatched the volunteer yeomanry which charged onto the field on horseback, wielding sabres. Eleven people were killed and over 400 wounded. (See Hewitt and Poole, eds., 2000; Reid, 1989). Speakers Henry "Orator" Hunt and Richard Carlile were arrested. The government not only endorsed the magistrates' actions, but put a series of repressive policies into place (the Six Acts) designed to quell further radical protest. In this light, it is hard to see how Peterloo could be said to have been "won"; however, in the wake of the event, the reformist movement grew, eventually paving the way for Chartism and women's suffrage.

"There was a report. I remember reading—But they were arrested, I thought?"

"Yes, outside, because they tried to hold a meeting in the street, where there was a crowd ready to listen to them; arrested for obstruction, and Christina was charged further with assaulting the police. From the report that *I* read, you would have thought they had behaved like wild beasts. Yet, if one of the men who asked a question that night had been set on and mauled by the others, it is the attackers and the maulers who would have been called wild beasts. But still the tide comes in. And the calling of names won't stop it. In fact"—Lady Henry's tone changed, and she smiled—"vile names are the concomitants of all causes, and the finer the cause, the viler the names."

The mist was lifting more and more; the sea carried silver gleams and the sun showed red.

"I believe it's going to be a lovely day after all," said Lady Henry. "We ought to have left our walk till later."

Walk! And Uncle Beauchamp? He had completely evaporated from Edith's consciousness: he loomed large in it now as she realised that it was already past the hour at which she had promised to return.

CHAPTER IX
AN INDEFINITE CALL

"We crave
A world unreal as the shell-heard sea."

E. Lee-Hamilton[1]

Edith was destined—there seemed no doubt about it—to see much of Cyril Race. When she went to the Dawnshire County Ball, he was there with the Bradleys' party; and when, early in the new year, she and her mother spent their usual month in London, she met him constantly.

At the ball he was the first person she saw on entering the dancing-room, but, having recognised him, she did not again glance in his direction. Of course he would not know her; a woman looked so

---

1 Eugene Lee-Hamilton (1845–1907), "Sea-Shell Murmurs" (1894).

different in a hat and a coat and skirt from what she did in evening dress; it was months ago and he would have forgotten the whole incident of their meeting; in any case she could not expect him to remember her, and she was certainly not going to scrape acquaintance on the strength of such an encounter as theirs had been.

But before many minutes had passed, he was beside her.

"Miss Carstairs, you of course haven't an idea who I am, but I have ventured—"

"Oh, but I remember you quite well. Your face is bound up—the only pleasant thing about it—with one of the most miserable days I ever spent."

"See what it is to be painted against a sombre background! I ought to have got Mrs. Bradley to introduce me, I suppose."

"It seems hardly necessary. She told you my name anyhow."

"Oh, I found that out before I left the market-place, on the day that was such a wretched one for you, but which I—I confess it—rather enjoyed."

"Well, your candidate got in."

"*Our* candidate, I hope? I somehow gathered—?"

"I don't know that I have a candidate, or whether I ought to do any more party work. But my sympathies are on your side."

"That's good. And a dance—may I have one?"

"Certainly." She handed him her programme. "You will see I am not 'full up' yet."

"I was wary and came at once. Two? May I have two?"

"If you like."

"Is three too many—for a man who has not been properly introduced?"

"I think our introduction should count for more than a formal one," said Edith, and then felt as if she had asked him to take four dances instead of three.

As Race turned away, other men came forward.

"May I have one?"

"I'm not too late, I hope."

"Any left for me?"

Edith's card was soon full, or nearly so; she kept two blank spaces in it.

Then the music began again, and her feet became impatient. Her partner—?

Ah, here he was! She moved away happily; the waltz was amongst her favourites.

Edith was one of the people to whom dancing is a pure delight, and the sound of waltz music an imperative behest towards motion. To-night the first dance was unadulterated enjoyment. The floor was good, the band perfect in time and tune; her partner danced as well—or almost as well—as she did; "the spirit in her feet" had its rhythmic will to the uttermost.

When the dance was over, as she was leaving the ball-room, there was a touch upon her arm.

"I suppose I haven't a chance?"

"Robbie! Why didn't you come before? I've had the greatest difficulty—But I've kept two for you; one of the supper ones and a two-step later on."

"Thanks awfully. Where are you likely to be?"

"Oh, you must find me." Edith laughed and passed on.

Robbie should take her in to supper; that was of course; as to the second dance it was more difficult to decide. It was hard to sacrifice a two-step, for she loved the skimming motion to the square tune (four-time was always square to Edith and three-time round); on the other hand a waltz with Robbie was misery; and the only polka had gone to old Sir Robert Dering, who claimed it as a right. For Robbie Colquhoun, red of face, fair of hair and deep of chest, was not a good dancer. He was a dear, but not a graceful dear; at any rate in a ball-room. His athleticism had broadened his shoulders and strengthened his muscles, but had conferred upon him none of the poetry of motion; and to Edith prose motion, when the band was playing poetry, was a misery. Nevertheless, because he was a friend, and a faithful friend, and because friendship had its debts as well as its privileges, she invariably dedicated two dances to Robbie, managing matters so that they supped or sat out through the greater part of them. Robbie was not exciting, especially as she knew him through and through; on the other hand it was no effort to talk to him, or, if she did not want to talk, it did not matter; Robbie either sat silent or kept up a smooth monologue. Somehow he always seemed to know which of these alternatives was most appropriate to her mood.

Could Mr. Race dance? It had not occurred to her that it was rash to give him three dances without a trial. When, after he had left her, the doubt arose, it was soon set at rest; she had but to watch him.

Now it was his dance. Would he come at the beginning? Absurd thing to ask! Her partners always came at the beginning. But Mr. Race was a stranger and could not know that she was the best dancer in the neighbourhood; unless, of course, he had watched her as she had watched him, which was hardly—Ah, here he comes!

"At last!" he said. "We'll start at once?"

"Oh yes."

She loved dancing, all dancing, if she had a partner who was even decent, but to dance with Cyril Race was, she told herself, divine; and Edith was not in the habit of using the adjective with the frequency and ineptitude with which it is commonly dragged into present-day vocabulary. They moved together in perfect accord with each other and the music; they moved over perfectly polished boards—in the air, through an enchanted land. The music led, followed, wrapt them in its magic. There was a wail in the violins, an indefinite call; to what? She could not tell, but it troubled her to the verge of pain; or was it happiness? Never mind; she won't think, but just dance on till—till—Ah, the music stops. It's over.

"What a splendid turn! Thank you ever so much. By Jove! Miss Carstairs, I knew you could dance; one had only to look, but—No wonder fellows fight for your programme."

"I love it."

Race led her to the space under the gallery. "I've found out that it's the best place to come to," he said, "the quietest; everybody rushes for the corridor." He made her comfortable with cushions, then turned and looked at her. "And so you have no politics?" he said.

Edith came down to solid earth, with a little bit of a bump as she landed.

"For the time being, no," she answered.

"That doesn't mean—" his tone was bantering, but she thought there was a note of anxiety in it—"it doesn't mean that you're going over to the suffragettes? I remember—that day in the market-place—you were keen on the fact that you were a suffra*gist*, a woman, not a—shall I say—warrior?"

"I should make a poor warrior, I'm afraid."

"You're hardly built that way." The tone and the look made the words a compliment.

"But I can't run down the suffragettes any more; because—I—I know one."

"I know several. That's why I run them down."

"I wonder which ones you know?"

"Christina for one."

"Miss Amherst, do you mean?"

Race bowed in apology. "I beg your pardon! Hers, as a public character, one perhaps hardly needs to beg. Is it she you have—whose acquaintance you have made?"

"No, it's Lady Henry Hill. Do you know her?"

"Quite well, and I congratulate you. She's an interesting and charming woman. But then you see, she doesn't mix up with the rabble of the movement, keeps to speaking and legitimate propaganda. There are, I admit, suffragettes *and* suffragettes. I assure you I'm not unduly prejudiced."

Edith was quite prepared to believe that Mr. Race was open-minded; her conception of his character would have been spoiled had she been obliged to own him ungenerous. Her next dance was with a man who, as she knew of old, had "no patience with women who want to ape men." Cyril Race gained by contrast, though she did not touch on the suffrage question with her present partner; nor indeed with any of her partners. It was a subject she had learned to avoid in Dawnshire, and it was not worth while to disturb the pleasure of dancing by discussing it with men who had not taken the trouble to master the ABC of it.

Nor did Race himself again refer to the question. After his second dance he took her to the chairs they had occupied before and she found herself talking to him about her likes and dislikes, the things she did and the things she would like to do. He had offered to forego the dance in favour of supper; but supper was to come later with Robbie Colquhoun, and it would have seemed desecration to Edith to eat when she could dance; above all, with such a partner as Race.

"Unless," she had said, "you are very hungry."

"Oh no, I would much rather dance; I have eaten many suppers, but I have never had such dances as we have had together to-night."

He liked dancing with her then, as much as she with him. She was glad; and glad to find herself sitting with him again under the gallery; and glad that he was so easy, so sympathetic to talk to. She almost got to the point of telling him about the lane and the fancies that were companions to her there; almost, not quite; she had never shared her phantoms with anybody, except Robbie Colquhoun and, strangely enough, Geraldine Hill. Robbie, of course, had always known of them, and Robbie, equally of course, understood; and Lady Henry would understand too and would not think her mad; she knew it intuitively. Mr. Race—well, she was not quite sure; he would think her silly perhaps, and that fancies such as hers were incompatible with the capacity for making proper use of the vote. It was better to be discreet, though she was tempted to be confiding during the dance they sat out together; for the waltz that followed theirs was an extra, he declared; an extra extra, not one of the ordinary ones. Mrs. Bradley had just told him about it, and if Miss Carstairs had not known of it and was consequently not engaged, he was sure it would do her good to rest a little. So Edith sat on and chatted. Race was more a man of the world than any man she had yet met; it was easy to draw her out; not difficult to bring the smile to her lips, the light—an added, leaping light that came with quickened interest—to her eyes.

When the music stopped Race asked her to introduce him to her mother; and while he and Mrs. Carstairs stood talking, Edith went over to Robbie Colquhoun, who was standing a little way off in a corner.

"You don't look much as if you wanted to dance with me," she said.

"What's the good of wanting? You've just cut my dance."

"Robbie! Oh no, that was an extra."

"I know; the second; my dance was the second extra."

"No, but I mean an extra extra. Mr. Race assured me, or I never—"

"It doesn't matter. I quite believe you didn't cut it on purpose. It doesn't matter, Edie, at all. Don't worry about it."

"Why didn't you come? Didn't you see where I was?"

"Yes, I saw, but—you looked quite contented, and I supposed Mr. Race would give you supper if you wanted it. I don't want you to go hungry, that's all."

He smiled at her, but Edith knew by the little twist in his upper lip—she knew him so well—that he was hurt.

She danced the two-step with him later on instead of making excuses to sit out, instead of having supper as he suggested—and she was really hungry by that time—because she knew that it would please him best if she danced with him; and Robbie showed no resentment, no sign of being the least little bit offended. Nevertheless when Edith got home that night and looked through her programme, kneeling by her bedroom fire, the initials R.C. opposite the second extra caused her a pang of compunction. To make the record of the evening a true one she must cross out those initials and put others in their place. Nay, she had only to turn them about and put C.R. instead of R.C. Odd that the two men should have the same first letters to their names! The same, but in the reverse order; as, she told herself, the two men were the reverse the one of the other: Robbie big and slow and what Edith at the moment called lumbering; Cyril Race of middle height, alert in movement and expression, full of brains and knowledge and intuition, of which, alas! poor Robbie had none.

Edith has that programme still and the two sets of initials standing side by side, bring to her mind all the pain and the joy bound up with the men whose names they represent; and all the stress, the strain and struggle and turmoil associated with the woman's movement in the first years of the twentieth century.

CHAPTER X
A BUNDLE OF PAPERS

> "'Tis strange what awkward figures and odd capers
> Folks cut, who seek their doctrine from the papers;
> But there are many shallow politicians,
> Who take their bias from bewildered journals—
> Turn state physicians,
> And make themselves fools'-caps of the diurnals."
>
> Tom Hood[1]

> "Deal with us nobly, women though we be,
> And honour us with truth if not with praise."
>
> *Aurora Leigh*[2]

---

1 Thomas Hood (1799–1845), "The Monkey-Martyr, A Fable" (1827).
2 Elizabeth Barrett Browning (1806–61), *Aurora Leigh* (1856).

Sally Simmonds took in *Votes for Women*.[1] She subscribed for three months in advance and had it sent to her, because it was so much more cheek (it was a word she had heard Mrs. Bilkes use and was that lady's way of pronouncing *chic*) than buying it in the street. She was as proud of the paper as if she edited, wrote and printed it all herself, and the week was not long enough for her to master its contents. It was all very well for the master to have his *Daily Mail* and his *Evening News*. Such papers as them was pore stuff and had to be brought out fresh every day to keep them going; but for her paper, once a week was enough; there was so much to study in it that it took a girl the whole of her spare time to find out all the suffragettes were doing and planning to do. Nobody could pretend they had not got plenty to say for themselves; and as for selling, why it went like hot cakes.

She offered to assist in the sale on one of her afternoons out, an afternoon that was damp and chilly, in the early part of February. For two hours she stood in the Strand,[2] eager petition in her eyes; a bundle of papers, which, to her encouragement, got smaller as time went on, under her arm; feet which became colder and colder; a nose which grew redder. All types of men and women passed her by, manifold types of the manifold attitudes taken up in regard to the question of women's enfranchisement. There was the irate old gentleman who hurried past with a wave of his hand and a "No, no, I've no patience with you"; the stiffly respectable woman who seemed to take Sally's presence on the pavement as a personal affront to herself; the maiden ladies who spoke to each other of "these creatures" as they went by; the smart young man who supposed she was out looking for a husband and was annoyed when Sally asked what price jokes of the year before last.

But there were the other types as well; the jovial man who wished her luck, and for his part he'd give the women anything they asked for; the timid woman who hastened past, paused, hesitated and scuttled back, thrust a penny into Sally's hand, murmured: "Just to see," and hid her *Votes for Women* under her coat; the man who raised his

---

[1] The newspaper published by the Women's Social and Political Union (WSPU) edited, until 1912, by Emmeline and Frederick Pethick-Lawrence.

[2] Just to the north of Victoria Embankment and the Thames River, the Strand is a busy thoroughfare linking the financial district in The City of London to the West End. The Savoy Hotel is just off Strand, and the area is famous for its theatres.

hat as he took his paper; the stout woman who didn't know much about it, but liked pluck, and didn't see after all, being a widow and in business and paying rates and taxes—and high ones at that—why she couldn't put a cross on a bit of paper as well as her foreman; the frank sympathiser, who said: "I take it in," and passed on with a smile and a nod.

And then, in the stream of strange faces, came a face that Sally knew. A girl with a theatre programme in her hand caught sight of the outstretched arm and the proffered paper, and, raising her eyes from the paper to the face above it, stopped and came forward to the pavement's edge.

"Why it's Sally Simmonds! Sally, do you remember me? Littlehampton?"

"'Course I do, miss; you was along of Lady 'Ill most mornings, for a week. A paper, miss? And you, sir?"

Edith's companions, her mother and Cyril Race, had stopped when she stopped; the latter followed her to Sally's side.

"Please. Here, Miss Carstairs, I've got two coppers handy."

"Do you know anythink of 'er ladyship—'ow she's gettin' on? I wasn't able to go to the last meetin'."

"She's very well, and all right in every way. We're just going to see her now, to have tea with her. I'll tell her I've seen you."

"Yes, do!" Sally's face and voice were eager. "She'll be pleased to 'ear as I'm workin' for the cause."

"I'll tell her certainly, and that—How have you been getting on? Sold pretty well?"

"Not bad." Sally held up the bundle of papers. "It's smaller than it was by a good bit, but there's a tidy few to get rid of yet."

"Well, good luck!"

The two girls nodded and smiled at one another, and Edith passed on.

"Dear me, Edith," said Mrs. Carstairs, "I don't know what you're coming to, talking so long to that common-looking woman. If you *must* buy a paper in the street, why couldn't you just buy it and pass on?"

"Because it was Sally, mother, Sally Simmonds, whom I saw at Littlehampton last summer, one of Lady Henry's protégées; and any-one who has once talked to Sally must want to talk to her again."

"Well, don't you think we might take a taxi now?"

"Certainly. I've succeeded in getting some air into my lungs after that stuffy theatre, and it's getting late."

Sally, from her cold corner, saw Race hail a taxi-cab, and the three get into it and drive away. How she would like to go with them; to whirl through the streets; to leave the cold wind and damp pavement for warmth and comfort; to go to tea with Lady 'Ennery 'Ill! But her dooty—that she must do. She was helping her dear ladyship more by standing here in the cold than if she were to go and share her tea.

Then, out of the gathering fog, a new friend came to her, but an unknown one. A woman, walking swiftly, paused as she saw the face with the growing weariness upon it; a woman, slender and upright, with finely cut features and unswerving eyes, and wearing a black lace mantilla on her grey hair. Many heads turned to look at her: yet all over London, Londoners knew the mantilla and the face; knew them as belonging to a woman whose courage was unquestioned, whose energy was unfailing, whose support of all movements in which justice and mercy were concerned, was as generous and un-grudging as the spirit which led her to hold no sacrifice too great on behalf of a principle. In the district in which she had made her home, the children ran to her as she passed their parents looked on her as a friend: in the wider world, where her name was well known to friends and foes alike, she was honoured by all save those to whom convention is the first of virtues. All the defenceless had a friend in her; women, children, animals; for her there were none too obscure, too feeble, too inarticulate, to stand within the sphere of justice; on her shield the arms of the faddist were crossed with those of the suf-fragette, and it would have been hard to say which were the more to her mind. When she stopped to speak to the little maid-of-all-work serving in the ranks of the movement in which she was one of the leaders, she was as unknown to Sally as Sally was to her; so that it is not to be wondered at that when she asked if Sally were nearing the end of her task, the girl should ask if she "belonged to us."

"To your army, yes; not to the same regiment. But whenever I see a soldier on guard, of whatever regiment, I always salute as I go by."[1]

---

[1]   Socialist and social reformer, Charlotte Despard (1844–1939) was president of the Women's Freedom League (WFL). NUWSS member Helena Swanwick writes "Mrs. Despard was

"When she had passed on, there was yet another surprise in store for the tired saleswoman. Out of the fog, crossing the street towards her, loomed figures, faces, that were surely familiar. Who—where? Why of course, the two youngest Miss Bilkeses.

"Lor'," said Sally to herself, "whatever will they say when they see me? Most like, nothink at all just pass me with a sneer. But shan't I 'ear about it from 'er, and especially from 'im!"

The two Miss Bilkeses passed her, to be sure, without speaking, but when they had gone a few yards they slackened their pace.

"Did you see, that was Ben and Emily's Sally?" said Georgina.

"Yes, did you ever?"

Then Sally saw them stop and talk together, with glances towards herself; finally they turned and came slowly back to where she stood, Georgina, the younger, leading the way.

"Do your master and mistress know what you are doing?" Georgina asked.

"Not at present." Sally's tone said, "Of course you'll tell them."

"We shan't mention it," observed Maria.

"You won't! I never!" said Sally. "Not as I'm ashamed of the cause," she added, "nor ashamed to be caught serving of it. I'd sooner serve the cause and Lady 'Ill, if it comes to that, nor wot I would Mr. and Mrs. Bilkes—no offence meant. But it makes ructions."

"And it's no business of ours to report your proceedings," said Georgina.

"No indeed, we are not our brother's keeper," added Maria, who felt that she was giving a high tone to their undertaking by the quotation.

"Let me give you a paper, miss, as a present. The reading's beautiful and such a lot for your money."

"We did think of—of buying a paper," said Georgina, "just to see the sort of things they put in."

---

one of the militant leaders whom one could not fail to revere. Partly this reverence was due to her picturesque aspect of a fiery old prophetess. Her speech, too, was sybilline and mystical rather than logical; she was no good at all on a committee, where she found it impossible to bring her mind to bear on a resolution. She was the soul of honour and looked a most gallant women, as she was. Her kindness had no end and she was always ready to strip herself of everything, first in her work at Nine Elms, then for the suffrage, then for peace while war raged...." (190–91). See also Linklater.

"There's all about the prisoners at Bow Street,[1] this week—them five wot went to Downing Street[2] to try an' see if they could speak to the Prime Minister."

"I don't see why we shouldn't," said Georgina to Maria. "We can throw it away if there's anything indecent," Maria answered.

"A month they've got," Sally went on, "same as if they'd stole a watch, and three weeks more than father got for kickin' mother next door to kingdom come."

"We'll take a copy, Sally, but we'll pay for it; and you needn't"— Georgina cleared her throat—"you needn't mention it to Mr. or Mrs. Bilkes."

"'Ow could I, miss," asked Sally, "without lettin' my own cat out of its bag?"

"Pore things!" she said to herself when the Miss Bilkeses had walked away, "they can't never give notice if it's ever so, from the place where *they*'re in, unless some feller comes along as'll offer them another."

CHAPTER XI
POINTS OF VIEW

"The first wrote, wine is the strongest.
The second wrote, the king is the strongest.
The third wrote, women are strongest: but above all things
Truth beareth away the victory."

1 Esdras 3:10–12

Meanwhile Edith and her mother and Mr. Race had reached Lady Henry Hill's drawing-room. They found quite a little company assembled there. There was Mrs. Carleton, Lady Henry's "Aunt Margaret"; Mrs. Merton, a journalist whose articles and sketches were welcomed by editors; Angela Sayte, a hospital nurse and a connection of Geraldine's; Sir Charles Martin, private secretary to a leading member of the House of Lords; and John Gorton, the playwright and novelist.

---

1 Bow Street Police Station and Magistrates' Court.
2 10 Downing Street is the official residence of the British prime minister.

All of these people had finished their tea, except the hospital nurse, whose chair was drawn up to the tea table, and who was eating leisurely.

"This is a meal to me," she said to Edith, who took a seat near her, "not just a polite snack. I can't tell you how good these nicely served things taste after the hospital food."

"I should think so, though I don't know much about hospital food. But I am sure I shouldn't fancy it; I imagine there would be a sort of a flavour of well—"

"Oh, it isn't the flavour, it's the lack of it," broke in the nurse gaily, "though to be sure, the things that ought to be flavourless, such as butter—I buy marmalade sometimes to hide the taste of it, but I've just read—in a wonderful book—that marmalade, shop marmalade isn't marmalade at all, but something quite disgusting. Have you read it 'The Soul Market'?"

"It's down on our Mudie[1] list," said Mrs. Carstairs, "but—I don't know that I should care for a book about marmalade."

"I've read it," said Mrs. Carleton, "and it's very well worth reading. Now there's a woman I can honestly admire. She really does something to help other women." She looked across at her niece; and Geraldine at once responded to the attack.

"As far as they *can* be helped without political freedom," she replied.

"She went through the most awful experiences, that Olive Malvery,"[2] Mrs. Carleton continued, "in order to show up the terrible things that go on."

"Just what we do," said Geraldine.

"You! Oh, Geraldine!"

"I should have said 'they,'" amended Geraldine. "I certainly have not done much."

---

1   Mudie's Select Library, established in 1842 by Charles Edward Mudie, charged subscribers a yearly fee of one guinea for which they might borrow an unlimited number of books. Mudie's Library was known for the "wholesome moral tone" of the books it made available to readers (Flint, 144; see also Griest, 1970).

2   Olive Christian Malvery investigated the plight of London's poor, particularly working women and children, by passing as one of them. She detailed her discoveries in a series of articles under the title, "The Heart of Things," in *Pearson's Magazine*, which were collected and published as *The Soul Market* in 1906. Money from the royalties of her book was used to build two shelters for homeless women (Walkowitz, 3–47).

"When I said 'you,' I meant your Society. I know that personally"—Mrs. Carleton addressed the company generally—"I know very well that my niece would never be guilty of the deplorable acts which make some of us feel ashamed of being women. But this Miss Malvery—is she Miss or Mrs.?—went about it so quietly, no fuss, no notoriety, no calling attention to what she did."

"She has called a good deal of attention to it now," observed John Gorton.

"Through her book? Yes, of course, but that's a legitimate way."

"It wouldn't have been worth doing what she did, if she hadn't called public attention to it," said Geraldine. "I assure you, Aunt Margaret, I quite share your admiration of her; she shows up some of the abuses we want to do away with."

"I do hope they're not going to begin and argue," remarked Mrs. Carstairs to Sir Charles Martin. "I can't bear arguments, and I'm getting so tired of the suffrage."

"It rather amuses me to hear people going for each other," returned Sir Charles, "so long as it isn't about anything that really matters. And this—of course it will never come to anything—is fizzling out fast. But I confess I agree with Mrs. Carleton—(mustn't let Lady Henry hear me!)—I do like a womanly woman."

"So do I, and I do wish we could get the vote in a womanly way and be done with it. My daughter, you see, she's very advanced—like her poor father—"

"Is your daughter a militant?"

"Oh no, certainly not. She's sitting over there by the tea-table."

Sir Charles was tempted to ask if militant Suffragettes never went near a tea-table, but he bridled his tongue, and a glance at Edith showed him the real significance of her mother's remark.

"She certainly doesn't look like one," he said.

"I should think not indeed." Then, hesitatingly, Mrs. Carstairs added: "But no more, for the matter of that, does Lady Henry Hill."

"She isn't; that's the answer. Imagination, you know, carried away by the idea, a bit *exaltée*.[1] Wise of her husband to let her have her head and work it off in speechifying. But Lady Henry at logger-

---

1 Excited.

heads with the police—! No, no, it's not her *métier*,[1] my dear lady, not her *métier*."

"I quite agree with you, and it seems so unfair to the policemen, because of course it isn't their fault, and I find them very polite at the crossings. One stopped the whole of the traffic in Piccadilly the other day for me to get across."

"I am sure you would always find a policeman much more useful than a vote when it comes to holding up traffic."

"Of course I'm in favour of the vote; when I pay the taxes for instance, I always feel I ought to have it, and I feel sure my husband would have liked me to be able to go on voting for the Liberals. But there are so many people on the other side, and especially in the country; and when you have relations who are against it and live near, it seems easier to do without it."

"That's Mrs. Merton's view, I believe," said Sir Charles. "Isn't it?" he asked, turning to the pretty journalist. "I notice that you never join in heated discussions on the subject. You smile, indeed, when others frown."

"I confess it rather amuses me to see people exciting themselves over a thing that women have done so admirably without. I'm not against it—not an anti—because, of course, logically speaking, there's nothing against it; but personally I find so many interesting things to do that I haven't time to think about it."

"But, then you've got a position," said Cyril Race, "and—if you'll excuse personalities—an unusual amount of brains. I imagine that the chief advantage of the vote would be to the obscure women. Isn't that so, Lady Henry?"

"Yes, in one way. In a sense, the obscurer and less capable the woman, the more she needs the protection and the status of the vote."

"Oh come!" said Sir Charles, "I thought women were claiming it on the ground that they are the equals of men."

"A woman with an ounce of tact can always get what she wants, whether she's clever or not; that's my experience," pronounced Mrs. Merton.

Lady Henry answered Sir Charles. "There are obscure men, if it's a question of equal claims, and men who are not very capable,

---

1 Occupation; vocation; a field or department of activity in which a person has special skill or ability; one's forte (*OED*).

and I think that what Mr. Race said applies to one sex as much as to the other. As a matter of fact, equality has nothing to do with the question. You probably would not consider my cowman on an equality with yourself; nor would you consider Lord Goresby, who is so stupid that his wife has to manage his estate for him, your equal in intellect; nor Archie Fisher, who is rarely sober, your equal in dignity. Yet the fact that one is a cowman, the other next door to a fool, and the third a drunkard, does not in the least interfere with their possession of the vote."

"That's all very well," said Mrs. Carleton. "All the same a woman—"

"Darling Aunt Margaret, please don't tell me that a woman's sphere is the home!"

"I wasn't going to say quite that, Geraldine; but put it as you like, a woman has her own duties, and they're different from a man's."

"I don't deny it; I agree. But it's just because of the difference in duties, in outlook, in needs, that women require direct representation."

"So sorry to interrupt the discussion, but I must be going on," said Mrs. Merton, getting up.

"Pretty, isn't she?" said Sir Charles to Mrs. Carstairs.

"Yes, very; a charming woman."

"Sort of woman a man likes to take in to dinner, amusing, easy to talk to, no equality, and all that sort of thing about her "

"Yes," said Mrs. Carstairs naively; "I always tell my daughter that men prefer women who are not their equals. She won't admit it, but what I say is that if a woman is cleverer than a man she mustn't let him see it." She rose and held out her hand. "So glad to hear your views. Edith dear, we must be going."

Edith, who had been talking to Angela Sayte, came over to her mother, then crossed the room to say good-bye to Lady Henry.

"I wish I could speak up as you do," she said, "without being afraid."

"If you had wanted to say something sarcastic, you could not have hit upon anything more cutting," Geraldine answered. She smiled as she spoke, yet Edith felt that in some way she was hurt or unhappy; the words were hardly a jest, though they were jestingly uttered.

CHAPTER XII
HUSBAND AND WIFE

"Shall I, lone sorrow past,
Find thee at last?
Sorrow past,
Thee at last?"

Christina G. Rossetti[1]

Mrs. Carleton left immediately after the Carstairs; so did Cyril Race; and Sir Charles Martin soon followed him. When they had gone, Lady Henry came and stood before John Gorton, who was leaning against the mantelpiece, his back to the fire.

"You didn't back me up," she said.

"I plead guilty."

"You said not a word of support, not one single word."

"Do you know why? Because I was afraid of saying too much. When I feel strongly about a thing, I'm apt to get carried away and say more than I—no, not more than I mean, but more than is helpful to my hostess."

"In a highly respectable society, such as was assembled here this afternoon," remarked Angela from her easy chair, "I am inclined to agree with Mr. Gorton and think that one spitfire is enough."

"Was I—I'm afraid I spat fire at dear Aunt Margaret. I hope I wasn't really—rude?"

"I think honours were divided as far as the fire-spitting was concerned," said John Gorton. "But seriously, Lady Henry, I stood out because I knew quite well I should never make them see my point."

"What *is* your point?" asked Angela.

"That though it's important that women should have the vote—for the women, it's far more important for the men."

"No, they wouldn't have seen that, I'm quite sure."

"It's true though, emphatically true. You want women's influence in public life, their driving power, their conscientiousness." ("Driving power! Shade of Sir Charles Martin!" murmured Angela.) "Men may be more physically courageous than women; I think they

---

1 Christina Georgina Rossetti (1830–94), "Confluents" (1875).

are; but they're not in it when it comes to moral courage. Women will face ridicule, they'll take no end of trouble, and they'll stick to a thing when a man will throw it over in boredom or disgust."

"I can bear you out in that—from my experience with patients. If a treatment is troublesome, a man will refuse to follow it out, put off doing it, do it irregularly; in any case, make an awful fuss. Women patients go through with it as a matter of course. There are exceptions, naturally, on both sides, but, as a rule, that's my experience."

"Look at women clerks; they are more careful, more diligent, more economical, more conscientious than men. It all means driving power, and it's just that driving power and the steadfastness and perseverance of women that would be of such immense value to men in the conduct of public business—more even in its influence on the men than on the business."

"It's just as well, perhaps, that you didn't say all that," said Geraldine. "The men certainly would not have liked it—nor you."

"Men don't as a rule like what I say, when I say what I think, and very often don't like me; just because I don't think on the usual man-thinking lines."

"Henry likes you," said Geraldine, "but then Henry—"

"No, Lord Henry is not quite the ordinary Englishman. The ordinary Englishman likes a man who will have a smoke with him, with perhaps a whisky and soda, talk a little about sport, a little about what's going on, a little—if the two happen to follow the same calling—a little shop; who will say the accepted things about the accepted topics, and take jolly good care not to go below the surface."

Angela Sayte got up to go and Gorton held out his hand to Lady Henry. "I'm afraid I've stayed too long chattering," he said.

"Oh no, you had to make up for lost ground you know."

Angela and Gorton went downstairs together.

"I think Lady Henry looks a bit worried," said Gorton. "Or is it my fancy?"

"Not altogether, perhaps; I fancied the same thing."

That evening Geraldine and her husband dined out together. From the dinner they went on to a political reception and it was late when they returned home. But Geraldine lingered in the hall.

"Are you going to smoke?"

"Yes, just a whiff or two."

"Then I'll come. I want to talk to you."

"No," Geraldine said presently, in the smoking-room, "I won't sit down. I'd rather stand by the fire. You sit. You love that old chair, don't you? I don't believe you'd like it half so much if the leather was mended and it was re-stuffed."

"It's jolly comfortable. Don't go and have it repaired, Jerry!"

"Not I; I never interfere with this room."

Geraldine stood with her foot on the fender, looking into the fire.

"Well," said Lord Henry presently, "I thought you wanted to talk."

"So I do." She paused. "I'm troubled, Henry."

"What about? Nothing really serious, darling?"

She turned and looked at him straight, with what he called her clear look. "I'm troubled about the promise I made you. I don't know how long—whether I shall be able to keep it."

"What promise? I don't remember—"

"When I joined the Union—that I was to do nothing but speak."

A shadow fell on the face that was looking into hers; the brows contracted, the eyes grew a trifle harder.

"You don't mean that you want to take part in any of these— confounded outrages?" He spoke quietly, slowly, almost gently, but Geraldine knew that she had said the thing which of all others he most disliked that she should say.

"I don't *want* to do anything," she answered, "very much don't want it; but I feel—I can't help feeling—it's borne in upon me— that I ought to do my part."

"Surely you do a very considerable part! I should have said that your part was a prominent one."

"That's just the word—prominent; but it's because of my title, not because of what I do. Oh, I speak well, I know—I don't underrate myself—as well perhaps as a dozen other women in the movement. And I'm listened to, talked about, mentioned in the papers, because of my name, because I'm Lady Henry Hill."

"Your name has been useful, I know; I knew it would be when first you joined in this—this movement; and I have never—have I?—objected to your making use of it."

"No," she said, "no. You've been—as I like to think of you."

"But when it comes to abusing it, Geraldine,—"

Geraldine! he called her Geraldine. She knew he must be really angry—

"Think of the parents!"

"I've thought of them," she said in a low voice.

"The Duke!"

"I know; and it's on you it would fall, in a great measure; that's the worst of it. But I can't help it. I feel such a coward, standing by, aloof from the real brunt of it all, letting the other women take all the kicks while I take the halfpence—such halfpence as there are."

"The other women haven't got your name. It makes a difference."

"That's just it. My name does make a difference. Nobody cares, nobody notices now, if a seamstress or a factory girl goes to prison, or a gentlewoman, if she has got plain Mrs. or Miss before her name. But if somebody with a title—"

"You're not here to tell me that you intend going to prison?"

"No; I only mean that in all that one does one must take the consequences, whether it means going to prison, or—hurting those that one loves."

"My father has been awfully good about your speaking. He hasn't liked it—you know what he is, prejudiced against what he calls platform women; but he's played up well, because you've always been a favourite and because, as he told me, he had confidence in your sense of what was becoming to your position."

"What is my position? what is it, after all? Lower, politically, than the meanest man's on the Duke's estate. Yet I am to be held back by it from doing anything towards attaining the position of a citizen! Like Aunt Margaret this afternoon, who took it for granted that in the drama which women are playing, I could never be anything but a walking-on lady—because I am her niece and your wife."

Lord Henry was silent a minute, then he said, "Well, what does it all amount to? Have you pledged yourself to active service?"

His wife overlooked the irony in his voice. "I have pledged myself to nothing, except, as you know, that I would confine myself to the kind of work I have done so far. But I don't know that I shall be able to keep the promise—always—perhaps not very much longer. And I felt bound to tell you."

"I shouldn't have expected you to feel anything else." Lord Henry got up out of his arm-chair. "There's nothing immediate, then? No particular raid you've planned to take part in?"

"No; it's only that if I come to feel I must—you understand?"

"Yes, a sort of needs must if the devil drives. Is that it?" Lord Henry smiled, but the smile was a wan one.

"Don't call the thing in me a devil, for it certainly possesses me."

Geraldine put her hands on his shoulders—the husband and wife were almost the same height—and her face close to his. "If it drives—the thing inside me—shall you cast me off?"

He let her cheek lie close to his, but his voice was cold as he answered, "How can I? I am bound to stand by you—publicly."

"But privately?" she whispered.

"It depends on how far you go." He drew back from her. "I have something I ought to do before coming up. Good night, Geraldine."

She took the word away with her; the seal of his displeasure; Geraldine.

CHAPTER XIII
THE SIGN OF THE CROSS

"The only plus sign is the sign of the cross."

A.W.L.[1]

Sally was growing restless. The bird in her breast, of whose fluttering Lady Henry had first made her aware was stretching its wings and becoming an unquiet inmate. At first the paper had sufficed, and the weekly meetings, and the converting of Joe Whittle, who was somewhat of a rice-Christian[2] and ready to sacrifice opinions for the sake of kisses; but all these things were negative, she felt. All that she could do was to send subscriptions to the Union and have the joy—the ineffable joy—of seeing her name in the list of subscribers. It was shown to Joe every time it appeared there, which was

---

1   Colmore dedicates her novel *The Thunderbolt* (1919) to "A.W.L. With whom I have often discussed the place of fact in fiction." It is unclear whose initials these were.

2   "One ... who adopts Christianity for material benefits" (*OED*).

almost every time that Sally received her monthly wage; and once Joe Whittle's appeared after it. She was proud indeed then.

But the pride and the joy of printed names made too concrete a return for the sacrifice of giving, and Sally, as she stood by her bedroom window, and looked across at the roof of Holloway Gaol,[1] felt that her shillings and sixpences were hopelessly inadequate as a contribution to the activities of the Union. How could she set about taking a share in these activities? She had her living to earn; she wasn't like a lady who had enough to live upon and could give herself up to the cause; no work meant no pay for Sally, and no pay meant absence of food, lodgings, clothes, the bare necessaries of life. "I think I see mother a takin' of me in for nothink," she was thinking; "nor I couldn't arst 'er, even if she was willin', nor take it, not if she was to press me." There were other ways, to be sure, of earning your living than by being in service; there were shops, for instance, and factories, and work in these meant that you had your evenings free. But Sally knew nothing about shop-keeping or factory work; she only knew that while those experienced in either had great difficulty in obtaining employment, she, the totally unskilled, would have no chance at all. And even if she did, Holloway Prison would put an entire end to her job and stand altogether in the way of her renewing it; and Holloway Prison, at this stage of the cause's progress, seemed to Sally to form an inevitable portion of the lot of active workers.

There were suffragettes over there, in the prison, at this very moment; the five women who had sought an interview with the Prime Minister. There were always suffragettes there now. She looked across at the sombre building and her heart sank. Should she ever be able to "stick it"? Alone in a cell! She who hated being alone. There were those who said the suffragettes only wanted to be noticed (Joe Whittle had said it once, but had never ventured to repeat the remark); for her part, it was the sort of notice she could do without;

---

1   Holloway Gaol figures largely in the novel as the North London prison to which women were sent as a result of their suffrage activities. The imposing structure (opened in 1852, but completely rebuilt between 1971 and 1985) resembled a medieval fortress with battlements, towers and heraldic beasts. The story told to staff and visitors was that the elaborate facade was intended to imitate Warwick Castle as a way to allay the fears of neighbours who were unhappy living next door to a prison (Rock, 16). For a description of the details of prison life see Purvis, "The Prison Experiences of the Suffragettes in Edwardian Britain," 1995; S. Pankhurst, 1931, 230–38.

following her inclination, she "wouldn't be taking any." To wake in the night and find yourself quite alone! It was a thing that had never happened to her in all her twenty-four years. Three in a bed and two on the floor; that had been Sally's home experience of sleeping accommodation; and now there was Miss Dorothy close beside her and Stanny, who frequently broke the silence of the night—and her own slumbers—by requests for a drink. That was another reason why she did not want to start out on a fresh line; to forsake what had come to seem to her the safe and peaceful shelter of the Bilkes household; forsaking it, she forsook also the children.

The children were often troublesome, but they were children, and as such made appeal to her; moreover, this particular trio, Dorothy, Stanny, and little Maud, had twined themselves about a heart inclined by nature to affection. And Sally, trusting and optimistic by temperament, had no very high opinion of her own kind—the "general" kind. Another girl might slap the children when their ma wasn't there, or dock them of their drinks, and would certainly not be able to tell them the stories, they liked best; even leaving out the story of the beautiful lady who spoke to people so as she waked up thoughts in them as had been fast asleep all their lives; thoughts as called out an 'arsted you things; "same as you, Master Stanny dear, when you wakes up in the dark and calls out to Sally to know where you is." No, she didn't want to leave the children, and she didn't want to be took notice of by way of Holloway Gaol.

So Sally in her kitchen and attic and Geraldine in her boudoir fought something of the same battle; were urged on by the same forces; held back, if not by the same ties, yet by ties the breaking of which would mean poignant pain to each.

From this battle, in which each knew nothing of the other's struggles, Edith Carstairs stood aloof. For her the woman's cause carried no call to arms; the methods by which to win it, by which undoubtedly it would be won, were methods of patience, of peace, of confidence in the men—gentlemen, statesmen—at the helm of political events. Such methods being right, the others, the methods of obstruction, of violence, must be wrong; and moreover unwise. It was unwise to hamper and harass a Government whose hands were so full, who had so many obligations which they were pledged to fulfil; it was wrong to distrust and persecute a Cabinet of which Cyril Race was a member. Persecute was Race's, word and Edith had accepted it. The by-election policy, the disturbing of Ministers' meetings, these things came under the heading of persecution; they were, in themselves, repugnant to her, besides being, as Race had pointed out, tactically unwise. If you want a Government to give you something, why put its back up? he had asked; and Edith had found no answer to the question, though she had tried to find an answer.

With the scene that Lady Henry had painted on the mist still vivid in her mind, with the sound of angry shouts and the calling of a girl's voice, "The question, the question! Answer the question!" still mingled with the breaking of tiny waves that fell upon her inward ears, she had asserted that the policy he combated had taken its rise in injustice and brutality. But Cyril Race had argued that all men make mistakes, that two wrongs do not make a right, and that it was ungracious, as well as illogical, to pursue a whole Cabinet with petty persecutions because some members of it were opposed to a measure of which the majority were actually in favour.

Edith had ended by agreeing with him, and it was delightful to find her heart and her head working in conformity. People did make mistakes, both men and women; even the leaders of the WSPU were not infallible. There were parts of their programme which, in spite of admiration for their pluck, of the comprehension of their motives and objects which Lady Henry had engendered in her, Edith could not but condemn; incidents in their policy of which even their own members—so she had been assured—did not wholeheartedly approve. If allowances were to be made, they should be made all round.

Back at the Pightle, and walking once more in the fancy-filled solitude of her beloved lane, Edith found that she had come back, in a great measure, to the attitude from which the meeting in the Free Trade Hall at Manchester had wrenched her. Not wholly: the meeting had left its mark; a deeper mark than it had made on many of those who in bodily presence had assisted at it; since she in spirit had been there, in spirit had perceived its significance, and since those who had been clothed upon with flesh had by that very flesh been shut out from the spirit's perception.

The mark was there, and she could no longer despise nor condemn the women whose methods were foreign to her nature and unconvincing to her intellect; but she was able to return to her allegiance to the Liberal Government, able to pursue once more with ardour and in confidence the policy in regard to women's enfranchisement, the efficacy of which for a time she had doubted. She was the same as she had been before going to Littlehampton, or thought she was; yet there was a subtle change in her, a change which was reflected in the atmosphere of the lane. The shadowy, impersonal forms of fairyland were shy of their former haunts; the elves and sprites were absent; the merry hobgoblins, if they still played at hide-and-seek behind the leaves, were too well hid to be seen of mortal vision; no numbkin peered at her from out the hedges. The forms that took a phantom life beside her now were human, with one that was dominant and made the others dim; one so full of mortal life and the attributes of mortal existence that he it was, perhaps, from whom the fairies fled.

Yet, fully as his phantom filled the lane, the lane, nevertheless, was lonely now, or so it seemed to Edith. Walking there one afternoon soon after her return from London, its solitude oppressed her; she turned and took the road to Pagnell; she would go and see Agatha Brand.

Through the village she went, past the little three-cornered slope of village green, past the pond on the left, and the cottage that had rambled into a house on the right; then, with the broad view facing her, on to the brow of the hill. It always seemed to Edith that it was here the real world began. You dipped down into it, leaving the isolated life of the village that was on the way to nowhere, since the two roads that reached it from the high road sank into grass-grown lanes before they had penetrated far on its farther side.

The trees were still unvestured, the brown of the young poplar leaves not showing yet; the slopes lay naked to the sight, the bosomed beautiful slopes that formed an intermediate country between the village and the outer world, a gateway to the one, a guardian of the other. Down the descent went Edith, and along the line of road that lay between the hills. There was a rumble and a roar and a white cloud rising from a hollow into the grey clouds of the sky, the pearl-grey clouds of February. That was the train, rushing from the confines of the world into the heart of it. Presently she would come to the bridge which crossed the line, and then she would see the main road that led to London and away from it, running right and left, with her own road lying at right angles, like the stem of the letter T.

The woods over on the hill towards the west were bare still, dark-stencilled against the sky, but touched here and there with the purple that comes to twigs and branches before they break into bud. The purple was in the hedges too beside her, invisible on each separate twig, distinct when the twigs were massed together; changing with the light, elusive, yet token sure of coming spring.

Edith, who had watched the spring come often, and knew its every step, forgot herself, forgot the suffrage and its problems, forgot Cyril Race, in beholding the signals of its presence. A gleam of sunshine fell upon the ploughed surface of the fields that ran down from the trees, showing the mauve tint which lurks in the brown of Dawnshire clay; ahead, where the woods paused and left the sky-line free, the clouds were breaking.

She was nearing the bridge now, with the railway line below running north and south, parallel with the main road which lay but a field's breadth away. The road she was on ran down from the bridge in a slope to meet it, widening at its issue into a space large enough to leave room in the centre for a plot of grass; to the left of the grass, uphill, was the way towards London; to the right, downwards, you went through Pagnell to the University town some seventeen miles away.

As Edith came towards the bridge, the thoughts which had been banished by the promises of the spring came back to her. She could not support the militant movement; that she had decided some time ago; but she would work for the suffrage nevertheless, as hard, as faithfully, as any militant; but in a way that would bring no discredit on the cause; in the way that Cyril Race declared to be worthy of women, the way that was void of violence.

She was near the main road now, and she saw it branching right and left, and saw the patch of grass which split the by-road into two. And on that grass she saw a cross. It stood, white against the hedge on the thither side of the road, one arm stretched out towards the north, the other southwards. Of all the many times that she had come across the bridge, never had she seen it till now. A sign-post stood there always, pointing out the way; but to-day for the first time she saw it in the form of a cross.

An omen was it, or just the outcome of her thoughts? for peace, surely, was the message linked with that sign, peace and goodwill.

Nay, but there were other words: "I come not to bring peace, but a sword."[1]

CHAPTER XIV
DR. DEAN

"I do not love thee, Doctor Fell,
The reason why I cannot tell:
But this alone I know full well,
I do not love thee, Doctor Fell."

Tom Brown[2]

For half a minute it was a cross, and then it was a sign-post again, and between the sign-post and the hedge a man passed on horseback. Edith recognised him, and hoped he would go straight on without seeing her; but as the hope was in her mind, he turned, caught sight of her, and stopped his horse.

"Miss Carstairs! I have been meaning to call at the Pightle."

"Indeed! My mother will be glad to see you."

"But I have been so busy." He was off his horse now, the bridle over his arm, walking beside her. "I seem to have so many patients. Just returning from a long round now."

"That's bad as far as the patients are concerned—I mean, that there should be so many people ill—but a good thing for you, isn't it?"

"It would be if I were going to stay here."

"And are you not?"

"No; I've had a very good offer—an appointment in the north of England, and I'm inclined to accept it."

"Indeed! I must congratulate you."

"You needn't. It's partly on your account that I'm going away."

"I'm sorry," Edith murmured.

"I don't believe you are. If you were—if I thought you were—pity is akin to love, you know, and—"

"Not all pity, and I'm afraid mine isn't of that kind."

"If you'd only give me a chance of seeing you sometimes! I know I was premature; I should have waited; I startled you. But if you'd

---

1   Matthew 10:34.
2   Thomas Brown (1663–1704), "Laconics," *The Works*, Vol. 4 (1715).

give me a chance of repairing my mistake, if you'd let us meet some-times, I believe, I do believe you could learn to love me."

"I'm afraid I can't share that belief." Edith spoke stiffly. It was all very well to be kind, but if this were the result, the kindness must cease. "Please don't say any more about it, Dr. Dean. And now that you are going away—"

"But I'm not—I mean I wouldn't if you would give me even the ghost of a hope. I'd throw up the appointment and stay on here—I've quite a good chance now old Frost is giving up; or I'd go to London and make my way there. I've got plenty of push, and with the hope of winning you—"

"But I have told you that such a hope is quite out of the question. Please do understand!"

"That is your final answer?"

Edith bent her head.

"I am not a man to be kept dangling. You understand? I shall never ask you again."

"I hope not."

"Good-bye, then, Miss Carstairs, good-bye. If that is your an-swer—your final answer, I won't intrude further on you. You will excuse me if I ride on."

"Certainly."

"Please make my excuses to Mrs. Carstairs. Under the circum-stances I feel that a visit to the Pightle would be both painful and unwelcome."

It was a relief to see him ride away. He had disturbed her thoughts and broken in upon that vision of the cross; she feared lest he should always stand side by side with it. She was sorry for him, of course, but such persistence would wear out any ordinary pity, and pity of a kind that was not ordinary he could not compel in her; he was not the man to inspire unusual emotion, especially, Edith thought, in a woman. For, though he had always been profuse of compliments, or perhaps because of the compliments, she was well aware that he was contemptuous of her sex; as fully persuaded of its inferiority to his own as he was convinced of his personal superiority to most of his fellow-men.

Agatha Brand was at home, and Edith spent a soothing hour with her. Agatha's society was particularly soothing at this time, inasmuch as she was a Liberal before she was a suffragist, and what Edith wanted most to hear just now was defence of the Liberal Government. And Agatha was an able champion. A clever woman, clearheaded, and well versed in political questions, she was capable of supporting any position she chose to take up; and the position of her choice, intellectually and temperamentally, was that of a member of the Women's Liberal Federation.[1] Confidence in Liberal statesmanship, trust in Liberal statesmen, these formed the foundation of her faith; and Edith, until her visit to Littlehampton the previous summer, had been amongst the keenest of her sympathisers.

The result of that visit had been to cool for a time the ardour of their comradeship; not that friendship failed, but that sympathy was not complete. Liberal statesmen, Edith had contended, had failed to reach the standard of Liberal tradition, had failed in the principles of Liberalism, and the principles were more valuable, she maintained, than the prosperity of the party. To Agatha principles and party were indissolubly bound together; the dissolution of the one meant the submerging of the others, a result which would be fatal to the best interests of the country. It was better to sacrifice something than to lose all; there were pressing questions, important reforms, which required the whole time, the entire energy of the Cabinet; and, ardent suffragist as she was, she was convinced that she best served her cause, best showed her capability for using the vote, by helping instead of hindering the men at the head of affairs; confident that when Ministers had fulfilled their pledges to the electors—"And you would not have them dishonourable, Edith"—they would not fail to reward the services rendered to them by women in the way that women wished.

To this Edith had replied—after that visit to Littlehampton—that it was all very well, but that this sort of thing had been going on for fifty years, and that she, for one, was getting a bit tired of it. The services were always recognised and women made much of at

---

1   From the 1880s, Women's Liberal Associations had been formed with the aim of drawing together women who wanted to educate themselves in political questions, and to support Liberal politicians (Rendell, 167–68). The Women's Liberal Federation was inaugurated between 1886 and 1887 and, by 1910, had 692 associations and approximately 104,000 members (169). The WLF became a forum for a wide range of political questions, including suffrage, and gave women unprecedented experience in public affairs and organisation (Rubinstein, 151). In 1892, a schism developed when, at the Annual Council Meeting, the WLF called on its associations to refuse help to candidates who did not support suffrage (Rendell, 170).

election times, but the reward never came; and it did seem to her farcical—or indeed she would say false—to talk big about the rights of the people, while a good half of them had no rights as citizens at all.

This she had thought after witnessing that act in the play of the evolution of women, which had been played to her on the Littlehampton sands. In a sense she thought it still, but it was a disturbing idea and not, as it had been at first, a stimulating conviction; and it was comforting to listen to Agatha's clear arguments, and to find, when all was said and done, and admitting even that Liberal Ministers might make mistakes, might even, under pressure be dilatory or—she went as far as to say—unjust; admitting all this, to find nevertheless that there were solid grounds for upholding the party as a whole.

"I quite see what you mean, Agatha darling, as to how difficult it is. People who don't know the inner workings find it easy to criticise; but since I have known Mr. Race and talked to him, I realise how complicated the inner workings are, and I feel I can't carp."

"Exactly; and which type of woman would be most likely to influence the men in authority do you suppose? those who carp with their tongues and fight with their fists, or women to whom they can talk reasonably, whose support and intelligence they can count upon?"

"Lady Henry Hill says that it's just because they can count upon it that they don't do anything."

"Oh, Lady Henry Hill! No offence to your friend, Edith. She's delightful, I know, from all that you have told me, but she is evidently *entichée*[1] of the suffragette leaders, and carried away, I should say, by her enthusiasm."

"I—I don't know. Perhaps. But I wonder—oh, quite apart from suffrage and suffragettes and anything of the kind, I wonder if anybody ever does anything much—great, I mean—fine, without the capacity, at any rate, for being carried away."

"Certainly they do; I should say that that capacity considerably interferes with fine action. The people who are carried away may create ideals—possibly; but it is the men of action who put them into practice."

---

1   Infatuated.

"Oh, I'm not speaking of dreamers; I mean people who do act, who are carried away—by their ideas, or ideals, if you like—into doing unusual things, things that some would call fine and others exaggerated or absurd."

"Yes, those are the people I mean too, but I evidently did not express myself clearly. I mean that people may create ideals by exaggerated action, by doing absurd things, but that it is only men with balanced minds, men who naturally express themselves in action, who can put the idealists' notions into working order. Do you see?"

"I see what you mean; I'm not sure if I agree with you."

The door opened, and Robbie Colquhoun came in.

"Robbie," said Edith, "are you a man of action?"

"Not just now. I want some tea. Why? Is there anything you want me to do?"

"She wants you to translate her ideals into action," said Agatha.

"Back her up if she kicks over the traces—is that it?"

"Would you if I did?" Edith asked.

"I think so."

"That's rash," said Agatha; "you don't know what direction she might kick in."

"None that wasn't like her."

"Thank you, Robbie. I accept the implied compliment."

"Will you accept my escort up the road? It's getting dark, and I don't think you ought to go back alone."

"I will, gratefully. It was so light when I came that I felt quite bold. I always do feel bold about the dark when it's still daylight, but when it comes I long for company and candles."

So Robbie Colquhoun walked home with her, and she congratulated herself on the fact that he was not Dr. Dean. If he had been Cyril Race—Yet in some ways Robbie was a more comfortable companion than Mr. Race. She knew him so well, and it was no effort to talk to him; she could say anything and everything that came into her mind; he was never shocked at anything she thought, never startled; that, perhaps, was just because he was not easily moved in any direction. Whereas with Mr. Race—To be sure she had never shocked him, but she had the feeling that it might be possible for her to do so; not, of course, by the sentiments which were shocking to Dawnshire, but by the expression of ideas which did not cause Robbie Colquhoun to turn a hair. Robbie, of course, was not particularly clever, but on the other hand he had not a mind in which balance was the predominant characteristic; while Mr. Race belonged to the category which Agatha had commended; the men who did the work of practical reform in the world and were not carried away by wild ideas. Mr. Race, probably, would not be thus carried away, even while he strained every nerve to accomplish that which he accounted worth striving for. But no more, for the matter of that, would Robbie Colquhoun. Of that she was sure, while it was just possible that Race might combine a touch of indiscretion with his sanity. Secretly she hoped that he did, in spite of Agatha Brand.

CHAPTER XV
ARRESTED

"Beneath this starry arch,
Nought resteth or is still;
But all things hold their march,
As if by one great will.
Moves one, moves all;
Hark to the foot-fall!
On, on, for ever."

Harriet Martineau[1]

It was the twenty-fourth of February, 1909.[2] Geraldine Hill sat at her desk and wrote a letter. It took her some time to write, and when it was written she sat still for awhile before putting it into its envelope.

---

1 Harriet Martineau (1802–76), "Harvests of All Time" (1834).

2 The date of the sixth Women's Parliament at which a resolution was passed "That this Parliament of women expresses its indignation that while every measure in the King's Speech vitally affects the interest of their sex, and while heavier financial burdens are to be laid upon women tax-payers, the Government have not included in the programme for the session a measure to confer the Parliamentary vote upon duly qualified women" (Lytton, 38). The deputation which carried this resolution to the House of Commons included Emmeline Pethick-Lawrence and Lady Constance Lytton, and they were among the twenty-eight women arrested, though not before they were treated with considerable violence (S. Pankhurst, 1931, 301). Lytton reports being repeatedly lifted into the air and thrown into the crowd (46–48).

That done, she addressed it without more waiting, and, taking it in her hand, went upstairs to her bedroom.

"I'm going out, Parker. No, I won't change; and my morning hat and coat, please. I shan't be in to dinner, and you needn't sit up; I'm not sure when I shall be back."

"Very well, my lady, but—"

"No, no buts, Parker. Go to bed in good time, like a good girl, and get rid of that cold of yours."

It was a pretty room, that bedroom in Upper Brook Street,[1] and comfortable, with its bright fire and gay chintz curtains, on the chill February day; Lady Henry looked round it before she went out of the door, with a look that was like a leave-taking.

Downstairs in the hall she gave the letter she was carrying into the charge of the butler. "If I am not back before his lordship, give it to him as soon as he comes in."

A taxi took her down to Clement's Inn;[2] she was often there now, sometimes just for a few minutes, and when that was the case she usually kept the cab that had brought her to take her away again. To-day she dismissed it. She was a well-known figure, and more than one passer-by recognised her as she entered the offices of the WSPU; indeed, her height and something about her that was distinctive as well as distinguished made recognition of her easy.

Meanwhile, in the Caxton Hall,[3] the Women's Parliament was assembling. It was the day of weekly meeting; it was also the day on which a deputation was to march to the House of Commons.

The room was full; of women, and of a sense of expectation. There were men too in the audience, but they were emphatically of the audience, whereas the women belonged to the actors in the drama which was in the fourth year of its playing, and on another act of which the curtain was to rise to-night.

Inside, in the hall, the enthusiasm culminated as those who filled the leading parts filed on to the platform. Outside in the streets the

---

1   Upper Brook Street is in the exclusive neighbourhood of Mayfair.

2   Clement's Inn, just north of Strand, was the home of Emmeline and Frederick Pethick-Lawrence, founders and editors of *Votes for Women*. From 1907 to 1912, it was the headquarters of the WSPU.

3   Located in Westminster, close to government offices and the Houses of Parliament, Caxton Hall was the venue for the WSPU's "Women's Parliaments," and their base for organising deputations.

people were gathering, the spectators; no lack there was of these. For in every portion of this play, as with all plays which are the translation of evolutionary law into concrete history, there was an element of the uncertain and the unforeseen; the playwright sitting in the chair of destiny unwound his scroll only as the play proceeded. Play-bills there might be, issued in advance, but never the exact text of the drama.

What would the text be to-night? Rival stage managers there were, designing different settings for the scene, but only one playwright; and the writing of that playwright was a definite decree, to be read as the scroll unwound. There was other writing as well; writing on the wall of the shadows of things to come; writing unseen save by the few. To all but the few the scroll alone was visible.

What would be on it to-night? No telling, till the curtain rose; the crowd in the street, a growing crowd, watched eagerly for its rising.

It rose just ten minutes before Big Ben at Westminster chimed eight; to the sound of the "Marseillaise"[1] within the hall; to the sound of cheers and applause without. Mrs. Patrick Lane[2] came first, the deputation's leader; and at sight of her the crowd broke into shouts, "Bravo, women! Hurrah!" It forced its way, that crowd, through the police line, and ran by Mrs. Lane and her followers as they set out at quick marching pace towards Great Chapel Street. Of all callings were these followers, of all ages, of all degrees of size and strength. One there was, noticeably tall, noticeably slender; as slender and as tall as Lady Henry Hill. But the police knew Lady Henry; she was one of the women they would be careful not to arrest; they did not know this woman.

So much for the rising of the curtain, so much for the opening of the scene. The action that followed that opening was quick and sharp.

Suddenly the street was alive with constables. They closed round the band of women, hemming them in; a wall of uniforms and

---

1 "The Women's Marseillaise," words by F.E.M. Macaulay, was published in *Votes for Women* on 28 January 1909. The sentiment of the chorus, "To freedom's cause till death/We swear our fealty," is echoed in the second stanza which sees martyrdom as part of "freedom's toll." Those women who have gone to prison, "have lead the way:/Who would not follow to the fray,/Their glorious struggle proudly sharing?"

2 Emmeline Pethick-Lawrence.

swaying helmets hiding the women from the crowd, and the crowd from the women. The crowd booed and cheered till the cheers and booings were merged in a great shout, as, forth from the wall of policemen, her face pale, but with a smile upon it, came the leader of the deputation. Others followed her; some in twos and threes, with linked arms, resisting the efforts of the police to separate them; others singly; and so, in straggling form, but determined, the body of women made its way along Victoria Street, the crowd running beside them, the police trying to hold them back.

Some reached Parliament Square and the Strangers' entrance[1] to the House of Commons, there to be forced back into the crowd, to be thrown again and again in amongst the people; some, penetrating to the Square, did not attain to the House; some got no farther than the street. Amongst the latter was the tall woman with the shabby hat pressed low on her brow and the collar of her coat upturned. It needed just that and a wig to save her from recognition, and to avoid recognition was important; for, though it mattered not how many women were arrested, titles must not figure in the list of prisoners, since titles meant people of importance. To Geraldine, diffident of her powers, humble in her estimate of herself, her title seemed the one asset of value that she could contribute to the cause she desired to serve; and if it was to serve her cause, it was essential that it should not protect her person. Her name, therefore, had not been read out amongst the names of those who formed to-night's deputation, for there were spies always at the meetings who would have given warning of her presence, and she had come forth from the hall nameless and unknown.

She was separated almost at once, as soon as the struggle to pass the police began, from the companion with whom she was to have walked, and she found herself carried along by the crowd, swayed this way and that, as uncertain of the direction in which she was being borne as she was unable to resist the force which bore her.

The evening was raw and cold, with a cold that was damp rather than keen, with greasy pavements underfoot, and overhead a dull, blank sky that threatened rain. Geraldine did not see the sky; she was conscious of the cold, conscious too of the stuffiness, the lack of air amidst the throng of people; but she was too bewildered to look

---

1   St. Stephen's Entrance is the visitors' entrance to the House of Commons.

about or above her; half blinded now and again by bright, sharp, sudden lights, the flash lights of the Press photographers; half smothered by the tighter grip of the moving mass around her as mounted policemen rode in upon it to disperse a crowd that was too friendly to the deputation.

Where was that deputation? The one clear thought in her mind was that she had lost her place in it, had failed in the purpose which had driven her into this nightmare of shouting, shoving people, of opposing policemen, of forces which pressed in different directions, and crushed the breath from your body, and the consciousness—or almost, for she was faint now, would have staggered, stumbled, fallen perhaps, but for the upbearing mass of humanity in which she was wedged—almost from your brain. The slippery damp pavement was difficult—to walk—or was it sand beneath her feet? And the rush and roar and the stifling sensation—was it the sea about her? was the tide coming in? and she—ah—it always roared and swirled about the rocks. Was it water surging in her ears? or was she herself that water, a wave flung—broken—breaking—? There were rocks all round, everywhere, pressing, grinding—But the tide was coming in; and she—for it was quieter now, calmer; she heard less, felt less—and she with it.

Then consciousness came back, consciousness of her actual surroundings, and she found that she was out of the swaying crowd; the voices were dimmed, the shouts more distant. She was upheld, supported still, but by hands that definitely gripped, arms that definitely urged her on. Her eyes were open now, and she saw that she was in a narrow passage, and that the men who held her wore uniforms.

So—the realisation came with a thrill of joy—they had arrested her! Her name would do what she had meant it to do; she had not failed. They were policemen who half carried her along, and the passage through which they bore her led to the Cannon Row Police Station.

CHAPTER XVI
SILENCE

"That night the empty corridors
Were full of forms of Fear,
And up and down the iron town
Stole feet we could not hear,
And through the bars that hide the stars
White faces seem to peer."

Ballad of Reading Gaol[1]

The white walls of the prison cell were not terrible to Geraldine, nor the hours which she spent alone. After the turmoil of the streets on the night of her arrest, after the ordeal of Bow Street, the little walled-in space, where she was at least alone, held for her a comparative peace.

She had said at Bow Street, before the magistrate, that she was proud to be where she was, prouder to have stood by her friends than she was of anything she had done in her whole life; and she had spoken the truth. For months the sense that she was holding back from risks which other women ran had been like iron in her soul; she had felt herself to be a defaulter, and the feeling had been a drag on all that she had tried to do. Now the false position was done away with, once and for always; she stood openly by her convictions and her comrades, and the house of her being was no more divided against itself. That was the fact which raised her above the sordidness and the suffering of all other facts. Though in prison, she was free; though she was subject to vexatious rules and a rigid discipline, she was absolved from the imputation of cowardice which had been cast at her by her own conscience.

The actual work which she had to do was not distasteful to her; she did not mind cleaning her cell; the polishing of the few utensils in it proved no irksome task; on the contrary, she took a pride in making them as bright as possible, and was thankful for the occupation. The discomfort of the prison dress, to be sure, was considerable; it was too short for her, in sleeves and skirt and waist, and she was conscious that she must appear grotesque; moreover,

---

1   Oscar Wilde (1854–1900), *The Ballad of Reading Gaol* (1898).

and this was a greater trial, the dress was not over clean, and was stained by former wearers. She sought amusement and consolation in trying to imagine what Parker would say if she could see her; Parker, who was so much more particular about the correctness of her appearance than she was herself; but the picture of Parker's face could not take the stains from the coarse garments, nor add inches to their length.

The solitary hours, the thought of which was a terror to Sally Simmonds, were, as had been said, no penance to Geraldine. What tried her was the absence of certainty that at any particular moment she was actually alone; the knowledge that at all times, through that peep-hole in the door, eyes might be upon her, day or night. At night, to be sure, you knew when the eyes were there, for the flashlight leapt into the cell, searched it and rested on you, revealing you to the gaze which you could never meet; but you never knew at what moment it might wake you out of sleep or drag you back from the inner world in which your mind walked free.

It was from the world of thought and not from the world of dreams that the flashlight, almost invariably, summoned Geraldine. She could not sleep on the plank bed, with its absence of pillow and its scanty covering. She was cold and consequently wakeful, and at night the prison atmosphere laid its grip upon her; the atmosphere that deadens the will and strains the nerves; that is imbued with some influence which seems to put those who breathe it outside the pale of humanity. Love languishes in prison, since all the impulses that feed and water it are quenched by rule. An attempt to help a fellow prisoner in any way is a punishable offence; a glance of sympathy is suspect; a wardress who is kindly to the women in her charge commits a breach of duty.

In the daytime Geraldine, in common with all those who were now, or had been, in prison for the same cause as herself, fought against this atmosphere, strove to lighten and to brighten it, pitted the hope and courage in her heart against the hopelessness and the destructive influences about her. And not in vain. The stream of women who for over three years had passed through Holloway brought with them something that was welcomed in their presence, missed in their absence, that was recognised as having in it elements of light and warmth and hope. The prisoners felt it; on the way to Holloway, one, sitting close to Geraldine in Black Maria,[1] said, "Prison ain't the same place as what it used to be before you ladies came." And the wardresses felt it, for on the morning of her release, one of them told her, "When the suffragettes are not here all the sunshine seems gone out of the place."

In the daytime she did her best to add to the sunshine; but at night, susceptible and impressionable as she was, the prison atmosphere and the prison stillness were often more than she could fight against. Yet was it the stillness or the breaking of it that disturbed and distressed her most? Dead the silence was at times, but there were sounds too, sounds which she could not account for, and which seemed to spring meaningless out of the darkness, only to sink into it again, for ever unexplained; sounds which were enigmas, never guessed; sounds which haunted her; fragments of dramas whose beginning was hid, whose end was never known. There was the night, for instance, when for hours Geraldine listened to the shrieks of a woman somewhere on the floor below her, and heard, mingled with the shrieks, sounds as of the shaking and the banging of iron gates.

"Let me out! Let me out! Let me out!"

What strength was it that sustained the wild voice, hour after hour, and the untiring arms that beat against the bars? Was it madness or drink or terror? She never knew. Questions were unanswered in prison, and if there were tragedies they were played out unseen by all save the authoritative few.

One morning when the prisoners were standing in line before going out for exercise, Geraldine's eyes caught the eyes of a girl who could not have been more than sixteen; eyes with a tendency to merriment in them, even in prison, eyes that lighted up with laughter if anything amused her. Why was she there? It was a question never answered. For three days Geraldine and the girl exchanged glances every morning, and she looked forward to seeing the smile

---

1   The black van which conveyed prisoners from the police courts to jail. Constance Lytton describes it as "a sort of hearse with elephantiasis" (63): "On either side [of the central aisle] are tiny separate cells, like the compartments of a cupboard, the doors of which when opened completely obstruct the passage so that only one prisoner at a time can be admitted or released. On first getting in it seems quite dark, and the sensation of being rapidly pushed into a very small hole, squeezed back, the door shut and locked to the accompanying sound of banging and much jangling and turning of keys, is extremely disagreeable" (64).

break over the young face. On the fourth day the girl did not come to exercise; on the fifth she was there again, but her face was changed and miserable, and her eyes were dazed as if they did not know what they looked at. As she passed Geraldine those eyes held tears, in place of the smile that had beamed in them at first. Every time they met on the round Geraldine tried to speak a word of comfort, but the wardress was watching her, and she dared not move her lips. Once she managed to whisper, "Cheer up"; she did not know whether the girl heard her; and once the girl muttered something as she went by, but Geraldine could not catch the words. That was all: after that morning they never met again. What had happened to change the face? What became of its owner?

She never knew; but she used to wonder, as she wondered about another face that haunted her, that of a woman who had come with her in the prison van, a woman who in a fit of despair had pawned the shirts she was making at sevenpence a dozen to buy bread for her starving children. She was in torture, this woman, because of the three children—little children—and the sick husband left at home; the youngest child, a baby, was in her arms. Geraldine heard an official tell her that this baby, young though it was, was yet too old to stay in with her, and heard her ask what was to become of it.

"It must go to the workhouse till you have done your time."

Her time was two months; two months of agony; the baby that she clung to and sobbed over, motherless in a workhouse; the three other children and the invalid husband with no one to care or work for them.

The sobs of this woman remained in Geraldine's ears; her face stood side by side with the face of the young girl; beside those faces, her own punishment, her own suffering sank into insignificance. She had been proud to come to prison for her cause's sake; she was glad to be there now, because out of her own experience she knew what wanted changing in the prisons, and in the laws which sent unhappy and misguided, as well as criminal, women there. These women, ignorant and inarticulate, had never been able to tell of the mistakes that were made, of the punishment that hardened, the discipline that weakened wills already weak. But she and her fellows, women who came to prison to serve a cause and not to expiate a crime, educated women who could speak and write; these could compel a hearing, had already spoken, already been the means of initiating reform; and would speak more fully, be listened to more surely, as time went on. This way of punishing such women as herself, a way devised, as the devisers thought, by their own perspicacity, was surely not theirs after all, but one of the mysterious ways in which God moves for the performing of those wonders which mean the advance of humanity.

CHAPTER XVII
"SHIPS THAT PASS IN THE NIGHT"

"The vilest deeds like poison weeds
Bloom well in prison-air
It is only what is good in man
That wastes and withers there
Pale Anguish keeps the heavy gate,
And the Warder is Despair."

Ballad of Reading Gaol

Geraldine was not left long in the solitude of her cell. The sleepless nights, the cold, the lack of fresh air, the insufficient exercise told upon her health, and she was removed to the infirmary. The change was not a welcome one; solitude meant at least privacy; and to Geraldine, who had been used to privacy all her life, the publicity of the ward was a greater trial than any of the trials of the first period of her imprisonment.

That which reconciled her to the change was the increased human interest. In the cells all speech between prisoners was forbidden, and no intercourse was possible save that which eyes could exchange with eyes; in the infirmary the inmates were allowed sometimes to talk together. There was opportunity for little acts of kindness, for friendly words and to be permitted to perform these acts, to speak these words, was a greater privilege than to lie on a mattress instead of on a plank bed.

She had not been long in the infirmary when she was visited by the chaplain. She had seen him each day in the chapel; but she had known him only as a face and a voice, not as a man. It was the man who came to her bedside, or that which prison had made out of a man, for it is not only the prisoners who are preyed upon by the hardness and the coldness of the atmosphere.

"What has brought you here?" he asked.

"Nothing that I am ashamed of."

"I fear you are hardened. You must be bad, or you would not be here. All the women who come here are bad."

"I don't agree with you. At any rate I have done nothing that I would not do again."

The woman lying on the bed was just a number to him, a unit in a mass of women who were all alike; sinners, outcasts, irreclaimably degraded, if not innately depraved; and his duty, as chaplain, was to impress their badness upon them. He did it to this number as to the other numbers; but when he came again he had learned that the new patient was not just a number, but Lady Henry Hill. That made a difference; good was foreign to inferior districts, but much might come out of Mayfair; he was no longer condemnatory, but servile. Geraldine preferred the condemnation, at least as far as she herself was concerned; it hurt and angered her to hear him pour it forth on the poor creatures who were her companions.

On Sunday afternoons he held a service in the ward; in the service itself there were words of hope and love; there were none in the sermon. No matter whence his text was taken, his exposition of it was always the same: his hearers were bad; his endeavour was to convince them of their badness. Most of these hearers listened, or did not listen, with stolid faces; the service, the sermon, were part of the punishment, amongst the things that they were forced to endure; but there was one woman who was moved by his condemnation to acute distress. An old woman she was, tall and gaunt, with grey hair, a face deep marked by the battle of life, hands that, whatever else they had done, had worked hard in that battle. She stood up one day while the chaplain was speaking, the tears running down her face, her hands shaking, forgetful of discipline, conscious only of the bitterness of his denunciation.

"Oh, sir, don't be so hard on us!" she pleaded.

She was seized upon at once, rebuked, suppressed; afterwards she was punished. She had committed a breach of discipline, and discipline must be maintained at all costs; at all costs.

That was the way the gospel of love, the glad tidings of great joy were preached to the spirits in prison in Holloway Gaol.

It was partly on account of this particular fellow prisoner that Geraldine was glad to have been transferred to the infirmary. She herself was ill in body; but this old woman, besides suffering physically, was sick in soul, and Geraldine found opportunity, scant though it might be, to lay a healing touch upon her hurt. What her crime was, or her folly, or her fault, Geraldine never discovered; all she knew of a long life was just this little bit of it that was passed within the infirmary walls. Had she known the woman to be as bad as the chaplain told her she was, it is doubtful whether Lady Henry would have shrunk from her. It was wonderful how class distinctions fell away, or rather how naturally she adopted the attitude of the class to which she now belonged: the class of prisoners. She was no longer Lady Henry Hill, but one of a body of women, at the command of another woman, absolutely subject to the prison authorities, completely at the mercy of the law's machinery. Similarity of conditions created a sense of fellowship; there is an *esprit de corps*[1] even amongst prisoners, and Geraldine was imbued with it. It was unjust that she and other women, sentenced for political offences, should be classed with rogues and vagabonds, with thieves and drunkards; but it was the classing she resented, not the consorting with a particular class. Good people and bad people are often, outwardly, very much alike, and, so far, she had found no cause of complaint in her companions. The chief sentiment evoked in her was pity, and after that came indignation; but this was not aroused by the prisoners.

Sometimes, for the official in charge was as kindly as she dared to be, the patients who were well enough to be up were allowed to sit round the fire and talk, and in this way Geraldine caught glimpses into lives utterly unlike her own; in this way too was able sometimes to bring interest and amusement into the faces about her. It was amusement she most liked to see there.

The time wore on, and the day of her release drew near: as it approached she felt that she hardly wanted to be free again. Obedience had become a habit and was developing into a necessity; in the whole course of the day there was never an occasion to exercise judgment, decision, will-power; she was told exactly what to do and had learned to do it without thought or question; and the idea of thinking for herself, of taking up responsibility, was one from which

---

1   Spirit of comradeship among members of a group or community.

she was beginning, after a month's imprisonment, to shrink. What must be the effect of such a system, she reflected, applied through many months; through years; and on wills feeble to begin with, characters whose need was to be built up and fortified? She, Geraldine, had friends waiting to welcome, to help and to strengthen her. What of those who were sent forth friendless, destitute, weak in resistance, strong in evil tendencies, on to the streets? With all her friends to back her up, she still shrank from facing again the world of action; even Henry and his love—

But there, as often as the thought came, doubt stepped in. How did she know what he would do? She had very little to go upon, but that little was hardly encouraging. As far as she knew, he had not come to the police station to bail her out on the night of her arrest; but then, he might have come after she had left. Mr. Lane had given bail for all those who were arrested, and she had gone straight to her sister, Lady Brinkworth, who, it had been arranged, would be prepared to receive her. To be sure, she had told her husband of that arrangement in the letter she had left in charge of the butler, and that might account for the fact of his not having come to Cannon Row; though she had thought perhaps that he would come nevertheless; it hardly accounted for his not coming to Montagu Square.

At Bow Street she had seen him for a moment after she had been sentenced; he had acted up to his promise, he had stood by her publicly; but the meeting had been a hurried one, with people about them, and she could not determine whether the absence of reproach in his words and manner meant that his heart upheld her or was due to courtesy alone.

Often during the monotonous hours of the last month she had tried to recall exactly what he had said, and what he had called her, and had never quite succeeded, though, as to the latter point, she had come to the conclusion that he could not have said her name at all. Jerry? She would have been filled with gladness. Geraldine? No, she would have been stabbed, as his use of the name had stabbed her that night in the smoking room, when she had told him that she could not keep her promise.

Certain it was that he had said nothing to hurt her. On the other hand she could recall no words which were an assurance of his sympathy. Well, she would soon know his real attitude. To the outer world, of course, he would be her champion. But privately? She remembered his answer to her whispered pleading: "It depends on how far you go." Was she too far away from him for sympathy, here in Holloway Gaol?

The Duke and the Duchess and her sisters-in-law and Henry's one brother; from them she knew what to expect; she had outraged their dignity and hurt their pride, of position and of race. She was sorry; outrage—whatever the papers might say—was not a method of her choice; but she was prepared to face the bitterness she had evoked because such bitterness was inevitable in the line of action she had laid down for herself. But Henry? If the bitterness were to come into the life, the inner life, that they two lived together, the life in which they were friends, comrades, lovers—She could bear it, of course, she would have to bear it, since there is no turning back or aside for one whose path is cut by conviction; but the path would be paved as with ploughshares and she would tread it with bleeding feet.

CHAPTER XVIII
IN THE PILLORY

"A woman in the pillory restores the original bark of brotherhood to mankind."

George Meredith[1]

Lord Henry came back from his constituency on the night of the 24th February, by the last train, a train which did not arrive at Paddington till eleven thirty-five; too late to make it worth while to go Cannon Row Police Station, even if he had wished to do so.

Reading Geraldine's letter, he was glad that he was too late, and the next morning he contented himself with a telephoned inquiry to Penelope Brinkworth, as to his wife's condition. Had she been ill, he must have gone to her, but she was not ill; on the contrary, she was what Lady Brinkworth described as "quite perky"; and hearing this account of her, Lord Henry hardened his heart; that is to say, he told himself that it would be better both for him and Geraldine that he should do nothing on impulse. Her action, in spite of the

---

1 George Meredith (1828–1909), *Diana of the Crossways* (1885).

warning she had given him, had taken him by surprise; he had not expected it to be either so speedy or so pronounced; and the fact that she had definitely kicked over the most cherished traces of Hill tradition had, to use his own expression, bowled him over.

He hardly knew whether he was angry with her or not; vexed, certainly; but angry? He had never been really angry with her; perhaps because she had never given him cause for anger; she had always been a reasonable woman—till she had taken up with these d—d suffragettes; the adjective was a comfort to him.

Reading in the morning papers the account of the "Suffragette Raid," with head-lines, "Arrest of Lady Henry Hill," "Lady of Title in Conflict with the Police," and the like, he made up his mind that he would not go to Montagu Square; he might say something for which he would be sorry. Bow Street was different; nobody should have the chance of talking about domestic disturbances; even the Duke would support him in standing by his wife in public. But Montagu Square—no, he determined that he would not go; all the more, that the picture of Geraldine, drawn by his knowledge of her, made strong appeal to him. He knew just how her face would be; she would have her clear look, and that little droop at the corner of her mouth which, perhaps, because it was not often there, never failed to move him. It was wiser not to go; his love of the woman might overpower his disapproval of the suffragette; or again, if the suffragette were uppermost (how would she seem to him, by the way, as a full-blown suffragette? what change would he find in her?), he might be unmanly enough to be brutal to the woman.

On his way to Bow Street he felt that the people in the streets were talking about her. She was discussed by the men on the omnibuses, as she would be discussed by the men in the clubs, by all the men, and the women too, of their own set and of all sets. She had laid herself open to discussion; neither he nor she had the right to resent it; she had become "one of those suffragettes," and must bear the onus of all the epithets with which the women to whom she had joined herself were laden.

These epithets were in Lord Henry's ears during all the month of her imprisonment. Some of them were spoken in the ducal tones which both he and Geraldine had anticipated; some were suggested in the remarks and inquiries of relations and friends; some reached only his inner hearing, sensitive now to inaudible words of public calumny and private contempt. He knew the epithets, all of them: unsexed, unwomanly, hysterical; and the phrases: to attract attention, for the sake of notoriety, an outcome of degeneracy; he had used them himself, had paraphrased them and made their substance into epigrams.

But his wife! That these things should be said of Geraldine seemed to him a desecration. Yet, when he came to reflect, why not of her as well as of another? She had done what the others had done, those other women, whose motives and wits and character were dismissed with curt phrases, a curl of the lip, a shrug of the shoulders. And she was in prison now, where, it was suggested, they went, these other women, for the fun of the thing, or for the sake of notoriety, or because they were driven by hysteria to self-imposed martyrdom; cheap martyrdom, as it was called. It might be true—of the others; not of his wife. Geraldine hysterical? She was the most reasonable being that he knew, man or woman, the least flighty, the most sincere. And thinking of her in prison, the expression, cheap martyrdom, that had seemed to him once so apt, became offensive. After all, where did the cheapness come in? To brave the disapproval, the anger, the disgust and contempt of her world, to risk a breach with those who cared most about her and for whom she most cared, this was hardly cheap. It occurred to Lord Henry for the first time that those other women had done as much, though their world was not her world, though each woman had a different circle to face, different ties of which to risk the breaking, different circumstances to defy or overcome. And to exchange her home with its comfort and luxury, its liberty, its love—and love, his love, he knew meant much to her; to exchange it for a prison cell, prison fare, prison dress, and subjection to coarse, rough, low-class women (that is how he thought of the wardresses—for the first time; hitherto, he had pitied them for the trouble caused them by the suffragettes), this was not cheap at all; not cheap, at least, for such a woman as his wife.

He hated to think of her, a prey to indignities and discomforts. It was misery to lie down in his comfortable bed and know how she was lodged; to eat luxurious meals, haunted by the thought of the food that was doled out to her. And she was fastidious about food, particular as to the way it was served; dainty, delicate, particular, in every thing that she did.

The other women were different, must be different; though they had homes probably, and some of them husbands; and—well, but when you came to think of it, prison dress and prison discipline would make no great appeal to most women. There was notoriety, of course, a diseased craving for prominence, to gratify which many women would do much. But Geraldine could not be of these. She was a well-known woman, in an assured position, prominent too through her speaking, having nothing to gain and everything to lose by associating herself with police-stations and magistrates' courts and prison life. That was obvious; people could not but see it.

But did they? He remembered that there were other women associated with prisons and policemen who had well-known names, who had no need to court notoriety or notice, and that these were still credited with a desire to be talked about, to make themselves into a target for the arrows of public observation. But Geraldine was different from them all; everybody who knew her, knew anything about her, must admit that her motives were absolutely pure and noble. Yet, even while he made the assertion, he was conscious that people did not admit it; only her husband—

He found himself wondering if the other husbands thought of their wives as he thought of Geraldine. Some of them certainly stood by their wives—in public, at any rate—as he did by his. What a bore it all was! And how tiresome of Jerry—Geraldine—to take an oar in that vexatious galley! It was all very well for women to have votes; he had nothing against *that*; though Geraldine would not have one if the Government did pass that confounded Bill they were all so keen about; but there were limits as to how far they should go in the getting them. He was not a prejudiced man, nor a prig, nor even very conventional; "But I'm bothered," he thought, "if there aren't limits."

It was practically what he had said to Geraldine, in that very room, standing by that very arm-chair. (The stuffing, by the way, was getting a bit too much exposed; he would have to have it repaired, after all; Jerry would see to—ah—Jerry was—well, when she came home.) That was what he had said, or implied, that there were limits. "Will you cast me off?" she had asked; and he had answered, "It depends on how far you go."

She had gone—well, pretty well as far as she could, except that she had not punched anybody's head. The question was, how far could *he* go in support of her; not in an official-figurehead sort of way, but, as she had expressed it, in private?

It was a question which occupied him during the whole miserable month of her imprisonment.

CHAPTER XIX
SAUSAGES

"A drudge disobedient;
And too fond of the *right* to pursue the *expedient*."

Oliver Goldsmith[1]

Sally Simmonds differed from Lord Henry Hill in a variety of ways; in none perhaps more than in the attitude towards Lord Henry's wife in respect of her arrest and imprisonment.

Lord Henry was filled with doubts and questionings; Sally had not a single doubt from the moment she heard the splendid, dreadful news; and she asked no questions except as to the behaviour of "them police," and the name of the—magistrate who had given the prisoner her sentence. Lord Henry had found comfort in an adjective beginning with a "D" made big by emphasis; Sally went one better, borrowed from the vocabulary of Joe Whittle, and chose as descriptive of the blackguard who had sent Lady Henry to prison a word whose initial letter stood close to the head of the alphabet, and which in conjunction with blackguard had the merit of alliteration.

The news of the arrest reached her on the morning after it took place, by the mouth of Mr. Bilkes, who was in process of chortling over it when she entered the dining-room with the breakfast tray.

Mrs. Bilkes laid the cloth for breakfast, but it was Sally's part to make the tea and fry the bacon; and the sausages, if there were no eggs; for Bilkes liked a good breakfast, an Englishman's breakfast, and as he was the breadwinner, he had a right to it, he said.

On Sally's tray there was a teapot, bacon, sausages, and hot water. She plumped it down on the sideboard at the same moment that Mr. Bilkes cried out:

---

1   Oliver Goldsmith (1730–74), "Retaliation: A Poem" (1774).

"Oh my! Oh lor'! Oh, here's a lark!" Then, changing suddenly from glee to pomposity, "And a disgrace to the British nobility."

"Whatever is the matter, Ben?" asked Mrs. Bilkes. "Sally, you're late again—a good five minutes."

"Matter? Why, here's one of the English aristocracy, that *should* be an ornament to the country, been breaking out against the law, along with those blooming, blasted suffragettes." The adjective expressed the two sides to Mr. Bilkes's view of the case, delight and disapproval; disapproval of suffragettes and all their ways, especially of Lady Henry Hill and the particular part she had played; delight because he had an opportunity of hitting Sally on a spot which he divined to be tender. Sally's heart, as a matter of fact, stood still for a moment at his words, before it bounded on at more than its usual speed; but she made up her mind that she would not give Mr. Bilkes the satisfaction of seeing her wince, and she proceeded with outer calm to put the bacon on the table. After all, there were numbers of titled ladies who belonged to the suffragettes.

"How shocking!" said Mrs. Bilkes. "Whoever is it? And what's happened?"

"What's happened is that she's gone and got herself arrested; and the name of the minx is Lady Henry Hill. Lord alive! what's got the gurl?"

Sally had put the teapot before Mrs. Bilkes, and was half-way to the table with the sausages; but the name of her beloved lady was too much for her; she stopped short and dropped the dish.

"Sarah! Good gracious! Upon my word! And to stand there staring! Pick 'em up, girl, pick 'em up, or the cat'll have them."

Mrs. Bilkes was out of her chair in her excitement, but Sally took no notice either of Mrs. Bilkes or the cat or the sausages. She stood still and looked at the grinning face above the newspaper.

"Took to prison, do you mean?" she said.

"Do you hear what I say, Sarah? They'll mark the carpet as sure as I'm born, and as for eating them now—You shall have them for your dinner. It's all you'll get, I bet it is." This from Mrs. Bilkes, kneeling beside the broken dish and the cooling sausages.

"Prison, of course," said Mr. Bilkes. "She'll do time, the same as other reprobate women."

Sally was not looking at him now, but at the opposite wall, and all that she said was "'*Er!*'"

"Sarah, *do* you hear? Give me a hand at once or take a week's notice."

"Sally," said Mr. Bilkes, "what price her precious ladyship now, eh? What did I tell you?"

Sally turned and looked at him as he spoke.

"Divorce court, or prison, along with thieves and drunkards—they're bound to come to it, women" (but Mr. Bilkes did not use the word "women," but a coarser one), "women like her."

Then Sally crossed the Rubicon. She had responded to Mrs. Bilkes's command, and had stooped to "lend a hand"; in that hand was a sausage, and as Mr. Bilkes paused in his speech to chuckle, the sausage went, not on to the bigger half of the broken dish beside its fellows, but straight for the face of Mr. Bilkes; and hit it.

Mr. Bilkes's grin disappeared with marvellous rapidity, and instead of a chuckling man there was a swearing one. Mrs. Bilkes was so "dumbfoundered," as she expressed it afterwards, that she could do nothing but sit speechless on the floor. Sally, erect, with flaming cheeks, said nothing either, but breathed hard.

"Gurl," panted Mr. Bilkes when he had let off steam a bit, "I'll have you up for this—prosecute—it's assault."

"An' make yerself a larfin' stock. Do!" said Sally.

"Whatever else happens," observed Mrs. Bilkes from the carpet, "out of this house you go. D'you hear me?"

"It's high time I made a change," retorted Sally, "an' would 'ave done it long ago if it 'adn't 'ave been for the children."

"Ben," said Mrs. Bilkes, "help me up!"

"You could have knocked me down with a feather," she told her mother-in-law later on, "if I hadn't been down already, and my legs were all of a tremble."

Once firm upon those legs, she pointed to the door. "Go," she said, "and pack your box." And Sally went.

She went upstairs to the attic that had been her bedroom for two years; she shut the door and she glanced at her box; but she did not begin to pack it. She sat down on her bed, as she had sat so often, thinking over the meetings and of "Lady 'Ill," and looked across the intervening roofs at the roof of Holloway Gaol. She would be there, the beautiful lady of whose wonderful deeds and attributes, as portrayed in Sally's stories, the children never tired; was there already, no doubt; for in Sally's imagination Lady Henry had been dragged direct from the streets to the prison; there, because she had chosen to take up the cudgels for other women, women like herself who worked, women like her mother who were "put upon." Everybody must admire her, everybody must see how noble she was and how unselfish. Lord Henry, considering the situation, had dreaded the criticism of the outer world; Sally had no such dread; to her it seemed that, learning what Lady Henry had done, the world would be converted. Bilkes, to be sure, had shown no sign of conversion, but Bilkes was a beast, and didn't count. Only, she admitted unwillingly, there were so many beasts about. And the bosses, of course (it was thus she designated the Government), they would be against her ladyship, else she would not be kept mewed up in the prison over there. The beasts and the bosses, they were her enemies; but the rest of the world would admire and reverence her as by Sally she was reverenced and admired.

Over there in Holloway Prison! That lady who was used to having servants to wait on her, and—There came a knock at her door.

"Who's there?"

"Ma says you're to hurry up."

"All right! Tell her I shan't be long. But just come in, Miss Dorothy."

Dorothy came into the room, and stood looking at Sally with one finger in her mouth. "Ma says you're a bad lot."

"That's as it may be, but there's some as is worse nor wot I am."

Dorothy came nearer. "What did you do, Sally? Did you cheek dadda?"

"'E cheeked me. But there, never mind about that. It ain't no business of yours, wot I done, nor it ain't no business of mine to turn yer against yer parents. And I thank the Lord," Sally added under her breath, "they aren't mine. Look 'ere," she said aloud, "you know that piece of ribbon I 'ad round my neck last Sunday, green, with the pink border, wot you wanted to tie round Minnie's waist?" Minnie was Dorothy's doll.

"Yes, and poor Minnie's got no sash at all now."

"Well, yer can 'ave it."

"Oh, Sally!"

"'Ere take it. An' go an' tell yer ma it won't be long afore I'm gone."

"'Tain't your day out, is it, Sally?"

"Yes, Miss Dorothy, and night out. Now cut!"

"I shan't tell them I'm goin'," she thought when Dorothy had gone. "Stanny'll cry his eyes out when 'e finds I ain't comin' back, and little Maud—but there, it's no good. It 'as to be and it ain't no good to funk it." Mr. Bilkes was not about when Sally went downstairs; it was Mrs. Bilkes who saw her off the premises, with half a week's wages in her pocket. Sally knew well that she was entitled to double that amount, but she would not, as she put it, demean herself to ask for it, and the only thing she said before leaving the house was:

"Miss Dorothy generally have a drink about the time you goes to supper, an' Master Stanny, 'e wakes up most nights an' wants one."

A couple of hours later a girl with a turned-up nose and wide bright eyes entered the offices of the WSPU.

"Well, and what is it? What do you want?" she was asked.

"Please, mum, I've 'ad to leave my place along of Lady 'Ill going to prison, an' I want to find a job where the people's suffragettes, and I can do my work without being baited and talked at all the time; and do something for you ladies too."

Did anybody want a servant? Sally could cook and clean, and do most things that a servant, a "general," was supposed to do. She did not want much in the way of wages; only some hours of liberty in the week, to work for the Cause; for Sally the word was always spelt with a capital letter.

It took some days to find out whether anybody wanted her; then a woman who had a small dressmaker's business, and needed somebody to help her in various ways, took her on a month's trial. Sally liked variety, and she and her new mistress, who was as enthusiastic as she was, suited each other exactly.

Thus it was that she left the Bilkes household, and became, like Lady Henry Hill, a full-blown suffragette.

CHAPTER XX
HUSBAND AND WIFE

"Let me but bear your love, I'll bear your cares."

Shakespeare[1]

It was the morning of release—the release of twenty-six prisoners from Holloway Gaol. At half-past seven, outside the prison, the suffragettes were collecting to receive their comrades. They all wore their colours, and the colours were on the seven carriages, draped and decorated, which were to bear those comrades to their homes.

There was plenty of life outside the prison, plenty to see and plenty to hear, for a band was playing tunes that, so Sally said, had plenty of go in them. For Sally was there, wearing her colours, proud to be known as a suffragette, excited, happy, waiting eagerly till the prisoners should appear. She was glad that Joe was there to see her and hear the music and realise the fine way in which the suffragettes received their champions. Joe was in the crowd of on-lookers and sympathisers, and she was glad he had come; but, for the moment, he was hardly more to her than one of the crowd; her thoughts, her interest, were concentrated on watching the prison gate.

Eight o'clock struck and the crowd drew closer to those gates; such a dense crowd that the police had to keep a pathway through it.

Inside, in the prison, Geraldine was thinking, "Will he be there waiting for me?" Outside, in the crowd, Joe Whittle was trying to edge himself close to Sally, and Sally was saying to herself, "Why don't they hurry up and let 'em out?" Everywhere there was a buzz of voices, and a sense of expectancy that grew tenser as the minutes passed.

It was a quarter-past eight when the small door in the great gates was opened and the prisoners filed forth; and immediately the band broke into the great world-known song of liberty, the song to which those same women had set out a month ago on their way to the House of Commons. Then they were marching to prison; now freedom was theirs once more; for a space, for a spell of fresh effort.

Forth they came, as they had come forth from the Caxton Hall, save that one who had been there then was absent now; their leader.

---

1   William Shakespeare (1564–1616), *2 Henry IV*, 5.2:59 (1600).

Mrs. Lane's sentence was double that of her followers, and there was not one of those released to-day whose heart did not carry the thought of her who was left behind, who would not willingly have gone back and served her sentence for her.

The crowd closed round them as they came, cheering, and through the crowd friends pressed towards them and they towards the faces that they looked for. Geraldine searched that sea of faces with trembling hope; then the tremor passed as the hope died. Her sister was there, waiting, brimming over with welcoming affection, but not Lord Henry. Well, if that was the trouble she had to face, she must face it, and she would not let her private disappointment spoil the sense of public rejoicing.

She had not much time to think; the procession was forming up, and she was called upon to take her place in one of the car-riages. A long procession it was, gay with banners and flags, with Christina Amherst, Annie Carnie, Madge Dewgall in the van of it; women whose names Geraldine had known when the movement itself was but a name to her. After these came the band, and after the band, groups of members of the Union, and behind the carriages containing the prisoners, more groups, and then a long line of cabs, carriages, and motor-cars; and these too were decorated with the colours, and flying tri-colour flags.

In a carriage with three others Geraldine was driven through a part of London absolutely unknown to her. Along Camden Road they went, then by Hampstead Road, into the Tottenham Court Road. Here Geraldine knew her bearings, but she had not much attention to give to where she was going. For all along the route the procession was cheered again and again, and continuously there were people waving from the windows, handkerchiefs, flags, the colours of the Union.

The popular sympathy was shown in many ways. In Camden Road they came across a huge dray, and the driver, having begged a flag from one of the carriages, added himself and his load to the procession.

Down the Tottenham Court Road, into New Oxford Street, and along High Holborn to the Inns of Court Hotel.

Geraldine was longing to get home; till she was there she would not be sure of her husband's attitude; but breakfast—a private break-fast, just for the released prisoners—had been ordered at the hotel, and it would be ungracious not to partake of it with the rest. So again she put her trouble on one side and concerned herself only with her immediate surroundings. Afterwards she was glad that she had stayed, glad to have the memory of that meeting together, presided over by the spirit of comradeship. There were the different experiences to relate, the various impressions; monotonous as was prison life, each one had something individual to speak of, were it only a point of view. And the sense of fellowship was strong and vital; Geraldine had been conscious of it ever since she had entered the movement, but she had never felt it so strongly as now when she sat comparing notes with those who had been her fellow prisoners.

Then the breakfast was over and the leave-takings, and she found herself in a taxi-cab, speeding through familiar places towards Upper Brook Street; shrinking, now that her home was so near, from what might await her there; steeling her heart that hungered for her husband's sympathy, to endure his displeasure.

She was there now, ringing the bell. Roberts, the butler, greeted her with a "Glad to see you back, my lady," as though she had returned from a lengthened week-end in the country: when it was a simple Saturday to Monday, it was his habit to say nothing.

"Thank you, Roberts. Is—is his lordship in?"

"Yes, my lady, in the smoking-room."

She went through the hall and up the passage beyond, to the door she knew so well, the mahogany door with the brass handle. She turned that handle very quickly and went in, closing the door after her. Whatever was to be between her and her husband, it should be shut out from all the rest of the world.

Lord Henry was standing with his back to the fire. He had been listening, and his eyes were on the door and on his wife as she entered. For a moment he stood and looked at her and she at him; then he came forward quickly, holding out his arms.

"Jerry!"

At that dear name all her fortitude forsook her and all the need for it; there was no reason now why she should not lay her head upon his shoulder and let the tears come; tears that had been unshed in Holloway.

"I couldn't come," he said, "to the prison. I couldn't have met you there, before the crowd." She was glad that he had not come: this was better.

Presently, with her cheek against his cheek, as on the night when she had asked him if he would stand by her, she asked him that same thing again:

"Are you going to stand by me, then?"

"Yes, dear."

"But privately, I mean?"

"Yes, altogether."

"Then you—? But you said it depended on how far I went."

"So it does; exactly."

"But, Henry—"

"But, Jerry. Just as far as you go I shall have to go too."

CHAPTER XXI
AN ADVOCATE

"The way's not easy where the prize is great."

Quarles[1]

Everybody said that it was extraordinary of Robbie Colquhoun to live in the country. He neither shot nor hunted, nor did he even fish, and life in the country unenlivened by even one of these pursuits must be destitute of interest and enjoyment. Especially was it extraordinary because he was not a clergyman, and consequently was not busied with, nor enchained by, parish duties; and more especially because he was well enough off to live where he chose. When Parliament was sitting he was obliged to spend a good deal of his time in London; but the inhabitants of Wenthorn, his own village, of Pagnell, and indeed of all the villages in the neighbourhood, decided that a house in London would suit him much better as head-quarters than the Manor House, and would have been positively annoyed with him for not seeing the wisdom of their decision, but for the fact that nobody wanted to lose him. He was one of the few bachelors in the countryside, and the only eligible one, and mothers who did not hesitate to characterise women desirous of the vote as

---

1 Francis Quarles (1592–1644), "Epigram 11 [O Cupid, if thy smoother way were right]" *Emblemes*, Book 2 (1635).

unwomanly, forward, and immodest were not ashamed to angle for him as a husband for their daughters.

So far no mother had got so much as a rise out of him. He was on amicable terms with all women, deferential to those who were elderly, friendly with those who were young; but he showed no desire to pass the impalpable barrier which divides friendship from love. He was popular nevertheless, in spite of the fact that the men thought the fellow rather a fool because he was no sportsman, and that the women were inclined to be piqued because he was no lover. The former were obliged to allow that he was a good sort, and the latter felt that he was to be trusted. Both declared him to be dull, but admitted that he was easy to get on with.

For a dull man he had unusually interesting friends; that also was almost a grievance in the neighbourhood; Dawnshire could not understand what they saw in him. He was very nice, of course—oh, of course; but that clever men, known men, men, who could pick and choose their society, should elect to come down and spend days at a time with Robbie Colquhoun was a fact that passed the comprehension of the intellect of the county. Agatha Brand suggested that the brains of his visitors needed rest, and found it, as well as very comfortable quarters, at the Manor House. Edith Carstairs, who never would allow Robbie to be laughed at when she was about, observed that because he found no pleasure in careering about the country killing animals, and had no idea how to flirt, it did not follow that he was incapable of reading the books in his library, an unusually large one; on the contrary, it was reasonable to suppose that that was how he spent part, at least, of his time. This she said, not so much because she believed it, for Robbie never talked about books, though, by the way, he seemed to know a good deal about what was inside some of them, but because he was a dear, and was not to be decried, even by her most intimate friend. Besides, he was understanding, almost always; understanding about things that other people would never understand; that fairies could be there, for instance, and not really there, at the same time. Edith, though she did not think him an intellectual swan, rated him, unconsciously to herself, considerably higher than did her neighbours.

She was especially glad of his understanding capacity at the time of Lady Henry Hill's imprisonment, the news of which came as a shock to the neighbourhood. That a woman of Lady Henry's position should belong to the suffrage movement at all was a revelation, and a startling one; that she should actually come into conflict with the police and positively go to prison were facts which played havoc with the ideas of Dawnshire. For a while it was a moot point whether the woman lent respectability to the cause, or whether the cause degraded the woman; then custom set its seal upon the problem, and perplexity was at an end. Mrs. Dallas, of the Firs, said that no nice woman would go to prison, and it was forthwith decided that Lady Henry was a blot upon her family, a black sheep in a flock of immaculate whiteness, a common wild weed in a garden of carefully cultured plants.

"How dreadful for her friends!"

"The poor Duke and Duchess!"

"What a trial for her husband!"

Such were the remarks made with what the French aptly term *une figure de circonstance*,[1] when Wenthorn went to call on Pagnell, or when Pagnellite met Pagnellite at tea. Commiseration for the relations of the offender, that was the note which effectually combined respect for the family and disapproval of the individual, and everybody united to strike it. Or nearly all. There were exceptions, such as Agatha Brand, for instance, who substituted angry resentment for mournful displeasure.

"It's abominable," she declared, "that when we constitutional women have been working quietly and steadily at work that really tells, gradually bringing our influence to bear upon the Government, proving to them that we are worthy of the vote, abominable that a woman whose position unfortunately makes her prominent, should come forward and aid and abet the senseless policy of those who are making the vote impossible. It's too bad, and I can't help, Edith, if she *is* your friend. You know I always say what I think."

"Yes, I know; but I hope you don't always think what you say. You are too generous not to give other women the credit of their convictions."

"I'm not talking about convictions, I'm talking about common sense. A lunatic may be convinced that the best thing he can do is to go and cut his own throat, but that doesn't prove that he is to be commended for doing it."

---

1   A sad or mournful face (as befitting the circumstances).

"After all, questions of policy must be questions of opinion. *You* think that the militant methods are mistaken; *they* think that they're the only ones which produce any result. As things are at present, I don't see how you, or anyone, can say positively whether they're right or wrong. When it comes to a question of principle, of course, it's a different thing altogether."

"Well, I'll take it on principle, if you like; it doesn't in the least diminish my objections, but, on the contrary, it adds to them. To my mind, these tactics, as they call them, sin against the very essentials of womanliness; and for my part, I think that the womanliness of women is of much greater value—greater to themselves and to the community—than the vote."

Edith sat silent; secretly she was inclined to agree with the present friend, but longed nevertheless to defend the absent one. It was then that she was particularly grateful to Robbie Colquhoun, who had a way of dropping in at Mrs. Brand's, and often, as on this special afternoon, when Edith happened to be there. She was passively grateful because he arrived just at the moment when she found nothing to say; she became actively so when, Agatha continuing to give forth her views, Robbie, in the slow, unimpassioned way peculiar to him, took up the cudgels for the other side.

"Of course a woman must be a woman," he said. "If she isn't, she's generally a beast. At least that's my experience. But suffragettes aren't beasts; they're much like any other women, except that they've got their backs against the wall, which makes a difference to everybody. At least that's my experience."

"What do you know about them, pray?" asked Agatha. "Nothing but what you read in the papers."

"There certainly isn't much about them in the papers," said Robbie, with the ghost of a grin on his weather-beaten face: he was as weather-beaten as the most inveterate sportsman. "Unless they've been on the warpath. Which might, of course, be partly why they go. But I've come across them, some of them, when I've been in London."

"Meetings, I suppose," said Agatha disdainfully.

"Gorton's rooms."

"They *would*, of course, go to men's rooms."

"Mrs. Brand," said Robbie, "have you never been to tea with me?"

"At the Manor House? That's different." Then Agatha laughed. "No, perhaps not so different after all. I confess I pushed it too far. But the whole thing is so repugnant to me," she said, taking up her serious tone again, "so utterly repugnant, that I can't express what I feel."

"I think you manage to express it pretty well," said Robbie. "Edith, I'm going to drive you home; I've got the dog-cart. You won't be cold?"

"No, not cold, but Agatha may think it's unwomanly to drive in a dog-cart without a chaperon."

"Oh no, she knows we're related."

The relationship was distant, consisting in the cousin-ship of their maternal grandmothers, but it served as a convenient sop to the Cerberus of convention.

"What I should call unwomanly," laughed Agatha, "would be if you were to punch his head because he wouldn't let you drive."

"I can answer for that not happening," returned Robbie. "If she wants to drive, I'll hand her over the reins."

Undoubtedly Edith had reason to be grateful to him, and on the way home she told him of her gratitude.

"Did you say it just to get me out of a hole?" she added, "or do you believe it?"

"I don't see much good in saying what you don't believe."

"But about the militants. I should have thought you would have been shocked."

"I am a bit."

"Not with Lady Henry?" she pleaded.

"No; with the Government; though I'm a Liberal." He paused while he gave the horse a flick with his whip. "Because I'm a Liberal; and more, not less, because I'm a Liberal Member. If a thing's just, it should be given—with some grace. Men shouldn't force women to fight."

"Perhaps they remember that they had to fight themselves."

"Very likely. But if women are different, they should be spared the fighting. If not, why blame 'em for doing it?"

"Oh Robbie, you *are* a dear!"

"Hold tight," was Robbie's reply. "There's a motor coming and we shall have to pretty well shave the hedge."

When the motor had gone by, he said, "How's Monty? Heard from him lately?"

"Yes, yesterday. He seems all right."

"You must miss them, the boys, both of them, when they go back."

"Yes, especially at first. One gets used to being without them."

In her heart of hearts, Edith rejoiced that Monty was not at home just now. He would have said horrid things about Lady Henry, things she could not have stood. It was a real hurt to her to hear her friend's motives belittled, herself abused; all the more so that she could not fight whole-heartedly in her defence. As to motives, oh yes; but it was useless to defend Lady Henry on that score; these people who were so much less noble than the woman they found fault with would never understand their purity. And as to conduct, Edith's reason and her temperament sided with the enemy.

When she got home that day after being with Agatha Brand, she went straight upstairs to her bedroom and over to the south window, a bay, with one narrow opening to the west. A row of poplars edged the path, a right of way, that ran between the garden fence and a neighbouring field, and the poplars were amongst the friends she found in inanimate things. All through the summer they whispered ceaselessly, however still the air. Edith used to wonder if the leaves had a life of their own, separate from the tree, because the branches, when they were bare, never stirred. Or was it that the wind had a special love for the poplars and rested in them, rustling the leaves, when it was too weary to wander through the world?

This evening the branches stood up, tall and straight, pointing to the sky; leafless yet, and therefore silent. But silence was what, just then, she needed most; one of friendship's most precious qualities, one of the charms which lay for her in things accounted speechless. They had a tongue of their own, these silent things; soundless, soothing; welcome when words would have jarred. More troubled than she would have owned, even to Robbie Colquhoun, the up-ward-pointing trees, in their bareness and their stillness, gave her consolation. The spell of evening was upon them, and upon the paling February sky, and on all the wistful awakening world of early spring. Kneeling by the window, the message of that world was given to her; hope, activity, effort, aspiration; given by the sprouting life in the garden borders, by the fields and hedgerows beyond, by the familiar trees. There was neither speech nor language, but their voices were heard.

CHAPTER XXII
PLOTTING

"Perfect scheming demands omniscience."

G. Eliot[1]

Mrs. Dallas, of the Firs, had a flat in London. It was partly the flat which gave weight to her pronouncement as to women and prison. A lady who could run up to London at any time for a few days, and was therefore, so to speak, in touch with the centre of political life, must, it was admitted, speak with authority; and a lady and authority in conjunction formed a combination than which none better could be imagined for passing judgment on the conduct of women. And Mrs. Dallas was emphatically a lady; there were those who in speaking of her prefaced the noun with "perfect," others with "thorough." Certain it is that, lying on ever so many feather-beds of refinement, she was capable, like the famous princess in the story, of detecting, beneath their softness, vulgarity even of no greater proportions than that of a pea; and the pea, in the case of Lady Henry Hill, was of the size of a potato; not a new one.

Nevertheless, though she held aloof from advanced ideas and un-ladylike conduct, she took an intelligent interest in the questions of the day, and was even a public propagandist, to the extent of sitting on platforms; an inability to express what she really felt prevented her from sharing her views with an audience. In private she had, as she herself put it, more flow. But there were those whose flow, extending to public utterance, presented accurately her private beliefs, and one in especial, a noble lord, commanded on this account her admiration and sympathy. This gentleman was to speak at a meeting to be held three days after the release of Lady Henry Hill, and Mrs. Dallas determined to go and hear him. It would be a refreshment, she said to Mrs. Leigh in the drawing-room of Vale End vicarage, and the meeting would be a particularly interesting one, very big, very important, marking, in fact, an epoch in the killing out of the women's suffrage movement.

---

1 George Eliot (1819–80), *Romola* (1862–63).

"I wish you could be there, dear Mrs. Leigh. He would so appeal to you, both to your sentiments and reason. His speech is sure to be an intellectual treat."

"I wish I could, I'm sure." Mrs. Leigh paused, and then spoke reflectively. "I should like—I wish I could have taken Edith. I am not satisfied about her. This local society—well, that doesn't matter so much, and if her mother is so foolish as to allow her to belong to it, one must just let it be. Though I must say that for a girl to stand about the streets, accosting every man she comes across, is not what either her uncle or I consider respectable; and I hope you quite understood, Mrs. Dallas, that we utterly disapproved of it."

"Oh, of course. I knew exactly the view you would take."

"To say she only spoke to voters," pursued Mrs. Leigh, "was of course to beg the question. All men are voters; even the most dissolute."

"Exactly. And yet women want to be like them!"

"I can't say that I think Edith shows any signs of—er—fastness; but, as I say, I'm anxious about her. She stood up for that Lady Henry Hill the other day in a way that, I could see, really shocked Lady Mercer. I assure you I was most uncomfortable, quite apart from my utter disapproval; and her uncle and I had a long talk about it after the choir practice."

"I understand what you feel so well, dear Mrs. Leigh, and I wish—I wonder how I could help you?"

"You are always so sympathetic, dear Mrs. Dallas, that I feel I can really speak to you of my anxiety. Poor Mary is so under the thumb of her children that it's no good talking to *her*; and Edith— well, I get so little out of her. She's not frank, either with me or her uncle."

To stand up hotly for Lady Henry Hill and to fail in frankness to her aunt! The position was really a serious one, and Mrs. Dallas reflected upon it while the maid brought in tea.

When the two ladies were alone again she brought forth the result of her reflections.

"Why not come up to the Queen's Hall meeting and bring Edith?" she asked. "I have one quite decent spare room, and a slip of a place where I can put a bed at a pinch, and I shall be delighted if you will accept my hospitality."

"Oh thank you! It's too good, really too sweet of you. I really don't know. Beauchamp—I so seldom leave him, you see—but in such a cause. And then, Edith; she's so—"

Aunt Elinor hesitated. "Supposing she refused to go?"

The two conspirators sat and looked at each other; they both recognised that Edith, with all her softness—and even Mrs. Dallas could not deny that she had nice manners—was a hard nut to crack; and the part of futile nut-crackers was an ignominious one to play.

Then Mrs. Dallas rose to the occasion. "If you would wish it, dear Mrs. Leigh, *I* will propose it."

Dear Mrs. Leigh was only too thankful to accept the generous offer, and Mrs. Dallas, fortified by a second cup of tea—"Very little milk, please, I should like it rather strong—" proceeded in her motor from the vicarage to the Pightle.

Edith, gazing out at the poplars, was roused from her dreaming by a knock at the door, followed by the entrance of Pierce, the parlourmaid. Mrs. Dallas was in the drawing-room with Mrs. Carstairs, and would like to see her.

"What on earth for?" thought Edith. "How tiresome she is!" But there was nothing to be done except to go downstairs.

"I've come to ask your mother to lend you to me for a night," said Mrs. Dallas. "Your aunt is coming to me in London for the great meeting at the Queen's Hall, and she would so like—we should both so like—if you would come with her."

"The Queen's Hall! On the twenty-second, do you mean? Surely—"

"No, dear child. Oh no! On the twenty-*seventh*; *quite* a different thing." She gave some details of the meeting and the names of the speakers. "Your aunt thinks you ought to hear these celebrated men, and I, for one, feel sure"—Mrs. Dallas became arch and tapped Edith playfully on the arm with her lorgnette—"I feel sure that dear little Edith is too open-minded to refuse to hear both sides of the question."

Dear little Edith felt that she wished to hear no side of the question in company with Aunt Elinor and Mrs. Dallas; but Mrs. Carstairs said, "I think it would be nice for you, darling"; and, after all, she might hear something from these well-known men which would contravene the thoughts suggested by the voices without speech or language which she had been listening to upstairs. It was always women speakers she had heard so far; men might bring forward arguments neglected or unthought of by her own sex; there *might* be something in the old-fashioned notion that the masculine mind had a fuller grasp of a subject, a greater logical force than the feminine. She would see; especially as it was easier in her present snood to give in than to resist. So she surprised Mrs. Dallas by replying:

"Thank you very much. There is nothing I should like better than to be an anti."

Mrs. Dallas, therefore, departed in triumph, and in triumph called in at the vicarage to tell Mrs. Leigh that there was no doubt dear little Edith was shaken. Whatever she might have said—out of sheer obstinacy, probably—it was evident that the impossible conduct of that woman (it was thus she alluded to the daughter-in-law of half a hundred dukes) had given her a shock, and it remained only for the noble lord, and the astute politician who were to speak at the Queen's Hall, to finish the conversion already begun.

CHAPTER XXIII
THE PLOT THAT FAILED

"Men may have rounded Seraglio Point: they have not yet doubled Cape Turk."

George Meredith[1]

"A great meeting, organised by the Women's National Anti-Suffrage League, was held at the Queen's Hall last evening, to protest against the parliamentary vote being given to women." Thus one of the leading morning papers, on the 28th of March, and the others were in similar strain.

There might be nothing that was worth reporting in favour of the women's movement: it needed columns to contain the remarkable declamations against it.

Mrs. Dallas and Mrs. Leigh perused the columns with delight; Edith did not even glance at them. The speeches as spoken had made such a profound impression upon her that there was no need to deepen it.

---

1   George Meredith (1828–1909), *Diana of the Crossways* (1885).

She had been impressed in many ways: in the first place, by the fact that the platform was crowded with women, and that a woman was in the chair; then, in conjunction with that fact, with the further one, that after the woman president had made a declamatory speech, the noble lord[1] who was the hero of the evening proceeded forthwith to denounce women who declaimed on platforms. Was this lack of logic or lack of courtesy or pure forgetfulness? Edith, who had come to look for logic and had donned the spectacles of favourable bias wherewith to find it, put it down to forgetfulness. The speaker would not designedly hurl the epithet "unsexed" at these many women who supported him and whom he was supposed to support. Yet he asked the audience if it were an imperial thought to dethrone woman from that position of gentle yet commanding influence which she now occupied, and substitute in her place the unsexed woman voting at the polling booth and declaiming on the platform?

His imagination, however, soared beyond the platform. The un-sexed one might even sit at the desk of the Cabinet Minister and decide some important question affecting the destinies of her fellow countrymen and women in the antipodes. Distance, indeed, seemed to lend additional disenchantment to the view, taken by the speaker, of women in possession of the vote. For not only did he refer to the inhabitants of the antipodes in general, but alluded separately to the settler in Australia, the backwoodsman in Canada, the ryot[2] in India, and the negro in the Sudan; all of whom were to be at the mercy of unsexed women. And sex, it seemed, was of all woman's attributes the most precious, creating ethical as well as physical differences be-tween her and man. It caused her action to be moral, whereas man's action was material; and, that being so, woman's action must not be allowed to intrude upon the domain of politics.

Edith wondered at this point if the danger of introducing moral-ity into politics was not exaggerated; for, if women, on entering a polling booth, became unsexed, out of that polling booth surely the dreaded attributes of the woman could not come forth to affect the negro in the Sudan and the ryot in India.

---

1   Evelyn Baring, Earl of Cromer and first British Viceroy of Egypt, (1841–1917) was President of the Men's League for Opposing Women's Suffrage. In 1910 he became President of the National League for Opposing Women's Suffrage, an amalgamation of the mens' and women's leagues.

2   Peasant, husbandman, or cultivating tenant (*OED*).

But she must not wonder; she must listen.

"Are you interested, dear?" whispered Mrs. Dallas.

"Immensely." And indeed she wished to lose not a word of the speech.

One of the difficulties which surrounded this question, she learned, was to find any common basis for discussion. The relative qualifications of a duke and a dustman to sit in the House of Lords could be explained, the differences between these individuals being merely those of class. But women did not constitute a class. They were a sex.

Edith stole a glance at her aunt at this point, and found the glance returned by a smile.

"Are you getting new ideas?" said Aunt Elinor.

"Yes, I always thought till to-night that there was a male sex as well as a female one."

"Hush!" said voices around, and indeed the speaker had come to his most interesting point; the statement of his principal objection to giving votes to women.

"Because they are not men."

Here was another new idea for Edith, who had always held that it was just because women were not men, were different in many ways from men, that it was important they should possess a means of political expression. She did not join either in the cheers or the laughter evoked by the masterly simplicity of the speaker's reasoning; but sat as quiet as the ladies on either side of her, who would have thought it irreverent to laugh and unwomanly to cheer. All they could do was to ask Edith if she were impressed, and Edith assured them that she was.

The sentiment which followed on the noble lord's main argument had none of the charms of novelty for her. She knew already that men honour and revere the mothers who leave on their minds high and sacred impressions, and that the really noble way of rewarding those mothers is to give them no say in the laws which affect their children. She knew that men cherish their wives, and delight in the society of female friends, who soften masculine asperities; being aware, at the same time, that there are husbands who substitute kicks for cherishing, encouraged in this manifestation of supremacy by receiving for the substitution a punishment less than that incurred by poaching on a neighbour's preserves; and that the delight of softening masculine asperities is not always equal to that of having them softened. She knew that women must not be sullied by being dragged into all the hurly-burly of political conflict; and knew too that the chivalrous guardians of sex delicacy had no compunction in persuading wives, daughters, and female friends to take a hand in the hurliest-burliest part of political life in order to win votes for their protectors at an election.

She knew all this, and much more that followed. It was the original parts of the speech which really made a mark upon her: the main argument against woman suffrage, and the, to her, novel ideas that there were no class distinctions amongst women because they were a sex, and that the sex of men disappeared when you compared a duke with a dustman.

The effect produced upon her by the noble lord was deepened by the astute politician who followed him. This speaker was at one with his predecessor in his chief argument, but he put that argument into a rather more elaborate form, and framed an utterance destined to be coupled with his name for the edification of posterity; an utterance combining the profundity of the statesman with the knowledge of the physiologist and the common sense of the man of the world. Man, he said, was man, and woman was woman. Nature had made them different, and Parliament could not make them the same.

"Well," said Mrs. Dallas, when she and her two guests were safely in the motor on their way to Mayfair Mansions, "I *am* glad I went to-night."

"And so am I," agreed Mrs. Leigh.

"And I," said Edith.

"A theatre is all very well," added Aunt Elinor, "but to-night's entertainment was, to my mind, much more interesting."

"And quite as amusing," said Edith.

Mrs. Leigh peered across at her niece's face, but the face, on which the light from a lamp happened just then to fall, was set in serious lines.

"The speeches were certainly very witty," she observed; "I am so glad you appreciated them."

"Was I not right," put in Mrs. Dallas, "in persuading you to hear the other side?"

"I am certainly glad to have heard it."

"I think I may venture to prophesy that you will take a *little* different view of the question in future?" Mrs. Dallas was in her playful mood.

"I'm sure I shall."

"And that that woman's conduct will strike you in an entirely different light," said Aunt Elinor.

Edith knew that "that woman" was Lady Henry Hill, and she replied, with earnestness, "Quite, quite different."

Sandwiches and lemonade awaited the propagandists and their pupil, and while the two ladies ate with appetite and talked with animation Edith sat nibbling a sandwich and screwing up her courage. It required a good deal of screwing; she was tender-hearted as well as timid, and shrank as much from causing disappointment as from raising anger. It was not till she had said good-night and had reached the dining-room door that she compelled herself to candour. Then, turning and facing the room, she said:

"I'm very much obliged to you, both to you Mrs. Dallas, and you, Aunt Elinor, for—for taking me to-night; but I think I ought to tell you—it wouldn't be fair not to—how I—I feel about it. I said I was impressed—and so I was; and that I take a different view—and so I do. But what they said made me understand for the first time why women join the—the militants."

Then, before the two faces had time to change from perplexity to indignation, she was out of the door and on her way upstairs.

She feared Aunt Elinor might come to her room to mingle tears with recrimination, and waited for a while in uncomfortable expectation; but Aunt Elinor did not come; and Edith, feeling guilty at having spoken, and telling herself that she would have felt still more guilty if she had not spoken, undressed and got into bed.

It was some time before sleep came to her; the speeches, the platform, the many faces and the two particular faces, beaming with satisfaction, stern with disapproval, all these made a jumble in her mind, which stood in the way of its quiescence. She dozed and woke, and dozed and half woke again; and in her drowsy half-consciousness was pursued by a problem—or a riddle—vague, foolish, but persistent: "If a woman has no class, how can she be *declassé*?"[1] She fell really asleep before she found even the semblance of an answer.

---

1   Reduced or degraded from one's social class.

CHAPTER XXIV
O EXCELLENT AND BENEFICENT SAUSAGE!

"The little waves make the large ones, and are of the same pattern."
Middlemarch[1]

Sally was serving her apprenticeship in street speaking; a difficult one, since the stringing together of sentences in face of a crowd was a task which seemed to her at first impossible of accomplishment. To make up stories for the children was one thing; the words came somehow, anyhow, to bear her meaning; to tell the truth to men and women was another; the words, it seemed at first, would come nohow. Especially at the start; that was the difficulty; to begin. Once launched, Sally found that talking to grown-up people was not so very different from talking to children after all. The same kinds of things seemed to please them both, or things that came to her in the same way—came into her head. The chief difference was that men and women were slower to believe the truth than the children were to believe the stories. But after a time Sally got into the way of making them care to listen to her. She had no lack of courage, and she knew what she wanted to say (the bird in her breast was fitted now for flight); and soon, as self-confidence developed, she found she could give the wags of the crowd as good as she got. They were not very difficult to answer after all, the field of their jocosity being limited; and the crowd, which at the questions was prepared to jeer with the questioner, was always ready to turn round and laugh with Sally.

"Don't you wish you was a man?" asked a weedy youth one day.

Quick came Sally's answer: "Don't you wish you was?" And there was no doubt who carried off the honours of the encounter.

"Where's your pore neglected 'usband?" a beery man called out.

"'Avin' a cup o' tea along of your cherished wife," answered Sally.

And then there was the man who told her: "Pity there ain't enough of us to go round; so as you could all get married."

"Time enough to count whether you'll go round when you've learned to act on the square."

---

1 George Eliot (1819–80), *Middlemarch* (1871–72).

Somehow there was always an answer not far from the tip of her tongue; and, finding that answers did not fail, she lost her fear of questions. She lost too her fear of starting a speech; became at home with these street audiences; spoke, in the vernacular that was theirs and hers, of the things she felt and meant that they should feel; let loose some of the fancies that had thrilled the little Bilkeses, on their brothers and sisters of maturer age; and held her listeners with a rough-and-ready eloquence which, if lacking in grammar, was not without a touch of oratory.

And all the time she scrubbed and worked and carried parcels for Mrs. Blake; and all the time her devotion grew to "the Cause" and to "them ladies at the orfice"; and all the time she drew nearer and nearer to the line of fire in the battle in which she was destined to be an active combatant.

She was at the opening of the Women's Exhibition at Prince's Skating Rink in May, and heard the speech of the only woman mayor in England, and was near enough to the front to hear too her dear Lady 'Ill's little niece say, as she presented a bouquet to the speaker, that when she was grown up she would always remember the day on which she was allowed to have the honour of giving flowers to a distinguished woman doctor.[1]

Sally wished the little Bilkeses could have been there to hear and see too. "Lor',''ow they'd enjoy theirselves, pore little things!" she said, "an' wot it'd be for them if they could be brought up in the Cause! But being born a Bilkes means bein' born a bat as far as seeing plain goes. An' wot eyes they *'ave* got as little uns, Bilkes'll put out afore they're in their teens."

Sally often thought of her former charges with longing affection. Once or twice she went and hovered about in the Bilkes neighbourhood to see if she could catch a glimpse of them, but without success. She used to wonder if the new girl gave them drinks, or if Stanny called out in the night in vain. Should she ever see Stanny again? Perhaps, some day, when the Cause was won, and she was

---

1 Elizabeth Garrett Anderson, who opened the WSPU's exhibition in May 1909, was Britain's first woman mayor having been elected, in Aldeburgh, in 1908. In 1865 she obtained the licence of the Society of Apothecaries which entitled her to have her name entered on the medical register, the first woman qualified in Britain to do so (*ODNB*; Holton, 1986, 31). Her sister, Millicent Garrett Fawcett, was president of the National Union of Women's Suffrage Societies.

married to Joe and had children of her own. Stanny would be a man by then, maybe; and "Lord alive!" thought Sally, "if I was to see 'im and 'e'd growed up like 'is pa, I should wish I 'adn't."

As for marriage, Joe Whittle was getting a bit restive. He had a good job now and leaned towards domesticity. But Sally was obdurate. She wasn't going to settle down yet, because she had something else to do; something that was the business of all women, and she was going to take her share. "Take me or leave me," she said; "but if it's takin', you can't take me yet."

Then Joe hinted darkly that there were others who might not be unwilling to take her place, and Sally said they were kindly welcome if he was such a silly as to go and bite off his nose to spite his face. "For you know as well as I do as there ain't a gurl in all London wot'd suit yer as I suits yer."

And then Joe would wait for another few weeks before he returned to the attack.

Sally worked her hardest for Mrs. Blake. She was unforgettingly grateful to the cheerful little dressmaker for allowing her, as far as possible, to do the household tasks at her own times and seasons, and was determined that her mistress should not suffer in consequence. So the house was kept in good order, the dinner was always well prepared, if not actually cooked, by the suffragette maid, and it was very seldom that a customer had to wait beyond the appointed time for the delivery of a new dress. Life was brimming over with interest, and Sally enjoyed it and her widened horizon to the full. And but for that sausage she might still have been general in Brunton Street, manoeuvring to escape the curiosity and the kisses of Mr. Bilkes! O excellent and beneficent sausage!

Her triumph, her day of days, came with the summer, in June, when she was allowed to be one of the girls who drew the carriage of Letitia Lockwood through the streets of London on the day of her release after three months' imprisonment.[1] Forty girls, all dressed in white, and Sally one of them; guided by silken reins of purple, white, and green; preceded by the drum and fife band of the Union;

---

[1] Patricia Woodlock was one of twenty-one women arrested while taking part in a deputation on 30 March 1909. This was her fourth arrest, and she was sentenced to three months in Holloway Gaol. Her release, on 16 June, was marked by the customary breakfast at the Inns of Court Hotel as well as an evening procession—in which she rode in a carriage drawn by women—in her honour (*Votes for Women*, 11 June 1909; 18 June 1909).

followed by a phalanx of members of the Union and of other societies, with a contingent of the Men's Committee for Justice to
Women bringing up the rear.

Sally's only regret was that the carriage was not heavier; she would
have wished to feel on her shoulders the weight of its honoured oc-
cupants; the girl released from prison for the fourth time, the woman, small and slight, who was at the head of the movement. Along
Kingsway and along Holborn and Oxford Street to the Marble Arch.
Crowds all the way and decorated windows; foreigners on the tops
of omnibuses gesticulating as they explained the movement to each
other or asked for information; words of sympathy, cheers.

"How many men would go to prison for each other?" was one
of the phrases Sally caught as she marched along.

She had looked at processions before; from the kerbstone,
perched on railings, once from a window. This was different, quite,
quite different, to be part of the procession and march through
gazing crowds, instead of being one of the gazers. And then, no
struggling for a place near one of the platforms; she was actually
on the platform, keeping humbly in the background, from which
Miss Lockwood spoke, and witnessed how the ex-prisoner turned a
bantering spectator into a friend who listened quietly. His chaff was
checked when, with a gracious impulse, she broke off a rose from
the beautiful bouquet of red roses presented to her by the Men's
Committee and handed it down to him.

"Look at that," said a man in a tall hat to the well-dressed woman
beside him. "See what happens when you treat us nicely. You can do
what you like with a fellow."

"Oh yes, turn him round our little finger. Do you think we don't
know that? So does the favourite in a harem. Cake? Oh, any amount;
but if we ask for bread, you cast stones at us and put us in prison."

"Not because you *ask* for it," said the man; and Sally, carried away
by interest, broke in eagerly: "No, but 'cause we won't be 'appy till
we gets it."

The man looked at her, smiled, and raised his hat; the woman
smiled too, and nodded. Then they moved away, and Sally never saw
them again. That was always happening. She came close to people,
in sympathy, interest, personal proximity, and then a wave of the
crowds swelled up and carried the moment's friends away for ever.
After the meeting there was work at Mrs. Blake's still to be done,

and Sally had no mind to shirk it. A lady was waiting for her dress; it had been promised for this evening, and she was not to be disappointed. Sally's legs ached a little, and her head too, now that the excitement was over. That didn't matter: the lady should have her dress, and she would sleep all the better for being tired. And sleep she did, soundly, dreamlessly, happily, proud of the place she had been allowed to fill, content with the work she was given to-day, utterly without presentiment of a very different day that was drawing closer on the inexorable path of time.

CHAPTER XXV
A FIRM HAND

> "When ye boast your own charters kept true,
> Ye shall blush; for the thing which ye do
> Derides what ye are.
> This is the curse. Write."
>
> E.B. Browning[1]

Edith Carstairs was staying in London with her father's sister, Mrs. Joyce. Mrs. Joyce's home was in Lancashire, but every year, in the season, she took a house in London, and every year she invited Edith to stay with her.

Aunt Lizzie was a very different person from Aunt Elinor, or Edith would never have left the country, in June, for what she called the stuffiness of London. As for the attractions of the season, they did not exist for her, save as they were connected with particular people; and while there were several people whom she strongly wished to see, the possibility of meeting them would hardly have lured her from the Pightle to Hyde Park Terrace. There was Lady Henry Hill, for instance; but—And there was Rachel Cullen; but—And Cyril Race; but—Indeed, between her and all the friends she most wished to be with, there stood a "but," and the dearer the friend, perhaps, the stronger the barrier.

The "but" which divided her from Rachel Cullen was the same as that which held her at a distance from Lady Henry, namely, the

---

1   Elizabeth Barrett Browning (1806–61), "A Curse for a Nation" (1860).

militant movement. Not that Miss Cullen had so far taken an active part in it; her body was too frail to support much physical hardship; but her mind, with its convictions, was what Edith felt at this juncture to be uncomfortably strong, and she shrank from coming in contact with its strength. The militant tactics were still repugnant to her, though the speeches at the Queen's Hall had enabled her to understand their genesis, and she did not want to have the reasoning which her friends were certain to mete out to her, and the affection which she felt for them, pitted against that inward feeling which was none the less powerful because it could not be intelligently stated.

Cyril Race, on the other hand, she wished to avoid for the precisely opposite reason; because he was strongly against the militant movement and had no difficulty in formulating his objections in convincing speech. These two reasons, taken in conjunction, certainly seemed to constitute a foolishness; but she kept the foolishness to herself, cherished behind the forbidding "buts" a desiring "if," had her trunk packed, and went to London.

She always liked to be with Aunt Lizzie, and besides the drawing power of Aunt Lizzie, there was also the driving power of Aunt Elinor to influence her decision; it was perhaps as much the desire to get away from the one as to go to the other, that caused her to accept Mrs. Joyce's invitation. For Aunt Elinor had been on a very high horse since the unfortunate expedition to the Queen's Hall. Edith was obstinate, ungrateful, and evidently under the influence of dangerous companions, she told her sister-in-law; and Mrs. Carstairs found nothing to say, except her usual statement that poor Richard had been very advanced and she supposed Edith took after him. Towards Edith herself, frigid compassion was the attitude taken up, though the nature of the attitude was only partially conveyed to the offender, for though Edith could not fail to observe the frigidity, she was entirely unconscious of the compassion.

As for Mrs. Dallas, dear little Edith had become Miss Carstairs, and Miss Carstairs was given to understand that she was no longer considered quite "nice."

Mrs. Dallas did not matter; she lived at Pagnell, between which and Vale End lay the delightful gulf of the intermediate country, and it was easy to dismiss her from everyday existence. But Mrs. Leigh was on the hither side of the gulf, and had many natural opportunities of obviously avoiding her niece, besides those which she went out of her way to make; so that Aunt Elinor's disapproval was constantly in the forefront of daily life, and was only varied by Uncle Beauchamp's course of sermons on the duty of woman as depicted by St. Paul. So it was pleasant to escape for a time, and Aunt Lizzie was a sympathetic loophole.

She was a woman who thought politically as Edith had thought hitherto, and as she wanted to go on thinking, and had moreover the merit of not being shocked at the idea that other people's thoughts might wander from the track which she, with her own mental feet, had beaten. Liberal in every sense of the word, she was willing to allow her niece liberty of opinion as well as liberty of action; and Edith never minded what she said to Aunt Lizzie, well knowing that Aunt Lizzie never minded what was said to her. It need hardly be stated that between Edith's aunt and her uncle's wife there existed no very cordial relations; but while Mrs. Leigh was much disturbed by Mrs. Joyce's disastrous influence upon her niece, Mrs. Joyce troubled herself not at all as to any and every influence brought to bear upon that niece by Mrs. Leigh.

Edith stood by the long French window in the drawing-room at Hyde Park Terrace, and looked out into the Bayswater Road and across into the Park. She was glad she had come, quite apart from the relief of being no longer continually avoided by Aunt Elinor; glad because, in spite of herself, her heart leapt up at the idea of seeing Cyril Race, at the knowledge that any one of the passing taxi-cabs might stop and deposit him at Mrs. Joyce's door, or that at any moment she might see him walking down the street.

"Edith, here's the tea. Come and have some. We won't wait for Mr. Race; he'll probably be late."

But Cyril Race was punctual, both by nature and habit, and Edith was still at her first piece of bread and butter when the door was opened and he was announced.

In that moment, at the sound of his name, in the knowledge of his immediate presence, the women's movement and its problems went quite away from her; she was conscious of but one woman, and that woman herself. She forgot that she had not wanted to see him, for fear that he should assail the stirrings of her heart with the unanswerable arguments which, at the same time, her reason longed for; the stirrings were lost in the heart's quickened beating; and all that she wondered, all that she cared about was, how would he greet her? Was he still—interested? Did he remember the things he had said to her in January? things that might mean a great deal—or nothing at all.

He came in with just the measure of eagerness, of friendship touched with tenderness, that her taste would have chosen. It was almost as if he had said, "I have no right to more than your friendship, and I will not compromise you before a third person by seeming to expect it. At the same time I cannot refrain from showing you how much this meeting means to me."

That, at least, was what his manner conveyed to Edith, and she felt that in her thought of him she had not rated him too high.

And what a pleasure to talk to a man who had his finger on the pulse of public affairs! After the dull diffidence of Robbie Colquhoun, it was delightful to listen to someone who knew, not only his own mind, but the minds of the men who mattered. At once Edith was lifted out of the doubtful, depressing atmosphere of the last few weeks and set in a firm place of assured convictions, set at the satisfying standpoint of Liberal administration as viewed by Liberal administrators.

But it was Aunt Lizzie who put the question which Edith longed to ask.

"How about to-morrow's deputation?"[1]

"Every possible precaution has been taken to avoid disaster. If disturbance takes place it will be because Mrs. Amherst and her followers are determined to assume the rôle of martyrs."

"Oh, are they going to be received?" The thought—child of an ardent wish—sprang to birth in Edith's mind, that at last a deputation was going to be received, that Mr. Race, by his force of persuasion and argument, had been largely instrumental in bringing about the longed-for consummation, and that on him would devolve the gratitude of all women. No more rifts in the lute of friendship; all her friends would unite with her in praise and admiration. But

---

1   In *Unshackled*, Christabel Pankhurst writes that "London was snowed under with the ... handbill" advertising the deputation of 29 June to lay before the Prime Minister women's demand for the vote: "Their right to do this is secured by the Bill of Rights which says 'It is the right of the subject to petition the King and all commitments and prosecutions for such petitioning are illegal.' Mr. Asquith, as the King's representative, is therefore bound to receive the deputation and hear their petition. If he refuses to do so and calls out the police to prevent women from using their right to present a petition, he will be guilty of illegal and unconstitutional action" (129).

this enchanting castle of desire was swept from the Spanish soil on which it had been so swiftly reared, and set down, a ruin, on solid English earth by Mr. Race's reply.

"No, but they have been positively assured that they will not be received. If, in spite of emphatic declaration, they persist in a futile attempt—" Cyril Race did not usually substitute gesture for utterance, but for once he let out-turned palms do duty for a tongue which found words inadequate.

"Of course they'll persist," said Mrs. Joyce. "Everybody must know that as well as they do themselves."

"Every preparation has been made, as I said, for minimising disaster if—and I agree with you in fearing it—it should be courted."

"I wish they could be given the audience they court," said Mrs. Joyce bluntly.

"Impossible, my dear lady, I assure you; quite impossible from the point of view of those who know the ropes."

"Is there no chance of a deputation ever being received?" Edith ventured.

"None; and therefore the kindest and wisest thing is to put down any attempts in that direction with a firm hand."

"It's a terrible thing—that firm hand," said Mrs. Joyce.

"Is it the hand or those who resist it that deserve the epithet? But, Mrs. Joyce, the last time I saw you, you were entirely against the militants. You are not, surely, veering round to that—well, I'll use no adjectives—section of your sex."

"No, I am thinking of no particular section, but just of my sex—which, by the way, cannot be divided into classes. *Vide* a certain speech at the Queen's Hall."

"Oh, that fellow! You know we don't take that view at all, and that many, if not most, of us are strongly in favour of giving the vote."

"I wasn't thinking of views so much as of action. Your views are well enough, but when it comes to action—you'll forgive me, I know—you staunch supporters of ours are a little inadequate."

"Men get so frightfully put off, you see. I just wish you could realise—Well, and why not? I came this afternoon with the intention of asking you to bring Miss Carstairs one evening to dine with me at the House. Will you come to-morrow? In good time, so that I can show Miss Carstairs round; and then we'll have dinner; and then, if there's anything to be seen, you can see it from a perfectly safe place."

"I don't know," said Mrs. Joyce. "I hardly—What do you say, Edith?"

"I'd rather—" Edith began. She was about to say she would rather not go, but Cyril Race cut in upon her words before she could finish them.

"Do come! Don't refuse me, please! I particularly want you to realise what men, and particularly members of Parliament, and more particularly members of the Government, what we feel on this subject and why. I want your sympathy, your inner understanding of our attitude, as well as your intellectual assent to our arguments."

So he had discerned what she felt, was subtle enough to perceive the conflict between her intuition on the one hand, her instinctive shrinking and her reason on the other.

"I will come if you wish it," she answered, "and if Aunt Lizzie is willing."

"You are sure you don't mind?" she asked when Mr. Race had gone.

"No, child; I simply wanted to make it easy for you to refuse if you didn't want to go, and I fancied somehow that you didn't."

"You were quite right; I didn't, and I don't, but I think I ought to. How is one ever to understand anything if one shuts oneself away from it? I think," Edith added, "I think I'll go along and see Rachel Cullen. It's not six yet, and you don't dine till eight, do you?"

"A quarter past to-night; I have a late engagement, so you have plenty of time. Don't be carried away by her, that's all."

CHAPTER XXVI
RACHEL CULLEN

"Out of the dark, the circling sphere
Is rounding onward to the light;
We see not yet the full day here,
But we do see the paling night."

S. Longfellow.[1]

---

1 Samuel Longfellow (1819–92), "Watchman, What of the Night?" Written for the Twenty-Fifth Anniversary of the American Anti-Slavery Society (1856).

A motor-omnibus took Edith from Hyde Park Terrace to Miss Cullen's little house in the Bayswater Road, facing Campden Hill Square. A sweet little house Edith always thought it was; a house that might have been transplanted from the country, as far as its outer form was concerned; and inside it there was a sense of country peace.

Rachel Cullen lived there alone, save for a widow woman, who acted as servant, and her little girl. It was characteristic of Miss Cullen to engage a servant who needed a home for her child. She had had a hard life. Of her mother she had no recollection; her father had died when she was twenty, leaving her penniless, and she had had to make her own way. She had made it, but at the cost of health and youth, and all that these mean to a woman. After fifteen years of battling with life, an uncle, who had taken no notice of her while he was alive, divided the money he had to leave between his niece and the Charity Organisation Society, and she found herself able to live in comfort.

Edith had first met her three years before at Aunt Lizzie's, Mrs. Joyce being the owner of Miss Cullen's house, and had been attracted towards her by that subtle sympathy which, when it exists between people, rapidly transforms them from strangers to friends, leaping over the period of acquaintanceship.

"Edith! I never knew you were in London!"

"No, but I knew *you* were. I only came to Aunt Lizzie on Saturday."

"I'm glad to see you." The words meant more from Miss Cullen's lips than did the "charmed" and "delighted" of more fashionable hostesses.

At forty, Rachel Cullen had, as the phrase is, lost her looks, yet she was in many ways a beautiful woman. Her face was worn and her hair was grey, but the tone of the face was good, and hard work and suffering had not been able to destroy the fine lines of the profile. Her eyes had lost much of their brightness, yet there was light in them, or, as Edith more truly said, behind them; her hair had a wave in it; there was a certain dignity in the carriage of her thin, bent figure.

The two friends sat by the window; it was open, and the roll of the traffic came to them across the little patch of garden.

"I never know whether to choose air or silence," said Rachel, "especially in the summer. I generally take them sandwich fashion, a quarter of an hour of one and then a quarter of an hour of the other."

"Let's have silence this evening. I want to talk to you."

"We'll have both. Come into the back room. It's not so cheerful, but it's quiet if we shut the doors."

There were folding-doors between the two little sitting rooms, furnished both alike with green hangings and rush-bottomed chairs; reposeful little rooms, very dear to their owner. The back window opened on to a tiny verandah, and beyond the verandah was another little space of garden, walled in, but with a real big tree in it, a tree in which birds were singing. There were always birds about where Rachel lived, and their enemies, stray cats, because she fed them both.

Sitting by the open window, in the sobered light, with the sound of birds in her ears and the restfulness of the room about her, Edith was able to speak of what she had come to say; so often she found that what she wanted to say was just the most difficult thing to talk about. But Rachel needed no very explicit statements; the tone of a voice, sometimes the turn of a head, told her much, especially when they were Edith's. She understood that Edith had wished to avoid her, and why; she perceived the warfare between the different elements in the girl's character; she knew that what Edith wanted to say and have said to her was "Peace, peace," and that there could be no peace until certain of those elements waxed strong enough to subdue the others. Which would gain the upper hand, it was not for her either to prophesy or determine. Rachel agreed with Browning, that

> "'Tis an awkward thing to play with souls,
> And matter enough to save one's own";[1]

and held that each one of us must work out his or her own salvation; in fear and trembling it might be, but never in the strength of another. To help? Yes, certainly, if it were possible, and most assuredly not to hinder, these were plain duties; but the help given must be in the direction of strengthening resolution, not in combating it.

"Do you think I am right to go to-morrow?"

"I think it's always better to see as much as you can."

"Have you ever seen a deputation?"

"Yes, once, from a window, last March. And I shall see to-morrow's."

---

1   Robert Browning (1812–89), "A Light Woman" (1855).

"Oh, where from? I should think Victoria Street—Where shall you be?"

"At the back of the deputation."

"But—Rachel! You! Do you mean to say you're going, so to speak, officially?"

"Yes."

"And you've done so much, writing, speaking, working in all kinds of ways. And you haven't the strength. Oh, why?"

"I'll tell you why. Because of something that happened to me when I was just your age, twenty-three. You know I had pretty hard work to make a living at one time."

"I know."

"Well, when I very badly wanted work, I got it at last in a shop—never mind where. I lived in and was supposed to be fed, but there were all kinds of fines and deductions, and the money I got was nowhere near enough to dress me as I had to be dressed, and to pay my washing and the many little things there were to pay. I tried it and couldn't do it, and then I went to the manager and told him so.

"'Little fool,' said he, 'whoever supposed you could? You must supplement it; you know we never ask what time you come in at night.'"

"Oh!" It was all Edith found to say. Things that she had heard of, read of, were true for her in that moment for the first time.

"I don't mean to say that because of that man—and others like him—I suppose all men to be the same. I've come across good men—men who have helped me, as well as men who have ground me down and done their best to degrade me. Why," Rachel said, and smiled, "I'm living now chiefly on money given to me by a man."

"Left after his death," put in Edith.

"Well, he might have left it all to what is called charity. But, Edith—"

"Well?"

"That's why I'm going to-morrow; because, though there are good men in the world, and men who really do their best for women, these things go on. They go on because people—oh, women as well as men, the comfortable, happy women to whom men will give anything and everything—except independence—because they don't know about these things; because the evils endured by women have to become crying evils, resounding in the ears of the public, stinking in the public nostrils, before anything is done to remedy them; because when any improvement is made in the condition of the workers, any safeguards given them, it is so much easier to leave the women out; and so perfectly safe, while they have not got the vote."

"I know. I know all that, and I—you know I do—agree. It's the methods, not the thing in itself that I—am doubtful about."

"I know you think so; I know you *think* that you want the vote; but do you? If you think it as important as I think it, you must think it important enough to fight for. Wait? Have patience? Oh yes, I know; there are numbers and numbers of women able to do both. And willing. And why? Because it doesn't really matter to them; because though they feel that they ought to have it, that it is absurd and unfair and illogical that they should not have it, yet, in their daily lives, they do not feel the pinch of being without it. They can get love, courtesy, comfort, influence, some of them practical independence, without it. They think they want it; they do want it in a sense, but they can afford to wait."

"They work for it, work hard, many of them," Edith said.

Rachel did not heed her. The voice that did not rise above its usual quiet tones went on as though she had not heard, the hands that had worked so hard lying crossed in her lap.

"But I have lived amongst women of a different kind, women who need the vote, but don't know that they need it; who are so crushed, so broken, so near the level of animals that they don't even desire it; because they desire nothing, are capable of desiring nothing, beyond food, sleep—just, and nothing more than just—what an animal desires. And these women cannot afford to wait."

"But you can't blame—statesmen, for not giving it if these women—until they ask for it."

If you wait till they ask for it, you will wait for ever. Did the agricultural labourers ask for the vote? Did the children ask to be educated? It is for the thinking classes to raise the unthinking. It is for the women who have intelligence and initiative to make it possible for the drudges, the fools, and the vicious to step up to a higher level. We can work philanthropically; we shall never work effectively till we have the lever of the vote."

"And you think that the only way to it is through this physical struggling, this fighting and imprisonment?"

"Else it had come without."

"How—what do you mean?"

"I mean that evolution has its own methods, and those who work them out are evolution's instruments. Individually the women who are working in all their different ways to bring about the next phase in the development of humanity are working, each one according to the behests of her conscience, her character, her circumstances. Cosmically they are tools, with just the qualities—and just the faults and failings, if you will—which fit them to do the work which at this particular time in the world's history has to be done. You may praise or blame them, but the things they do have been planned by a mightier than they."

"But the little—the petty things, the stone-throwing and break-ing of windows—?"

"Very petty, very small, and without meaning, unless you attach to them their true significance."

"I can't see any significance at all."

"It was thought no small thing when Clerkenwell Prison[1] was blown up, no little or petty thing when buildings were wrecked and blood was shed; and all these things were done by men when men fought for political freedom. Women could do as much; it requires but little strength, but little courage, to set fire to a building; and there are many women who would wish to follow faithfully the traditions set by men. Not so the leaders, in whose hands the guid-ance of this movement ostensibly lies. Storms there may be within and around the movement, yet it inaugurates an era of greater peace, and so, instead of repeating the crude acts of the past, women take the meaning of those acts and embody it in symbols."

"I don't quite see—"

"No, I forget; it's all so clear to me, that I forget how it looks to people who haven't thought it out. And yet I know very well how it looks to them—ridiculous, contemptible, small. To throw a stone, deliberately, in cold blood, through the window of a Government office seems stupid, absurd, compared with the crude, hot-blooded act of destroying the whole building; and the fact that women have

---

1   In November 1867, Richard Burke, who had been employed by the Fenians to purchase arms in Birmingham, was arrested and sent to Clerkenwell prison in London. While he was awaiting trial, a wall of the prison was blown down by gunpowder; twelve people were killed by the explosion, and 120 were wounded.

chosen to make only symbolic protests, that they have shed no blood, have destroyed no property except a few windows in buildings which they help to maintain, has been marked down, not to their self-restraint, but to their discredit."

"But people say—many people say—of course it may be just for the reason that you give, that they don't understand—but, *as* they don't understand, don't you think that these things which seem to people in general petty and absurd are likely to put back the clock?"

"If they do, it means that it is not yet time for it to strike. When the hour for striking comes, nothing can put or hold it back."

"Is it near, do you think?"

Rachel Cullen shook her head. "Hardly. I believe that there are worse times ahead than any we have come through yet."

"Are you ever afraid?"

"Sometimes. But I know it has to be. And the end is bound to come."

Edith thought of Geraldine Hill and the words she used so often: "But the tide comes in."

"You are very sure, some of you," she said, "of evolution, of its inevitable force."

"Some call it evolution, some—" Rachel paused; looking at her, Edith saw the light behind her eyes grow brighter. When presently she spoke again, it was to quote from a poet's hymn:

"'God moves in a mysterious way
His wonders to perform;
He plants His footsteps in the sea,
And rides upon the storm.'[1]

And the sea is His, and the storms come at His bidding."

So that was Rachel Cullen's point of view! Edith, in the little green-room with its reposeful atmosphere, called up a picture of a lighted hall, and heard a man's voice say that women were not men and therefore must not be citizens. The man was famous and typical: the woman sitting here beside her was all unknown. Was she typical too—of the women who were fighting for other women?

---

[1]   William Cowper (1731–1800), "God Moves in a Mysterious Way" (1774).

Rachel was speaking again. "I like, when I say those lines—and I say them often—I like to think of the whole movement as a sea, and each wave of it a separate, striving woman." She waited a moment.

"But it is a sea," she added, "that will have its dead, one day, to give up." She waited again. "And perhaps in that day the soul of the movement will be set free from the vile body in which it has been constrained to dwell; and men, and women too, looking back, will see and recognise that to which, beholding it near at hand, they were blind."

When Edith went back to Hyde Park Terrace the sun was setting, but she took no heed of the sunset; she was too busy thinking over what Rachel Cullen had said. But when she had reached Aunt Lizzie's house, and while she waited on the doorstep for the door to be opened, she glanced down the Bayswater Road and became aware of the splendour of the sky. Bright red it showed between and above the houses; the colour of blood.

CHAPTER XXVII
A SHOW

"My soul, sit thou a patient looker-on;
Judge not the play before the play is done:
Her plot has many changes; ev'ry day
Speaks a new scene; the last act crowns the play."

Quarles[1]

Edith hardly looked forward to dining at the House of Commons; yet when she got there, she enjoyed herself. Mr. Race was charming; deferential, sympathetic, not only towards herself, but also towards the question which, as he seemed to divine, was holding a foremost place in her thoughts. Edith did not wish to discuss it with him; she was not in the mood for discussion; but it pleased her to listen to his incidental remarks upon it, to note the understanding and the fairness which characterised them; and it was comforting to be able to assure herself that he was broad-minded and generous, and that whatever his views might be as to the suffragettes, the suffrage itself had in him a true and staunch friend.

---

1   Francis Quarles (1592–1644), "*Respice Finem*" (1635).

He had asked a fellow member to square the little party, and though Mrs. Joyce was supposed to be Race's partner at dinner, it so happened that she and the member guest talked together most of the time, and Race was free to give the greater part of his attention to Edith. That he wished to please her was obvious, to Edith as well as to Mrs. Joyce, and a happy elation took possession of her, driving out the dull dread that had lain heavy on her all day. She was glad—she could not but be glad—to find him looking at her with eyes that were more than kind, to hear his voice sink low so that only she could catch its utterance; to feel his love—she knew it was love—shutting her and him away from those two elderly people talking composedly together, away from all the world, into a world in which he and she were alone. It was a happy and rather bewildered Edith who went out into the June evening after dinner and took a turn on the Terrace and looked at London's water-way flowing by towards the sea.

Silence fell between Edith and her host, filled with a sense of unspoken words and a consciousness, growing with the moments, that utterance could not long be kept back; then, when the silence was becoming tense, it was broken by Mr. Golder, who said that it was time for them to go and take their places at one of the windows overlooking Parliament Square.

She hardly knew whether she was glad or sorry for this prosaic interruption, whether she quite wished Cyril Race to say the thing which she felt was not far from his lips, or whether she was relieved to have it left unsaid. As they left the Terrace she was not sure; a little later and the Terrace, the silence, the words which went before it, Cyril Race himself, though he stood beside her, were swept headlong from her consciousness by the torrent of events and impressions which overwhelmed it.

Half an hour before eight women had left the Caxton Hall, following on a despatch announcing to the Prime Minister that a deputation would wait on him immediately.

The deputation, unlike that of which Lady Henry Hill had been a member, was not held back by the police. Mounted policemen cleared a way for it, and on either side of it policemen marched, holding back the pressing crowd from the women they cheered. Mrs. Amherst walked first, alone; and behind her two women, old and grey-headed; and behind them, again, two and then three together, the other five women who made up the number to which a deputation is legally limited.

The crowd had no jeers to-night, and indeed the cheapest wit, the most ribald scoffer would have found it hard to suggest that these women walked there in search of husbands or notoriety or for the fun of the thing. A roar of cheering went with them all the way, from the people in the roadway, on the pavements, on the stone balustrades, at the windows. Straight ahead, marching quickly, they went, policemen making their way easy. Were they to be received, then, after all? On, without let or hindrance, past the Westminster Hospital and the west end of the Abbey; on past the wall of police, mounted and unmounted, which stretched across the road on a line with St. Margaret's Church, and, opening, let the deputation through; on to St. Stephen's entrance; and then a pause.

All around the crowd, dense, eager, anxious, filling the spaces about the Abbey and the Houses of Parliament, stretching up to Whitehall and along Whitehall; at the entrance to the House of Commons eight women facing a row of police; at the windows of the House and in the Square, protected by police, protected from these eight women—two of them grey-headed—and their followers in the crowd, members of Parliament and friends of members, looking on.

Standing at Cyril Race's side, Edith saw the eight women advance, saw them pause, saw an inspector speak to the leader.

"That is Inspector Jervoise," said Race. "You see how perfectly respectfully he receives them."

From the open window, near the entrance, Edith could see plainly, and hear too; but as yet no word was spoken by any member of the deputation. In silence Mrs. Amherst took a letter which was handed to her in silence she read it; and in silence dropped it on the ground.[1] Then Edith heard her say:

"I stand on my rights as a subject of the King and demand to enter the House of Commons. We are firmly resolved to stand here until we are allowed to enter the House. We have come through a

---

1   "The Prime Minister, for the reasons which he has already given in a written reply to their request, regrets that he is unable to receive the proposed deputation" (E. Pankhurst, 1914, 140).

great crowd of people who believe that the opposition is at an end, and that we are to be received. I will not answer for the consequences if we are not."

No message could be taken.

But the message was a simple one, harmless, without offence; only to tell those in authority that the deputation was there.

"Do you refuse to take that message?"

"I refuse," and the refusal was followed by a command to the eight women to disperse.

Perhaps the woman of seventy-six, who had been a schoolmistress, and who had worked under the English Red Cross Society at Sedan and Metz for seven months during the Franco-Prussian War; perhaps she thought she ought not to be treated as a school child;[1] perhaps she and the seven other followers of Mrs. Amherst felt it incumbent upon them to maintain the principle which had brought them hither, the right of every subject to appeal to the King in the person of his Minister; but not a woman moved.

"We absolutely support Mrs. Amherst."

Twice more the command was given to disperse; twice more the answer came: "We absolutely refuse."

Then the police began to "move" the deputation, to seize the women, and push them away from the entrance. Mrs. Amherst was the first to be seized, and as the inspector laid hold of her, Edith saw her raise her hand and strike him in the face; heard him speak to her and her reply; and saw her then, a second time, raise her hand, and a second time strike him.

After that it was difficult to tell what happened. A great confusion set in, and in place of the quiet of expectation was movement, hubbub, shouting, struggling, cries. The members of the deputation were separated and were taken out of the square, half carried by the police. Edith had never seen women in the hands of policemen before, except, on two occasions, drunken women in the streets. One of these women had struggled, kicked, hit out with her fists: that was horrible, sickening. Mrs. Amherst had hit too, had done what Edith had been told that suffragettes always did—but—it had

---

1   Dorinda Neligan. The other members of the deputation were Georgiana Solomon, Catherine Corbett, Hon. Evelina Haverfield, Maud Joachim, Mildred Mansel, and Catherine Margesson (C. Pankhurst, 130).

hardly seemed like hitting, it was so coolly done she had seen village women at Vale End slap their children with immensely greater vigour. And the inspector had hardly seemed to take it in ill part. "I know why you did that, Mrs. Amherst," Edith had heard him say.[1] It seemed as if—Ah, Mr. Race was speaking to her.

There were people speaking all around her; a little way off a man laughed, and the sound jarred on her.

Cyril Race was far from laughing. "You're looking so white and tired," he said. "I'm sorry; I'm afraid it's been too much for you. I should have thought—known—And yet," he said to Mrs. Joyce, "it was really not so bad to-night—in here, in the Square, I mean. You saw that there was no unnecessary violence used. Out there, in the crowd, well—I expect the police will have their work cut out for them."

Out there in the crowd! Rachel Cullen was in that crowd. The little room of yesterday evening, with its green hangings and restful atmosphere, was empty now; and the delicate face and frail body—

"Yes, Aunt Lizzie, whenever you like, whenever Mr. Race thinks we can get a cab. Yes, certainly, we might go and sit down in the meantime."

The crowd that had waited in cheerful expectation had changed its mood; its temper was not of the best; its first friendly attitude towards the police was changed to antagonism; there was a tendency to interfere when arrests were made, to rescue and free the arrested. The police had a hard night's work, but they made the best of it. The Metropolitan force was never hard on the women with whom they were forced into conflict, and many a captor was more in sympathy with his captive than with the authorities whose orders he was bound to carry out. But even policemen have human weaknesses, and Sally Simmonds, struggling towards Westminster, got a

---

1 In *My Own Story* (1914), Emmeline Pankhurst writes "I now knew that the deputation would not be received and that the old miserable business of refusing to leave, of being forced backward, of returning again and again until arrested, would have to be re-enacted. I had to take into account that I was accompanied by two fragile old ladies, who, brave as they were to be there at all, could not possibly endure what I knew must follow. I quickly decided that I should have to force an immediate arrest, so I committed an act of technical assault on Inspector Jarvis, striking him very lightly on the cheek" (141). The *Times*, on the other hand, reported on 30 June that "Mrs. Pankhurst struck the inspector three times in the face with her open hand," and subsequently "dealt him two severe blows, and a member of the deputation knocked his hat off" (12).

kick from a leg that was vehement with irritation. Never mind! It's all in the day's work. It hurts—yes, it hurts a bit, but it doesn't matter, if only she can get to them ladies, find out what has happened to them. She gathers, of course, that they have been turned back, refused a hearing; but have they been hurt, arrested? What has become of them? She must press on and see.

And then, in the hands of big policemen, Sally saw a woman with a white delicate face and grey hair. Very unfitted she looked, Sally thought, to be pushed as she was being pushed, very unfitted for prison. The crowd apparently thought so too, or some of them; there was a rush in her direction, and Sally rushed too; with the result that, instead of effecting the grey-haired woman's release, she was herself arrested.

It all took place so quickly, she had acted so entirely on impulse, that she did not realise what had happened till she found herself on the way to prison, one of the hundred and eight women arrested that evening. To Sally there was neither pride nor pleasure in the situation. What did people mean by saying that women went to prison because they liked it? Sally felt quite sure that she was not going to like it at all. As for having your name in the papers, there was only one person who would be pleased to see it there, and that was Mr. Bilkes. His delight, to be sure, would equal that of six ordinary people, but that fact could hardly be a consolation to Sally. And the little Bilkeses, Stanny and Dorothy and Maud, what would they say? They would be sorry; she felt sure they would be sorry—unless Bilkes and their ma had set them too much against her. But Stanny—she thought, Stanny would be sorry all the same; and little Maud—if she understood. She saw the children in the bedroom she had shared with them. Would they take her to Holloway, the police? And would another girl stand at that window, as she had been used to stand, and look as she had often looked, across the forest of roofs to the roof of Holloway Gaol?

"Come along, come along!" said the constable.

"I'm comin' along as quick as ever I can," said Sally.

The next morning Edith read Sally's name in the paper, and she thought of Littlehampton and the sands; of Annie Carnie and Christina Amherst; and of the tide that was coming in.

There was another name she knew in the list of prisoners to be charged at Bow Street; that of Rachel Cullen, who had broken a window in the Home Office.[1]

CHAPTER XXVIII
A LEADER

"O, I but stand
As a small symbol for a mighty sum."

George Eliot[2]

Edith Carstairs was in two minds as to whether to return at once to the Pightle or to stay on with Aunt Lizzie. Monty was at home now, and that was against return, for Monty was in that crude stage of orthodoxy which necessitates the hurling of names at those who diverge from its obvious paths. Speaking as a Conservative, the Liberal Ministers were liars and traitors; speaking as a man, the suffragettes were fools and viragoes.

Edith felt that she might possibly support abuse of the Liberal Ministry at this juncture with greater equanimity than was usual to her, but she knew that she would find it particularly trying to hear Rachel Cullen called a virago; and she finally decided to stay on in London. In London, to be sure, there was Cyril Race, as against Monty at Vale End; but it is easier to avoid a man who is no relation, in a town, and that town the metropolis, than a brother who is living, not only in your particular village in the country, but actually in your own home; and so Edith gave up the Pightle and the poplars and the lane, all that made life most lovely to her in the summer time, and stayed another fortnight at Hyde Park Terrace.

---

1 Sylvia Pankhurst writes that this was the first instance of window-breaking by the suffragettes, and that only Government panes were attacked: "This new departure was a protest against the violence done to women who offered themselves for arrest. Since we must go to prison to obtain the vote, let it be the windows of the Government, not the bodies of women which shall be broken, was the argument; for a window-smasher was at once taken quietly into custody" (1931, 309). Pankhurst does not note whether the Home Office was specifically targeted, but since this is the branch of the government dealing with, among other things, law, public order, prisons, and the police, such an attack might have had symbolic significance.

2 George Eliot (1819–80), *Armgart* (1871).

After all it was not necessary to let Mr. Race know that she was lengthening her visit; and perhaps—perhaps after that night at the House of Commons, even if he did know she was in London, he would be as careful to take no step forward as she was that he should hold back. For Edith had an intimate conviction that Cyril Race's love for her—and she was far too intuitive a woman not to know that the love was there—was held in check by his doubt as to the attitude she held, or might assume, in regard to the franchise agitation. His wife would mean much to him, but politics, she felt, would mean more; that was to say (she hastened to justify him), if his wife and his convictions were on opposite sides. To what he felt to be right, he would sacrifice everything, even political office, but he could not be compromised by views or actions to which he was opposed.

What conclusions he had drawn from her behaviour on that memorable Tuesday evening she could not know, hardly knowing, in fact, exactly what her behaviour had been. On the way home from the House—for Race had insisted upon escorting his two guests to Hyde Park Terrace—she had been silent or nearly silent; it was Aunt Lizzie who had discussed with him the events of the evening. But of the time before that, when she had stood by the open window, watching the deputation and the scrimmaging crowd beyond, she remembered nothing, save the scene in which she had been absorbed; how she had looked, what she had said, of all that she had no recollection.

She was well aware that she was supposed, both by Aunt Lizzie and Mr. Race, to suffer disillusion; supposed to agree with Aunt Lizzie in thinking that the deputation should not have persisted in their refusal to go away; supposed, having seen Mrs. Amherst hit the Inspector on the face, to be disgusted at this visible demonstration of the truth of charges brought against the suffragettes. Yet, aware of all this, she was aware too of having felt, deep down in her, that these eight women, pitted against the whole machinery of law and order, were somehow in the right; that the small, slight woman who led them had been actuated by no impulse of violence or sense of antagonism, when she had committed her seemingly violent act; that her own sense of fitness had been shocked, not by the deputation, but by the refusal to receive it.

But how much of the inner workings of her consciousness she had shown in her outward demeanour she could not judge; and could not judge, consequently, how far it was probable that Cyril Race would seek an opportunity of saying what, on the Terrace of the House of Commons, he had so nearly said. He must not say it, not just now; for to give him the answer that she wanted to give him meant to pledge herself to a line of conduct, present and future, which she felt she could not bind herself to pursue. Had she been obliged to give her decision at once, she must have said no.

But in the days to come, those days which hold for youth such boundless and beautiful possibilities, all sorts of changes might take place, which would sweep away not only any present divergence of feeling and opinion, but the bare chance of any such divergence in the future. The tide might come in, at any time; and the tumult of its flow be stilled for ever. No mixing up then, any more, of conflicting issues, no warring between dear traditions and compelling ideas; loyalty would be free to walk once more untrammelled; and, loyalty firm clasped with the one hand, she might hold the other out to love. She did not want to cut herself off from this sweet hope; and so, in the meantime, she must cut herself off from Cyril Race.

It seemed not very difficult, not quite so difficult as perhaps, in her secret heart, she would have wished it to be, though each day that she did not see him she told herself that she was glad.

But his absence and the necessity for it did not by any means hold the sum of her thoughts: there was very much to do and to think about in those anxious days, the anxious and the pregnant nature of which was conveyed to her, not only by an inner sense of foreboding, but by the convictions of Geraldine Hill and Rachel Cullen. Both were of opinion that the twenty-ninth of June had ushered in a new phase of the movement; both looked forward with dread to the coming time. The immediate future seemed worse to Edith at that time, and certainly more important, than days farther ahead; for Rachel had no doubt that when her case came on she would be sent to prison; and Rachel in prison was a possibility which Edith could not bear to contemplate.

"It's impossible," Edith said. "Prison is not meant for women like you."

"Women like me are meant, I think, at this time, for prison."

"I don't believe it. Oh, why did you go?"

"I thought I had told you."

"Well, in any case, you need not have thrown that miserable stone."

"I thought I had explained that too. But I did it partly, I confess, in self-defence. If you do nothing in particular, you see, you get terribly hustled and knocked about. If you throw a stone you are immediately arrested and taken away at once, out of the turmoil."

"The police—" Edith began.

"No, don't blame the police. They have most difficult work to do, especially when the crowd is as ugly as it was that night; no end of rushes there were, and attempts to release the women arrested. Oh no, I don't blame the police."

"I feel that I must blame somebody."

"According to the newspapers, you ought to blame me."

Rachel refused to be pitied. "Those who break the law must perish by the law," she said, "and unfortunately we seem driven to break it, since, by keeping it, we can get no hearing."

It was on the ninth of July that Mrs. Amherst's trial took place. Edith went with Lady Henry Hill to Bow Street, to hear her defence. That was the comfort of staying with Aunt Lizzie; she let you go where you wanted to, without reproaches, veiled or bare, and she would listen too to what you told her, when you came back, without unfair comment.

Edith was glad she had not returned to Vale End; a letter from Monty in which he described Mrs. Amherst as an unfeminine ass was quite as much as she could stand. Aunt Bessie also wrote, in a style of sweet womanliness, which was quite as irritating as Monty's crude denunciation.

What interested Edith most at Bow Street was the fact that Mrs. Amherst's explanation of her assault upon the inspector corresponded exactly with her own impression of the act. She was glad to understand the reasons which gave rise to that impression, and she listened with special eagerness to the particular portion of the speech in which those reasons were set forth.

"Then Inspector Jervoise took hold of me. Well, I will ask you to remember that we women do not belong to a class who are accustomed to have hands put upon them, or are accustomed to be treated in a very ignominious way. In addition to the crowds of people, there were members of Parliament filling the windows of the House of Commons, there were members who had brought ladies with them, and strangers with them, to see the 'show,' to see eight humiliated women making, in the only way they could, an attempt to assert their constitutional right. It was a show for them."

Yes, Edith knew that, had felt and known it at the time. In herself she was guiltless, since there had been nothing in her attitude of the sensation-loving spectator; but she had felt that attitude about her, and it was one of the factors which had sent her sympathies forth to the group of women outside.

"They had come, many of them, to see the humiliating struggle that was inevitable. But we refused to leave the door of the entrance to the House of Commons. I was seized. Standing behind me were two elderly women, one very frail, very much over seventy years of age, and although I have shown in the course of this agitation that I do not mind very much what violence is done to me, I did feel for those women who were standing behind me. I knew what the inevitable result would be. I knew that we should be humiliated, and that we should hear members of Parliament, who thought it consistent with their duties as representatives of the nation, to jeer at women who had no political power, jeer even at them. I have seen it before. On the last occasion we went there to do what I tried to do on June twenty-ninth members stood for a very long time smiling at the pushing which was inflicted upon the women.

"And I determined, not for my own sake, but for the sake of the women behind me, to cut short the struggle. I did not do it before force was used to make us go away. Inspector Jervoise seized hold of me—I am willing to say that he did it as gently as he could; but the police are strong men, and we are delicate women, and the pushing of the police is not the kind of thing that women ought to be subject to when they believe that they are acting in accordance with the laws of the land. Well, then I did what I am quite ready to apologise to Inspector Jervoise for doing. I do not think I hurt him. I struck his cheek with my open hand, and he said, 'I know why you did that.' But the pushing still continued, and I said, 'Must I do it again?' And as far as my memory serves me, and I think I was quite cool, he said, 'Yes.' And I did it again. Then he said, 'Take them in!' And we were arrested."

The speech went on, and Edith listened still, losing no word; and indeed, Mrs. Amherst was easy to hear, for her voice, though it sounded low and soft in a room, filled easily much larger places than Bow Street Police Court. But the part of the speech which stood out in Edith Carstairs' mind was the part in which the leader of the deputation explained that her design in committing a technical assault was to spare her followers, and especially the two elderly women, close behind her, the humiliation and the danger of a prolonged struggle. For assault led to immediate arrest, and the arrest of the leader meant the arrest of her followers. And arrest, it seemed, was the best treatment meted out to women who sought in the only constitutional way that was open to them the constitutional liberty enjoyed by men. For behind Mrs. Amherst's words were Rachel Cullen's words: "If you do nothing in particular, you get terribly hustled and knocked about. If you throw a stone, you are arrested at once and taken away out of the turmoil."

There were other words of Rachel Cullen's recalled by a passage at the end of the speech, and words of Lady Henry Hill's; the opinion expressed by them both that the twenty-ninth of June had prefaced a new phase in the struggle for political freedom.

"I want to say to you here," said Mrs. Amherst, "standing in this dock, that if you deal with us as you dealt with other women on similar occasions, the same experience will be gone through—we shall go to prison to suffer whatever awaits us there. But we have reached a still more serious stage in this agitation. We are not going to conform any longer to the regulations of that prison if we go there. There are one hundred and eight of us here to-day, and I do not want to say this to you from any disrespect for you; but, just as we have thought it our duty to defy the police in the streets, so, when we get into prison, being political prisoners—and there is no doubt about that to-day, sir—we shall do our very best, when we get into that prison, to bring back in the twentieth century that treatment of political prisoners which was thought right in the case of Cobbett and the other political prisoners of his time."

And then Mrs. Amherst stated the policy which had been determined upon, if women political prisoners were to be treated differently from men political prisoners, and classed as ordinary criminals.

"In the last resort, we shall do what Miss Bruce-Gordon did."[1]

---

1   Marion Wallace Dunlop was arrested for stencilling "it is the right of the subject to petition the King, and all commitments and prosecutions for such petitioning are illegal"

Edith knew what that meant. Miss Bruce-Gordon was the first woman to adopt the hunger strike.

Edith and Lady Henry did not wait for the magistrate's decision. It was reserved until after lunch, and Lady Henry had an engagement to speak in the afternoon.

They did not talk much on the way home. Both were thoughtful, thinking possibly of the same things, feeling no inclination, and perhaps no need, to put their thoughts into words. When they were nearing the Marble Arch,

"Will you come and lunch?" Geraldine asked.

"No, thank you. Aunt Lizzie will be expecting me."

"She won't eat you instead of her lunch, because you have been to Bow Street?"

"Oh no. Whatever she thinks, she does not force her opinion on other people, even when they are younger than she is, and related to her. And, besides, I believe that, though she thinks it's unwomanly to go on a deputation, I believe she thinks, at the same time, that the deputation ought to have been received."

"If it had been received it would have been considered all right, I suppose. I verily believe it is the things that are done to women, and not the things they do, which makes the part they play in this movement seem unwomanly to many people. If their legitimate questions at meetings were answered, for instance, as the questions of men are answered; if their petitions were received, all this cry of unwomanliness would cease. And, on the other hand, I suppose we should be considered unwomanly just for speaking in public, if every time we tried to mount a platform there were policemen told off to prevent us. Anyhow, if we have to take to fasting, they can't say that's unwomanly. At least," said Geraldine, with a smile, "they can't say we're trying to imitate men."

on the walls of St. Stephen's Hall in the House of Commons. She was sentenced to one month in prison but, having been refused political-prisoner status, fasted for ninety-one hours after which she was released.

CHAPTER XXIX
A HUNGER STRIKE

"Wrong makes wrong. When people use us ill, we can hardly help having ill-feeling towards them. But that second wrong is more excusable."

George Eliot[1]

Rachel Cullen was right: she was sent to prison; for six weeks, because the glass she had broken was plate glass, the difference between that and ordinary glass being valued at a fortnight. Those women who had broken ordinary glass received a month; and a month was also meted out to Sally for her attempt to rescue Miss Cullen.

Poor Sally! She could have escaped her sentence by binding herself over,[2] and for a minute the temptation was strong to accept the easy way out. Not only did she not want to go to prison, but Mrs. Blake was sadly in need of her services; it was a busy time, and there was more than one customer waiting for parcels which it would have been Sally's duty to deliver. What would Mrs. Blake do without her? And oh! if Holloway looked so gloomy from the outside, what would it be like within? Then she caught sight of Lady Henry Hill. Lady Henry was looking at her, and as her eyes met Sally's she smiled, and Sally hesitated no longer. She would not be bound over, she said, she would go to prison.

In Black Maria she was next to Rachel Cullen, and before they reached Holloway Sally's courage and her gaiety had come back to her.

"Lor', miss, if you can put up with it, I'm sure *I* can. You ought to be in yer bed, that's where *you* ought to be by the look of you; but as for me—I ain't so very tall nor yet so very stout, but I'm wiry. Most of us gurls is, gurls as pore as me, else we wouldn't grow up at all."

Rachel indeed was noticeably delicate looking, but she had the nervous energy which is the birthright of highly strung temperaments, and that energy endured throughout the term of her imprisonment and carried her through its conditions.

---

1 George Eliot (1819–80), *Scenes of Clerical Life* (1857).
2 "To make (someone) give a recognizance not to commit a breach of the peace" (*OED*).

Those conditions were harder than any which had fallen to the lot of previous prisoners, because of the protest which this group of fourteen had decided to make against being treated otherwise than as political prisoners. The protest took the form of refusing to conform to the regulations until such time as the prisoners were placed in the first division, besides the breaking of cell windows, in order to secure ventilation. The protest was made, and then came the punishment.[1]

Sally was brought before the visiting magistrates, and charged with rebellion and breaking her windows. Was she sorry for what she had done?

"No, gen'elmen, I ain't. If it was a case of bein' sorry, I shouldn't 'ave gone an' done it. I done it cos I ain't no criminal an' didn't ought to be treated as such. An' as for winders, I broke 'em 'cos I 'appens to be one o' them as can't breathe without air."

Then Sally was told that she would be put in a cell where there were no windows to break, and was sentenced to eight days' close confinement.

"Will you go quietly?" one of the magistrates asked.

"I'll be *took* as quiet as I can, sir, but it ain't in our line of action to go. If I was to go along with the wardresses as quiet as I walked in, it ud look as if I thought you was punishin' me fair, an' that I don't think, nor never will."

So Sally was "took"; by several wardresses, not in the best of tempers. These suffragettes were giving a lot of trouble with their tiresome ways, and the wardresses had plenty to do as it was. So, outside the magistrates' room, two of them began to pommel this tiresome little Cockney girl with no light hands. The pommelling hurt, and Sally's temper took fire; she forgot all about being "took quiet," and, her arms being held, hit out with her feet, and caught the wardresses on the shins. Then she found herself lifted up in strong arms, arms

---

1   Of the 108 women who were arrested on 29 June, fourteen were charged with window-breaking and attempted rescue. They began their fight for political status by refusing to change into prison clothes, at which point they were "forcibly stripped by a crowd of wardresses" (S. Pankhurst, 1931, 310). They smashed the windows in their cells and began to hunger strike at which point they were sentenced to solitary confinement. Pankhurst describes the punishment cells as having little light and poor ventilation: "The floors were of stone, in some cases never dry; the only seat was a tree stump, rising through the floor, even the plank bed being removed during the day" (310).

that were cruel as well as strong, with hands at the end of them that twisted her own arms, that tore at her hair, that half throttled her. The wardresses carried her across the courtyard, into her cell, and threw her on to the wooden shelf let into the wall, which did duty as a bed. There for awhile she lay, overcome with a mingled sense of outrage and exhaustion; then, by and by, she raised herself on her bruised arms and looked about her.

When she realised what sort of place it was in which she was to be confined, it was as much as she could do to keep her tears back. She had thought, standing at that attic window in Brunton Street, that it must be dreadful to be in Holloway, but this was worse than anything she had imagined. The cell was underground, very dirty, with hardly any ventilation, and with no light except that which came from a thick skylight in the ceiling. The worst of all, Sally thought, was the smell, a thick indescribable smell of dirt and damp, which clung to everything in the cell and then seemed to cling to Sally herself.

Her first feeling was that she must give in, must promise that she would not break any more rules or any more windows; and certainly, bad though the air was in the cell from which she had come, it was pure and fresh compared with the atmosphere here. Then she thought of Miss Cullen; it must be much worse for that pore shadder-like lady than for herself. And she thought of Lady Henry Hill. Lady 'Ill, she'd never give in, not 'er; and so no more wouldn't Sally. And she thought of the women outside, who were "put upon," who did men's work for less than men's wages; as far as the kind of work they did was concerned, nobody seemed to care whether they were womanly or not. And with these thoughts Sally's spirit grew strong again. If she stuck it, it would make it easier for other prisoners, if others were to come after her; and, for all she knew, Lady 'Ill might be there again. Oh yes, she'd stick it, let the place stink as it might. She blinked her eyes hard, to get rid of the threatening tears, and started to sing the Marseillaise; very flat and not quite accurately. Sally had not much ear for music.

She could not sing long; for one thing, the closeness of the atmosphere made her feel faint, and it was dark and dreary in the windowless cell, into which the light came, unwillingly as it seemed, through the thickened glass in the ceiling. Sally began to feel very lonely, and her thoughts went to that house not so very far away, in

Brunton Street, where she had lived when Holloway Gaol was no more than a name to her. It had seemed altogether outside her life in those days; a place where people were put when they stole or murdered, the people whose portraits appeared in halfpenny papers. Only bad people, it had seemed to her then, went to prison: she had never thought she would do anything to bring her to such a place. Then, later on, before she left the Bilkeses, she had seen Holloway as a possible stage through which she might have to pass; but it had not occurred to her that, if she went through that stage, she would do so in solitary confinement, in a cell with but little light, and still less air.

The ordinary life in prison, so far as she knew about it, had seemed quite bad enough; but in that life you went out every day for exercise: only in the prison yard, to be sure, but still outside, and you could look at your fellow prisoners, though you might not speak to them. There was chapel too, when there would be a voice speaking; that was something. Sally was not very fond of church-going, but preaching, however dull, would be welcome in prison; it would at least make a break in the silence. The silence was what she had dreaded, and it seemed dreadful now in actual experience; yet it was perhaps hardly so bad as she had expected it to be. For Sally, though she was hardly more used to being alone than in the days when she had viewed Holloway Gaol across a series of roofs, was better company to herself than she had been in those days. There was more in her mind for her mind to feed upon: that made a difference. It is the empty mind, the mind with no inward picture, save that of the crime or misery which cut its possessor off from the rest of humanity, that makes solitary confinement such a terrible punishment to the uneducated.

Sally's crimes played no very prominent part in her consciousness, and were girt about with no thoughts either of remorse or vengeance. She had tried to save Miss Cullen from arrest. Good; she would do the same again if the chance came her way and there seemed any prospect of success. She had kicked two wardresses on the shins. Bad, up to a certain point. She ought not to have done it, she supposed; but she was riled—and who wouldn't be? she asked herself; and she could not have hurt her tormentors much, seeing that she had had on her own shoes, indoor shoes, which she had refused to exchange for the prison ones. Those kicks on the shins with her worn old shoes couldn't have hurt anything like that kick which she herself had received in the stomach from the policeman's boot. Policemen's feet, she supposed, had rights denied to ordinary folk. Her own feet were getting very cold now, for the wardresses had taken away the offending shoes, and stockings alone were not much of a protection from the damp floor.

Sally did not sleep much that night. Unlike Rachel Cullen, who could not bring herself to make use of the foul-smelling mattress and rugs which were supplied at bed-time, she wrapped herself up and lay down to rest; but she was bruised and sore and stiff, as well as weary, and the close heavy air made her feel as if she must choke or be sick. And this was to go on for eight days and nights! No, not if Sally knew it. In any case; food with the smell in it that was in everything that entered the cell, was not inviting; she would do what Miss Bruce-Gordon had done, what the other prisoners, every one of them, she felt sure, would do. The next morning Sally began the hunger strike.

The first twenty-four hours were the worst. In spite of the atmosphere; in spite of the close confinement, in spite of the untempting food, the hunger habit asserted itself, and Sally, who was what she herself styled hearty, had a hard struggle to keep herself from yielding to its cravings. Then came intolerable nausea, and feelings that she could only describe as all-overish. She half thought she was going to die then, and found herself wondering how long it would be before Joe Whittle took up with somebody else. And she didn't seem to mind somehow whether she died or not; it would get her out of this old prison anyhow. She would like to have had another sight of Joe, though—and Lady 'Ill—and little Stanny Bilkes—would Bilkes laugh when he heard she had died in prison? or would he take his solemn line and tell the children she had gone to hell? "An' no way of lettin' 'im know as I ain't—s'posin' I was thought decent enough to be let in to 'eaven." It was an aggravating thought, or would have been if it had not been so vague. It was all rather vague: Bilkes and Lady 'Ill—and Stanny—and that window that she could not break.

Then Sally got better. Her head cleared and the dreadful feelings went; the pain and the giddiness and the craving for food; and she was content just to lie still, or would have been, if the wooden bed had been less hard, for in the daytime the mattress and the rugs were taken away; and if only she could have had clean water to drink. She was thirsty, not hungry any more, but very thirsty, and the india-rubber "water glass" and its contents were repugnant to her.

Five days Sally passed in the close damp cell; then, on Sunday evening, she was taken to the hospital. The food there was tempting to her, but, longing for it, she refused it nevertheless; as she refused the medicine; lest it should be a form of food. Determination is sometimes broken down by opposition, and sometimes, in answer to a strain upon it, grows in strength. Sally's determination increased with the call to exercise it; and still, on Monday afternoon, with her head very bad again and her mind so apt to wander that she hardly knew what she was doing, she would not give in. And then, on that same evening, she was released; weak, emaciated, sensitive in every part of her body, but proud in heart; she had not gone back on them ladies, she had stuck it.

So Sally served her apprenticeship, and was made ready for that which was to come.

CHAPTER XXX
INVENTIONS

"My mind goes on working all the same. In fact, the more head downwards I am, the more I keep inventing new things."

Through the Looking Glass[1]

To go to prison for causes not accounted great may seem ignominious; it is certainly a difficult task to defend those who encounter the ignominy. So poor Edith found when, towards the end of July, she returned to the Pightle. Monty was to start for Switzerland in a couple of days, but two days were amply sufficient for him to discharge all the arrows of wit, contempt, and ridicule contained in his mental quiver.

Edith had found it impossible to sit by and hear Rachel Cullen spoken of as an hysterical fool, to hear Monty, who would not miss a meal even for the supreme pleasure of going out to kill an animal, sneer and jeer at the hunger-strikers as if it were as easy for a

---

1   Lewis Carroll (1832–98), *Through the Looking Glass, and What Alice Found There* (1872).

woman to fast as for a man to swear. It had seemed to her disloyal to listen in silence which might appear to give consent to his strictures, and she had accordingly rushed in where an angel perhaps would have deemed it wiser not to tread, and had made herself responsible in Monty's eyes for any and every deed performed by any and every suffragette since the beginning of the militant movement.

The kicks which Sally Simmonds had bestowed upon the wardresses' shins had been held up to opprobrium in the House of Commons, together with a bite reputed to have been given to another wardress by Miss Garland. Honourable members were shocked at the unwomanliness of women in prison; it had been expected evidently that life in the cells would have a refining influence. But Monty was jubilant.

"That's the sort of thing you stand up for, is it? Kicking and scratching and biting. I'm jiggered!"

"There's nothing said about scratching," returned Edith, "and as for the biting and kicking, I'll wait and see what is said on the other side when the trial comes on. But this I can tell you, Monty, that if I were a prisoner and you were a wardress, and you were to go on as you are doing now, I am quite sure I should kick *and* scratch *and* bite you."

"My dear Edie!" said Mrs. Carstairs, "how can you?"

"There, now you see what it is, mater. 'Pon my word, a fellow comes down from Cambridge and finds his sister hand-in-glove with a lot of female criminal lunatics! I'm bothered if it isn't enough to make a man forget he is a man."

"I'll remind you what you are, old chap," said Tommy, "when your moustache has got a bit bigger. Till then," he said, dodging round the table, "let's be boys together!"

Tommy acted for the moment as an effective red herring, but Monty returned with persistence to the attack, and Edith was heartily glad when he substituted "good-bye" for "suffragette."

She reproached herself with being unsisterly, for she had a tender conscience as well as a tender heart. "But really," she said in self-exculpation, "a brother *can* be more aggravating than any other kind of man."

When, a few days later, Miss Garland was absolved from the charge of biting a wardress, she wrote post-haste and in triumph to inform Monty of the fact; but Monty wrote back undaunted.[1] A bite more or less made precious little difference, he said; anyhow, one of her friends had kicked; that was proved; and probably most of them had had a try at biting, if the truth were known. There was no smoke without fire. He ended up with the remark that women had no sense of fairness.

Poor Edith found that his view of the situation was the common one. The charge of biting had been widely spread, the refutation of the charge had a more limited circulation; and Edith found that from that time on many people had an idea that suffragettes were afflicted with a species of hydrophobia.

Aunt Elinor and Uncle Beauchamp indulged in no gibes. They took it for granted that Edith must be shocked at "these women," and Edith hardly knew which she found the more trying, the approval of all acts, real and fictitious, on the part of the suffragettes imputed to her by Monty, or the disdain which it was assumed by her aunt and uncle that she must necessarily feel.

In the presence of the latter, she kept silence, chiefly on her mother's account.

"Don't, dear child, say anything before the vicarage people," Mrs. Carstairs implored. "Your uncle never quite approved of my marrying your poor father; he thought him too advanced; and if you stand up for these poor dreadful women, he's sure to blame me for bringing bad blood into the family."

But with Agatha Brand she could not avoid discussion, and Agatha was bitter with a sectarian bitterness which obtains in causes as much as in creeds. It seemed to Edith that it was possible to view the question from both points of view, the militant and the constitutional; but she knew that Agatha would never see it from any standpoint but her own, and excuses, explanations, arguments, alike seemed futile. She had still the lane and the poplars and the delightful world of fancies and impressions of which these formed the frame; and she turned to them at this time with a longing to lose herself in the peace and the beauty of them, which was almost passionate. But alas! the trail of the serpent lay over all. She had eaten

---

[1] Sylvia Pankhurst writes: "Theresa Garnet was acquitted of the charge of biting a wardress. She had been wearing the brooch I had designed for presentation to WSPU prisoners, and she was able to demonstrate that the marks on the officer's hand, mistaken for those of teeth, were made by the points of the portcullis" (1931, 310).

of the fruit of the tree of knowledge, and the gates of her Eden were closed to her.

To Edith the beauty of the outer world, and the thoughts which emerged from and were merged in that beauty, had been hitherto the essence of life; her true existence lay in the perception of it and in the mental condition with which perception was allied. She had been none the less happy because she had walked almost alone in that secret world of hers, save for the creatures of her fancy; avoiding instinctively the commonplace mind, shrinking from the conventional remark, she had spoken to but few of her joy in the loveliness of nature's garment; and none knew, save Robbie Colquhoun, and he but dimly, what, behind that garment, she sought and found.

Edith was one of the artists who do not paint, the poets who do not sing. She could hardly be called inarticulate, since she had no desire to put into concrete form what she saw or felt or thought, and so did not suffer with the suffering of those who, craving to express themselves, are denied the faculty of expression. The foundation stone of her nature was receptivity, and she was spared alike the pangs, the ecstasy, and the imperious behests of creative impulse.

She had been happy in the life which had appeared to no one to be lonely, because no one knew that the chief part of it was lived alone; but now the simplicity of her happiness, the rare sweet quality of it, had been taken away. The outer forms of things were still as beautiful, nay, more beautiful perhaps, than they had ever been; but the heart at the back of them had lost its joyous beat. Knowledge had crept in; of the reality of suffering in human life, of the complexities of its conduct, the confusion of its motives. Right and wrong were no longer opposed, but interwoven; and the ugliness which found no place in Edith's hidden world was rife and rampant in the life of her fellow beings. The sight of the conflict in Parliament Square, the actual sordid sight of it, had broken the simple melody to which hitherto her consciousness had attuned itself. Later on she might be aware of the chords which make the finest music, might hear in their blending the fuller sweep of harmony; but for the moment the tune halted, and life was robbed of its song.

What song could there be when prisoners and prisons stepped forth from the unsubstantiality of newspaper reports and marshalled themselves as facts which concerned your friends? What song when women worked like men at chain-making, starved as seamstresses, drew their highest wages on the streets? What song when sex, held high as woman's proudest possession, was degraded from an attribute to an instinct threatened by political freedom, so that it was held more womanly to be a prostitute than a voter? What song when all the safe approaches to citizenship were closed to women, and when, women having been forced into the hateful ways of warfare, convention derided what injustice compelled?

Edith would no more have dreamed of voicing these thoughts to Monty than she would have spoken to him of the hidden inhabitants of the lane; the only method of replying to Monty was by *tu quoque*[1] of an obvious kind; but the thoughts rose within her vigorous and keen, and she kept them and pondered them in her heart. She kept them and added to them; as when Sally Simmonds was sentenced to a further imprisonment for her attack on the wardresses' shins, and went through a second hunger strike and was released after three days; as when, week after week, the prisons were full and emptied again of women who preferred starvation to the denial of their rights as political prisoners; as when all questions were allowed and answered at political meetings, save only questions, even when put by men, on the subject of women's enfranchisement.

Agatha Brand said it was all because men were sickened by the militant methods, and for her part she didn't blame them, she was sickened too. Robbie Colquhoun said little, beyond remarking dryly that it was conceivable that the militants were as much sickened by Ministers' methods as Ministers were by the militants'. Lady Henry Hill was abroad with her husband, and silent as far as Edith was concerned. Rachel Cullen was ill in bed, and silent too. It was perforce that Edith kept her thoughts to herself and pondered them in her heart.

---

1   This Latin phrase meaning "you too" or "you also," also refers to a logical fallacy in which an argument is made that an action is acceptable because one's opponent has also performed it. The fallacy is a form of personal or *ad hominem* argument because a person is attacked for doing what she or he is arguing against.

CHAPTER XXXI
MRS. BROWN

"While he
Struck midnight, I kept striking six at dawn,
While he marked judgment, I, redemption-day."

Aurora Leigh[1]

Monty Carstairs had gone on from Switzerland to the Bavarian Tyrol with the three companions who, like himself, had come abroad to "read hard." They were staying at a small hotel on the borders of a lake round which, on every side, mountains rose up in the shape of a cup. Certainly there should have been no difficulty in devotion to study, since the outer world was completely shut off, since there were not many people in the hotel besides the four undergraduates, and since only two of these people were English. And yet Monty and his friends found that boating expeditions, and walking expeditions, and meals, and the rest necessary after meals, took up so much time that there was not a great deal left to give to books.

"And when there's a damned pleasant woman about, to talk to, why a fellow talks to her," said Monty to Marjoribanks of King's; and Marjoribanks answered:

"Yes, if that's your line. I'm not much of a woman's man myself."

Monty, indeed, was greatly attracted by Mrs. Brown. Her husband wasn't half a bad chap, but hardly worthy of her. So he wrote home to Edith, proceeding to descant on the charms and merits of Mrs. Brown. Never before had Monty shown himself such a voluminous correspondent, but Edith was not slow to discover that his letters—and he actually sent her three in the course of a month—were written not so much to, as at, her. For Mrs. Brown, it appeared, was the very antithesis of a suffragette, or Monty's conception of a suffragette. She was charming to look at, very well turned out, *extremely* feminine. She was not always airing her own opinions, but was willing, and indeed eager, to listen to a man's views on the questions of the day.

---

1   Elizabeth Barrett Browning (1806–61), *Aurora Leigh* (1856).

It was all quite true. Mrs. Brown was not only pretty, but well dressed, and had, moreover, the supreme merit of being a good listener. When she spoke, it was more often to ask a question than to make an observation, and she would sit knitting silk ties while Monty, to his own satisfaction—and hers apparently, since she smiled from time to time—monopolised the conversation. It was especially when Monty let himself loose on the relations of the sexes that she seemed impressed: sometimes she would let her knitting lie on her lap and fix her eyes upon his face. Monty was always spurred to additional eloquence when this occurred.

"A woman's home is her castle," he announced one evening after dinner, when he, Mrs. Brown, and Saunders were sitting in the verandah that overlooked the lake, while Mr. Brown, Marjoribanks, and Selby paddled lazily in a boat not far from the shore. "A woman's home is her castle. There she is queen, and within its walls she is man's equal."

"I have always understood that the man was the head of the household."

"So he is," said Saunders, "unless the wife happens to have the money."

"Technically," amended Monty, "and as far as authority goes. A woman rules by her influence; her weapon is persuasion."

"The difficulty is to know how to use it."

"She should always, for instance, welcome her husband with a smile."

"Even when he comes home drunk?" asked Mrs. Brown.

"In our rank of life, men don't drink nowadays, not decent men."

"Don't they? But I was thinking of other ranks"—Mrs. Brown took up her knitting again—"ranks in which the castle is extremely small. But how delightful for your mother and sister—I think you told me you had one sister—that you hold these chivalrous views as to their supremacy in the home."

"A fellow's views are often thrown away on his relations," said Monty.

"So many brothers tease their sisters," Mrs. Brown went on, "and don't at all give way to them."

Memory and conscience combined to keep Monty silent for two minutes, during which the blunt Saunders remarked that he found it much easier to give way to other fellows' sisters than to his own. Then Monty returned to the attack.

"It's all very well to give way, of course; up to a point; but there *is* a point. If a chap sees his sister taking up with outrageous ideas, he's got to put his foot down. Don't you agree now?"

"Doesn't it depend a little on where he puts it?" asked Mrs. Brown. "Some men's feet are rather heavy, you know."

"He puts it down where a woman stops being a woman, and becomes a—a—"

"A suffragette," suggested Mrs. Brown.

"That's it; you've hit it. They're just awful, those suffragettes. You think so, don't you?"

"I'd rather hear what you think," was Mrs. Brown's reply.

It was after this conversation that Monty wrote to Edith and said that Mrs. Brown was not always wanting to air her own opinions.

As to Monty's opinions, Mrs. Brown knew what they were in regard to most subjects before she went away. He was young enough to have formed opinions on every question within his cognisance, naive enough to think they were of importance, fresh enough to be eager to pour them forth. Satisfied that his new friend was on the right side in the matter of the suffrage, he did not launch forth with his full strength of argument in that direction; mild contempt took the place of the violent invective which had fallen to Edith's share.

One day he discovered that the tie Mrs. Brown was knitting was composed of the WSPU colours.

"By Jove!" he exclaimed; "do you know what colours those are?"

"What are they?" asked Mrs. Brown.

"Why, the colours of the militants—purple, white, and green."

"So they are. They go very well together, don't you think?"

"Oh yes, they're well enough artistically, but—I almost wonder you care to use them, associated as they are with those unsexed viragoes."

"Oh, I don't mind at all. It's a combination I often wear, and it never occurs to me to associate them with any body of women I should be ashamed of belonging to."

"I can't bear to connect you in any way with anything unfeminine."

"That's the way with you men—you think so much more of our surroundings than of what we are in ourselves."

"You men" appealed to Monty: he thought it particularly femi-nine, and he hastened to disclaim any idea of valuing the husk more than the kernel.

"No, no, I assure you," he cried. "When a woman is a brick—I mean a true woman, as you are—her surroundings don't matter one little bit."

"Not even if they are the colours of the WSPU?"

"N—o, no. Because," cried Monty in a burst of eloquence, "women like you take the colour out of any colours."

"How kind of you! But I am sure even you, with your large views, would be affected by surroundings. Prison, for instance?"

"No," said Monty, with determination. "Of course," he went on, "if I were choosing a cook or a housemaid, I should avoid a felon; but if you, for instance, were sent to prison, I should know there was a miscarriage of justice. You would be a martyr, not a criminal."

"You are very broad-minded, Mr. Carstairs; but I can't help think-ing that you could not avoid being influenced by public opinion. If a woman were notorious, universally condemned, even though she had committed no real crime, I fear you would not stand by her."

"However much she was condemned, and if she *had* committed a crime, I would stand by her, if that woman were you."

The next time Mrs. Brown was alone with her husband—

"Henry," she said, "I really feel as if I were playing it low down with that young man. He is quite chivalrous when you get through the things that he thinks he is."

"Low down or not, you'll stick to your bargain."

"I'm afraid he'll be so mortified when he finds out, and he's sure to, sooner or later. Why, he must have recognised me from the pic-tures in the papers, if they had been in the very least like me."

"The young ass must look out for himself. You promised you'd be Mrs. Brown and not discuss women and votes for a whole month, and that promise you'll keep. I'm not quite sure you've stuck to it as it is."

"I have, I assure you I have. Whatever he says, I reply by a ques-tion or a request for his opinion. You can't call that discussion."

"N—no; but just you look out and keep to the spirit as well as the letter."

It was the evening before the Browns were to leave the Königsee, and Mrs. Brown and Monty had gone for a last stroll.

"Have you ever been," she asked him, "to any of the suffragette meetings?"

"Certainly not. Wouldn't waste my time."

"I wish you would do me a favour and waste an hour in that way. I have promised to go to the Queen's Hall on the fourth of October, and I should so much like to meet you there."

"Oh, if *you're* going, I'll try and manage it. It would be rather fun."

"It might be."

"Who's going to hold forth? Do you know?"

"Lady Henry Hill, I believe, for one."

"Oh, *that* woman! Now there's a man I pity—her husband."

"Poor fellow!" murmured Mrs. Brown.

"I'm told she's good-looking," Monty went on. "Well, she may be—for a suffragette. But my eye! if you'd seen her portrait in the papers—Perhaps you did."

"Yes, in more than one."

"And didn't you think her frightful?"

"Hideous. But perhaps," Mrs. Brown added, "they were not a fair likeness."

"Flattered her, I'll bet you anything."

"You may be right. But about the Queen's Hall—you'll come, then?"

"Oh, I'll come. How shall we meet? You couldn't lunch with me, I suppose, or anything? Or could I fetch you?"

"Thank you so much, but I'm afraid we must meet at the Hall. The best way will be for you to go straight in."

"And keep a seat for you? Is one allowed to? Are the places reserved? I'm afraid we shall miss each other."

"You are sure to see me, but I can't be there till the meeting begins."

"But it'll be no fun if I don't sit beside you."

"I think you'll find it quite funny enough, and we can talk it over afterwards, if you care to."

"Well—er—of course I'll do as you say. And, I say, Mrs. Brown, I wish you'd—may I come and call upon you in London?"

"I shall be delighted if you will—after the meeting."

"This is my card. If I might have your address?"

"I'll give it to you—after the meeting. Perhaps," Mrs. Brown added, "I may also see your sister?"

"Oh, Edith! I'm afraid you wouldn't hit it off with her. She's far too much inclined to uphold the suffragettes."

"It's an inclination," said Mrs. Brown, "that always makes either a bond or a barrier."

CHAPTER XXXII
CONTRASTS

"Look here, upon this picture and on this."

Shakespeare[1]

The great Bingley Hall meeting at Birmingham was over, and the great Minister had delivered his message to eager multitudes; not without difficulty.[2]

Elaborate had been the preparations, manifold the precautions to keep out interrupting women. Armies of police around the hall, barricades at either end of the street in which it stood, armies of police again at the railway station; an underground passage and a circuitous route, to secure the safe conduct of the speaker; all the forces at the service of the law to secure and maintain order. And against order, a dozen women, safely lodged in the houses enclosed by the barricades, some days before the barricades were erected.

Inside the hall, on the platform, a hundred and fifty women, so firmly imbued with Liberal principles that there was no fear of their putting any question as to the political existence of their sex; in the gangways and at the entrances, groups of policemen and posses of stewards; in the body of the hall, hundreds of men singing heartily and fervently songs of freedom.

---

1 William Shakespeare (1564–1616), *Hamlet, Prince of Denmark*, 3.4.54 (1603).

2 The Birmingham meeting was one in a series undertaken by Asquith's government in an attempt to promote David Lloyd George's "People's Budget." The WSPU took the opportunity to demonstrate outside the halls in which the meetings took place and, because women had been barred from political meetings, male sympathizers heckled Cabinet Ministers on the women's behalf (C. Pankhurst, 135). Women who wanted to attend Liberal meetings had to purchase tickets in advance through recognized Liberal offices. Tickets were not transferable, and had to have the ticket holder's name written on the front (Rosen, 122).

"Keep the light of Freedom shining,
Still the cause of right defend."

A band of trumpeters led the singing; freedom, fortified by wind instruments, is a glorious thing.

"Save thy people from oppression,
From injustice set them free."

The hearts of the multitude were stirred; against injustice their fathers had fought, and failing, fainting not in the fight, had won freedom for these, their descendants; and these descendants, fired with that same sacred spirit, would fight, if need were, to win fresh freedom for their sons. For their sons alone; for when, the Minister had waxed eloquent on the rights of the people, and a man rose up and asked that these rights should be extended to the wives and daughters of the nation, a holy horror took the place of the noble heroism which had inspired the singers.

Instead of "Save thy people from oppression," "Boot him!" rang through the hall; and one of the descendants of the fathers who had fought for freedom was kicked and dragged from the assembly.

Outside, in the streets, incessant turmoil; the whole populace, as it seemed, abroad; the crowd, led by women, rushing the barriers again and again; the leaders ever more tightly wedged in between the rushing, pushing crowd and the charging mounted police.

Inside, the speech proceeding, eloquent, lucid, with bursts of rhetoric.

"Was John Stuart Mill a Socialist?"[1] queried the Minister.

"No, sir," rang out from one of the side galleries, "he was a champion of Votes for Women."

---

1   John Stuart Mill (1806–73) was a philosopher, politician, economist, reformer, and friend to women's suffrage. A Liberal MP for Westminster, in 1866 he presented a petition to Parliament with 1,499 signatures in support of women's suffrage. In the debates over the 1867 Reform Bill, Mill proposed replacing the word "man" with the word "person" thus giving women the right of suffrage. In *The Subjection of Women* (1869), he argues that "the principle which regulates the existing social relations between the two sexes—the legal subordination of one sex to the other—is wrong itself, and now one of the chief hindrances to human improvement; and that it ought to be replaced by a principle of perfect equality, admitting no power or privilege on the one side, nor disability on the other" (5).

The man who sent that answer was seized upon, roughly handled, and cast out. Every man who mentioned the word "woman" that night was seized and roughly handled and cast out. The seizing and the ejections caused constant interruptions; and there were others.

Crash! Bang! the sound of shivering glass! One of the tall windows was broken; and another; and now on the roof, sounds as of hurled missiles.

Outside, on a neighbouring roof, two women flinging slates, dislodged by an axe; men below turning the fire-hose upon them, hurling stones and bricks at them; policemen, climbing up in their rear, dragging them to the ground, bruised and bleeding.[1]

"Serve them right!" Such acts as these deserve and get from all right-thinking people no pity. The ancestors of the men applauding freedom in the hall below rased buildings to the ground and did not pause at bloodshed. But women, debarred from asking questions at meetings, debarred from receiving answers to questions put for them by men, debarred by their own instincts from deliberately violent acts, must not use the blunt weapon of interruption, even though the risk be to the lives of the interrupters, not of the interrupted.

Men hurled missiles at their fellow men; women, at the roof of a building to which they are refused admittance; and they are careful, these women, as the Minister emerges from that building, to touch neither him nor his chauffeur.

But stay! Are they careful? Nay, for what is this? A slate, flung on to the roof, bounds downwards, hits the motor, breaks lamps and a window. Unpardonable and cowardly assault! In spite of the scores of stewards, of the hundreds of policemen, miserable women have hit the Minister's motor! Of a piece it is with the rest of their conduct on that memorable night, conduct for which the freedom-lovers throughout the country can find no adequate epithets.

"Frenzied and dangerous"; "It is worthy only of criminal lunatics whose minds are so warped that they think any violence excusable as a means of advancing political ends." Violent indeed! a score or so of women pitting themselves against a hall full of British males and

---

1   Mary Leigh and Charlotte Marsh were among the first suffragette prisoners to be forcibly fed. For having thrown slates from the roof of a nearby house at police and at Asquith's car, Leigh was sentenced to three months and Marsh to two, both with hard labour.

a thousand policemen! The odds in favour of the women make such a proceeding infamous. Respectability is affronted; Mrs. Grundy[1] stands aghast; then, making the round of the Press, whispers into every editor's ear; and most of them listen.

But it was all over now. His Majesty's Minister was safely back in London, and ten women lay in Wenlock Gaol, no longer dangerous, but weak with hunger; the head of one was bandaged; it was cut open on the night when the Minister's motor was in imminent peril. Foolish women, to fast when they might eat; more than foolish, when fasting means something beyond mere abstinence from food.

One of them is lying very still; not asleep, for her eyes are open. The hunger strike is apt to dim the vision, and perhaps she does not see very plainly with those open eyes, as she lies there; listening. Whether the hunger strike has dimmed her sight or no, her hearing is as acute as ever: hunger does not touch the hearing, perhaps, or else, to counteract the hunger, there is something else to quicken it. She is listening, and her hearing is as acute as ever it was; nay, more acute than ever in all her life.

They are coming now; in a minute the hand will be on the door, and the door will open, and then—

No more picturing of what is to be; the hand is there, and the door is open, and they are in the cell, the two doctors and the four wardresses.

Foolish woman, to endure what she is about to endure, just to uphold the rights of political prisoners, just for the sake of a principle! Men have been as foolish in days gone by; but not to-day.

She must sit up, this woman who was lying down; the four wardresses see to, that, and to the holding of her still. She might struggle voluntarily, or perhaps involuntarily, so needs firm hands upon her, while her mouth is prised open with what, as far as she can judge by the feel of it, is a steel instrument. Very wide the doctors open her mouth, just as wide as the jaws will stretch, and the gag is fixed so that the teeth cannot close. Then down the throat goes an india-rubber tube, not too small.

---

1 The surname of an imaginary personage (Mrs. Grundy) who is proverbially referred to as a personification of the tyranny of social opinion in matters of conventional propriety (*OED*).

She is choking now, or feels as if she were; all the agony and the horror of suffocation is upon her. It seems as if it would never stop, the passing of that tube; the delicate mucous membrane is hurt and irritated; the choking, the sensation of not being able to breathe, grow worse and worse. An instant's relief as the food is poured into the stomach, and then the stomach resists, and deadly sickness sets in. Need now for the wardresses' strong hands to hold the writhing, straining body of the woman who is no longer foolish. For the moment her folly has gone from her; she forgets why she is there, forgets principle, hope, fellow prisoners; forgets everything save her own suffering.

Meanwhile, in London, in the House of Commons, a member of the Labour Party was asking questions about this very woman and her fellows. It had been rather a dull sitting: honourable members were disposed to yawn; the questions, sharply asked, and the answers, coolly given, formed an agreeable variation. Honourable members sat up and listened attentively; cheered when they were informed that forcible feeding had been adopted in Wenlock Gaol; cheered, for this was a fine new policy; and added laughter to their cheers, for it was a humorous one.[1] Very humorous it was to pour food through an india-rubber tube into a woman's stomach. Honourable members, whose own stomachs were filled regularly without external pressure, were moved to mirth by the information supplied. The atmosphere of the House, which had been wearisome, was lightened by friendly jocosity, for here was a subject on which all could agree, a subject which bridged over the differences of party. On both sides of the House honourable members sat approving and amused; one touch of that primitive instinct of Nature which causes the schoolboy to laugh when he sees a fellow being fall down, had made the whole House kin. A few protested; they were almost as funny as the women who chose to be fed through tubes.

Funny, those women, yes, and typical; it showed, all this business, how impossible it was to take them seriously, and how unfitted they were for the vote.

---

[1] In a letter to the *Times*, Keir Hardie, MP for Merthyr Tydfil (Wales), wrote that he was "horrified at the levity displayed by a large section of members of the House when the question [concerning the forced feeding of suffragettes] was being answered. Had I not heard it, I could not have believed that a body of gentlemen could have found reason for mirth and applause in a scene which I venture to say has no parallel in the recent history of our country" (28 September 1909, 10).

There was the serious side too, though; afterwards, in the lobbies, men of both parties remembered the missile and the motor, and, as a leading Liberal paper put it, sympathy was reserved for the great Liberal leader whose life had been in danger. And then, the dinner hour approaching, honourable members repaired to the dining-room to renew the strength necessary to the task of dealing with the important affairs of men and the foolish outrages of women.

Sweated women in the slums, who could not eat; foolish women in the prisons, who would not eat; and wise men in the House of Commons dining cheerfully.

CHAPTER XXXIII
WAS IT WORTH WHILE?

> "Oh! would I were dead now,
> Or up in my bed now,
> To cover my head now,
> And have a good cry."
>
> Tom Hood[1]

"An' so," said Sally, "we shall 'ave to part."

Joe Whittle sat on one of the wooden chairs in Mrs. Blake's kitchen twisting in his hands a red cotton handkerchief with white spots. His eyes were on the handkerchief, and the expression of his face was sullen. So had it been on the few occasions on which, since her release from prison, he and Sally had met.

On the first occasion Sally had felt still too ill to heed him— though, indeed, he had not come to see her till she had been free a fortnight—and she had put down his silence and constraint to solicitude. On the second occasion she had thought that he was "a bit off his chump"; on the third it occurred to her that what he was off was herself. So she had summoned him to an interview, and the interview was turning out pretty much as she had half feared it might.

Joe had stuck by her when she joined the Union; he had endured the street speaking and the processions; he had even pressed her to marry him, poor Joe! who wanted a home, and Sally in it, more

---

1 Thomas Hood (1799–1845), "A Table of Errata (*Hostess loquitur*)" (1839).

than any other woman he had ever set eyes on; and who thought that at bottom that was what Sally wanted too, and that she would settle down in her home like any ordinary wife when she had let off some of the steam engendered, by those other women, in her emotional boiler. But prison had been too much for him; and the hunger strike; it seemed so d—d silly not to eat out of sheer contrariness; and his mates were always asking him how his fasting girl was getting on.

Sally had been doubtful before he came as to whether the change in his manner was due to her refusal to contemplate marriage at any near date, or whether he was beginning to repent of his bargain. It did not take long to find out. She was good at leading questions, and Joe had no desire to beat about the bush; it was soon evident that he was tired of her goings on. Nevertheless, she was quick to perceive that it would not be very difficult to win him back again. The exercise of what are called woman's wiles: a little appeal, a little flattery, a judicious blending of smiles and tears; above all, an impression that she loved and longed for him, and a promise to marry him whensoever he would; and Joe would have been hers again, to possess for evermore.

But speedy marriage was not on Sally's programme. She had to stand by them ladies till the vote was won, and a feller that wanted a wife at once must go elsewhere. So when Joe reproached her with bringing him into ridicule, and avowed that he did not hold with the tomfoolery she had lately indulged in, she offered no blandishments in reply, but simply accepted his point of view.

"You looks at it different to what I look at it," she said, after Joe, with some forcibleness, had expressed his sentiments, "an' if we was to sit jawrin' 'ere till midnight, I shouldn't no more see it your way than wot you'd see it mine. An' so we shall 'ave to part."

Joe raised his eyes from the twisted handkerchief. "Looks like it," he said. Then, his heart growing hot within him, "I must say as I think you 'aven't treated me fair," he went on, "leadin' of me on all these years, an' now to go an' leave me in the lurch."

"'Tain't me as is leavin'; it's yerself."

"It's you as druv me to it, carryin' on with ways more fit for 'ooligans than women."

"'Ooligan yerself. Lor', you don't know what 'ooligans is made of, nor women, or you wouldn't talk so foolish. You men, wot your god is your belly, you can't never understand 'ow a woman can go 'ungry for the sake of something she 'olds to. You'd give in, *you* would, sooner than go without yer dinner."

"I'd sooner 'ave my dinner than go an' vote for one of them Parliament blokes, if that's wot you mean. Wot do I care which of 'em gets in? An' if *I* don't care about the bloomin' franchise, why should *you*?"

"'Cos of the others, them as is put upon; women like my mother—an' yours, Joe, for the matter of that."

"Wot's that got to do with it?"

"They can't stand up for theirselves unless they've got somethin' to stand on."

"An' they're goin' to stand on the vote, is that it? By Gawd, they'll find it bloomin' rotten."

"Joe, you've been deceivin' me all this time. I thought you was for us."

"An' so I was, an' I ain't agin you now, in a manner of speakin'. I don't see no reason why you shouldn't 'ave a vote if you wants it; an' I like pluck, an' some of them suffragettes 'as got it. An' besides, I wanted to please you, Sally. But when it comes to doin' a man out of 'is 'ome, and doin' yerselves out of yer dinners, well, then, I ain't got no more patience with you, an' I don't know as any man as *is* a man would 'ave."

"Well, then," said Sally, returning to her former contention, "I don't see no way out of it. We shall 'ave to part."

"It's all very well for you to take it so cool; you don't seem to care about 'avin' a 'ome. But 'ere am I, done out of 'ome an' sweet'eart an' wife an' everything."

"You'll soon take up with somebody else. There's Mary Ann Dobbs now—"

"Blow Mary Ann Dobbs!"

"I don't say she'd suit you as well as me; I don't know as she's got a firm enough 'and, for you want somebody as won't be too much on the givin' in side. But she's a good 'earted gurl, an' partial to you, or I don't know nothink about gurls."

"I don't want 'er, so that's enough. I s'pose," said Joe, turning to sarcasm, "that as you ain't goin' to 'ave me yerself, I'll be allowed to choose who I *will* 'ave."

"No offence meant, I'm sure. I only want to see you 'appy; an' men are so silly that, as like as not, you'll be took in by some flashy gurl as ain't good enough for you."

"That's as it may be. An' so," said Joe, getting up, "we're to part; an' that bein' so, I think I'd best be goin'."

"Good-bye," said Sally.

"Shall I give you a last kiss?"

"I'm willin'."

She held up her face, the face with the turned-up nose and the wide bright eyes, the face that was thinner than it used to be; and Joe kissed it.

Then he turned and went out of the door and up the area steps, and Sally was left alone.

Was he really gone? Never to come back? Would she never feel those fervent and somewhat moist kisses on her face any more? Never the pressure of his arm about her waist? She had counselled him to take up with Mary Ann Dobbs, and perhaps, after all, he would take her advice. At that moment she hated Mary Ann. To think of that round-faced young woman walking out with Joe, her Joe! No, she couldn't stand it. She must run after him, write to him, beg him to come back. Oh no, she didn't want to part.

Love seemed very sweet; and so did a home—with Joe. And she was giving up both; and for what? For a life of struggle and humiliations, for prison and the tortures of prison. She felt as if she could not stand by her choice. She was more easily tired now than before she went to prison, and she had pain sometimes where the policeman had kicked her; the paper-selling and the street-speaking and the jeers and insults of the crowd, all these tried her more than formerly. There were women here and there in the Union who had been hardened by the violence used against them, who had become, to a certain extent, inured to the methods of militancy; but Sally was not of these. She had a brave little heart, but she was not fearless; neither was she insensitive, nor had she by nature much physical courage, for all her cheery disposition and her cockney impudence. The bird in her breast, which had fluttered first in response to something in the words, and something in the voice, and something in the personality of Lady Henry Hill, had notes in its song inspired by the soaring instinct; notes whose significance was not always understood by Sally;

notes which were sometimes dumb, but which, dumb or uttered, were an integral part of the singing.

To-night they were dumb. Sally tried to think of the women who were "put upon," but they seemed far away; it was her own womanhood that was insistent in her. And she thought of Lady Henry and Rachel Cullen and of all the women who had gone through the hunger strike; but, "was it worth while?" came side by side with the thought to-night. And those other women who had been fed by force, who, at this very minute, as she stood by the kitchen table, were living through the scenes that Sally had had described to her. It all seemed far away, unreal, a sort of dream, and not a pleasant one. The reality was Joe, and Joe's arms and kisses, and the home she might have had. Somehow she had thought that he would wait for her, till she was ready, till the vote was won, and she was free to settle down. She had taken him with a high hand in the days before she went to prison, had told him he could take her or leave her, feeling so sure that he would choose the taking—at such time as suited her; thinking that he understood why she had to wait, and was willing to take his share in the sacrifice. But he didn't care enough, either for her or for the Cause; he wouldn't wait. Yet, was he to blame? Hardly. Sally, longing after him, seeing him at his dearest, recognised nevertheless that she had put too great a strain upon his steadfastness, and exonerated him from blame.

"'E ain't got no 'ero's blood in 'im," she said to herself; "an' if it ain't inside a man when he's born, 't'ain't no good tryin' to pour it in after."

Then she sat down in the chair that Joe had sat in, and put her hands before her face and cried.

CHAPTER XXXIV
THE PASSING OF MRS. BROWN

"Quoth he, 'If my nag was better to ride,
I'd follow her over the world so wide,
Oh, it is not my love that begins to fail,
But I've lost the last glimpse of the grey mare's tail!'"

Tom Hood[1]

---

1 Thomas Hood (1799–1845), "Equestrian Courtship" (1826).

Monty Carstairs returned in high feather to the Pightle. The Königsee had seemed rather dull after the departure of the Browns, and the increased facilities for reading hard had not made up to him for their absence. But now anticipation was taking the place of regret; he was beginning to look forward instead of back, and it was a contented, not to say cock-a-whoop Monty who talked to Edith of "Mrs. Brown and I."

"Mrs. Brown and I" were going to have tremendous fun at the suffrage meeting. "At least," said Monty, "if she isn't too much upset by the whole thing to see the funny side. That's my only fear, that she'll be too disgusted to be amused."

"Where does this paragon live?" asked Edith. "In London? or is she coming up from the provinces on purpose to join in your jeers?"

"Provinces! How ridiculous you are! Anything less provincial you can't imagine."

"Well, I haven't seen her, you see. And perhaps I shan't agree with you when I do."

"What do you mean? When are *you* likely to see her?"

"I'm going up to the meeting, and I presume you'll point her out to me. Oh, in the distance; don't be afraid! I assure you I don't want to be introduced."

"Oh, *you're* going up, are you?" Monty was half taken aback, but on the whole more pleased than displeased; he would like Edith to see the sort of woman who really appealed to a man.

"Yes, Lady Henry Hill's going to speak, and I particularly want to hear her."

"So do Mrs. Brown and I. If her speaking's no better than her face, it'll be an uncommon poor show. Mrs. Brown agrees with me that she's hideous."

"Mrs. Brown and you don't know what you're talking about, then. I don't believe you've ever seen her."

"No, I haven't, but I've seen her portrait in the newspapers. Nice thing that—a woman's portrait bandied about in halfpenny newspapers for the scum of the earth to jeer at."

"The portrait wasn't the least like her, so it doesn't much matter who jeered at it."

"That's what Mrs. Brown said, that it *might* not be like her, might not do her justice. Awfully generous that woman—and gentle. What are you looking at me like that for, you little silly?"

"Darling Monty, any woman who set herself to do it could so easily take you in."

"Oh indeed! That's what *you* think. But I'll tell you one thing, I won't ever be taken in by one of your blooming suffragettes. So, if you've joined them, you know what to expect."

"I haven't yet; I'm only thinking about it."

"Edith," said Mrs. Carstairs, "don't provoke your brother."

"Oh, *I* don't mind her," said Monty loftily. "A silly girl who's got ideas into her head."

"It's to make up for you and Mrs. Brown," laughed Edith, "who don't appear to have an idea between you"; and then she made her escape into the garden.

In truth, Edith was in no laughing mood; she was unhappy at this time, torn by inward conflict; but it would not do to let Monty see that.

The brother and sister went up to London together on the fourth of October, that is to say, they went by the same train, for Monty travelled in a smoking compartment. Arrived at the terminus, he asked his sister what she was going to do. Edith replied that she was going to lunch at an ABC,[1] and Monty said he was bothered if he was. Why couldn't she go to a restaurant or some place where you could get a decent meal? Even a club—he thought all women had clubs nowadays.

Edith said she didn't mind; you got more for less money at an ABC, that was all. "But if you like I'll go to the club, and treat you if you care to come too."

Monty, after intimating that he had but a poor opinion of women's clubs, accepted the invitation, and they went off together to Piccadilly. They could have found an ABC much nearer to their final destination, but they had plenty of time; "so what does it matter, so long as he's pleased, poor boy?" thought Edith. But alas! her hospitality was wasted, for Monty was so excited at the prospect of seeing Mrs. Brown that he could not eat anything like the amount of food provided, and was moreover engaged during the greater part of the meal in comparing his watch with the clock near by and wondering how long it would take to get to the Queen's Hall, and if they ought not to be starting.

---

1   A chain of tea shops that originated on the premises of the Aerated Bread Company.

On the way there he asked Edith if she intended to sit with him, and Edith, knowing what was in his mind, instantly reassured him.

"Oh no; I want to listen to the speakers, not to the remarks of you and Mrs. Brown upon them. We'd better each be on our own, and if we don't happen to meet before, we'll meet at the station."

"Perhaps that *will* be best," said Monty.

Arrived at the entrance he looked eagerly around. No Mrs. Brown, but then, she had told him they were not to meet outside. He went in—he was very early—and secured a seat, two seats, in the body of the hall. She had said she would not be able to sit beside him, but he would see to that; he placed his hat and umbrella on the chair next him, and told all comers he was keeping it for a lady.

His eyes were on the door; his neck was getting stiff with keeping his head constantly turned towards it; she had said he would be sure to see her when she came in, could not miss her. He had either missed her, or she was very late. Monty was bothered, he was jiggered, he was even damned, but still Mrs. Brown did not come. He was beginning to be alarmed, hurt, mortified, angry. If she had thrown him over, forgotten, played him false—! He remembered Edith's words: any woman could take him in; had she been right, after all? It was late now, almost three o'clock; the hall was quite full, and it was very difficult to keep the seat for Mrs. Brown. Finally, as the hands of the clock touched the hour, he couldn't keep it, didn't keep it, let it go in a rush of vexation and disappointment. He would go away, shouldn't wait any longer, wasn't going to be made a fool of. But—she *might* have been delayed. Hadn't she indeed said something about not coming till the meeting began? He would give her a few minutes longer.

And now the meeting was going to begin; the speakers were filing in. A lot of gawky frights! but Monty must turn from the door for a moment, in order just to glance at them.

The glance became a stare, and the stare a prolonged gaze, first of incredulity and then of utter astonishment. He was—it is impossible to write what Monty was—if there was not Mrs. Brown on the platform!

The chairman was half-way through her opening speech before Monty recovered from his astonishment, recovered sufficiently to think consecutively, and to remember that Mrs. Brown had asked him to come to this meeting because *she* had already promised to do so. Whom had she promised? Perhaps—perhaps she actually had a friend amongst these suffragettes, had given her promise to the friend, and had not liked to confess to him why and how she was to be there. Poor little woman! (She was two inches taller than Monty.) Well, he wouldn't be hard on her; after all, it was very feminine of her to shrink from telling him. But now he understood why she had said she could not sit by him, why he was sure to see her, why—he understood it all; but oh, Mrs. Brown, Mrs. Brown, with your roundabout ways, and your foolish, though perhaps natural fears, what a thorough woman you are!

Was she looking out for him, trying to find his face amidst the sea of faces? He thought so; almost thought she had found it, but was not quite sure whether he had caught her eye.

And now the chairman had finished her speech, and was saying words often heard in those days, words which had heralded a new epoch in the life of Sally Simmonds: "I will now call upon Lady Henry Hill."

The audience broke out into clapping, clapping and cheers; and then, to the sound of the clapping, Mrs. Brown got up from her seat and came and stood at the front of the platform.

"Madam Chairman, ladies and gentlemen," she said.

The clapping had ceased and the audience was listening attentively; all but Monty Carstairs, who heard not a word, but sat back in his seat with his mouth open. The speech went on, punctuated by applause and cries of "Hear, hear!" Monty heard vaguely the cries and the applause; heard too, in a sort of way, the voice he had admired so much, in sustained utterance; but of words none. Only blurred sounds, indistinct and meaningless, came from the lips of the tall figure on the platform.

How charming she looked! He had told Edith that she would altogether cut out those unsexed suffra—But she *was* a suffragette; not unsexed, though. Mrs. Brown was absolutely different from— But she wasn't Mrs. Brown, but that woman, that shameless woman, whose portrait had been in halfpenny papers for the scum of the earth to jeer at. Anyhow, she wasn't hideous, not the sort of woman suggested by the portrait. Mrs. Brown had said that perhaps it didn't do her justice. He had thought it so generous of her, but just the sort of thing that Mrs. Brown—Oh, damn it all, she wasn't Mrs. Brown, but the woman that he and Mrs. Brown together were going to make fun of. Monty found himself trying to find out where the fun came in. There was certainly to have been fun; but if Mrs. Brown was not Mrs. Brown, but the woman who had pretended to be Mrs. Brown, how did—

His brain was in a maze, and "blasted" was the mildest of the terms he hurled at his mental confusion. Then his brain cleared a bit; the throbbing in his head and ears grew less violent, and he was able to perceive that some huge blunder had been made. This was not a suffragist, but an anti-suffragist meeting, of course, and Mrs. Brown was declaiming against the militant movement. He would listen— he would listen now; it would be great fun. He caught words, then sentences, then sequences of sentences, and—No, she certainly was not an anti.

She really was, then, Lady Henry Hill! The idea gradually became definite. She was Lady Henry Hill, and she had deceived him, taken him in, made fun of him. That was the most unkindest cut of all. She shouldn't have the chance of doing it again, anyhow, nor the chance of crowing over his discomfiture. He would go as soon as ever the audience began to stir, as soon as he could move without attracting attention, *her* attention.

No, he wouldn't, by Jove! He wouldn't; he'd have it out with her, fair and square. In the meantime he had to sit still and listen to what she had to say. Bosh, of course; nevertheless, Mrs. Brown spoke well, or would have spoken well, if she had been Mrs. Brown—Mrs. Brown of the Königsee—and not Lady Henry Hill. Well, Lady or no Lady, suffragette, shameless, vulgar, as she had shown herself to be, with her wretched practical joke, he wasn't going to funk her or her joke either. So when Geraldine was coming out of the artists' room she was confronted by a young man with a pale face, a determined air, and eyes that flashed reproach.

"You see I have kept my appointment, Lady Henry Hill," he said.

"And you are angry with me; I can see you are, and I'm—so sorry."

Monty bowed.

"Will you give me the chance of an explanation or—?"

Lady Henry paused; her look said, "Is this to be the end of our friendship at the Königsee?"

She had all the charm, all the feminine appeal that had belonged to Mrs. Brown, and Monty was conscious of both appeal and charm; but he hardened his heart.

"The explanation is obvious, surely," he said. "You intended to make a fool of me. I acknowledge that you have succeeded."

As he stood there, hurt, angry, not without dignity, Geraldine felt she had never liked him so well.

"I am not to be heard, then?" she said. "Yet if you had kept your promise—"

"A promise I made when—"

"Under a misapprehension. Yes, I acknowledge you are not bound to keep it. Nevertheless, I am going to venture to ask you—I told them to wait with the car a little way up Portland Place—to ask you to walk with me so far."

"Of course I am at your service."

Edith would not have known this calmly polite young man for her gibing brother, and, indeed, Monty hardly knew himself: the afternoon had turned out so differently from his expectations that he felt as if he were in a dream.

He walked along by the side of Mrs. Brown; she really was Mrs. Brown to him, the very same woman who had aroused his reverence and admiration in Bavaria, though here, in London, he knew with his mind that she was Lady Henry Hill; and as they went she told him how she had promised to rest absolutely from work and discussion for a month, how it was impossible to avoid discussion if people knew who she was, how Lord Henry had held her to her promise, in spite of her desire to break it before leaving the Königsee, and how finally she had agreed that it was best to say nothing.

"Because, you know, you might have turned upon me, and the one thing I was to avoid beyond all other things was a scene."

"I don't make scenes."

Geraldine smiled to herself; then she said, "You must agree that I was right not to give you my address. It would have been awkward for you to find out the truth in my own house, where you could not very well have denounced me."

"You might have written."

"I might; but I confess I wanted you to hear me speak—hear what I had to say."

"Well, I didn't. I was far too much upset—except just a little towards the end."

"Here is the motor. And so you won't come to tea with me, after all?"

"Thank you, but I have to meet my sister at the station."

"Edith! Oh, I wish I had seen her! What time does your train go?"

"Six-thirty."

"Not till then? What a long time you will have to wait at the station!"

She *was* Lady Henry Hill, of course, a militant suffragette, shameless, unsexed, altogether abominable; and yet, somehow, the woman who presented herself to him was the feminine Mrs. Brown. The end of it was that Monty went to tea in Upper Brook Street; and enjoyed himself very much.

CHAPTER XXXV
A DECISION

"But O the truth, the truth! the many eyes
That look on it! the diverse things they see,
According to their thirst for fruit or flowers
Pass on: it is the truth seek we."

George Meredith[1]

Edith uttered not one single gibe on the passing of Mrs. Brown. She did not take long to grasp the situation, and Monty was spared more than a few sentences of abashed and hesitating recital. Inwardly Edith was shaken with joyous merriment; outwardly she was a demure and agreeably intelligent recipient of tidings not too easy to convey. Monty was grateful to her for the generosity of her behaviour, and Edith was grateful to circumstances which must put a stop to Monty's teasing attacks. Henceforth, she knew, she had a weapon ready to her hand, though she did not intend to use it unless driven to extremities; if Monty would be a sleeping dog, she was content to let him lie.

---

1   George Meredith (1828–1909), "A Ballad of Fair Ladies in Revolt" (1876).

Monty, however, was temperamentally incapable of lying low for any length of time; he might be subdued for a few days, but was bound to bark before a week was out. It must be allowed that he had something to bark about; for, on the Saturday following that memorable Monday, Lady Henry Hill was arrested at Newcastle. Edith had more than half expected the arrest. She knew that Geraldine had been overwhelmed with horror and indignation at the treatment meted out to some of the women in Wenlock Gaol,[1] women not socially prominent, and that she had declared her intention of taking her stand by these women, of sharing their fate and seeing if she, a known woman, would be treated in the same way as the women who were unknown. Edith knew too that Geraldine had gone to Newcastle, and that the occasion of her going was the visit to that town of one of His Majesty's Ministers. She was, therefore, not surprised to find her name amongst the names of the twelve women who had been arrested; but to Monty the news came with all the shock of news which is alike unexpected and unwelcome.

The news was in the Sunday paper, and Monty, coming down late to breakfast, and taking up the paper in leisurely fashion, let it drop with an expression of disgust.

"They really are beyond everything, some of these women!" he exclaimed. "Here are twelve of them arrested yesterday on all sorts of disgraceful charges."

He helped himself to bacon, took up the paper again, and then, almost immediately, for the second time, let it drop.

"Good God!" was all he said.

"What is it, Monty dear?" asked his mother, who had finished her breakfast and was putting the marker in her prayer-book against the eighteenth Sunday after Trinity.

"Mrs. Br—, Lady Henry Hill is arrested. She—she's thrown a stone."[2]

---

1   The hunger-striking suffragettes were first forcibly fed in Winson Green Prison, Birmingham.

2   In October 1909 Lady Constance Lytton travelled to Newcastle with Jane Brailsford and Christabel Pankhurst on the occasion of a speech by Chancellor of the Exchequer, David Lloyd George. Seeing a car driving through the crowd and, thinking Lloyd George might be in it, Lady Constance threw a stone at the car hitting the radiator. According to Christabel Pankhurst, her stone was labelled: "To Lloyd George: Rebellion against tyrants is obedience to God" (142). Lady Constance, along with other stone throwers, was arrested. She was charged with assault on Sir Walter Runciman (Lloyd George's host whose

"I hope it didn't hit anybody," remarked Mrs. Carstairs.

"I know she meant that it shouldn't," said Edith.

"You know?" from Monty. "What do you know about it, pray?"

"When the prisoners come before the magistrates you will see for yourself."

"Oh I daresay, I daresay. Of course she'll—But, by Jove! I—I—it's really too much. She hit the speaker's car. Did you see?"

"If she had been a man she would probably have hit the speaker."

"She's got a month," said Monty, "a month! By George! I—I give her up."

"For throwing the stone or being given a month's imprisonment?" asked Edith.

"For heaven's sake, don't begin to jaw," said Monty.

"Don't aggravate him, Edith," said Mrs. Carstairs. "I suppose you're going to church?"

"If you particularly want me to; otherwise—I had thought—"

"Oh yes, you must. I'm sure Monty won't want to go, and Aunt Elinor will be coming and calling tomorrow if two of us are not there."

Three days later Lady Henry was released from prison, together with Mrs. Bridford, the wife of a well-known journalist. A specialist had been sent down to Newcastle to examine the hearts of these two prominent women, and had declared that they were not fitted to undergo forcible feeding. The unknown women, on whose behalf Lady Henry had made her protest, were still in prison, and were subjected to no examination, were exposed only to a continuance of the treatment which had roused Geraldine's indignation.

On the journey from Newcastle to London she was nearly silent. She was tired, perhaps, or exhausted; and well she might be; but no, Lord Henry observing her as she leaned back saw, from the expression of her face, that she was thinking, not resting. At St. Pancras she roused herself, talked on the way to Upper Brook Street, talked again during dinner. Afterwards, sitting in the smoking-room with her husband, she fell into silence, and Lord Henry, who knew her,

---

car she hit), malicious injury to the car, and disorderly behaviour in a public place. Both she and Jane Brailsford refused food, but were examined by doctors and released after two days as medically unfit. (See Appendix C.)

in some ways, as well as she knew herself, let her be. By and by she turned her eyes from the fire to his face. She had her clear look, the look dear to him, but which now he had learned almost to dread, so often had it been associated with some enterprise which meant for him apprehension and anxiety.

"Henry," she said, "I can't let this thing be."

"What thing?"

"This intolerable injustice of setting me free because I have position and a title."

"But, Jerry, you're *not* fit to go through the forcible feeding."

"Perhaps not; but as fit as the women who have had it practised upon them for weeks, who are undergoing it still; now, perhaps, while I'm sitting comfortably here."

"I think you're hardly just to the authorities. Sorristone knows you, and knows that you can't stand very much."

"Yes, he knows me," said Geraldine, "socially, that's just it, and he doesn't know Mrs. Law and the others. Their hearts may be quite as weak as mine or Mrs. Bridford's, but what does Sorristone or anybody else care? It would not be noticed, perhaps, if *they* died in prison; it would make a stir if I did."

"I think you're a bit biased, you know, a bit unfair."

Geraldine looked at the fire again, sat with her eyes upon it for a minute without speaking; then she said, "Before I've done, I'll prove to you that I'm not unjust and that you are too generous."

That same night, when Geraldine had fallen fast asleep, Edith Carstairs knelt by the bay window in her bedroom and looked out into the darkness.

She had had a trying afternoon. Agatha Brand had come to tea, and Mrs. Dallas of the Firs had called; and Mrs. Dallas, at this juncture, was like mustard on a raw wound. Agatha was hardly a sympathetic companion just now, but Agatha at least was intelligent. However much she might be down on the militants, however strongly she might disapprove of the hunger strike, however ingenious she might be in finding excuses for the infliction of forcible feeding, she at least understood the point of the fasting—that it was a protest against being treated as common criminals, instead of political prisoners; she even admitted that it was the only protest possible, in the circumstances, to those who made it. But Mrs. Dallas persisted in believing that what the hunger strikers were striking against was the fact of being sent to prison at all, and continually repeated the statement that if you behaved in a certain way you must expect to be sent to prison, and that if you were in prison it was wicked and hysterical not to eat.

"As for suffering, they deserve all they get, and more," she said. "Look at the awful things they do and the awful things they threaten. They are always sending the most terrible letters to the poor Prime Minister's wife, threatening to steal her children and do all sorts of dreadful things."

"Lady Brinkworth, Lady Henry Hill's sister, wrote to Miss Amherst about those letters," said Edith, "and I happen to have seen Miss Amherst's reply. There are always mischievous people who write anonymous letters about any prominent subject. The leaders of the WSPU constantly receive abusive and obscene letters, some of them written on House of Commons paper, but they do not dream of holding the Cabinet responsible. The suffragettes do not fight against women and children, I assure you, Mrs. Dallas, but *for* them."

But Mrs. Dallas was not to be convinced; she had it on the best authority that such letters had been received, and, though she was not a Liberal, she could feel for an anxious mother as one woman for another.

"It is not disputed that they were received. What is denied is that the anonymous writers had any connection with the Union."

But Mrs. Dallas still shook her head; the letters had been received, and that was enough for her; and then she turned her guns on to Lady Henry Hill. Mrs. Dallas was especially shocked at her release.

"So ignominious to be turned out of prison." Even Agatha laughed at instead of with her, in consequence of this remark, and Monty, who had maintained a frowning silence, was heard to mutter "Fool!" Under his breath, to be sure, but with a vigour which caused his mother to shake her head at him behind Mrs. Dallas's back.

It had been a trying afternoon, but it was not of the afternoon and its trials that Edith was thinking, as she knelt by the window and looked at the dim forms of the poplars, which showed only as a denser darkness under a sky so thick with clouds that the moon was shut away. Dark outside and dark within the room, for Edith had put out the light; she, who usually was afraid of the dark. But to-night she had no fear of it, nor of anything it might contain: fear lay heavy upon her, but it was fear caused by that which lay waiting in the daylight, in the light of the next, the coming day.

Edith had put her hand to the plough, and there was no turning back; but oh, how she longed to turn! The thing before her was repugnant to every habit of her mind, to every attribute of her temperament. Her being had been shaken to its foundations, when she had heard about the forcible feeding and what it meant; when she had read the questions and answers connected with it asked and given in the House of Commons, and been told how they had been received. Then, at last, she had done that which she had not been far from doing for many weeks, she had given in her adherence and offered her service to that body of women whose courage and devotion seemed to her now to outweigh any of the charges that could be brought against them. And then, having offered to work, she had been given work to do; work from which she shrank in dread and horror.

Often, when she heard in former days of interrupted meetings, she had thought of the women who interrupted, with no pity, no sympathy, for it had seemed to her that they needed neither; the women who did such things did not mind doing them. Annie Carnie and Christina Amherst were different: when they had gone to the meeting in the Free Trade Hall at Manchester, they had had no intention of interrupting, had thought that they would be given an answer to a legitimate question. But the women who followed them knew that they would not be answered, knew what to expect, interrupted solely as a protest against the treatment which had been accorded to genuine questions; and Edith had supposed them to be of a fibre which made such work, if not alluring, at least not actively distasteful. Then Rachel Cullen had told her how many of the doers of the work shrank from doing it; how for nights beforehand they could not sleep, but lay awake wondering if they could bring themselves to go through the ordeal, to face the anger and bitterness, the rough usage, the physical risk which the work entailed. That had made her think; the pictures drawn by Rachel were amongst the things she had kept and pondered in her heart, the things that had haunted her. But till tonight she had not understood, had certainly not realised the full meaning of the pictures: to-night that meaning was vivid in her consciousness.

Her head lay on her folded arms; outside, the dark, still night passed slowly over the earth; but night, darkness, quiet, the known and loved trees and fields on which they lay, had no existence for the kneeling, trembling girl. In her torn mind there was light, hideous revealing light, which showed her plainly; and stir and movement, shouts and jeers, and rough, hurting hands.

No, she couldn't; she couldn't face it; she must draw back; anything was better than the naked publicity and the degradation and the physical pain. She decided that she could not face it; and behind that decision, unswerving, inflexible, resolute, was something that said she must. Her heart failed her, her soul rebelled and shrank from the task ahead; and still the spirit that commanded both reiterated its order: "Go!"

The dawn came, and still Edith kneeled by the window; the chill of dawn stole in and closed round her body, and with cold hands dragged her to the realisation that the day was actually here. Looking round, she saw dimly the well-known objects within and without the room struggling into view; and knew then how cold she was and how very tired; and her physical nature, very kind to her then, cried out imperatively for warmth and rest. She crept into bed and lay shivering, till, as the sun rose, sleep came to her and blotted out the morning of the dreadful day.

CHAPTER XXXVI
A PROTEST

"While we are coldly discussing a man's career, sneering at his mistakes, blaming his rashness, and labelling his opinions, ... that man, in his solitude, is perhaps shedding hot tears because his sacrifice is a hard one, because strength and patience are failing him to speak the difficult word, and do the difficult deed."

George Eliot[1]

Edith was back in the beloved solitude of the lane. The peace of it, the healing, the exquisite tender voices of silent, natural things which had neither language nor speech! She needed those voices to

---

1 George Eliot (1819–1880), *Scenes of Clerical Life* (1857).

still the rough, harsh sounds that rang in her inward ears; she needed the peace and the silence, to wash away the stains which lay dark on memory's latest pages.

The hall with the bazaar stalls round the walls made a clear picture on those pages; clear and clean compared with the pages which followed. Parts of those pages were blurred, parts were vividly black; on one was a little white space of wondrous peace.

She had stood in the chattering, careless crowd waiting for the opening of the bazaar. She had presented the ticket of admittance provided for her, and who should know her for a forbidden, disturbing suffragette? She looked as gentle as she was, more than usually timid, far less aggressive than most of those about her.

Edith was in a dream, and a dream that had the tense, terror-laden atmosphere of nightmare. Longing intensely to flee from her surroundings, she yet was constrained to remain; the paralysing spell of nightmare was upon her, and the curious dream influence which makes strange unexpected things seem hardly strange. Otherwise, to raise her eyes to the platform and see, beside the minister who was to open the bazaar, the man whom of all men she most at that moment desired not to see, would surely have been bewilderingly startling, instead of seeming the cruel climax that she had waited for. Not that it made any real difference; all that there had been or might have been between Cyril Race and herself had ended when she entered the hall that afternoon; and yet his presence intensified, if anything could intensify, the horror of the ordeal through which she had to pass.

That was another of the things that people did not seem to realise when they spoke of cheap martyrdom; the pain of forfeiting the approval of those whose good opinion was amongst one's most precious possessions. It was hard enough to go against the outside world, but a hundred, a thousand times harder to thwart the ideas, brave the affection, of one's nearest and dearest; relations, friends, a lover that was or might have been. The opinion of the outside world was nothing compared with that.

Edith was glad she was smaller than the average woman; Race would not notice her in the crowd; till the inevitable moment she was likely to remain unseen.

The Minister had begun his speech now; all chattering was hushed; attention was concentrated upon his words. For two minutes he spoke, and then, from the back of the hall, the cry rang out: "Votes for women!"

What followed was ugly: a rush of stewards, shouts of "Out with her!" mingled with cries of "Fair play!"; a scuffle; a woman dragged and hustled through the people and out of the door.

Quiet again; the stewards cast searching glances here, there, everywhere; were there any more of those accursed suffragettes about? None, at any rate, whose looks betrayed them. The speech went on; Edith knew that it would continue uninterrupted for five minutes; her eyes sought the clock.

"Sir, will you give justice to wom—"

Before the words were out of the second interrupter's mouth she was set upon, seized, dragged out by many pairs of hands. How strong these suffragettes were supposed to be! So many men combined to throw them out; yet having made their protest, they offered no resistance to ejection. Edith caught sight of the face of interrupter number two as she was borne past her; it was white, and there was blood upon it. She herself was number three. Four more minutes and then—What was it she had to say? "Women tax-payers demand the vote." Was that it? "Women tax-payers demand the vote. Women tax-payers demand the vote. Women—" "To give the vote to those women who pay rates and taxes—" Where was she? In the market-place at Charters Ambo, begging rough men for signatures? Hateful it was. Then Cyril Race had come along, and Cyril Race—certainly she had seen him just now, while she was still able to see. Now she could see nothing; it was all half dark and blurred about her; nothing—and yet—there was something she must—she *must* see. The clock, yes, and the moving hand.

She is not at Charters Ambo, not in the market-place. No, she is indoors—of course—in the hall, and when the hand touches the next figure—she can see it now, the hand, and how near to the figure it is. To call out before all these people, and be set upon and hurt! Can she? Yes, for she must—if—if her voice will come.

The hand moves; moves, there, it has touched the figure. Now; she must speak now; but—but—

The hand has touched the figure and passed it and the speech goes on. Edith has not spoken. She has failed; utterly and miserably failed. Her throat was dry and hard; her voice would not come;

because, as she tells herself in an agony, she is a coward, has failed for very fear. It seemed to her then that the suffering of the shrinking and the dread was nothing, nothing at all compared with the agony of self-reproach which overwhelmed her now. If she could only have her chance again, she would brave it all, the pain, the humiliation, everything. But the chance is over; she has failed utterly.

Five minutes more had passed; it was the turn of number four. She was braver than Edith, and promptly the words came: "The women of England—"

She got no further. A hand was over her mouth; hands dragged her head back and grasped her throat. She was not far from Edith, and Edith could see.

How dry her throat was! Her tongue seemed fast to the roof of her mouth. Could she ever manage to get out the sentence that her comrade had not been able to finish? Yes, for the power that had forced her here was paramount now, and her voice came to her and rang out clear: "The women of England demand the vote."

And then a miracle happened. All at once, or so it seemed to her, she was caught up out of the turmoil and the dread, and set in a place of peace. The angry shoutings were very far away; the hustling crowd and those advancing hands had surely no power to hurt; in any case, the dread has gone from her, and she has no more fear.

They have found her now, the little slender figure amidst the taller ones; very easy is this suffragette to drag across the hall and send flying from the door. In truth, she hardly knows what is happening to her; she is hurt, but feels no pain; is roughly handled, cuffed, bruised, but, in her half-consciousness, is alive only to a sense of movement and confusion. Stewards and policemen convey her out of the hall; she stumbles on the step outside, puts out a blindly groping arm, strikes something, clutches, and is clutched. When sight and sense come back to her she is in custody; she has assaulted a policeman.

Is it really all over, and she back in the haunts she loves? Oh, blessed, beautiful sights and sounds of the kind familiar country! Stand very still, Edith, and fairies may flit there from tree to hedge; for it is twilight, when fairies are most prone to show themselves.

She hardly knew whether she had been grateful or not to Cyril Race for bailing her out; yet she was grateful when she found herself with Rachel Cullen in the little green quiet room, and felt that but for Race she would not have been there. He came the next morning and took her to the police-court; and afterwards to the station. His evidence was sufficient to rebut the charge of assault, and Edith was free to go home.

On the platform she thanked him for what he had done. Hitherto she had hardly spoken; on the previous evening she had felt too dazed and too ill, had been in too much pain to speak; and this morning, so grave and quiet and withal so peremptory was he, that she hardly knew whether she was in the company of a friend or in the custody of a gaoler.

"I thank you very much for what you have done for me," she said. "I am grateful, though I cannot say it properly, and all the more so that I know very well that you entirely disapprove of me and my doings."

"You poor little girl," he answered, "do you think I don't know that you have been pushed into this, that you have been led on and carried away by a mistaken impulse of loyalty?"

Edith shook her head. "Not much impulse about it. It was a long-drawn-out deliberate resolve that went before—before yesterday."

"You are not meant for that sort of thing. It's not your rôle."

"Is any woman meant for it?"

"Most certainly I think not."

"Then why are we driven to do these hateful things?"

"Heaven only knows. I don't."

"The Government does."

Race shrugged his shoulders. "Don't let us get into argument," he said after a moment's pause, "because I might get angry with you. As we are parting, we may as well part with as little bitterness as may be."

The train was alongside the platform now, and Edith held out her hand. "Good-bye and thank you. If there is any bitterness, it is all on your side," she said.

"Good-bye. You should rest altogether when you reach home."

"Is there any bitterness?" she asked. She was in the train now, seated, looking out at him. He looked straight back at her.

"I wanted you," he said, "for my very own. You must have known that. And now—"

"You don't want a suffragette."

His eyes, that were hard, softened a little as he looked at her. "I haven't only myself to think of. If I had—But it would be incongruous and absurd, as things are, for a member of the Government to think of—as you say—a suffragette."

The train was moving; away from love, from hope; though Edith had told herself that hope was dead, it had an extraordinary vitality and seemed to be standing now beside Cyril Race on the platform. Yet she had plucked up spirit enough to give him an answer.

"And quite impossible for a suffragette to think of a member of the Government."

"And that was quite true," she told herself, as she paused in the peace of the lane, recalling her words.

At that moment, indeed, she wanted nothing more than peace.

CHAPTER XXXVII
CONSEQUENCES

"The game of consequences to which we all sit down, the hanger-back not least."

R.L. Stevenson[1]

Monty had received her without positive jeers or violent invective; for that she thanked the fictitious Mrs. Brown, who was indeed in a large measure responsible for the restraint of his demeanour, but not entirely so. Edith was undeniably ill and exhausted; you could hardly hit anybody so obviously down; and moreover, however abominable her conduct, she had shown pluck. It was all very well to rave at women you knew nothing about, but when your own sister ran the risk of having her head battered in, and did, in fact, get some battering, you couldn't help seeing that such a proceeding was hardly gone through for the fun of the thing.

So, in the two days which elapsed between Edith's return and Monty's departure for Cambridge, he prevailed upon himself to spare her.

Mrs. Carstairs was divided between tears and reproaches, and Edith, who had expected the reproaches and not the tears, was more

---

1   Robert Louis Stevenson (1850–94), "Old Mortality," *Memories and Portraits* (1887).

upset by the tokens of her mother's love than she would have been by the displeasure which she had braced herself to meet.

It was not till she had been back a week that she went to call at the vicarage.

"Your aunt and uncle will be offended if you don't go, I'm sure," said Mrs. Carstairs.

"I'm afraid they'll be more offended if I do; but I'll go, of course, if you like."

"If only it hadn't been in the papers we needn't have said anything about it."

"Perhaps they didn't notice it."

"Notice it! Why, the whole neighbourhood noticed it. My life has been a misery ever since, with people writing, and stopping me on the road. The least you can do, Edith, is to do what I ask you to."

"All right," said Edith; "I'll go."

So she started, and just outside the gate of the Pightle met Robbie Colquhoun. It was dreadful seeing people for the first time. How would he take it? Then, when he looked at her, she was ashamed of her doubts. There was only one way in which Robbie ever took anything; the kindest.

"I've been away, or I should have come before. How are you? Let me look."

"I'm all right."

"No, you're not. And how could you be? You're not meant for that sort of thing."

Cyril Race's words, but said differently: Race had seemed to arraign her for a fault; in Robbie's voice there was only solicitude.

"I have to go to the vicarage. Will you come?"

"If you want me to."

"I do want you to, very much."

"How do they take it?"

"I don't know. That's the point. I haven't seen them yet—not even in church. I could not face church last Sunday."

Going through the village, Edith said: "Robbie, if you were a member of the Government, could you imagine yourself marrying a suffragette?"

"Certainly I could, if you were the suffragette."

Edith laughed; knowing him so well, she knew that he was joking.

No more time for jokes though, for here they were at the vicarage gate.

"Perhaps, after all, you'd better not come in," Edith said. "You can't knock Aunt Elinor down whatever she says, and it might make it more awkward if you were standing by. Good-bye."

"No, I shall wait and walk back with you."

"Oh don't, Robbie! I may be a quarter of an hour or so."

"Yes, I shall."

Edith walked up the drive alone, her heart beating quickly. It would be nice if Aunt Elinor were out; no, it wouldn't; it would only mean postponing the evil day. She was not out anyhow; Edith could see her in the drawing-room as she passed the window. Uncle B. was there too, and he saw her, they both saw her, for they looked round as she passed, and Uncle B. got up and went over to the door. He was coming to let her in, then; that was kind; they really could be kind. Edith's heart grew lighter, warmer; she would be as gentle, as humble, as pleasing to them both as she could.

Uncle Beauchamp opened the door, in truth—not too wide— and stood in the aperture.

"How do you—" Edith began and stopped; Uncle B.'s face had a freezing influence.

"Your aunt and I regret that we are unable to receive you. You have brought disgrace upon a family that has never till now been disgraced."

Then the door was shut.

Edith did not look in at the window as again she passed it; she looked neither to right nor left; she was tingling all over, with pain and mortification and anger.

Half-way down the drive Robbie met her.

"Out?"

"No, but they won't let me in."

"Not let you in? What do you mean?"

"Uncle B. says I've disgraced—Oh, Robbie, where are you going?"

"To punch his confounded head."

"No, don't, Robbie, I beg of you! For my sake! I'd so much rather you didn't."

"All right; just as you like. But—by—Jove!" Robbie said the last three words very slowly, and shook his fist at the house; then put the fist, unclenched now, and the arm beyond it, across Edith's shoulder, with a gesture that meant protection, not only from aunts and uncles, but from the whole world.

"You poor little girl!" he said.

Cyril Race's words again, but again differently said. There had been a trace of contempt in Race's voice; there was only tenderness in Robbie's. There were tears in Edith's eyes, welling up from the hurt in her heart; she could not see clearly, because of them, and was glad of the guidance of that protecting arm down to the gate.

To the two people at the drawing-room window the arm was the centre of observation.

"Do you see that, Beauchamp?"

"I cannot fail to see it, my dear."

"Well, upon my word!"

"What else can you expect?"

It must be acknowledged that when you have turned a young woman from your door in righteous censure, it is disconcerting to see her walking away with a young man's arm across her shoulder.

"Perhaps they are engaged," said Uncle Beauchamp.

"Not they," returned his wife.

Edith and Robbie Colquhoun walked back to the Pightle in silence.

"Will you come in?" she asked, as they reached the gate.

"No, thank you. I came to see how you were, and I've seen. It will be more comfortable for you to tell Mrs. Carstairs about this outrage without me."

Edith smiled faintly. "Hardly an outrage. The outrage is all on my side, according to them—and most people. Thank you, Robbie, for sticking to me."

"I wish to heaven I might!"

"Well, you may and do, and I'm very grateful."

"Good God, Edie, don't you know that you're all the world to me? There, forgive me! Of course you don't, and I never meant to tell you. I know I haven't a chance. But—but—don't throw me over altogether because I've been a blundering fool and gone too far! Good-bye! I'll come soon and—you needn't be afraid—in my right mind."

Robbie Colquhoun was striding down the lane; he walked well, though he did not dance well; and Edith stood and looked after him. Robbie in love with her! Robbie, her good friend, her comrade, the person she could say anything to and had never thought of as a lover! It was amazing; and amazing that she had never found it out, because she knew him so well, could read him like a book, knew him through and through. Not quite through, though, or she would have found out this—this absurd idea of his. If he were in the Government, she had asked him, could he imagine himself marrying a suffragette; and he had answered that if she were the suffragette, he certainly could. That was true; if Robbie cared for her, he would not consider whether it was incongruous or absurd or anything else. In that he was different from Cyril Race. But alas! alas! he was different in so many ways from Cyril Race, and Cyril Race's ways had a glamour over them for Edith at that time. Just because he condemned the thing she had done, it was all the nobler of him, she told herself, to give her his help and countenance. Robbie would stand by her whatever she did, as staunchly, nay more staunchly than Race; but there did not seem to be any special generosity in the fact; he would do it as a matter of course, just because—well, because she was Edith and he was Robbie.

CHAPTER XXXVIII
ON REMAND

"With bars they blur the gracious moon,
And blind the goodly sun:
And they do well to hide their Hell,
For in it things are done
That Son of God nor son of Man
Ever should look upon!"

Ballad of Reading Gaol[1]

Sally had been obliged to leave Mrs. Blake, greatly to her regret, for she and the little dressmaker got on well together; and yet Sally was very proud. For now she was one of the regular workers for the Union, and all her labour, all her mind, all her energy, could be given to the cause to which she had already given so much. She

---

[1] Oscar Wilde (1854–1900), *The Ballad of Reading Gaol* (1898).

was not always in London now; she was sent hither and thither, to work under the direction of one or other of the organisers; to do, in this place or that, work that by her could be done. In October, at the time of Lady Henry's short imprisonment, she was in Bristol; in November she was back in London; in December she found herself in Brummage.

Sally worked cheerfully, loyally, her pride in her work and her position making her humble. She was proud in that she had been accorded honours which to her were of the highest; she had been entertained at a breakfast on her release from prison, had been cheered, applauded, welcomed, had been received with as much enthusiasm as if she had been Lady 'Ill herself. If only Mr. Bilkes could have seen her! Bilkes had never been cheered in all his life; of that she felt sure; whereas she, the "general," whom he had kissed in private and tyrannised over in public, had been driven in procession through London, never more to do the bidding of Bilkes and his kind.

But she was humble, in that, or so it seemed to her, she had done so little. She had been to prison once, but there were others who had passed through the ordeal twice, thrice, many times; and just because Sally had hated prison, she admired those who had endured more of it than she had. She had undergone the hunger strike; but that, to her, seemed a little thing, since, at the time she had gone through it, the terror of the forcible feeding had not been added to its pains. Lady 'Ill had braved that terror, and though she had not actually experienced it—"an' the only decent thing them bosses ever done was to say as she wasn't fit for it"—she had faced it nevertheless. Sally's imagination was not of the strongest kind, but she shrank from the forcible feeding.

There were many enduring it now, in this very town of Brummage, in Wenlock Gaol. Mrs. Law, the working woman, on whose behalf Lady Henry Hill had had herself arrested, to see if there were any difference made in the treatment of women of known position and women of none, had been released at last and taken to a nursing home; but there were others in her place; and still honourable members in the House of Commons treated the woman's movement as a joke; and still women, who worked prominently in the political field on behalf of men, held meetings to protest against other women working politically on behalf of themselves and their fellow women.

In Christmas week Sally found herself at Belton Head. It was a sorrowful time for Sally, for every year since she and Joe had kept company they had spent Christmas together, and now there was to be no more Joe. But a day or two before leaving Brummage she had had a letter from him, in which he told her that he had followed her advice and taken up with Mary Ann Dobbs. It was the best thing he could do; it was the thing she had told him to do; and yet when Sally heard the news she knew that she had had a secret hope that he would find it impossible to take up with anybody but herself. She, like Edith Carstairs, had had visions of golden days, ahead, when the vote would be won, and there would be no suffrage question to stand between a girl and her lover.

Well, it was a good thing there was work to be done; it was a good thing, if the bosses, when safe in the House of Commons, refused to listen to women, that one of them was coming to Belton Head, where it might be possible to get speech of him. Possible, it perhaps might be, but not easy; for the suffragettes, lightly spoken of as futile demonstrators, were, in fact, recognised as a formidable force; and wherever a Cabinet Minister went, he was surrounded by numberless precautions and protected by large bodies of police. The strange thing was that, in spite of police and precautions, the suffragettes generally managed to reach the place where they meant to be; and outside the Reform Club, on the twenty-first of December, a dozen of them were waiting when the Minister's motor-car drew up.

Sally had thought much about the bosses, had wondered often what they looked like, but she had never seen one till now. He did not look very different from anybody else, not more imposing, not more formidable. But she must not stand staring there; she had her part to play. That part was not to address the Minister, but to distract attention while her companions surrounded him. She was glad she had not to speak to him; she did not want to speak; she could not, she told herself, talk grand enough. A street crowd she did not mind, nor one of her own degree; but a boss needed a lady to address him.

Her own part, however, she could do, and she did it deftly. She had an empty ginger-beer bottle in her hand, and she threw it into the car from which the Minister had alighted; she threw it, without hurting anybody, exactly where she meant it to go. The act called attention to the car; it also called attention to Sally, who was arrested for disorderly conduct, and taken before a magistrate. She could not be tried then, so was remanded for a week. That was good; whatever her sentence, she would not, at any rate, have to spend Christmas in prison; she knew that she would be bailed out, and, later in the afternoon, applied for bail.

"So that I can have my Christmas dinner at home," said Sally. Joe was gone for ever, but she had still the mother who was "put upon."

But no, even though she promised to be of good behaviour till after the time of remand, bail was not allowed; Christmas must be spent in prison after all.

Sally's heart sank; it was a dreary prospect; more than dreary, for the spectre of forcible feeding stood waiting in the foreground; and in her mind was the knowledge of what had been done, in divers ways, to the prisoners at Wenlock Gaol, besides the recollection of her own imprisonment in Holloway. Then comfort sprang up within her; she was not convicted, had not been tried yet, was on remand; she could meet with no very bad treatment.

The treatment, she found, was just the same as if she had been convicted, except that she was allowed to wear her own clothing; and she had no choice, therefore, in her loyalty to the plan of campaign, but to protest against it. She remembered the dark, damp cell of her previous imprisonment, and her body was less strong than it had been at that time; but she remembered too that other women had gone through worse sufferings than her own, and made up her mind to put up with whatever might be in store for her.

She refused the prison food, and had, at any rate, the satisfaction of knowing that for that night, whatever might come later, she would breathe fresh air. Before lying down to sleep, Sally broke her windows. The air smelt doubly sweet coming through those broken panes, perhaps because the air inside was so close and stale; but whatever the reason, the fact remained, and she made the most of it.

But now, she knew, she must expect the worst; the refractory cell would be her lot, cold and airless and damp; and solitude and feeding by force. But her spirit rose to the call upon it; and even while her dread became more definite, her courage grew. "In for a penny, in for a pound," she thought; and in the morning, half in fear and half in defiance, she barricaded her cell. There was not a great deal wherewith to construct a barricade, but Sally made the most of what there was, and for a good little while kept the officials out. It was exciting, the most exciting experience she had ever had; the joy of battle awoke in her, and coolness developed as the contest lengthened; there was satisfaction in circumventing the enemy, and for a time, in spite of her empty stomach, in spite of her scanty clothing, for her clothes were still wet with the snow of the previous day, and she was clad only in her under-garments; in spite of all this, Sally almost enjoyed herself.

But the battle was an unequal one, and she was bound to lose it. The barricade was broken down, her cell was entered, and then there was no more enjoyment and no more triumph for Sally. It was natural, perhaps, that the head wardress and her subordinates should be angry; natural, perhaps, too, since human nature has its ugly side, that they should vent their anger by an unmerciful pommelling of the refractory prisoner. Sally, when defeat was certain, had retreated to the bed, but she was pulled from off it and left, when her summary punishment was over, lying on the floor.

She lay there for some time, pain-stricken, exhausted, unable to move; and, as she lay, the thought of Joe Whittle came to her, and of Mary Ann Dobbs. She seemed to see them walking together along Camden Road, where she and Joe had often walked; free in the open street, all London theirs to walk in, the whole world theirs. They were happy, and she did not grudge them their happiness, not she; they seemed too far away for her to have a thought of envy. She hardly envied them even their freedom, for freedom was not much use if you could not move, if it hurt you every time you stirred; and it did hurt—oh yes; it was best to lie still. It was cold, though, horribly cold on the floor; better to try and crawl slowly—it doesn't matter how slowly; there is plenty of time in prison—back to the bed. Never mind though it hurts; it will be better when she is once in bed; never mind the getting there! Ah, that's it; at last! Yes, it is better; she can rest now more comfortably; it is good to rest.

Rest truly is good; but, just because it is good, there is none for the wicked; Sally, at any rate, did not have much of it. She had not lain long upon the bed when the doctor came in; a man dapper, young, with a poor opinion of women at best, and none at all for the genus suffragette.

"You have refused your food," he said.

"Yes."

"Do you mean to go on refusing?"

"Yes."

"Then I shall feed you at once."

Sally made no answer; there seemed to be no answer with any point in it; nor did the doctor seem to expect one. He went away almost immediately; Sally, shivering with cold and dread, asked herself for how long.

It was but a few minutes later that the cell door opened again. So he was back! No, he wasn't; it was women who entered now.

"Get up and put your clothes on!"

"They're wet, 'orrid wet."

"Put them on, I say!"

"I dunno as I can. I'm bruised an' sore."

"We'll soon see."

Sally was dragged off the bed and forced into her clothes, and then came—well, she had foreseen it, of course, had known that it was bound to come—the punishment cell.

Very cold that cell was on this December day; but it must be always cold, in June as well as in December, for no sun could ever reach it, no warm outside air could ever penetrate to its gloomy depths. So Sally thought as she was led into it; so she thought while her hands were handcuffed behind her back; so she felt, more and more certainly, as she lay and shivered on the damp floor, unable to raise herself. She did not see Joe any more now, nor Mary Ann; she was too cold to see anything, and too tired; had it not been for the utter discomfort of the position in which she had been left, she must have slept from exhaustion.

She lay there for some hours, conscious only of pain and cold and stiffness. If she could free her arms! or even just turn over! It was very quiet; it was almost like being dead and buried to lie there, hearing nothing, seeing almost nothing; only that dead people did not feel; at least she hoped not, oh, she hoped not; for it would be awful to be left—left as she was left—left—forever, in cold and pain.

A wardress came in at last and lifted her on to the board that served for bed. It was better than the floor, and her clothes were getting drier now; but oh, the pain in those arms, dragged backwards, that she could not move! So the day passed.

In the evening the doctor came again, and Sally was removed to another cell, which, he said, would be warmer. The mere prospect of warmth was a boon, but alas for Sally's hopes, the warmth was only prospective; the second cell proved to be as cold as the first. Yet the night was better than the day, in that the handcuffs were removed for a minute or two, and her arms brought to the front of her body before they were put on again. At least she could lie on her back now; that was something; at least and at last, she was able to fall asleep. And while they are asleep all prisoners are free.

CHAPTER XXXIX
THE LONG NIGHT

"Our chain on silence clanks.
Time leers between, above his twiddling thumbs."

George Meredith[1]

The next morning Sally was taken before the visiting magistrates. It was true that she had broken windows; but Sally, on her side, had charges to bring against the prison officials. They had no right to treat her as she had been treated while she was on remand.

Yes, said the magistrates, the wardresses were justified in what they had done.

Sally tried again. They had no right to threaten her with forcible feeding while she was on remand.

She found that a suffragette on remand could be threatened or treated as the prison officials thought fit.

Then back to the cell; and the second day was as long and as lonely as the first; but a worse day, taking it as a whole, because of the evening.

In the evening several wardresses came to Sally in her cell.

"You are to come to the doctor's room."

"I ain't coming; not of my own will."

"You had best come quietly. You'll have to come."

"I ain't comin'."

Foolish Sally to resist the irresistible! What is the good of it? None, in a sense; in another sense, it was sticking to the protest against being treated other than as a political prisoner. To give in would mean

---

1   George Meredith (1828–1909), *Modern Love* (1862).

to sanction the treatment awarded to suffragette prisoners, would mean to fail in carrying out the plan of campaign; "them ladies" would never submit; no more would Sally.

"I ain't comin'," she said.

The wardresses had been upheld by the visiting magistrates, the wardresses could do as they would. They dragged her to the foot of the stairs, with her hands handcuffed behind her; then, face downwards, they carried her by the arms and legs to the doctor's room. After all, they had to do as they were bid, these wardresses; their task was to bring Sally from her cell hither; they had accomplished their task. Or part of their task, for there was more to do yet. The prisoner had to be placed in a chair, the handcuffs removed and her arms held firmly, so that she could not move, while the doctor and his assistant forced down the stomach-tube into the prisoner's stomach, and then poured in the food.

It is well to feed the hungry, and so, and thus, in His Majesty's prisons, in the years of grace 1909 and 1910, prisoners, who adopted the hunger strike, were fed.

The feeding over, Sally was handcuffed once more and walked to the head of the stairs. Strange that she, who had looked with shrinking dread from the attic window in Brunton Street, across roofs and chimney-pots to Holloway Gaol, and had told herself then that prison was a thing she could not face, strange that now, after the worst that prison could bring her, she still had some spirit left.

"I ain't goin' back to that there cell," said Sally.

There were three wardresses with her: two seized her by the shoulders, the third kicked her from behind. So she went down the stairs, till she reached the bottom step, and at the bottom step the wardresses relaxed their hold. Then, with her hands secured behind her and no means of resisting the impetus of her descent, she fell forward, on her head.[1]

That was the end of the trouble, so far, at any rate, as the wardresses were concerned. Sally made no further resistance; indeed,

---

[1] Colmore draws on the prison experiences of Selina Martin and Leslie Hall who were arrested in Liverpool, and sent to Walton Gaol, after Martin threw a ginger-beer bottle into Asquith's empty car. Sylvia Pankhurst writes that Martin "was carried face downward by the arms and legs—'frog marching' as it is called—her face being allowed to bump on the steps. The doctor jeered at Leslie Hall, telling her that she was 'mentally sick,' and that feeding her was 'like stuffing a turkey for Christmas'" (329).

she lay quite still. The wardresses picked her up and carried her to her cell.

Meanwhile, on that same evening, Mrs. Merton, the successful journalist, who, as Sir Charles Martin had said, was the sort of woman a man liked to talk to, was entertaining a small company at dinner. Sir Charles was one of her guests, and Robbie Colquhoun was another. The talk was animated, as talk always was at Mrs. Merton's. The subject under discussion was John Gorton's new play.

"Oh, it's clever of course," the hostess said, "but he's getting tiresome—preachy. I don't like problems on the stage."

"Except the sex problem, I suppose you mean," said Robbie Colquhoun in his slow way.

"Love's young dream is always interesting," said Sir Charles. "Eh?" He looked round the table for support.

"It's the sort of thing everybody understands, at any rate," somebody said.

"I thought plays and books were to make you understand things you don't," remarked a girl rather timidly.

Robbie Colquhoun nodded at her across the table, but nobody else paid any attention to her observation.

"It doesn't matter what a play's about, so long as it's a good play," said a short dark man. "The subject's nothing; it's the way you treat it. Take any problem you like as far as I'm concerned: it isn't the problem, it's the treatment that matters."

"Hear that, Race?" asked Sir Charles mischievously.

"Yes, I hear; but what has it got to do with me? I'm not a playwright, nor a novelist, not even a critic."

"No, but you're a member of the Government, and you've got your problem, and you've got your treatment."

"The eternal suffragette, I suppose," said a lady, with a very high colour and a very low dress.

"Oh, I'm so sick of her," sighed the short dark man.

"So is Race, I expect," laughed Sir Charles.

"And the Press," said Robbie Colquhoun. "Not in London, of course; the London Press is like a well-trained dog, it don't bark at the well-dressed; but the provincial Press is getting a bit sick over the treatment."

"The forcible feeding, do you mean?" asked the timid girl.

"Disgusting!" said Mrs. Merton.

"You think so?" exclaimed Sir Charles, opening his eyes very wide.

"I mean those very tiresome women. I approve of the vote, as you all know—in principle, logically I mean, though what the good of it is supposed to be I don't fathom; but I've no patience with women who think they're going to get it by behaving like naughty children."

"Suck it in through a stomach-pump, eh?" said Sir Charles.

"Colquhoun is glaring at you both," observed Cyril Race.

"So sorry," answered Mrs. Merton. "I forgot. You're one of the flowers of chivalry, aren't you?"

"Nothing so pretty, I'm afraid; the fruit of brutality is quite good enough for me."

"Brutality, ha ha!" from Sir Charles. "Now we shall have Race's back up."

"Don't be afraid. My back is hardened."

"What do you think," Mrs. Merton went on, addressing Robbie, "of women concealing themselves on a roof, in order to interrupt a meeting? I was in the house when they were discovered; and what do you think they did? Giggled."

"Some women will giggle at any occupation."

"Do you call sitting on a roof an occupation?"

"Temporary," said Robbie. "I have known women to giggle when a man would swear. Don't know that I could say one's more futile than the other."

"Now tell me this"—Mrs. Merton looked round the table—"have you ever met a suffragette whom you would care to *marry*? Honest Injun."

"Honest Injun, certainly," answered Robbie.

"Honest Injun, no," said Race.

"Honest Injun, the only woman I want to marry is not a suffragette," said Sir Charles.

On that same evening Rachel Cullen and Edith Carstairs dined with Lady Henry Hill at the Lyceum Club, and after dinner the three sat in a corner of the drawing-room and talked.

"It's no use saying anything more," Geraldine said. "I have quite made up my mind."

"What does Lord Henry say?"

"Nothing: because he knows nothing. If I told him, he would be miserable. Nobody knows or will know, but you two."

"Except the leaders, at the office, of course."

"Certainly not; no. I am doing it entirely on my own responsibility. They know nothing about it; whatever happens, I alone am answerable. I wanted you two to know, because if I were to get very ill, or—or anything, it must be known what becomes of me. And I can trust you not to talk."

"You don't know when?" asked Rachel.

"No; the next time a protest is necessary."

"I'm afraid that is not very far ahead. Did you see about Angela Sayte, how her wrists were hurt with the handcuffs?"

"Yes. I'm wondering how they are treating Sally—Sally Simmonds. She's a working woman, you see."

"The trying part of it is," said Edith, "that people don't seem to be able to understand *why* women go through these things."

"Does anybody ever see why people do things," Rachel answered, "until years after they are done? Then they look back over their shoulders at the things, and seem to see, and begin to applaud."

"Obviously, it is difficult to see a thing in its right character," said Geraldine, "when you are close up against it, unless it is quite small. Take a mountain, for instance. It's the same with movements. That is why it is so much easier to be a politician than a statesman."

Edith was staying the night with Rachel Cullen.

"You're not going to prison again, Rachel?" she asked on the way home.

"Not if I can avoid it. I'm going with Geraldine on her tour, because I can help her in many ways."

"I never understood what it meant, the going to prison and the rest of it, till I went to that awful bazaar."

"Poor Edith! It isn't everybody, fortunately, who takes it as hardly as you do. Still there are many—"

"Yes, there must be many. I wonder if Sally—how she's getting on?"

"Poor little Sally!"

Sally lay in her cell; awake, because the hunger pangs would not let her sleep. The feeding had made her sick and had added pain to faintness; her throat was swollen and sore; her mouth was dry. If only she had somebody to give her a drink as she, in past days, had given drinks to thirsty little Bilkeses!

The night was very long, as nights are in December, and the day, when it came, always lagged in forcing its way into that dark place. Sally lay and thought of those who were thinking of her: of Miss Carstairs with her delicate face, of Lady 'Ill. Those two together always led to Littlehampton. What a time she had had there! a rippin' time. Perhaps, when she came out of prison, she might be able to go to Littlehampton again. She would need what she had gone there for before; a thorough change. To walk along the sands with Lady 'Ill and watch the tide come in! That would make up for all the loneliness, all the suffering. The tide; that was what Lady 'Ill had said about the Cause. "Nobody can hold the waves back, Sally. In the end the tide must come in."

"We can't hold it back," she had said, "but we can help it on by clearing away the rocks."

She, Sally, was helping it now, perhaps. Perhaps; but the night was very long.

CHAPTER XL
A PUBLIC SERVANT

"Their services are, clock-like, to be set
Backward and forward, at their lord's command."

Ben Jonson[1]

Edith was in the train on her way to Lightpool,[2] to stay with Aunt Lizzie. She had been very glad to accept Aunt Lizzie's invitation, because she knew that Geraldine was to be in Lightpool that week, and now, owing to a letter received that morning from Rachel Cullen, she was particularly anxious to see her two friends.

The General Election was in full swing. Right honourable gentlemen were stumping the country, informing electors that taxation without representation was tyranny, the while women were impris-

---

1   Ben Jonson (1573?–1637), *A Pleasant Comedy Called: The Case is Altered* (1598?).
2   Liverpool.

oned for upholding that very principle. The Liberal papers were jubilant over Tory meetings interrupted by democratic voters; Edith had a paper in her hand, which told her, under the heading "Baffled Tories," how a speaker "entirely failed to get a hearing, owing to the pertinent and searching questions and deadly interruptions of stern Democrats, seething with indignation." Yet some women who had asked one of the Liberal leaders a few questions as to the granting of the suffrage to their own sex were accused in that very same paper of disgraceful conduct, although so little was the meeting disturbed that the majority of the audience were unaware that they had spoken. "If these disreputable but futile tactics are really intended," the correspondent went on, "to influence the election results, it only shows how little do women understand political warfare in England." Edith, reading the two accounts, felt that women were to be excused if they did find it a little difficult to understand English political manoeuvres.

She began to wonder if the politicians eagerly seeking election meant anything they said; if the papers, reporting their doings and sayings, really believed what they wrote. Was there any reality of principle or ideal behind all this clamour of "seething indignation" and the like? or were all the noble sentiments party cries, and politics a mere game? It was pain and grief to her to behold the Liberal party devoid of the halo that, till lately, had always surrounded it in her eyes. Alas! had it been only in her eyes? That was the doubt that hurt her. Nay, but it had noble traditions; splendid deeds stood on the register of its achievements. If it would only act up to those traditions! Add to its achievements one which lay on the direct path of its principles! To deny those principles, to juggle with them, interpreting them now in one way, now in another, to suit or excuse a policy; that was mean, that was degenerate. In the pain which Edith suffered through and because of the suffrage movement, there were pangs, many and acute, due to her love of Liberalism, her grief at the stains cast upon it by the setting up of one standard of political honesty where men were concerned, and another in dealing with women.

Her thoughts went on from women as a whole to the particular women in whom, at that time, she was particularly interested: Geraldine Hill, Rachel, Sally Simmonds, Angela Sayte. Something of what Sally had undergone had leaked out; it was not to be wondered at that there was to be another protest. But Geraldine—Edith's heart sank, knowing, as she did, what Geraldine meant to do; and it was no use to remonstrate with her, to argue or to implore. Well, she could see her to-morrow, and have, at any rate, the meagre satisfaction of knowing the worst.

At Lightpool, on the platform, trying to point out her trunk amidst a heap of luggage, she suddenly heard her name.

"Miss Carstairs! It is an unexpected pleasure to see you in Lightpool."

"Dr. Dean! I certainly never expected—That's it"—to the porter—"over there, the brown leather one with 'E.C.' on it. I sometimes come, because my aunt has a house a little way out in the country."

"May I get you a cab?"

"Thank you; my aunt has sent her motor. It's waiting—over there."

As she walked on, Dr. Dean walked beside her. "Odd, my meeting you," he said. "I've just been seeing somebody off."

Edith was thinking of the last time she had met him; on that spring day just after she had seen, in the place where the sign-post ordinarily stood, instead of the sign-post, a cross.

"I was surprised, too, to see you, at first," she said, "but, of course, I remember now, your appointment is here, in Lightpool."

"An appointment, Miss Carstairs, which some of your sex make a difficult one. I have had to add a new petition to the Litany: 'From the vagaries of the suffragettes, good Lord deliver us!'"

Edith had been doing her best to feel friendly in her mind, to be pleasant in her manner, but now her old dislike of the man came back in its strength.

"Indeed?" she said coldly. "May I ask in what way my friends have annoyed you?"

"Your friends! Ha ha! Very good. But I'm not so easily taken in, Miss Carstairs."

"I have no desire to take you in, I assure you. I am quite serious."

"Of course, of course." From his tone, he evidently still thought she was joking. "Well, if you want to know, I'm senior medical officer at Belton Gaol."[1]

---

1 Walton Gaol.

"Oh!" Edith had been about to step into the motor; she faced round. "Then you—then it's you—then Sally Simmonds—you must know her."

"Know her! I should think I do; wish I didn't."

Edith's whole tone and manner changed; she was no longer the dignified Miss Carstairs.

"Oh, Dr. Dean," she said beseechingly, "be good to her!"

"Upon my word! Then you really do know her? But she's a—quite a common woman; no class, no education. By Jove! you stagger me, Miss Carstairs."

"We don't think of class, or education, in our Society; and I—I'm miserable about Sally. From what I hear—know—Oh, will you do what you can for her?"

"Very sorry, Miss Carstairs, but a public servant, as I happen to be, has to put his duty before the pleasure of obliging his friends. It's a thing, I know, that women don't understand; but that's the way men look at it."

It was pleasant to have the tables turned. The last time they had talked together he had been the suppliant and she, or so he put it to himself, had scorned him; now the supplication was on her side, and it was for him to take down her pride a little.

"I beg your pardon!" The supplication was entirely gone from Edith's voice and eyes; her glance went past him, her tone was like ice. "I apologise for imagining that it was possible for us to think alike."

She drove away, saying to herself that he was odious—odious, and that to appeal to a man like that would make him worse, not better. She was glad of the ten miles drive; it gave her time to cool down; but Sally and Angela; and Dr. Dean doing his duty as a public servant!

"Do you know anything of the doctor at Belton Gaol?" she asked Mrs. Joyce.

"How should I, my dear? You should ask the suffragettes?"

"By reputation, I mean."

"No, nothing. But, as I say, you should ask—"

"Oh don't, Aunt Lizzie! I'm miserable about the women in prison; I know two of them, Angela Sayte and Sally Simmonds, the servant girl, you remember, that I told you about; and the treatment—well, I simply can't speak of it."

"I confess I think they've gone too far with the feeding; it's a brutal thing."

"Brutal! Just look at the scores of doctors who have protested against it. And no notice taken."

"At the same time, you must remember that it's a most difficult position for the authorities."

"I remember nothing, except that what women are asking for is a thing which morally and logically they ought to have, and that everything, *everything*, Aunt Lizzie, that has happened, is happening, and will happen, is because of the refusal to give it to them."

Aunt Lizzie did not agree with her, Edith knew; but that was the comfort of Aunt Lizzie, she didn't mind what you said; and even if she didn't agree, she was always reasonable, not blindly prejudiced. It was a relief to be with her after Agatha Brand, who was intelligent but limited; after Monty, who was loyal to the re-incarnation of Mrs. Brown, but superior and dogmatic; after her mother, who was like a reed shaken by the wind. The wind, at that time, blew from the vicarage, and Mrs. Carstairs was continually engaged in trying to stem the blast, both to secure peace for herself and rehabilitation for Edith. The only comfort in the situation at Vale End was that Monty had pronounced it damned cheek on the part of Uncle B. and Aunt Elinor to shut the door on his sister.

The next day Edith went into Lightpool to see Lady Henry. Geraldine had told her that, though she was not lodging in the house to which Edith was to come, she would be waiting there, ready to receive her; and Edith, arriving in a flush of eager expectation, conscious too that she was a little late, and full of apologies, was acutely disappointed to find that Geraldine had not yet come. Rachel Cullen, for whom she was to inquire, was there, and in the room with Rachel a working woman, judging from her dress, a member of the WSPU of course, possibly a new recruit; but no Geraldine.

"This is Anne Heeley," said Rachel. "Geraldine wanted you to see her."

"How do you do?"

The woman—she had a delicate face—bowed her head and looked at Edith through thick glasses, but did not speak.

"Where is Geraldine? Isn't she coming? I thought she *said* she would be here before I was."

"It's all right, then. As you don't know me, nobody else will."

Anne Heeley took off her glasses. "Edith!"

"Oh, Geraldine!" The tears came into Edith's eyes. "You've—I can't bear to see you like that—and you've cut off your beautiful hair."

"It had to go. It's never any use doing a thing by halves."

"Certainly no one can accuse you of that. And when Rachel told me in her letter that there was to be a protest."

"I should think so. What they've done to Sally—well—Did you hear of the frog-marching, and the letting her head bump from step to step of those stone stairs? I can't tell you what I felt and feel about it."

Edith had not heard of that; she had much to hear, of what had happened and of what was to take place. And all the time that she was listening, she had a vision of Dr. Dean standing by the motor, describing Sally as a woman of no class.

Anne Heeley would be a woman of no class and Dr. Dean would have dominion over her. Oh, if Edith had only taken more trouble to propitiate him, been more friendly in those bygone days, when he was at Pagnell, she might have had some influence with him now. But no; there was no mean course, she knew, with Dr. Dean; propitiation was useless, friendship impossible; she must either have agreed to marry him or made him her enemy. "A public servant has to put his duty before the pleasure of obliging his friends." In those words he had conveyed to her that she was not forgiven; by those words, and the look on his face, and the note in his voice.

She motored back to Aunt Lizzie's with those words and that look and that tone distinct in her mind, and, side by side with them, the knowledge that, on the morrow, Geraldine was to make her protest.

CHAPTER XLI
EDITH AND DR. DEAN

"The Devil has no stauncher ally than want of perception."

Philip H. Wicksteed[1]

On the morrow the protest was made. Edith, waiting in a sickness of dread for news, heard the news that same evening.

A great crowd, consisting largely of the men of the city, had marched to Belton Gaol to protest against the treatment meted out to Sally. Geraldine had led them; outside the prison she had addressed them, calling upon them to follow her within the prison precincts, and then, moving across the road, had been arrested.[2]

Edith had expected the arrest, had known that it must take place; but the knowledge that Geraldine was actually in prison, not as Geraldine, but as a working woman, who would be treated as working women had been treated lately, caused her almost as much distress as though she had been unprepared for it. And she must not show her distress; for Geraldine's secret was in her keeping, and she must not, by any symptom of grief or anxiety, run the risk of betraying it.

The next day she learned, late in the day, that Anne Heeley had been sentenced to fourteen days in the third division with hard labour. There was the option of a fine, which was, of course, as Edith knew it would be, refused; suffragettes did not admit the criminal character of their protests by paying fines, and Geraldine's object on this occasion was to prove that the treatment of suffragettes in prison varied with their social position.

The arrest and the sentence attracted no attention in the outer world. When Lady Henry Hill had been arrested most of the newspapers in the kingdom had recorded the fact; the Press took no notice of Anne Heeley. Who was Anne Heeley? Nobody. And so many women were arrested and imprisoned and forcibly fed in those days

---

1   The source of this quotation is unknown. Philip H. Wicksteed (1844–1927) was a noted economist and philosopher.

2   In January 1910 Lady Constance Lytton disguised herself as a working-class woman and gave herself the pseudonym Jane Warton. She was arrested in Liverpool for exhorting a crowd to protest against forcible feeding, and for dropping stones over the prison governor's hedge (see Appendix C1).

that accounts of them had become a drug in the journalistic market. Nobody took any notice, nobody cared; Aunt Lizzie went on quite unconcernedly with her canvassing and her getting up of meetings on behalf of the Liberal candidate.

What was Edith to do? She could not speak, she could not act, and all the time she was haunted by the picture of Geraldine as a "woman of no class" and Dr. Dean doing his duty by her. What could she do? Nothing; and yet something must be done, something, at any rate, attempted. She might not succeed; she might even make matters worse; nay, that was not possible when she thought of Sally; certainly she would try. Pride? that was nothing; to put pride in her pocket for Geraldine's sake was almost a joy. Persuasion? There lay the doubt; she feared that no powers of that kind remained to her in connection with Dr. Dean. But she would try, she would use her utmost endeavour; in any case, it was better to try; even if she failed, it was better than to do nothing.

So she wrote to Dr. Dean. Would he be so kind as to see her, to give her but a few minutes? She would come to the prison, or, if he preferred it, would receive him at No. 12 Drayton Street, at any time that suited him, but the sooner the better. She particularly wished to speak to him.

Rachel Cullen was lodging in Drayton Street, and Edith knew well that Rachel would give her the use of her sitting-room.

It was on Sunday that she wrote the letter, on Sunday morning after breakfast; and all the time she was in church she was rehearsing the interview between herself and Dr. Dean, rehearsing it as far as her own words, her own demeanour, were concerned; refusing to ascribe to him the words and looks which her knowledge of him prompted her to allot to his part.

One of the men servants was going in to Lightpool in the afternoon, and to him Edith confided her letter, to be delivered at the earliest hour possible. Then, having spent the morning in rehearsing the scene between herself and Dr. Dean, she spent the afternoon in wondering whether it would take place. Would he see her or would he refuse? There was no possibility of knowing: she could only wait.

Never had she looked so eagerly for a letter; but, thank heaven, the letter was there; suspense as to that, at any rate, was at an end. She gave a little gasp as, opening it, she read that Dr. Dean would see her. He was not so bad, perhaps, after all; he would see her, but—it was a big but—he had a horrid way of putting things. He would be happy to meet her that afternoon, Monday, at three o'clock, at 12 Drayton Street; he did not consider that to come to the prison was quite the thing for a lady.

A lady! no; it was only bad women, common women, working women who were not out of place in prison. Never mind; she must make the best of it; he would see her at any rate, and that was something. She told Aunt Lizzie that she wanted to go in to Lightpool that afternoon, to Rachel Cullen's rooms, but that she would take the tram-car; it was not far to walk, she would find her own way.

"Very well; I do rather want the car this afternoon; we have a meeting at a village farther out. Is Lady Henry still in Lightpool?"

Edith hesitated; was she or was she not? She decided that, as Anne Heeley had taken her place, Lady Henry was no longer there, and answered, "No."

"Gone home again, I hope."

"No," Edith answered again.

"Poor Lord Henry! It's really hard lines on him to have his wife stumping the country instead of looking after him."

"He's stumping the country himself just now, at least, his constituency."

"I suppose I mustn't say that she ought to be helping him?"

"Most certainly, dear Aunt Lizzie, that is one of the things that you must not say."

Three o'clock! Long before then Edith was in Drayton Street, had seen Rachel and explained to her what she was about to do, had walked from the fire to the window and back from the window to the fire many times.

Dr. Dean was a little late, and apologised for keeping her waiting. It was a good beginning, and his manner was polite; he seemed, indeed, disposed to be conversational. This was all very well, but Edith had not come there to be asked how she liked Lightpool and to discuss that city and its inhabitants, and she was wondering how she was going to ask what she had come to ask when he himself gave her an opening.

"And now, Miss Carstairs, may I ask to what I owe the pleasure of seeing you?"

"Certainly. I—I don't want to take up too much of your time. I asked if you would be so kind as to see me because I wanted to know—to ask—there is a woman in Belton Gaol"—she saw his face darken—"a woman that I—"

"Oh, you mean the woman you spoke about the other day—Simmonds? She was released this morning."

"Yes, I know. No, it isn't her; it's—she was arrested last Friday—Anne Heeley. I am very much interested in her."

"'Pon my word, Miss Carstairs, you've got very democratic since I last had the pleasure of seeing you. Then you were inclined to snub people, such people as my humble self, for instance; and now you seem to be hand-in-glove with all the low-class women in the country."

"In our Society we are all comrades, whether we have titles, or whether we work for our living."

"In your Society! You really are, then, a suffragette? 'Pon my word, I thought you were joking that day on the platform. A suffragette! Miss Edith Carstairs, a suffragette! By Jove!"

"I don't know why you should be so surprised."

"Because you always seemed to me so dainty, so—so sort of high bred, you know. I never thought you'd go and mix yourself up with a lot of women who go to prison."

"Some of those women are of a higher class than I."

"Never heard of any, except that Lady Henry Hill, and her they let out at once."

"I know; because she had a title."

"Blue blood is more delicate than red, Miss Carstairs, and it would have been mighty awkward if she'd popped off under the feeding."

"There are other women quite as delicate as she is; this woman I came to speak to you about, she is a very delicate woman, not fit, really not fit, Dr. Dean, for hardship and rough treatment."

"Why does she put herself in the way of them, then? You don't suppose the penal system's going to be turned upside down to make prison a bed of roses for the suffragettes?"

How hard it was to be humble and not haughty! But Edith would lie down and let him trample upon her, if by so doing she could serve Geraldine.

"I don't want to criticise the system," she said. "I only, want to ask you, as a personal favour, to be kind—as considerate as your duty allows you to be—to this woman who is really delicate. You must have a good deal of power—of influence—"

"Just enough to make it worth your while, if you think of going in for this martyr business, to get yourself arrested here in Lightpool. I promise you I won't be hard on *you*, Miss Carstairs."

"I have no intention of being arrested." Edith hesitated, then made an effort, and spoke in her most winning voice, in her most winning way, the voice and the way that Robbie Colquhoun, ever since her childhood, had never been able to resist. "Won't you be kind to me by proxy, to this woman I am interested in?"

Dr. Dean looked at her, and Edith's heart contracted; she knew before he said it what he was going to say.

"I will be very kind, just as kind as I know how, to anybody you like, if you choose. It rests with you."

Edith shrank away. "How?"

"I said that day, the last time I saw you before leaving Pagnell, when you refused—even to consider my proposal—I said, I told you, that I was not a man to be trifled with, and that I should never ask you again. Well, I'm a man of my word, and I assure you I didn't go on hankering and pining after you; indeed, I have been paying attention to a young lady here in Lightpool, who is not likely to say no. But after I had seen you that day on the platform—"

"Oh, don't, don't!"

"After seeing you," he went on, "I felt I wouldn't mind throwing the other one over and having another try, if you gave me any encouragement."

"Oh, but I haven't."

"You have rather queer notions, Miss Carstairs. You write to an unmarried man and ask to see him alone, ask to come to his rooms, or for him to come and meet you, and you expect him to believe that he's not to make love to you?"

"I—I never thought of—of—"

"Come now, Miss Carstairs, come, Edith! I know a woman's got to pretend to hang back—it's one of the ways you lead us on; and, of course, you had to have an excuse to find out if I had changed my mind. But now that I've been frank, now I've shown you that it's all right, don't keep it up any longer. Drop Anne Heeley and come—Edith, I love you!"

Edith got up; she was utterly dismayed, completely miserable; she got up and went farther away from this man who was smiling at her.

"It's a mistake—altogether a mistake—I never—thought—dreamt—Oh, Dr. Dean, can't you understand—believe that, on the strength of our old—our former friendship, I have ventured to ask a favour of you?"

The smile went from the face on the other side of the table. "Do you mean to tell me that you're serious, really serious about this—what's her name?—this Heeley woman? That you came for nothing else but to try and wheedle me into showing favouritism to a prisoner you happen to be interested in?"

"I did come, yes, just to ask you to be gentle to a very delicate woman."

He stood silent, his brows drawn together, his face sullen. He had given himself away, a proceeding than which to a small nature there is nothing more humiliating.

"Well," he said at last, "you've made a fool of me for the second time; but don't think I'm a big enough fool to be made a cat's-paw for nothing. My love and my services go together, and I offered you both just now. If you're wise you'll accept them. I told you before I could make you care for me if I had the chance, and I'm not afraid. Promise to be my wife, Edith, and I'll answer for the rest."

The idea was deeply rooted in him that every woman was anxious to be married; a little pressure and all would be well.

Edith sat down again; she did not answer; she sat, one elbow on the table, her head resting on her hand, sat silent and thought. Should she do it, do what he asked her, and make it easier for Anne Heeley? It might mean the saving of Geraldine's life, might mean so much in many ways. Should she do it? If she did, there could be no drawing back; having gained her end, it would be utterly impossible to refuse afterwards to pay the price. Should she do it? She thought of Geraldine as she had seen her last, in the working girl's clothes; she thought of her as she had seen her first, on the smooth bare sands, with the tide, very gently, with a plashing of tiny waves, coming in. And thinking of her thus, and of what she had said that day, Edith knew very well what she ought to do, and what, most certainly, she should abstain from doing. It was womanhood that Geraldine cared about, not the advantage, when that advantage conflicted with the end she had in view, of any one woman, last and least of all when that woman was herself. It would hurt her far more that Edith should degrade her womanhood than any hurt that could be done her by prison officials; yes, even though that hurt should rob her of life itself. It would be an insult, not a benefit, to Geraldine to fall in with Dr. Dean's proposal.

Edith looked up and met his eyes. "I'm sorry. I could never return your love. It would be unfair and wrong to accept your offer."

"You mean that?"

"Absolutely."

"Then there is nothing more to be said."

She just shook her head; she could not speak.

She heard the door open and shut and knew that she was alone. When by and by Rachel came in she found her pale, dumb, trembling. It was some time before Edith could speak and tell what had happened.

CHAPTER XLII
WHAT IS IN A NAME

"Who would despise the people that have among them such women."

Judith 10:19

Anne Heeley had entered at once upon the hunger strike. It was true that Geraldine did nothing by halves; what Sally Simmonds had endured, that she intended, if necessary, to endure; and she would prove to the public that a working woman of precisely the same physique as the daughter-in-law of a duke received entirely different treatment from that accorded to the owner of a titled name.

On that Monday, while Edith was talking to Dr. Dean, she was in the punishment cell, taken there for refusing to perform hard labour. Outside, a winter sun was shining, but in the cell it was twilight; the only window was high up in the wall, small, barred, and of thickened glass; and through a similar tiny window over the door a gas-jet flickered, casting eerie shadows on the white-washed wall.

A wooden platform, raised a few inches from the ground, served as bed-board; and on it, her head on the wooden pillow, Geraldine lay. She had always suffered greatly from cold, and she suffered intensely now. She was weak from hunger; there was a curious feeling about her heart; with the best will in the world, she could not have performed hard labour. She lay there; she could only lie, she felt worse when she sat up; comforted by the knowledge that her husband was able to go on with his candidature undisturbed by any idea of what had befallen her, that the authorities had no suspicion of her identity, that nobody knew or could grieve over her condition, save only the two friends who would bear the knowledge bravely, for her sake who bore the suffering.

Towards evening a mattress was brought in and rugs; by dint of them, she was, if not warm, a little less cold. She slept fitfully, wakened constantly by the damp chill of the atmosphere, lulled to rest again by weakness and exhaustion.

It was not till five o'clock the next day that, for the first time, she was forcibly fed. No medical examination preceded the operation, no testing of her heart. What had been necessary in the case of Lady Henry Hill was quite superfluous where Anne Heeley was concerned.

Geraldine's imagination was stronger than Sally's, and had painted the horror of the process in no neutral tints; but the reality surpassed in every detail the worst that she had imagined. Afterwards, when she came out of prison, she refused steadfastly to cast blame upon the officials for the treatment she received from them; they were but the instruments, she maintained, of higher authorities, and could not be held responsible for the tasks set them to do, nor for the brutalising effects those tasks had upon them. But, at the time, it was hard, beyond even Geraldine's magnanimity, not to feel resentment at the indignities heaped upon her, not to feel that wardresses and doctor might have been a little less callous, a little more kindly.

After the feeding she was taken from the punishment cell to an ordinary cell, where she had daylight, when it was day, for there was a window opposite her bed. It looked only on to a narrow prison yard; but light will find its way into the dreariest places, if it be given a bare chance; and light came into Geraldine's cell and made it better for Anne Heeley than the punishment cell had been.

Yet light, entering in the morning, had its burden of dread, for it meant that with a new day the feeding must be gone through again.

Geraldine's delicacy made the forcible administration of food especially difficult, both for her and for those whose task it was to feed her. All the time it lasted her writhing, straining body rebelled against it; all the time her stomach rejected the food poured into it; and this physical weakness on the part of the woman of no class made the doctor angry.

"You did that on purpose," he said. "If you do it again to-morrow, I shall feed you twice."

If Edith had known! But Edith, fortunately, miserable and anxious as she was, did not know.

Twice a day and every day the feeding took place; twice a day Geraldine passed through the torture of it, the intolerable sickness, which was not only a misery to herself, but disgusted the wardresses and infuriated the doctor. She met the daily ordeal with a physical dread she was quite unable to overcome; as the time for it approached she waited trembling, suffering in anticipation the inevitable pangs and degradation; and when her tormentors were actually there, it was an added trial that she was incapable of concealing from them what she deemed a cowardice.

And yet it never occurred to her to take the only way of escape, to put an end to it all by submission. She had but to take a mouthful or two of the food provided, and all this agony would cease at once. Was it worth while to endure it? That was a question Geraldine never asked herself. She was there for the sake of the working, the unknown women; women whose treatment while they were in prison was unscrutinised, whose accounts of that treatment when they came out were unheeded. But the experiences of Anne Heeley would be recounted by Geraldine Hill, and it never occurred to her to cut them short.

Yet each day became more difficult than the last; each day the things which tried her in the prison routine tried her more acutely; each night the putting out of the lights jarred ever more painfully on her nerves. At eight o'clock it began, at the farther end of the long, long landing; a sharp rap with a key on the little glass spy-hole, and the wardress's voice shouting, "Are you all right?" Nearer and nearer it came, sharp, continuous, sometimes repeated at the cell of a prisoner too drowsy, or too poorly, it might be, to answer at once; and once it had begun, it was impossible to do anything but listen to, and for, the rasping, insistent sounds, growing ever more distinct and aggressive, till her own cell was reached, and on her own spy-hole came the clatter, and to her was shouted the inquiry, "Are you all right?"

"All right," she had to answer, and then came darkness, and the noise passed on.

One night, when the lights had long been out and it was quite quiet in the prison, Geraldine awoke. It was the cold that had waked her, she supposed; perhaps that special dead cold which comes before the dawn, for her body was numb, chilled through and through, the circulation seeming to have ceased in hands and feet, seeming as if it soon would cease in all her frame. Life seemed ebbing away from her, gently, peacefully, without struggle, without pain. So—was she going to be released—that way? through the door that needed no key?

Happiness, full and exquisite, took possession of her. Oh, the joy of it! To escape, so easily; to slip out from the weakness and the hunger and the cold, and the horror of cruel hands and the suffocating tube! She had not known till now how great the suffering had been; till now, when it was almost—almost over. For she had but to lie still and let the cold creep up and up, and so, quite easily, glide away. She had always heard that it was peaceful to die in the snow; it was true, must be true; strange that the cold which always, all her life, had brought her suffering, should be so gentle now, so kindly, such a friend. In the morning her cell would be empty, alike of Anne Heeley and of Geraldine Hill; there would be one less suffragette to feed; and the others—

The others! They would be still there; in the world; within and without the prison; working, suffering, enduring; while she—Ah no, no, and alas! The door is open, freedom is beckoning; but she must not go. Coward to slip away, leaving, the burden she has shrunk from bearing, to be borne by other shoulders! It must not be, she dare not let it be. Rise up, weak spirit that has faltered and almost failed, and spur the body, that is your link with the world, into being again!

Geraldine sat up in the prison bed: with a great effort sat up, and began to rub and chafe her hands and feet. Then, when some little movement seemed to be in the stagnant blood, when some little power er seemed to awake in the numbed limbs, she left her bed and paced and paced the few yards of her cell, till the ebbing life came back.

And as she walked, all the sorrow of the world was about her; all the pain of weak, defenceless, struggling, suffering beings swept through her soul and across her vision. Sweated women she saw, gaunt, ugly, starved, with half the womanhood and all the charm of it crushed out of them; street women she saw, buying with their bodies the food they might not earn; children she saw, stunted, joyless, ungainly; animals, helpless, dumb, used in all sorts of cruel inhuman ways. There was much work to do, for her and for all women, work that, save by the help of women, would never be done. And she had almost fled from the doing of it. Almost, but not quite. She had been given another chance. She hailed it with humility, and in thankfulness took up once more the burden of physical being.

CHAPTER XLIII
THE VALLEY OF VISION

"Out of the woods my Master came,
Content with death and shame
When death and shame would woo Him last,
From under the trees they drew Him last:
'Twas on a tree they slew Him—last,
When out of the woods He came."

Sidney Lanier[1]

One of Anne Heeley's neighbours in the cells was a girl who was nervous and could not sleep. So long as there was light, daylight, or the electric light provided when daylight failed, she seemed to get on fairly well; once, or perhaps twice in the day, she would rap upon the dividing wall, making speechless appeal for human sympathy, but that was all. But after the lights were out, loneliness seemed to grow upon her; it seemed as if fear came with the darkness; and time after time, through the long night, Geraldine would be roused by the beseeching reiterated knocking on the wall. Her own bed was not against the wall which stood between her and the cell whence came the knocks, and every time the rapping came Geraldine had to get up, in order to answer it. It was a service she never failed in, no matter how often she was called upon to perform it; the thought of the lonely, frightened girl craving for some sign of life, some sense of companionship, was one which made irresistible appeal to her.

One night she heard the girl's bell ring, and she wondered what could have happened, for the electric bell was only to be rung in

1   Sidney Lanier (1842–81), "A Ballad of Trees and the Master" (1880).

cases of emergency. Listening, she heard footsteps, voices, sounds that seemed loud and many as they fell on the heavy silence; then she heard her neighbour's door unlocked and flung open, and then loud and indignant scolding. The girl had grown so restless and nervous that she could not stand the dark loneliness any longer; she had thought that if she might have a light—just for a time—she might read a little, and so find sleep. The officer was horrified at such a request; it was unheard of; naturally it was refused.

The next night there was no rapping on the wall, but Geraldine heard much movement in the passage outside, much going up and downstairs, much whispering and talking. After that, all was quiet, and in the morning the girl's cell was empty. Geraldine did not know her name, so was not able, after her own release, to find out anything about her. She never saw her again.

Her own nerves were tried to the uttermost. The forcible feeding, the waiting for it, the pain of it, the exhaustion which followed, were a tax upon her nervous strength which was almost more than it could bear; and it was not the pain and fear alone, but the indignities, the sense of outrage which told upon her, and the feeling of utter helplessness. For there was no hope, no appeal, no possibility of aid in prison. Outside, in the hands of evil doers, there was always the chance of rescue, of discovery; but here, she was in the hands, not of lawbreakers, but of upholders of the law; the instruments of a penal system, the aim of which seems to be the deliberate lowering of self-respect in the individuals under its charge, by arbitrary restriction and punishment. That was the worst of it; if she could have appealed to this man and those women, as to fellow beings, asked for mercy, sought for sympathy, it would have been less terrible; if they had been even brutal individuals, at any moment a more kindly intelligence might have been awakened in them; but they were officials, imbued with the idea of conscientiously carrying out an official duty, and, as such, impregnable to appeal.

She had tried appeal, not to mercy, but to reason, with the doctor. "I can never take much food at a time," she said one day. "I think if you were to give me less in quantity, the result might be better; and if you would not press the tube so far down into my body."

The voice and manner were the voice and manner of Lady Henry Hill, but Dr. Dean was not sensitive to qualities of voice or manner, and he saw only the woman who had been arrested as Anne Heeley, a working woman, a woman of no class.

"Your stomach must be longer than mine," he answered, "because you are taller. Do you think I don't know my business better than you do?"

And so it was useless to speak.

Once, indeed, Geraldine was so faint, so obviously very ill after the feeding, that even Dr. Dean was alarmed, and called in his assistant to test her heart. But it was Anne Heeley's heart that was tested; a very superficial examination was considered sufficient; and the heart was pronounced to be sound.

But even worse than the feeding, even worse than the anticipation of it, were the hard faces and the callous attitude of the beings whose business it was to carry out the operation. To her there seemed a sort of moral poison about this treatment of one human being by others; it seemed to her to sin against the fundamental law of humanity; it was hideous. After the first once or twice, she used to shut her eyes when the officials entered her cell. Feel, she must; from feeling there was no escape; but she would not have the scene of her suffering imprinted on her vision, would not look at the faces and the movements of those commissioned to make her suffer. She hoped thus to escape resentment, to shut out dislike; but in vain; in spite of her efforts she grew to hate those men and women, to hate still more the powers that stood behind them, to hate all those who, in blindness and prejudice, turn aside from the misery in the world, refusing to look at, or to listen to, what is going on under their very eyes.

She tried hard to get away from these thoughts, from this hate, by thinking of the heroic men and women who, ever since the world began, have tried to help the world; by thinking of the martyrs; by thinking of the courage and devotion of many in the very movement which had brought her to this place. But in vain; the hatred grew, and she found no strength to combat it.

No strength at all she found, till one strange evening, when she was lying on her bed on the floor of her cell. In pain her body was, her heart full of bitterness, her soul darkened. Then she looked up towards the light that came in through the window. In that window were three panes of clear glass, and on them, as the light fell, there came shadows of the moulding, that looked like three crosses. They brought to Geraldine's mind the familiar scene of Calvary, and she thought, "What did they stand for?" And after the thought in the question came a thought in answer. "One for the Lord Christ who died for sinners, and one for the sinner who was kind, and one for the sinner who had not yet learnt to be kind."

And then, behind those crosses, she saw the hateful faces, the faces of the self-righteous; and the hateful institutions of superior goodness and the moral blindness of officialdom, of all the injustice done, not only in prison, but in the world outside. And Geraldine thought: "It is surely for these that Christ died and is dying still and will have to die until they begin to see." It seemed to her that her hate, the hate she felt for them, was standing between these people and their better selves; and the hate sank down and ebbed away from her and never came back.

On a spring day in February Edith had seen, passing at the end of the road she was following, the man who, some minutes since, Geraldine had hated; and between him and her, as he passed, there had stood a cross. Now between this man and the woman, whom of all women Edith most reverenced, a cross was reared, raising them both; ay, even though he knew not, this man, that he was raised; knew not that by the forgiveness of the woman, whom, as a working woman, he despised he was brought a little nearer to the glory that waits, far onward on the upward path of evolution, for every living soul.

CHAPTER XLIV
BUMBLEDOM

"Say gentle soul, what can you find
But painted shapes,
Peacocks and Apes,
Illustrious flies,
Gilded dunghills, glorious lies,
Goodly surmises
And deep disguises,
Oaths of water, words of wind?
Truth bids me say, 'tis time you cease to trust
Your soul to any man of dust."

R. Crashaw[1]

---

1 Richard Crashaw (1613–49), "To the Same Party Counsel Concerning Her Choice" (1652).

Lord Henry Hill was engaged in fighting officialdom; not an easy task.

Geraldine, released from Belton Gaol five days before the term of her sentence was up, released because she was too palpably ill longer to endure the forcible feeding and live, had made known on her return to the outside world the experiences of Anne Heeley.

Speaking of those experiences, in public and in private, writing of them, she had been careful to attach no blame to the prison officials.

"I wish to make it clear," she said, "that I accuse no man or woman officer of being by nature brutal."

Brutal actually they often were; that could not be denied; but it was the penal system, the machine in which they were as cog-wheels that was responsible.

"Is it surprising," Geraldine asked, "that sometimes the turn of the machine causes these human cog-wheels to enact brutalities, regardless of the human material which they grind?"

In her speech at the Queen's Hall, delivered a week after her release, she struck the same note; the officials were helpless, the tools only, of a higher authority. Very measured was the account of Anne Heeley's experiences which she gave to the outside world; underdrawn, as was well known to the intimate friends to whom she told in full the story of her imprisonment; well known to her husband; well known, too, to the officers, men and women, in Belton Gaol. And yet her statements were denied; officially and authoritatively: officialdom, afraid of the rain of public opinion, put up the umbrella of hysteria. Anne Heeley had not passed through the experiences which Lady Henry Hill affirmed her to have passed through; officialdom indignantly repudiated such a possibility; officialdom consisted entirely of men, and was consequently impartial, unprejudiced, infallible; whereas Lady Henry was a woman and necessarily hysterical.

When the denial of her statement first appeared, Geraldine was ill in bed. For a week after her release she had kept about; to be at liberty, to be back in her home, to have about her the love and sympathy of husband, sister, friends; to breathe pure air and see the sky and the sun; this surely was enough and more than enough to make any woman well. And yet it was not enough; in spite of it and of her joy in it, she flagged and failed; and after the Queen's Hall meeting and her speech there and the effort of the speech, she could hold out no longer, but was obliged to betake herself to bed and rest, and submit to the dominion of doctor and nurse. Not Dr. Dean any more; it was a woman's hands to which she was confided now; and Angela Sayte, herself not long out of prison, was her nurse and chief companion.

Geraldine was quite unfitted to war with officialdom, and Lord Henry, without even telling her that war must be waged, took up the cudgels on her behalf. Not that war or the methods of war came within the intention of his activities; his wife's veracity had been impugned, and he asked, but asked quite civilly and peaceably, for a public inquiry into the statements in question. He was told in reply that the prison officials had been closely interrogated and had denied entirely every one of the charges made; therefore, said officialdom, no useful purpose would be served by granting his request.

It seemed to Lord Henry, to Geraldine's friends, to all who knew her, and to many who did not, that a specially useful purpose would be served by such an inquiry as would prove whether or no the closely interrogated officials were honest in their denials; but officialdom would permit no stirring of the waters of its penal system, and in spite of Lord Henry, his efforts, and his influence, the depths of those waters remained unplumbed.

From the beginning of February till the end of March, Lord Henry strove with officialdom, and, finding that officialdom was impervious to all appeals, he wrote a statement of his proceedings and their failure and sent it, in the form of a letter, to the organs of the Press. In that letter certain facts were made plain; that whereas, as Lady Henry Hill, Geraldine had been examined by a specialist and speedily released on the ground of heart trouble; as Anne Heeley she had been kept in prison for nine days, forcibly fed for six, and no heart trouble or tendency to heart trouble had been discerned in her. No amount of officialdom, Geraldine said, could wipe those facts away; they spoke for themselves and could not be silenced.

And moreover, out of these facts and others like them; out of the things that she and her fellows had done; out of the hunger strike and the forcible feeding, had come a measure of reform.

In April the new prison rule came into force and the need for rebellion within prison walls was over; for some of the demands made by the suffragettes were granted, some of the conditions which they had denounced, with which they had refused to comply, were to be done away with; in their cases and in the cases of those whose offences did not "involve dishonesty, cruelty, indecency or serious violence."[1]

The women who had protested, suffered, and endured, had won for themselves, and for all those to come after them, both men and women, whose sins were of no more criminal a character than theirs, at least exemption from the worst indignities. That was solid, that was actual; what matter if officialdom gave her words the lie, seeing that, from the facts denied, real benefits came forth?*

When Geraldine was well enough to see her, she sent for Sally. Sally had been ill too, had been for weeks in a nursing home, but was quite well now, she said, except for what she called a sort of toothache pain, from time to time, in the place where the policeman had kicked her.

"But, Lor'," said Sally, "there's many 'it as 'ard by 'usbands, an' there ain't no gettin' away from *them*. A p'liceman, well, 'e 'its or 'e kicks, an' if you 'it back, it's a week or a fortnight or a month as may be; but with a 'usband it's a life sentence. So I'm better off than some, you see, after all."

She looked very thin, Geraldine thought; her nose seemed to turn up more decidedly than ever, and her eyes, always big, seemed

---

* She could not foresee that the new regulations would be swept aside to suit the convenience of officialdom. [During much of 1910, in the wake of the General Election, the WSPU called a truce to allow the government to decide "in an atmosphere of peace and calm, what would be their action in regards to votes for women in the new Parliament" (C. Pankhurst, 148). Churchill proposed Rule 243A during this truce, a fact that Sylvia Pankhurst called an "ominous harbinger of further hostilities" (334). The truce was strained when it became clear that the Conciliation Bill would fail. Two members of the Men's League "assailed Lloyd George with the familiar cry. Refused the benefits of the new rule 243A , they hunger struck and were forcibly fed" (S. Pankhurst, 1931, 340). Apart from this incident, however, Rule 243A seems to have ameliorated prison conditions for suffragettes to the extent that hunger-striking was no longer necessary.]

1   Rule 243A, proposed by Home Secretary Winston Churchill, increased the privileges allowed to prisoners, as long as the crimes did not involve "moral turpitude," and the offender's "previous character [was] good." In such cases, "the Prison Commissioners may allow such ameliorations of the conditions prescribed in the foregoing rules as the Secretary of State may approve in respect of the wearing of prison clothing, bathing, hair-cutting, cleaning of cells, employment, exercise, books, and otherwise. Provided that no such amelioration shall be greater than that granted under the rules for offenders of the first division" (*Votes for Women*, 18 March 1910, 387).

bigger. Seeing her standing there, with her little, impudent, wistful Cockney face, and knowing what she had gone through—ah, how well she knew!—Geraldine was moved to a great tenderness, and, stooping, put her hands on the sloping shoulders and kissed the colourless face.

"Oh, ma'am oh, m'lady, oh Lady 'Ill!" Sally was too much overcome with pride and astonishment for aught but exclamations. That she, Sally, the erstwhile "general," should be kissed by *the* lady of all ladies, was a bliss of which she had never dreamed. It made prison worth while, apart from the Cause; it was compensation, consecration, and reward. "Mr. Bilkes, 'e ain't never been kissed by no lord," she thought, "nor never will be. 'E made fun o' the Cause, but look wot it's brought me to!"

Then Geraldine thanked her for what she had done, and Sally was more astonished still.

"I ain't done nothink, Lady 'Ill," she said. "I got took, along of that ginger-beer bottle—which I couldn't 'ave throwed it straighter if I'd been born a man—an' bein' once in quod—in prison, Lady 'Ill, there I 'ad to stop. Specially as they wouldn't let me out on bail."

"Yes, but, Sally, you went through the hunger strike and the feeding."

"I couldn't go back on you ladies," said Sally, opening her wide eyes wider.

Geraldine smiled. "That's what I'm thanking you for—for what you couldn't do. And Joe?" she added, "how is he?"

"I give 'un up Lady 'Ill, afore I left London, an' now 'e's bin an' gone an' married Mary Ann Dobbs, which I advised 'im to take up with 'er, but I never thought 'e would."

"If he could take up with Mary Ann, I am sure he could not have been worthy of Sally."

"You don't seem to think about whether 'e's worthy or whether 'e ain't, when 'e's your sweet'eart. It's kissin' an' such like I used to think about with Joe. Wot they reely are you never know till they're your 'usband; an' then it's too late. Any'ow," said Sally, with a sigh, "Mary Ann knows now."

CHAPTER XLV
A TRUCE

"Terrible as an army with banners."

Song of Solomon 6:10

The summer of that year was a summer of processions, of truce, of hope. Anne Heeley had done more than prove that class distinctions obtained within prison walls; she had roused the husband of Geraldine Hill from passive to active sympathy with the woman's movement. It was much, for Lord Henry showed himself to be one of the most valuable friends the movement had ever had.

In May all the suffragist world and the anti-suffragist world were talking of the Conciliation Committee, of its honorary secretary, Mr. Bridford, and its chairman, Lord Henry Hill; of the Conciliation Bill drafted by that Committee; of the probable introduction of the Bill in the coming session.[1] Pending the introduction of the Bill, pending the possibility of its passage through the House of Commons, there was a cessation of militant methods; in the militant camp, women who had fought hard were only too glad to welcome a space of peace. Christina Amherst, as spokeswoman of that camp, said that while the Bill did not give all that she, her fellows and her followers asked for, it still gave much; enough for women to accept, in that it broke down the barrier which stood in the way of effective co-operation between men and women, the barrier of sex.[2]

There was truce; and not one woman in the land but rejoiced in it, save only those who, clinging to sex influence, shrank from sex equality. Liberal women renewed their trust in the Cabinet;

---

1 The 1910 Conciliation Bill was drafted by a committee of fifty-four members of Parliament from all parties, and chaired by Lord Lytton with Henry Noel Brailsford as Secretary.

2 The Conciliation Bill proposed to extend the parliamentary franchise to women householders or occupiers. H.N. Brailsford writes that the householder "will get a vote if she inhabits any house or part of a house, be it even a single room, and however low its value, provided she has full control over it, as will the occupier of "premises valued at £10 per annum. This will bring in the small shopkeeper, or the typist who has an office of her own. It also enables women living together in a house to rank as joint occupiers, provided the house is worth £10 for each occupier" (4–5). The bill would have enfranchised one million largely single, widowed, or working women. Married women were not disqualified, per se, "provided that a husband and wife shall not be both qualified in respect of the same property" (Brailsford, 1910, 6). See Appendix D1.

Conservative women turned confidently to those of their party who had joined the Committee and would support the Committee's Bill; individual women thought gladly of individual men who, sinking party differences, were committed to the women's cause.

Edith, amongst women, was of the first class and the last. Her heart beat high with pride and hope; after all, it was by a Liberal Government that women were to be accorded the vote; after all, the party was going to stand by its traditions, carry out its principles; after all, she might be able to return to her allegiance. And Race was a member of the Committee; in that fact she took a more joyous pride, found a sweeter hope. He had always said that he was on the women's side, always maintained that, disapproving of the suffragettes, he approved of the suffrage; and now he had proved his words. Perhaps in those long months of strain and separation and struggle, she had a little doubted the genuineness of his convictions, but now there was no more room for doubt; she might respect, admire, look up to him, convinced of his sincerity. Therein lay the chief source of her rejoicing, that he had not fallen below her conception of him; that she could maintain her ideal, though she had lost her lover; in the secret territory which she entered from the lane she might meet him still admitting him to that select company whose credentials were honour, generosity, chivalry. And behind her avowed pride there lurked a secret hope. If the Bill passed, there would be no more militant methods, no more interrupted meetings, no more law-breaking in protest or symbol; in a future where further offence would be uncalled for, there was the sweet possibility that the deeds of the past might be blotted out.

It was a cold, wet summer, but the warmth and sunshine of summer as it should be, was in the hearts of the women of all ranks, of all societies, of all shades of opinion, who had worked so long for that which now seemed near; and even the outer weather was kind to these women, showing a smiling face to their processions.

The first of these, organized to bear witness to the demand for the passing of the Bill, took place on the eighteenth of June, and from all parts of the kingdom, women flocked into London to swell its ranks. Not women only; more and more, throughout the country, men were giving in their adherence to the women's cause, and men were there, bodies of men, on the crowded Embankment, to join in the march and add to the number of its banners.

Amongst those men, actually one of the banner-bearers, was Monty Carstairs. If Geraldine had done nothing else, by taking on the semblance of a working woman, she had at least made a profound impression upon Monty. It was her pluck which appealed to him, taken in conjunction with that knowledge of her temperament, her character, her womanliness, which had first made a captive of him at the Königsee. As Mrs. Brown, she had enchained his fancy and won his respect; as Anne Heeley she had compelled his admiration. For a long time he had clung to Mrs. Brown; she was the better half, the higher self of that disconcerting personality, Lady Henry Hill; she had never been quite dislodged till Anne Heeley came upon the scene. But now Mrs. Brown was gone for good, dead and buried; Anne Heeley was in apotheosis; and Geraldine, unadulterated by any *alias*, held his complete loyalty. Suffragettes there might be, vulgar, coarse, flippant, unwomanly, but not *his* suffragette; Geraldine *á la* Monty was feminine, modest, gentle, everything—except perhaps a little too clever, in her speaking, for instance—that a woman ought to be; and the light of her glory cast its reflection over all the movement.

Monty was far back in the procession, past, a long way past, Cleopatra's needle,[1] a mile or more from where Geraldine waited amongst those who headed it. All the way from Westminster to Blackfriars Bridge stretched a line of waving banners; all the way, in file four deep, close pressed together, ranks of women, ranks of men; massed densely on either side, crowds of spectators; and beyond the Embankment wall, the river rising in its banks, swelled by the flow of the incoming tide driven upward from the sea.

It is six o'clock, but most of those who are to march through the West of London are there, all ready in the ranks. Twenty Societies there are, besides the Union; actresses; artists; graduates, men and women; writers; representatives from New Zealand, Australia, Norway, the countries where women already have the vote; representatives from America, Italy, France, from Germany, Sweden, Denmark, Holland, the Colonies; leagues and branches of leagues from Scotland, from Ireland, from all parts of the kingdom: and in front, forming the first group, the prisoners.

---

1   Cleopatra's needle is an Egyptian obelisk that stands opposite the Victoria Embankment Gardens, overlooking the Thames. It is one of a pair originally erected in Heliopolis in 1475 BCE, and was presented to the British people as a memorial to Admiral Nelson in 1819.

It is half-past six. The group captains, who will keep the ranks unbroken, the officials who will manage the banners, are in their places, but the procession is so large that it is long before the whole length of it can be got under way. No movement yet far back where Monty waits impatiently, no movement even where Edith stands, west of the Temple; but in the front, the bands are playing and the crowd is cheering; the first group has started.

Ahead of it, first of all, goes the colour bearer, the woman who for three whole months endured the forcible feeding;[1] then comes the band of the Union; and following the band, are the six hundred and seventeen prisoners. They are dressed in white, and carry wands tipped with the broad arrow. Geraldine Hill is there amongst them; Mrs. Amherst, Christina Amherst with her girlish face, Mrs. Patrick Lane, Annie Carnie; all those suffering from that hysteria which furnishes the courage to fight for a cause and stand fast by a principle, against contempt, against convention, against physical force. And Sally was there, dressed, for the first time in her life, in white, and carrying her wand with its arrow top, with pride inexpressible.

At first she was too excited, too much overcome with the honour of her position, to be conscious of aught, save of the mere fact that there she was, in the very head of the great procession; amongst "them ladies." Then, when she had grown used to the music, the marching, the cheering and the crowds, she began to think; and first she thought she would like Joe to see her, to see and understand that for which she had foregone the sharing of his home; though it was not really for that, the triumph which all the world could see, but for something which had led her through dark places, hidden from every eye. In truth Joe had seen her; he had been on the Embankment with his Mary Ann, and Sally's face had been distinct to them both, though in the crowd their faces had not been visible to Sally. They had looked, half in admiration, and half in mockery, at Sally in her white dress; had looked, wondering, at the procession in its length; and after looking, had gone home to supper. They had what they wanted; Joe had a home and Mary Ann had Joe; but in them both there, stirred dimly a sense that Sally had gained something that they had not, something they would never have.

---

1   Charlotte Marsh was arrested, along with Mary Leigh, in September 1909. She was one of the first suffragette prisoners to be forcibly fed.

As she went on and on, growing gayer, more confident, beginning now really to enjoy herself, Sally thought it would be grand to be seen by Mr. Bilkes. And Mr. Bilkes did see her and what was quite as much to the point, she saw Mr. Bilkes. There he was, at the corner of St. James's Street and Piccadilly, nudging a friend, "jawring away," as Sally expressed it, with all the sneering pomposity she remembered so well. She saw him give his friend an extra nudge, and point his finger; he saw her then. Splendid! Sally held her head very high and looked straight in front of her! it was not for her to notice such as Mr. Bilkes. And yet the touch of bedevilment in her which had not been quite killed, either by her devotion to her cause, or the force of prison discipline, sprang up and incited to mischief. She meant to pass him by without a glance, but, almost in spite of herself, as she reached the place where he stood, she half turned her head. There he stood with his mouth a little open, half jeering, half impressed. It was too great a temptation, the mischief in her was too strong; as she passed him, she winked at Mr. Bilkes.

On the procession went; truly "an army with banners"; scarcely a space there was above the marching women, where was no flying silk or streaming pennant. When the army's head had reached the Albert Hall, the end was at St. James's Palace; longer it was than Piccadilly and Knightsbridge; and all the length of it the pavements and the roadways were crowded with people looking on.

At a Club window Edith saw Cyril Race. He did not see her, but that hardly mattered; it was enough to know that he was on her side, enough to know that he, a member of the Government, was pledged to support the Bill.

Poor Monty, at the far end of the procession, was tired, not to say bored, before his group was able to start, but once started, his spirits revived. He walked with a certain jauntiness, pleased with the part he was playing, for was he not the supporter, not to say the protector, of all these women ahead? They had ceased to be unsexed, these women, since Monty had given them his countenance, and had become oppressed; they were no longer viragoes but pioneers. It was fine, he thought, marching to music and giving the strength of his manhood to the service of the weaker sex; it was a splendid procession, and he was glad to be in it. What matter if Jones of Jesus[1]

---

1   This refers to Jesus College, Cambridge.

grinned at him from the pavement? Jones of Jesus would jolly well have his head punched if he presumed to grin when Monty was not officially engaged. A whipper-snapper, not fit to black the boots of Lady Henry Hill!

A fine procession, thought Monty; a fine procession, thought Edith, and Geraldine and Sally; a fine procession, thought those who led and followed in it; and those, too, who looked on.

A fine procession it was in truth; but upon it lay, unseen of the public eye, the shadow of the Veto; not of the House of Lords, not of the House of Commons, but of half a score of men in the Cabinet.

CHAPTER XLVI
ONE HUNDRED AND NINE

"These are the Times that try men's souls."

Thomas Paine[1]

Rachel Cullen and Edith Carstairs sat together in Rachel's little sitting-room. It was dusk, the airless dusk of a summer night in London, and the breeze that came in through the open window had no freshness in it. Across the little space of garden the sound of the traffic was distinct; the heavy roll of omnibuses, the whirring of motors, the fall of horses' feet, the rumble of carts.

A little more than a year it was since the King's Representative in the House of Commons had refused, by the mouth of Inspector Jervoise, to receive the Deputation of eight women, headed by Mrs. Amherst. The object of that Deputation had been to beg that measures might be taken to extend the political franchise to women; and now, within the House of Commons, the Second Reading of a Bill to grant that extension was actually in progress. A year ago, from the House of Commons window, Edith had witnessed the expulsion of the petitioners from Parliament Square: now, far from the House, she sat and thought of what was going on within, of the measure which was occupying the attention of the Members, the measure which was to carry into effect the principle which the eight women had set out to advocate. Then Cyril Race had been beside her, and

---

[1] Thomas Paine (1737–1809), *The Crisis* (1776).

she had felt dimly within her the first stirring of those convictions which were to make a gulf between them. Now he and she were separated by three miles of space, or more, and yet, it seemed to her, that they were, in sympathy, nearer than they had been a year ago. For then, they had been speeding towards the parting of the ways, and now, in thought and aim, they had come to a meeting point. He would not be thinking of her now: his thoughts would all be given to the business in hand; but she, thinking of that business, could think of him as well. He was part of it, had made himself part of it, an important part; for it mattered greatly how members of the Government voted, mattered much more than the voting of private members. If enough of them supported the Conciliation Bill and supported it strongly, surely the foremost men in the Cabinet would be influenced and won over. And Cyril Race was working very hard; that she knew; she had heard through Lord Henry that he had been much in the company of the Ministers who were opposed to the enfranchisement of women and who intended to oppose the Bill, as well as being in constant intercourse with one particular Minister who had undertaken to give the Bill his support. Edith had been elated when Lord Henry had given her this information, elated and proud to think that Race was using all his influence to win over the opposing Ministers, and she had been angry with John Gorton, who had shaken his head over it. John Gorton was a depressing person; he had never taken a hopeful view of the chances of the Bill; he had no trust, he said, in the Government's intentions in that direction, nor in that of the individual members of the Government. As Cyril Race was one of those members, it was natural that Edith should feel irate, and she told herself that suspiciousness was, of all traits of character, the one she most disliked.

Rachel was thinking too; of how much was at stake that night; of how much the Debate meant to the women who might rest or must fight again, according to the results of it. Was the hour really near? would the clock strike? or was there more weary work, more humiliation and struggling and pain before the ever-advancing hands touched the destined point of peace? The Conciliation Bill had risen like a star of hope in the sky of women who thought as Rachel thought, who strove as Rachel had striven. Would it brighten and endure, or fade and fall? A year ago the outlook had been dark: a year hence, what would it be? A year hence, would the struggle be over? Ay, Rachel, for some of you it will be over. But that she could not know, sitting in the little quiet room, looking out across the patch of garden, seeing beyond that patch of garden only the Bayswater Road and not the future.

"Don't you think we'd better go to bed?" Rachel said at last.

"Oh no. I couldn't sleep; I'm too excited. If we could just have a sort of supernatural hearing and know what's going on!"

"I'm afraid we must wait for the newspaper; and it can't come before morning, even if you sit up all night."

"Oh, Rachel, how calm you are! You don't seem as if you minded having to wait."

"I've waited so much. Perhaps, when you're as old as I am, you will have learned how to do it."

At last Edith consented to go to bed; indeed, it was getting chilly by the open window; dusk had long given place to dark; and her eyes were not so wide open as they had been. Once in bed they closed altogether, and the night went quickly by. It was Rachel who lay awake.

"A majority of a hundred and nine! Oh, Rachel, how splendid! Bigger than the Budget, bigger than the Veto! It must, it must come now!"

Edith stood with the newspaper in her hand; her face was radiant, her eyes sparkled; in her heart she was disposed to think that Race's efforts had had much to do with the fine majority. And then she betook herself to reading the list of names in that majority.

"A—B—F—; R came near the end: Radford, Randies, Rawson—Roberts, Roberts, Roch—Rachel, I can't see Mr. Race's name! He must have been taken ill—wasn't there, and nothing but illness would have prevented him. Oh, what a pity! Every one makes a difference, and especially those in the Government."

Rachel took up the paper and looked at the lists of names; more than one list Rachel looked at. Then she said—it had to be said somehow:

"John Gorton was right to shake his head."

"What do you mean? You don't mean, you can't—Let me look at the paper!"

Rachel handed it to her, and again Edith searched for the name she had thought so soon to find; but this time she read more than the one list. There were three: "M.P.'s who voted for the Second

Reading and supported the proposal to send the Bill to a Grand Committee"; "M.P.'s who voted for the Second Reading of the Bill, but voted against sending the Bill to a Grand Committee"; and "M.P.'s who voted against the Second Reading and who voted against sending the Bill to a Grand Committee."

Cyril Race's name was in the last list, in company with the strenuous opponents of the Bill, in company with that Minister with whom lately he had had much intercourse and who had let it be understood that he was in favour of the Bill. The two had decided, after all, to row in the Government boat, and had performed that manoeuvre vulgarly known as "ratting."

Robbie Colquhoun's name stood in the first list. Edith hardly looked for it, hardly cared to find it; it was a matter of course, not a matter of pride that Robbie should be amongst the genuine supporters of the Bill.

In the programme which lay in her drawer at home, Race's initials had ousted Robbie's from their place: it was bitterness to know that now Robbie's name stood alone where Race's should also have been.

CHAPTER XLVII
DELAYS ARE DANGEROUS

"Now *here*, you see, it takes all the running *you* can do, to keep in the same place. If you want to get somewhere else, you must run at least twice as fast as that."

Through the Looking-Glass[1]

"I think, you know," said John Gorton, "that it's one of the chief things that women have to learn, to act altogether independently of men."

"I don't agree with you," Lord Henry answered. "Politically speaking, they haven't the experience of men, don't know the ropes so well, and would do better, it seems to me, where political manoeuvring is concerned, to take advice."

"No, my dear fellow, no. If the mere granting of the vote were in question, possibly; though they've shown themselves uncommonly

---

1   Lewis Carroll (1832–98), *Through the Looking-Glass, and What Alice Found There* (1872).

astute in gauging the sincerity of professed supporters. But for their own best and ultimate benefit, for the good of the movement in its width, not just where it touches the outer instrument of the vote, absolute independence, the habit of thinking apart from men, standing apart from men, is of the utmost—well, I should say, vital importance."

"All very well, but they're jolly apt to make mistakes in the process of getting it."

"Never mind; it's worth it. I'd rather see them make mistakes on their own than be ever so wise under the direction of men."

"Sound enough, Gorton, I daresay, from your point of view, but mistakes mean delay."

"I don't know," said Gorton, getting up and standing with his back to the fire, "that delay's a bad thing. Oh, don't suppose that I wouldn't give the vote to-morrow if I had the power. I'm sick enough of seeing men blundering on, trying to stamp out, through the bodies of women, a fire that's alight in their souls. But all the same, delay is no evil. I tell you what it is, if the vote had been given years ago, even five years ago, nine-tenths of the women who ought to use it would have valued it not at all."

"I acknowledge," Lord Henry agreed, "that every year more and more women are keen to have it."

"Every year! Every day, my dear fellow, and not keen about the vote only, but about the questions that can be affected by it. Women have learned to think in these last years, have waked up to all sorts of things that meant nothing to them at the beginning of the century. They are becoming a force, of opinion and activity, and the longer they are without the vote, the stronger their force will be when they get it. If the men who want to hold women back, to keep them ignorant, weak, dependent, if they had been wise, I say, they would have enfranchised them long ago. They wouldn't, the great majority of them, have cared about the franchise then, have valued it, known what use to make of it. Now they will know how to make the most of it, and every month they are kept without it, the more women there will be to use it and the more independent will be their action, when it comes."

"As to its coming," said Lord Henry, "I have no doubts."

"Who has, except certain reactionaries of the ostrich type, and of Honourable Members a foolish and decreasing few?"

"Who say that it's not for the good of the community."

"That they are sure to say; it's the thing people always do say when they can't say anything else. There are three things that are always said about movements which have moral force at the back of them and the benefit of an oppressed class ahead of them. First: the evil is for the good of the community; secondly, it's for the good of the oppressed; thirdly, the people who want to do away with it are hysterical sentimentalists. All these things were said about slavery, the slaves and the abolitionists. The slaves liked it, the world would go to the devil without it, and the abolitionists were hysterical fools. They are said about vivisection—so good for the animals and the community; and those who would do away with it: Lord! what sentimentalists! And it's the same thing about the women; so much better for them and the community that they should have no political rights; and it's only sentimentalists who can possibly take any other view—like you and me."

"Which proves that the Committee's got its work cut out."

The Conciliation Committee had worked hard and was working still; its Chairman and Honorary Secretary had done and were doing their utmost in every possible way; but its first Bill was dead, or practically dead. In spite of meetings, demonstrations, memorials, representations, facilities for its passage had hitherto been refused, and all the high hopes that had heralded its advent were laid low. During the nine months of truce a constitutional agitation had been carried out on a larger scale than was attempted by any of the men's political parties. All over the country great halls had been filled and refilled and resolutions passed, urging the granting of facilities for the Bill; in London, there were meetings many and large, and in one week the Albert Hall was twice filled. Nevertheless, facilities were refused; and now the truce was over, or all but over, and war was imminent, if war it was to send a Deputation to the House of Commons.

On the very eve of war it was that the Australian Senate, beholding with troubled and critical eyes the efforts of women in the Mother Country, passed a resolution affirming, "That this Senate is of opinion that the extension of the suffrage to the women of Australia for States and Commonwealth Parliaments, on the same terms as to men, has had the most beneficial results. It has led to the more orderly conduct of elections, and, at the last Federal elections, the women's vote in a majority of the States showed a greater proportionate increase than that cast by men. It has given a greater prominence to legislation particularly affecting women and children, although the women have not taken up such questions to the exclusion of others of wider significance. In matters of Defence and Imperial concern they have proved themselves as far-seeing and discriminating as men. Because the reform has brought nothing but good, though disaster was freely prophesied, we respectfully urge that all nations enjoying representative government would be well advised in granting votes to women": and a second resolution was passed to the effect that a copy of the first one should be cabled to the British Prime Minister.

The cable was sent and received; but no attention was paid to it by the Government; no attention was paid to it by the daily Press; no more attention was paid to it by officialdom and the London newspapers than was paid to the widespread constitutional agitation, with its nine months of thronged, enthusiastic meetings.

But in the meantime the Government had made no official statement of its intentions with regard to the Bill, and hope, crushed and thwarted, still struggled for existence.

Before the date fixed for the Deputation, if a Deputation proved to be necessary, Sally, at one of the Albert Hall meetings, had a surprise, for just outside the Hall, and evidently about to enter it, she came upon the youngest Miss Bilkes.

"Lor', miss!" she exclaimed, "wotever's brought *you* 'ere?"

"Why, I declare it's Sally," said Miss Bilkes. "I've—I've come to the meeting."

"I never! And Mr. Bilkes, wot does 'e say?"

"He doesn't know; and if he does, I can't help it. It was all you, Sally."

"Me!"

"Yes, I never forgot what you said that day about—don't you remember?—when my brother said woman's place was the home, and you said there were lots of women who had no homes to have a place in. I thought of it again and again; and then I bought the paper—you remember that; and then somehow I took to it more and more. Only I have to keep it sort of secret, because—well, you know what ma is and Mr. Bilkes and all of them."

"I do, miss. I see 'im the day of the big procession—the first one. He didn't look no different."

Miss Bilkes shook her head. "No, he isn't."

"An' Stanny?" asked Sally. "'Ow is the little feller, an' Miss Dorothy, an' Maud?"

"Quite well. Dorothy, and Stanny have lessons now, a governess in the morning."

"'Ave they forgot me?"

"I don't think so. But, Sally, isn't it dreadful to be a suffragette?—a regular one, I mean."

"Dreadful? It's stunnin', that's wot it is. It's religion an' politics; an' woman's place-is-the-'ome all in one. For religion's 'elpin' them as is put upon; an' that's wot we do. An' politics is fightin' agin the Government an' that's wot we do; at least, we shall soon 'ave to take to politics again 'cos they won't pay no 'eed to you, if you leave 'em alone. An' woman's-place-is-the-'ome, is lookin' after children and widders an' such like; an' that's wot we want to do if they'd only let us 'ave a look in."

Georgina was observing her. "You've got very thin, Sally."

"Ain't never been fat since I come out of prison; an' I don't sleep so sound as I did 'cos of a sort of toothache down 'ere, where the p'liceman wiped 'is feet. But I'm all right; all I want is a thorough change; an' by an' bye Lady 'Ill says, I'm to 'ave it."

That night Christina Amherst was speaking, and Miss Bilkes, who had been more and more surprised as the meeting went on, was most surprised of all when a girl, looking no more fierce or extraordinary than any other girl, stood up on the platform. Was this the awful Christina? Then Ben was quite wrong; Ben was often wrong, she found. She only wished he could speak as Miss Amherst spoke; then she wouldn't mind having to listen to him so often as she was obliged to do. It seemed wonderful to Miss Bilkes that a girl, no older than herself, could hold that vast audience, for Miss Bilkes had been told that women could not say anything worth listening to and, in her simplicity, had believed it. She went home, wishing many things; amongst them that she had asked Sally for her address.

CHAPTER XLVIII
BLACK FRIDAY

"Out of the dark, the circling sphere
Is rounding onward to the light."

Samuel Longfellow[1]

In the House of Commons the Prime Minister was making his statement as to the fate of the Conciliation Bill. In the Caxton Hall, women, who had waited for nine months, were waiting still, assembled together, to hear what that statement might be. By four o'clock they knew. Facilities for the Bill would be given, not next session, but next Parliament. At what period in the life of the Parliament? No time was named; it might be seven years hence. That was not enough for women, who had waited nine months and, before that, fifty years. The Deputation would start at once. But the House had risen, it was said; it was useless to go to an empty House. Then, said Mrs. Amherst, to Downing Street.

The streets were full of policemen, some in uniform, many in plain clothes; not, as far as could be judged, the Metropolitan police, who had always, to the extent to which it was possible, been considerate to the women; but, as it seemed, a rougher lot of men, used apparently to work of a rough kind.

For hours the battle lasted, not limited to any one place, but fought, simultaneously in many places; in Parliament Street, in Downing Street, in Parliament Square. Deputation after deputation came up from Clement's Inn, and was broken up and dispersed; and here was a wild turmoil of struggling men and women; and there a woman lay upon the ground; and there again were women hurled by the police into the crowd, and back from the crowd against the line of police. Women doctors were there in the thick of the tumult, well-known writers, hospital nurses. Woman who had been told they must not have the vote because they could not fight, showed they could fight that day; there was nothing to be done but fight, since all around was warfare; since well-dressed men and youths amused themselves by striking women; since a man ap-

---

1   Samuel Longfellow (1819–92), "Watchman, What of the Night?," a poem written for the twenty-fifth anniversary of the American Anti-Slavery Society (1856).

pealed to for help, turned on the girl who appealed to him and hit her again and again.

And all this because a man in power refused to receive twelve women who had none.

Sally was not in the crowd; she had meant to be, but the tooth-ache in her stomach had grown too strong to fight against, and she had had to take to her bed. She lay in a little room that Geraldine had taken for her, with a window looking west, and from her bed she could see the sun go down in a blood-red sky like the sky which Edith had seen on the eve of a former deputation. That same sky, brilliant with the colour of glory, lay, a fierce background, behind the Houses of Parliament clearly outlined against it, the House of Commons rose up, and against the doors of the House stood wom-en, refused admittance.

In the crowd were Rachel Cullen and Angela Sayte, carrying, as many women carried, little purple bannerettes, with the motto, "Our Bill is vetoed." Suddenly the police bore down, snatched them away, and began to tear them up. The policeman who took Rachel's scratched his hand badly in destroying it.

"You will probably hear that you did it," said Angela; and so it was; in one of the Liberal dailies it was stated that the policeman's hand had been slashed with a knife.

There were bullies in the crowd, who had come there to give their instincts free play; there were men who were friends of the women, cheering them as they tried to force their way; crying to them, "Go on! We'll push you through"; calling to the police: "Let her through! She has a right to go"; and more than once the lines of police broke and gave way. They applauded, some of these men, when Angela stuck to her dismantled banner-pole, and made a dash and got half-way to the door of the House, before she was seized and stopped and spun round like a ninepin; and one of them fought hard for Rachel, when a policeman struck her with all his force and she fell to the ground. A tall man he was, and strong, but three or four police seized hold of him and bundled him away.

Indeed, it was not easy for the police; their orders were to make as few arrests as possible; and what could they do, save try to wear out the women's strength by violence?

Edith was there that day; not actually in the crowd, but helping in her own way. She had persuaded Robbie to bring her; she wanted to see for herself how far the papers were accurate in their accounts; and Robbie, much against the grain, had brought her. What she saw sickened her; a little of it was enough for Edith; and then she and Robbie formed themselves into a sort of rescue committee. They found that the police brought many disabled women to one of the small streets behind the Abbey and laid them there to recover as best they might. Many were dazed; some could not walk without help; some, strangers to London, had no idea where they were or how to find their way back to the thoroughfares. These women were helped and guided by Robbie and Edith. Some Robbie put into cabs; some were taken to the Caxton Hall; some were led or directed to spots whence they could find their way.

And then—how it happened Edith never knew, but she found herself separated from Robbie, and borne, by the will of the crowd, away from Westminster, towards the Mall. The crowd thinned, and she could breathe now, and think; consider how she should find her way back to Robbie. Or would it be better to go straight to Bayswater, to Rachel's house, where she was to pass the night?

And then, suddenly, she found herself face to face with a man she knew, or had known; with Cyril Race. She was in a little knot of women, and he in the centre of it. His hat was off, and some of the women were hustling him. Policemen were in sight, but they did not interfere, nor did Race call upon them; he was looking round, angry, flurried, seeking seemingly a way of escape. And then their eyes met, his and Edith's, in a swift glance, instantly averted. Race turned quickly; and turning, seemed to stumble, to twist his knee in the effort to get away. He cried out and bystanders rushed to help him; and a tall man, in a silk hat, offered him his arm and led him limping away.

Afterwards, whenever Edith thought of Cyril Race, she saw him, as she saw him that evening, limping away from her. He danced so well, and he walked well too; she did not forget the ball, when she had waltzed with him in an abandonment of delight; she remembered his carriage, firm and upright, when he walked: but always, in her thoughts, she saw him limping away from her.

CHAPTER XLIX
"CHEAP MARTYRDOM"

"'And oh, for a seer to discern the same!'
Sighed the South to the North!
For a poet's tongue of baptismal flame,
To call the tree or the flower by its name!'
Sighed the South to the North!"

E.B. Browning[1]

Cyril Race limped away, and the next day there appeared in the
newspapers highly coloured accounts of the harm that had been
done by women to a well-known man.[2] The newspapers, or most
of them, were silent, or all but silent, as to what had been wrought
by men on the bodies of unknown women. And yet, not far from
where Race had stood, there were women lying prone; beaten,
kicked, hammered on the head, with arms twisted and pinched, and
twisted thumbs.

Robbie Colquhoun, separated from Edith, seeking her in the
crowd, was aghast with the horror of the fear that in that crowd
she might be cut off from his protection. Edith treated as he saw
women treated that day! It would kill her, delicate, tender, sensitive
as she was! Yet he saw women, as delicate as Edith, as slender and
as slim, struck with clenched fists again and again; he saw a woman
sent on to her knees by a blow at the base of the skull; he saw at the
St. Stephen's entrance to the House, a woman knocked down the
steps, with the words: "You'll find which is the hardest, the stones or
you." He saw things which, done to women in Russia, would have

---

1 Elizabeth Barrett Browning (1806–61), "The North and the South. The Last Poem"
(1861).

2 This account refers to the injuries suffered by Augustine Birrell, the Chief Secretary for
Ireland, who was "swarmed" by a group of about twenty suffragettes "who pulled me
about and hustled me, 'stroked' my face, knocked off my hat and kicked it about.... I struggled to get free and in so doing I twisted my knee ... and slipped the kneecap." (Rosen,
143; Wilson, 36). The incident occurred four days after Black Friday (on 22 November
1910) in response to Asquith's statement that facilities for proceeding with a suffrage Bill
would be granted in the next Parliament, not necessarily in the next session (Rosen, 145),
leading to another violent clash between suffragettes and the police. Asquith, in a memo
to Churchill the day after Birrell was injured wrote: "The assault on Birrell seems to have
been a serious one, and I think the case should be proceeded with: also all cases of *serious*
assault on the police" (Churchill, 1457).

aroused in England a blaze of indignation, with admiring plaudits of those who served liberty; but which, done in England, brought forth, when he spoke of them afterwards, only the comment: If women take to forcing their way, they must expect to be repelled by force.

Through the crowd in which Robbie searched, a devil stalked, whose name was Licence, and, as he went, he tore from the minds of men the restraints of civilisation and stirred up in their hearts latent impulses of the bully and the savage. Men there were, like Robbie himself, past whom the devil slunk, abashed and silent, but these were few in that wild concourse; the hearts that were ready to that devil's touch, the ears that were open to his coward's cry, were many on that day.

More than once, Robbie was delayed in his search for Edith by his attempts to help other women; more than once, seeing women seized by the throat and flung backwards on the ground, he stopped and helped to raise them. One of these women was flung almost under the wheels of a motor-car; the head of another—a grey-haired woman this—was grazed by a passing vehicle. That devil of Licence who dared not accost Robbie was yet visible in his deeds. Robbie saw him, with the hands of men, grip women by the throat, forcing the head back as far as it would go; saw him seize the head of a woman struggling for breath, and rub her face against an iron railing; saw him clutch the breasts of women and twist them with hand after hand.

And side by side with that devil, he saw the spirit of courage flit unceasingly through the crowd; saw women, led by that spirit, fly to the rescue of fellow women; saw once or twice, in the effort to rescue, and only in that effort, women lift their hands against the police, knocking off a helmet or dealing a blow; the while the police more than once used their helmets as weapons, striking with them the heads and faces of those who were to be conquered by physical force.

And all this because a man in power refused to listen to twelve women who had none.

Rachel Cullen found herself in the very thick of the battle. Before and after her fall, she was beaten about the body, thrown backwards and forwards from one to another, until she was dazed with the horror of it. Once she was dragged out of the crowd into a side street and beaten on the spine till she could not stand. Then, with a shove she was released; a shove and the words: "I'll teach you a lesson; I'll teach you not to come back! I'll punish you, you—" The devil of Licence chuckled then all through the crowd. In the devil's speech that day the second letter of the alphabet was much to the fore, both in regard to noun and adjective.

Angela Sayte had stuck as long as she could to Rachel's side, doing her best to protect her, seeking to stand between her and the devil of Licence that swayed the crowd. But, after a time, she and Rachel were separated; and Angela, having striven to thwart that devil, was singled out by him for special savagery. For, besides trying to protect Rachel, she had sought to help other women, and one in especial, a woman who had been hurled within a foot of a motor, and who was lying quite still, unconscious as it seemed. The devil was angry when Angela, bending over her, cried out to the policeman who had thrown her there: "Oh you have killed her!" and, in the policeman's body, kicking savagely at the prostrate form.

Onward went Angela, never ceasing in her efforts to give a helping hand to other women, or in her attempts to reach the goal she had come out to reach, till, at last, she was arrested. That was comparative peace; just for a little while; but simple arrest was not enough for the devil, whose power increased as time and the battle went on. The cry of "Prostitute" was raised, and, with her skirts held high by the police, Angela was made to pass for several yards through the crowd.

Not far away, and all over the country were thousands of womanly women, secure in womanliness and safe in circumstance; women who would reap where others sowed. Some were happy in their homes; some were winning or losing money at bridge; some were returning from the killing of otters and foxes. None ran the risk of insult or indignity or violence. All were very far away, in spirit and in aim, from the women struggling in the streets round Westminster.

About the towers of Westminster the sky was red like blood. There were touches of red, very like to blood, on the pavements; stains, very like to blood, on the bodies of women; something, very like to blood, on the heads of men who were not in the crowd that day.

CHAPTER L
ROBBIE COLQUHOUN

"He who's for us, for him are we."

George Meredith[1]

All through the country there was sympathy with Cyril Race. Suffragettes had attacked him, kicked and injured him, said the Press; and not him only; another member of the Government had been surrounded, had been obliged to flee in a motor-car, and the window of the car had been broken.

Complaints of the devil of Licence had been lodged at Scotland Yard, but no notice was taken of them; a long letter was written by one of the injured women to officialdom, but no notice was taken of it; of the many women crippled and injured on Black Friday and the black days which followed it, no notice was taken. The notice and the sympathy were all for Cyril Race's knee.

A week later, a Right Honourable gentleman was addressing a meeting at Bradford, and waxed eloquent on the delinquencies of the Lords; but, said he, "a one-sided struggle, often averted, long debated, long delayed, but always inevitable, has come at last to the final stages."[2]

There was a grey-haired man at the meeting, whose wife was one of the prisoners in Holloway.

"What you say applies equally to the women who are demanding the vote," he interjected; and immediately five stewards were upon him. Outside, in the passage, they were joined by four more; he might have been a woman, so many pairs of hands, so much strength, seemed necessary to his ejection.

---

1   George Meredith (1828–1909), "A Ballad of Fair Ladies in Revolt" (1876).

2   One of the reasons Asquith dissolved Parliament in November 1910 was because of a long-standing clash between the Liberal Party and the House of Lords over David Lloyd George's proposed land tax in his 1909 "People's Budget." This tax would have had a serious impact on large landowners, and the Conservative opposition, many of whom were large landowners, had a large majority in the House of Lords. As a result of this dispute Asquith introduced a Bill to limit the power of the Lords which the Lords voted down. As a result, Asquith, with the assent of Edward VII and, after his death, George V, threatened to create sufficient new Liberal peers to pass the Bill if the Lords rejected it. One of Edward's provisos, however, was that Asquith call a General Election to see if there was support for this constitutional change (Searle, 74–75).

"I will go quietly," he said. "You needn't knock me about."

But the Liberal stewards, keen on justice, dragged him to the top of the staircase, and sent him flying with a kick in the middle of his back. He fell on his knees and one of his legs was broken; but that did not satisfy the zeal of the League of Young Liberals; they lifted him up and flung him outside the entrance hall on to the pavement. He was longer in recovering from his injuries than was Cyril Race, but the sympathy of the Liberal Press was all for Mr. Race, and there was none left for the grey-haired man. Besides, the case of the latter was but an instance of democratic zeal; no speaker pouring forth fine sentiments on the necessity of overcoming tyranny by justice should be hindered in the flow of his eloquence; whereas Race had been the victim of an outrage, inasmuch as he had been surrounded by women when he twisted his knee.

The General Election was in full swing. Geraldine was working for her husband against the Government. Her sympathies were with the people, but to Geraldine it seemed that fully half the people were women, and she gave all her energies to helping the man who was not only her husband, but the champion of women.

Rachel Cullen was in prison, maimed and ill; she had been terribly mauled by the men who had been ordered to turn back women without arresting them; and the punishment given on Black Friday lasted throughout the punishment of her detention in Holloway.

Angela Sayte has been discharged from Bow Street. The charge against her was withdrawn, and she had had no opportunity of stating in court what, at the hands of the devil of Licence, had befallen her.[1]

Sally was still in the little room, high up, with the window that let her see the sky. Ever since she had been in prison Sally had loved the sky, because it was so big and stretched so far. It was the next best thing to the sea, and to get to the sea again was what Sally wanted most.

"It would set me up, Lady 'Ill, at once, I know it would," she said. "Wot I want is a thorough change, same as I 'ad that time after the little Bilkeses 'ad the measles, an' I was wore out an' sent to

---

1 Charges against most of those arrested were dropped, not without some controversy. Only those women who had been charged with damage to property or assaults on the police were prosecuted. This course of action denied the women who had been brutalised the right to a public trial. According the *Times*, Winston Churchill, the Home Secretary, had considered the matter, and had come to the conclusion that no public advantage would be gained by continuing the proceedings (see Appendix D3).

Little'ampton. If I could get there, I'd be all right again in a day or two. There's nothing picks you up like a thorough change."

She should have it, Geraldine assured her, when she was just a little bit better.

"If I could be along of you, Lady 'Ill, same as I was before, an' see the tide come in, an' 'ear yer talk about the waves an' the women, same as yer did that other time, it would sort of soothe me. I b'lieve it'ud make that there toothache better."

Geraldine said she should go and she would go with her. In the meantime she was under the care of Angela Sayte, who wrote often about her to Geraldine.

Edith Carstairs was at home, touching the stir of the election only through the newspapers. It was quiet enough at the Pightle, peaceful too; but Edith found no peace. Her thoughts were with Rachel in Holloway; with Sally in the little room with the window looking west; with Robbie Colquhoun who had lost his seat at the beginning of the election, and had gone to help a friend in the north.

And then, one day in the paper, Edith came upon an amazing thing: the arrest of Robbie. For what? For doing what he had once said he would like to do, on the day, namely, after the division on the Second Reading of the Conciliation Bill, for punching Cyril Race's head. Race, it seemed, grown bitter since that day, had said at a public meeting things anent suffragettes, which Robbie, as he afterwards put it, could not stomach. The bitterness, of course, was not apparent to the newspaper reporter; to him, it seemed that Race was well within his rights; to all respectable people, it seemed that Race was well within his rights. But the two men had travelled south together and Robbie, having no longer a seat in the House, and being therefore, as he told Edith afterwards, free to please himself, had taken the opportunity of indulging his desire to bring his fists in contact with Race's head. Race's head did not suffer, for, like all members of the Government, he never travelled without plain clothes detectives to shield him from the futilities of women. Nevertheless, he suffered enough insult and indignity to warrant the arrest of Robbie, and to enlist the sympathy of decent people.

Edith's heart rejoiced as she read about it; not that she wished any harm to Race, nor bore him any malice; but it was a delight to know that Robbie had done, was capable of doing, something that was ardently unconventional. In past days, thinking of Robbie and

Race together, she had thought it conceivable that Race might be carried away by the pursuit of an ideal or possibly by the impulse of a passion, to over-ride convention: she had never dreamed that such a course would be taken by Robbie. She had thought that a capacity for indiscretion might be latent in Race, because, as she reasoned, she knew him only in part: she had dismissed the possibility of anything of the kind in Robbie, because, as she told herself, she knew him through and through.

But did she? Had she ever known him? It was evident to Edith that she had not known him at all, this Robbie Colquhoun, who had been convicted of assault, had been sent to prison, had shocked Aunt Elinor and Uncle B., and pained inexpressibly Mrs. Dallas of The Firs: this was a new acquaintance, and a very interesting one. Considering him, it was borne in upon her gradually, that this unknown man had done all the things that she had once expected Cyril Race to do, had the qualities she had most admired, so long as she had supposed him to possess them, in Cyril Race. She had suffered acutely when she had been obliged to separate him from those qualities, when the Race she had set on a pedestal had been cast down and slain by his actual individuality, and had given up the ghost of her ideal. She had sought to bury that ideal, to lay that ghost, never hoping to find for it another habitation in any living man; but the ghost, as it seemed, had been equal to the occasion, and had gone straight home, to the body of Robbie Colquhoun.

CHAPTER LI
AN INTERLUDE

"Demetrius, king of Macedon, had a petition offered him divers times by an old woman, and answered he had no leisure. Whereupon the woman said aloud, 'Why then give over to be king.'"

Bacon[1]

The elections were over; the country was at rest; and the marks made on the public mind by the events of Black Friday had been blurred over or wiped out. Cyril Race's knee was better, and the

---

1   Sir Francis Bacon (1561–1626), *Apophthegmes New and Old* (1625).

window of the motorcar had been mended. There were women, many women, still suffering from the violence of that day; some of them tended in their homes, some of them still undergoing punishment in prison. But this was not in the public mind, nor within the public knowledge.

Sally still lay in bed; Geraldine came to see her every day, and talked to her in the way that Sally said did her good; but she could not take her away from the London room for the change that Sally craved for. And Sally craved less as the days went by, or grew more patient. A thorough change would set her up at once, she continued to say; but she would wait for it till Lady 'Ill thought the right time had come.

Geraldine was very sad at this time; she knew much that was not known to the public mind; knew that a heavy toll had been levied on the health and strength of the women with whom she worked, on Black Friday and before Black Friday; and in the youth of the new year the question was constant: What waits for us in the year's maturer months?

Edith was sad too, and anxious, thinking of Rachel in Holloway; of Sally; of the many women whose lives henceforth would be crippled lives. Cheap martyrdom! To go against party, family, friends; to thwart love's longings and forfeit liking; to give up the pleasant side of life and walk in the mire of crowds and police-courts and prisons; to lose health and strength and see youth die before its time; this, it seemed to her, was not cheap, and this, she knew, was what many women, despised of comfortable folk, had done. She knew something of what it meant; she had been saved from contempt of other women, saved so as by fire, by the agony of the ordeal which that half-hour at the bazaar had been to her. But Aunt Elinor and Uncle Beauchamp and Mrs. Dallas; these knew not at all, and never could know; and there were so many of them; the world was thick with Aunt Elinors and Uncle B.'s, and Mrs. Dallas was indigenous to the soil of respectability.

Thinking of these things, Edith felt almost ashamed that, through the grey of them, should run a thread of gold; but she could not pluck it from the fabric of her consciousness; it was there, interwoven, and seemed to widen as the days went by.

It was broad and bright the day that Robbie Colquhoun came out of prison; it was like sunshine on that January afternoon, when she walked in the lane, knowing that he would come to her there. A wild wet day it was, with a drizzling rain that blew against her face. Edith did not mind the rain, and the rushing clouds carried no dreariness. On such a day no fairy showed itself; even the rain fairies, the numbkins as she had named them long ago, hid away from the sweeping wind. But the phantom company that had companioned her since her girlhood was with her to-day; the heroes and the knights were with her, to meet Robbie, the new Robbie, a stranger and yet well-known. And if she told him they were there, he would understand; he had always understood; it came upon her fully, walking there, that he was the one person in the world who had never failed to understand what she wanted and what she meant; the one person in the world to whom she could say anything and everything that came into her head.

That was why, when he came, it was so easy to show her heart to him; that was why, as they followed the lane together, her phantom friends faded away from her, and her anxious thoughts were hushed and her fears cast out; why for a little space, the thread of gold spread out into a broad band, overlapping the grey; why she was conscious only that she was with Robbie, and that with him was happiness and confidence and strength.

CHAPTER LII
A THOROUGH CHANGE

"All was ended now, the hope and the fear and the sorrow;
All the aching of heart, the restless unsatisfied longing,
All the dull deep pain, and constant anguish of patience."

Longfellow[1]

The next day, the last of the Black Friday prisoners were released; certain of them to return to work; two of them to die. Rachel Cullen lived three days after she came out of prison; her comrade lingered not much longer.

Rachel made no complaint. It was good to be back in her own room, in her own bed, to hear the traffic in the Bayswater Road,

---

1   Henry Wadsworth Longfellow (1807–82), *Evangeline: A Tale of Acadie* (1847).

which had worried her sometimes in past summer days when the windows must needs be open and air could not be had without sound, but which was welcome now because it was familiar and belonged to the outer world and told her with untiring voice that prison days were over. It was good to see Geraldine and Edith and Angela; good to dwell for a little space in the outer world before passing on to the world invisible. Rachel was glad she had not gone direct from the prison cell without another glimpse of places that she knew, of loved and loving faces.

There were many storms in the early part of the year, and in a storm her spirit passed, riding forth upon it, away from contempt and misunderstanding, from privation and pain; not afraid and not alone.

It was February before there was much change in Sally. She seemed to have got over her desire to go to Littlehampton; it was Geraldine now, and Angela, who talked of Littlehampton; but she liked to hear, liked more and more to hear, Lady 'Ill talk about the waves, and the tide that was coming in. She would lie very still and listen, and, like a child, she liked to hear the same thing over and over again.

"Tell me about them waves, Lady 'Ill, a dashin' theirselves agin the rocks."

"Tell me about the tide, Lady 'Ill, wot can't be stopped by nobody."

Geraldine came every day and told her, and always after the telling, Sally said: "Thank you, Lady 'Ill. It's a bit farther in, that tide, ain't it, nor wot it was yesterday?"

But one day, after the telling, Sally did not speak; and something in the way she lay and something in her face caused Geraldine to start up and call for Angela. Yes, it was as she had thought, as she had long known it must be; at last, Sally had got her thorough change.

CHAPTER LIII
"OUR GOD IS MARCHING ON"

"He has sounded forth the trumpet that shall never call retreat,
He is sifting out the hearts of men before His judgment seat;
Oh, be swift, my soul, to answer Him! be jubilant, my feet!
OUR GOD IS MARCHING ON."

Julia Ward Howe[1]

AUTHOR'S NOTE

This is a story which cannot be finished now. The happenings in it, in so far as they have to do with matters political, with prisons and public meetings and turmoil in the streets, are true happenings; and the end has not happened yet. Whether that end will come before more women have died in what is called cheap martyrdom, is a question the answer to which lies hid in the unborn months. It may be that to the women of England will be given that which is already possessed by the women of England's Colonies, while there is still some little grace in the giving. It may be that the forces of strife have done their work and that wisdom will lead the way to peace. It may be that God, riding no more upon the storm, will plant His footsteps on the heaving sea and say to the waves "Peace; be still"; so that the tide may come in gently. It is bound to come in, since the forces of evolution are stronger even than the force which draws the material tide; it may not pause in its coming; but, till it has reached its appointed place, the end of this book cannot be written.

February 23, 1911.

---

1   Julia Ward Howe (1819–1910), "The Battle Hymn of the Republic" (1861).

Appendix A: Additional Writing by Gertrude Colmore

[One of the contentions of the suffrage movement, and of *Suffragette Sally*, is that women with votes would be a formidable force for social change. As Geraldine Hill puts it, "there was much work to do, for her and for all women, work that save by the help of women, would never be done" (256). Such work requires a vote and that, combined with women's particular domestic concerns and abilities, would lead to the amelioration of the lives of the downtrodden. In Colmore's writing, her work for the Theosophical Society and her commitment to anti-vivisection, the same impulse to social reform is evident. Her speech to the Theosophical Society below indicates her belief that many forms of oppression have the same cause: the double standard for men and women. It also, she feels, has the same cure—"the raising of the standard of men to the level of the standard of women."[1] "Broken" deals with this specifically, as the suffragette window breaker confronts a man who has just left a brothel. Both Colmore's speech on the topic of "social purity" and the two short stories are concerned with the status of female sexuality and the relationship of the suffrage movement to conventional forms of femininity. To the man in "Broken," the suffragette is a shameless hussy because she has committed a crime against property, whereas the prostitute is simply invisible. Although the two women begin the story moving in opposite directions, at the end they walk off together and we might assume that, in the eyes of the man watching, there is little to choose between them. In "The Nun," Muriel gives up the trappings of her upper-class femininity—pretty clothes, a hat from Paris, lunches at the Ritz, and marriage—to "take the veil." Though Muriel complains that "Anti's have no sense of antithesis," her Anti

---

[1] The discourse of social purity is one inherited from the nineteenth century. Colmore's arguments, for example, are close to those that Josephine Butler, campaigner against the Contagious Diseases Act, made in 1879: "The root of the evil is in the unequal standard in morality; the false idea that there is one code of morality for men and another for women" (5). In 1913, Christabel Pankhurst published *The Great Scourge and How to End It* in which she argued that prostitution, and the consequent spread of venereal disease, were the direct result of men's failure to live up to women's moral standards.

Aunt is perfectly clear that, in the way *she* defines "womanhood," the opposite of what a woman ought to be is a nun. Or, even worse, a suffragette. While she sees the suffrage movement as a renunciation of conventional womanhood, Monica characterizes it as a spiritual mission "to serve the most oppressed, the most degraded." In both stories, the moral force of this specifically gendered mission is underlined as one of the rights and responsibilities of securing the vote.]

1. "Broken," *The Suffragette*, 26 September 1913

There was nobody in the still night street save two women going in opposite directions and gradually drawing nearer the one to the other, and, at the far end a policeman. It was a street of shops, all made fast for the night, some with shutters and bars, some with the protection only of strong plate glass.

As the man turned the corner, cigar in mouth, hands in overcoat pockets, thought in the scenes he had left, he saw the woman walking ahead of him look round, and, not perceiving him in the shadows, quickly raise her arm. Bang! bang! bang! went the hammer, and crack! crack! crack! went the great sheet of glass. In half a minute, before she could attack another window, before she could flee, he was upon her, and had her by the arm.

The policeman had disappeared: doubtless—the hussy!—she knew his beat and had timed his absence.

"I've got you," cried the man, "and you shan't escape—by George! you shan't. Women like you are a shame and a—"

"A shame and a disgrace, ain't they, my dear?"

The voice, coming from behind, caused him to turn suddenly. The second woman had come up, and was standing under the lamp-post. A painted face, a smile that was slightly vacuous, clothes tawdrily fine, pathetically shabby. *She* didn't count.

"Get along with you!" he said, then turned to his captive. She had not struggled, she had not attempted to break away; she stood quite still, and looked at him.

"Aren't you ashamed of yourself?" he asked. Because she stood so quietly, because she had a refined face, because she looked like a lady, he was all the more angry. "Aren't you ashamed of yourself?"

"No. Aren't you?"

"I? What do you mean?"

"Three hours ago I saw you go into a house—I noticed you because you had in your buttonhole then an orchid of a rather rare kind with which I happen to be acquainted—a house in which such as she," she pointed to the lamp-post, "are bred. Women like her are made by men like you."

"And women like you—"

"Women like me will fight till we have won the right to alter the conditions which drive girls on to the streets because they cannot earn enough honestly to keep them alive—will fight till what is destruction to a woman is not made easy for a man."

"Don't mind her, my dear," said the figure under the lamp-post. "You come with me!" She stepped forward, and with a gait not too certain; she spoke again, in words not too clear.

The girl with the hammer—she was not much more than a girl—pointed with her free hand first at the window, then at the painted face. "Look," she said. "Broken glass and a broken woman. I break windows, and you—how many women have you helped to break?"

He made no answer. He dropped the arm he held and pushed aside the arm that would have held him, and went upon his way. Once, near the end of the street, he turned his head, and, looking back saw the window breaker leading away the broken woman.

2. "The Nun," from *Mr. Jones and the Governess*, London: Women's Freedom League, 1913, 107–11

"You will be called unsexed."

"And over-sexed."

"Yes, I know; and sexless—all at the same time. It is curious how little sense Anti's have of antithesis."

The three, the woman with the pale face and marked features who had spoken first; the woman with the radiant colouring and beautiful clothes who had spoken second; and the girl, with the charm of youth upon her who had spoken last, were in a room overlooking the Park; a pretty room, gay with flowers and bright chintz and fresh muslin curtains.

"When I was your age, girls didn't talk about sex."

"It isn't the *girls* who talk about it now, dear Anti-Auntie."

"Well, it's talked about anyhow, and all owing to those shameless women. Oh, it's all very well, Monica, but I must say what I think."

"I know you must," said the pale woman.

"And you can't say I'm not broad minded. I consented to Muriel—hoping it would cure her—working for three months at that abominable office."

"A fair novitiate."

"Novitiate, indeed! I wish it was. I wish she'd do anything so decent as go into a convent. I wish *all* you women would be nuns and be done with it. It's all you're fit for."

"Perhaps. We *are* nuns, in a sense."

"Funny sense. Nuns give up the world."

"So do we."

"Not in the same way."

"That is true. They renounce the world as a whole, its struggles as well as its pleasures. We give up the pleasures only."

"It's nonsense to talk like that. Nuns spend their time in doing penance and fasting."

"We may be called upon at any moment to fast and do penance."

"Oh," impatiently, "that's different. And besides, they do it, nuns do it, I am told, to lighten the sins of the world."

"If it were not for the sin in the world, the shame and the suffering, we should not be in prison cells nor face rough, angry crowds."

"You are illogical, Monica, and absurd. Convents and crowds, in-deed. As if any two things could be further apart!"

"In form, no. Yet it is the same spirit which impels certain women towards the one and the other."

"You will say, next, that like the nuns you are the brides of Christ, I suppose?"

"No, for we aspire only to be His servants, serving Him in that we seek to serve the most oppressed, the most degraded, the least of His brethren."

"Brethren? I thought it was only women you stood up for."

"I read no sex into the word 'brethren.' But, as a matter of fact, you can't stand up—or be knocked down— for women without helping men too, any more than you can purify one-half of a pool of water and leave the other foul. Humanity is a whole and indivisible."

There was a pause while three pairs of eyes looked out between the muslin curtains into the green spring glory of the Park. The pause was broken by a little laugh.

"Well, Muriel," said the owner of the room, "which way is it to be? You have passed your novitiate according to Monica, and now you must choose; once and for all. From this morning I do my best to make your life what a woman's ought to be, or wash my hands of you. I am lunching at the Ritz. Will you come? There's a new frock waiting upstairs, and a hat I brought back with me from Paris last week—*your* hat; exactly; I know your style. We shall be eight—some of the people you like best; and Sir Harry—wealth and good looks and a title—to be picked up as easily as your table napkin. On the other hand, Monica and her nunnery. Which is it to be?"

The girl was still looking out into the Park with eyes that had grown a trifle wistful. Then, all at once, they shone.

"I take the veil," she said.

3. From "Standards and Ideals of Purity," *Theosophical Ideals and the Immediate Future, Lectures by Mrs. A. Besant, Mr. Laurence Housman, Mr. Baillie-Weaver and Mrs. Baillie-Weaver*, London: Theosophical Publishing Society, 1914, 78–94

[...] It is especially of what is commonly called social purity that I am to speak this evening; commonly called, I say, because social purity, rightly speaking, is a much wider thing than the relations between the sexes. It includes commercial purity, municipal purity, legal purity, political purity, purity of diet, purity of amusement; and indeed all these things are bound together, are mutually inter-de-pendent, and a nation cannot progress far in purity in one direction if it maintains corruption in the others. But the term social purity is commonly restricted to sex morality, and it is in that restricted sense that I am using it now. [...] We hear much about the chivalry of men, much about reverence for womanhood. It is not chivalry which causes the average man to clamour for purity in his wife, his daughters, his sisters, but simply the sense of ownership, impel-ling him to keep in innocence and ignorance certain women—his own. And here I want to say that I wish to make no too sweeping statement, that I recognise that there are many men living above the ordinary standard, many fine and noble men who are fighting by the side of women for purity, as there are certain women, not of the ordinary outcast class, who are living below that standard. I am speaking of the average man, and facts, impossible to deny or explain away, prove only too clearly that reverence for womanhood belongs to the average man's conventions and not to his convictions.

What are these facts? First, the number of women on the streets. Secondly, the existence of white slavery, arising out of the impossibility of keeping up the supply of outcast women equal to the demand. Thirdly, the large number of cases of criminal assault, and, fourthly, the inadequate sentences passed upon offenders of this kind.

First, as to the number of women on the streets. The number has been variously computed, varying from 30,000 to 90,000 in the streets of London. We might halve that number but I will not even do that, I will take it at the lowest figure, 30,000. Thirty thousand outcast women in London alone; women who are described as fallen; but these women are not really, as regards very many of them, fallen—these women are broken. [...]

Now why are these women outcast, what is it that has induced them to lead this life? Amongst them is a certain number who have taken to the life from what may be called choice, who have vicious propensities or are led into it through idleness, love of ease, love of amusement, or vanity. But these are, comparatively speaking, the few; experts who have studied this question unite in affirming that it is a very small percentage who live this life from deliberate choice. Then there are the numbers, and they are large, of those who are drawn into this life from the fact that they have been ruined in childhood. [...] And then there are those who are driven into the life by what is called economic pressure, that is to say that the utmost they can earn, strive as they may, work as hard as they will, is insufficient sometimes to keep body and soul together, and constantly insufficient to do more than keep them in a state of semi-starvation. It is a marvellous testimony to the innate purity of women that girls will go on year after year struggling in this semi-starved state to keep themselves in purity and honesty: the wonder is not that so many give way but that such large numbers refuse to give way. For these girls are constantly watched and constantly tempted by the white slave traders, always on the look out for fresh victims, and if the white slave trader comes across a girl in a moment of weakness or despondency or depression, she, having refused to give way for months, may, in this bitter moment, yield to his offers and persuasion. And yet in spite of all this, in spite of the large numbers of women who through all the causes that I have enumerated are living in the service of vice, the supply is not equal to the demand. And just in this inadequacy of the supply lies the possibility of the white slave traffic. [...]

Then we come to criminal assaults; and I think that the common standard is indisputably shown by the trivial sentences passed upon the men who commit these assaults. If these sentences are compared with the sentences given for offences against property, if you note these things in the newspapers, you will see how much higher is the regard for property than the regard for the person and for human life. It is the Woman's Movement which is bringing these things to our notice. In former days such things as this, such things as I have been speaking of to-night, were hidden from the knowledge of women. But the movement has brought to light these horrors that were tucked away out of sight, and to woman has it been given to assert the truth that life is of more value than property. [...] Take the case of that councillor of Bradford who committed a criminal assault on his little servant not 16 years of age, and was sentenced to fourteen days' imprisonment in the first division. Compare that with the sentences passed on Suffragettes for the destruction of property. [...]

And now before I end, a few words as to the ideals at present before the nation. I have said that a low standard necessitates a low ideal. What then is the ideal which goes with the actual standard of sex morality amongst the generality of men to-day? It is two-fold. Not to be found out, and to escape the consequences of vice, that is the ideal. And here is an instance of the interdependence not only of ideal and standard, but of all movements for reform and of all forms of abuse. For here, against this desire to avoid only the consequences of wrong, the Woman's Movement, the Purity Movement, and the Anti-Vivisection Movement are linked together, since by means of vivisection scientific men are engaged in seeking to nullify those consequences. They are seeking, by inflicting upon animals, living as Nature meant them to live, a disease arising out of the vices of men; seeking in this cruel and infamous way the means of escape from the results of those vices. Far be it from me to say that no effort should be made to combat the terrible disease from which suffer many who are themselves wholly innocent. But I do say that it is a shameful thing to seek by such means as these to avoid the consequences of wrong-doing, and I say that by means so cruel and so foul no real or lasting benefit can ever be attained. The only thing that can combat impurity is purity, the only way to get rid of disease and suffering is clean living, right food and a striving towards purity.

And this brings me to the ideal for which women are battling to-day: the ideal of like purity for man and woman, of doing away with the double standard of morality, the raising of the standard of men to the level of the standard of women. There are some who would do away with the double standard, but seem to advocate the extension of licence to women instead of self-control in men. To me that seems a greater disadvantage. Better to remain as we are, better to have half of the race striving for purity than the two halves discarding the strength that is in them. But the women striving after true emancipation are preaching a gospel of salvation to men, a gospel of strength and hope. They are saying to men: You are not the slaves of your lusts, you are stronger than your passions: you have in you the power to live as purely as women are able to live. Come up and stand beside us! fight with us shoulder to shoulder and together we will cleanse and purify the world. That is the ideal which women are holding up to-day, that is the ideal towards which we are striving and which we are bound to reach. It may be ages before it becomes the standard instead of the ideal, but in the new era that is dawning it will be strengthened and made clearer, and we shall inevitably approach it with ever quickening steps. And when from the ideal it becomes the standard, what then? Why, then we shall see before us ever new heights rising up, loftier, nobler. What those heights may be, whither those ideals may lead us, I cannot say. I only know that we shall go on and on from height to height, from strength to strength, with ever widening conceptions, ever clearer sight, till at last we shall reach the point where the Divine Vision will open, till at last, our hearts made pure, we shall see God.

4. From *The Life of Emily Davison, An Outline*, London: Woman's Press, 1913, 56–61, reprinted in Ann Morley and Liz Stanley, *The Life and Death of Emily Wilding Davison: A Biographical Detective Story*, London: The Women's Press, 1988

[The following excerpt is taken from the final chapter of Colmore's *Life of Emily Davison*, one of the two works, along with *Suffragette Sally*, for which she is best known.

On Derby Day, 4 June 1913, suffragette Emily Wilding Davison was mortally injured when she ran onto the Epsom racecourse and into the path of the racing horses. She may have intended to wave the WSPU colours; she is reported to have tried to grab the bridle of King George V's racing horse Anmer. She was knocked down by the horses, received head injuries, and died, without regaining consciousness, on June 8. In her purse was a return train ticket, and inside her coat were pinned two WSPU flags. Whether she had intended to gain publicity by waving the flags, or whether she had intended to kill herself is still debated.[1] Suffragettes, however, claimed her as a martyr and gave her a funeral which Lisa Tickner describes as a "last, tragic occasion for public spectacle in the suffrage campaign" (138). In *Unshackled*, Christabel Pankhurst writes that "Emily Davison paid with her life for making the whole world understand that women were in earnest for the vote. Probably in no other way and at no other time and place could she so effectively have brought the concentrated attention of millions to bear upon the cause" (254). Constance Lytton writes, in *Prisons and Prisoners*: "It was her opportunity of proclaiming to the whole world, perhaps heedless till then, that women claim citizenship and human rights.... Millions of people, not only in our own but other countries, knew from this act, that there are women who care so passionately for the vote and all it means that they are willing to die for it" (213). Not everyone saw her actions in the same light. Among the Papers of Emily Wilding Davison (GB 0106 7/EWD) in The Women's Library in London is a short piece of anonymous hate mail, signed "An Englishman," which begins: "I am glad you are in hospital. I hope you suffer torture until you die. *You Idiot*," and ends by asking "Why don't Your People find an Asylum for you?"]

Derby Day. Packed trains and rushing motors, and the rank and fashion of England and the scum and riff-raff all hastening towards Epsom Downs. A woman took a third-class ticket to Epsom; a return ticket. Not fashionably clad this woman was, but in quiet, unnoticeable garments; round her body, under her coat, was wound a flag; another rolled tight was carried in her hand. Early that morning Emily had rushed into Headquarters. "I want two flags."

---

1   See Crawford, 159–63; Morley and Stanley; Tickner, 136–40; Sleight.

"What for?"

"Ah!"

"Perhaps I'd better not ask."

"No, don't ask me."

The crowds were great all the length of the course, and very close and dense at Tattenham Corner. Now it is the great race of the day; fine horses, long watched and tended, carefully trained, are waiting for the start, with jockeys cool and keen and weirdly small; and one horse and one jockey of great interest to the crowd; the King's jockey, the King's horse.

They are coming! Hark to the sound of them, and how the hoofs thud upon the turf! There are women in the crowd; one has a flag wound round her, hid by her jacket, and in her pocket the return half of a railway ticket. None notice her, or the other flag, held close to her side.

With a rush the horses come in a great swinging sweep round the curve of Tattenham Corner. There is a woman on the course, there, in amongst the horses, and a flag waves, the colours of it purple, white, and green. A hand grasps at a bridle; the King's horse swerves and falls; the King's jockey is hurled to the ground; cries and confusion everywhere; one only heeds them not. For her there are no more sounds, of icy, rushing water, of comrades' cries, of prison voices. The life so often risked has been given; the time has come.

At that same hour, in a house at Longhorsley, a woman stood in a room alone. She had risen that morning with a feeling that she knew, the feeling that always came when one far away from her was running into danger. And as she stood, something went by her—a bird it seemed. But how had it entered, how escaped? for the window was shut and the door, and looking she saw that there was nothing in the room, no living thing, save only herself.

Emily's physical body lay for four days ere the physical life went out of it, but her consciousness left it, for even as she fell beneath horses' hoofs, at that same moment that "something" went with a flutter of wings through a room in her Northumberland home. "I never let myself think of you when I do things," she had told her mother. But her thought surely had gone to that mother as her soul drew back from life.

Many processions Emily Davison had been in, but never one like this of the 14th June, 1913, when the marchers and the crowd were silent, and the face of the queen of it was hid. Close to where it started, a ragged man stood, holding a rose, ragged too, drooping, half faded; and as the coffin passed he threw the rose upon it. "Gawd bless 'er," he said. "'E's bin waitin' this two hours to do that," said the woman beside him.

There were tears on the faces of many men, gibes on the lips of very few: silence was in all the street through which her body passed, half awe, half wonder. Midway for some of those who marched was a burst of sound; a dim church filled with the singing of women's voices; not sad singing, but triumphant, almost glad. "Nearer my God to Thee," they sang, "E'en though it be a cross that raiseth me." And the words that might have been Emily's own: "Fight the good fight with all thy might!"

Then through the streets again, through crowds, poorer, more ragged, denser. Women were in the crowds, with faces, some worn, some wicked, some hunger-stricken; women for whom Emily had died. Most of them knew it not; some never till now had seen "the suffragettes." Through these to King's Cross Station, whence the coffin was sent, "covered with most lovely flowers," as her father's had been in her description twenty years before, to Morpeth Church—"very old-fashioned, with a lich gate."[1]

The writer first saw that church on an evening in July. A paved path leads through the lich gate edged with great squares of yew to the church's door; and beyond the door the path goes on between borders of mown grass on which are clumps of rhododendrons, and behind them cedar pines and Irish yews. On the Sunday of Emily Davison's funeral the rhododendrons were in bloom.

The bloom had gone on the evening in July and twilight lay grey upon the many yews and cypresses and tall cedar pines that stand amidst the graves. But about the rail-enclosed burial place of the Davison family, sight has a wider field, and looking upwards—for the ground rises all the way from wall to wall of that graveyard—the sky was bright with the sunset, a brilliant red; and looking downwards towards Morpeth very pale and clear, and hanging in the pallor, was a half-formed moon. Looking, the sight went on, beyond the churchyard into the width of the world, beyond the evening

---

1   The roofed gateway to a churchyard under which the corpse is set down, to await the clergyman's arrival (*OED*).

into the years ahead, and saw, from far away and from near, feet coming, many, many feet, treading the paved path through the lich gate till the stones were hollowed and worn; the feet of pilgrims to the Church, "very old-fashioned," and on beyond it, upwards, to the grave of Emily Wilding Davison; who died that other women might find it possible to live truer, happier lives; who fought that other women might have freedom; who gave herself to the Woman's Cause, without grudging and without fear, convinced, as every apostle of liberty has been convinced, that rebellion against tyranny is obedience to God, and never doubting that God will give the victory.

Appendix B: Suffrage: Militant, Constitutional, Anti

[Reading *Suffragette Sally*, one could be excused for thinking that the WSPU was the only suffrage society of any importance in women's fight for the vote. Although the Women's Freedom League (WFL) comes into the novel through Colmore's portrait of its leader, Charlotte Despard, and the National Union of Women's Suffrage Societies (NUWSS) appears through the constitutionalist Agatha Brand, clearly the heroes of the story are WSPU members. While a focus on the WSPU is not uncommon in latter day thinking about the Women's Suffrage Movement, it is important to note that they were not the only game in town, even if they were the most spectacular. There were suffrage societies for women and men, for various religious affiliations, for different regions within the British Isles, for many trades and professions including artists, textile workers, nurses, writers, teachers, as well as for university graduates. There were those who agreed with militancy, and those who did not; and those who were pro-suffrage and those who were "antis." Some blamed the WSPU for spurring the government into peevish delay, while others thought that the actions of the WSPU in the years prior to World War I had a considerable impact on the government's decision to grant a limited franchise in 1918.

The WSPU did, however, keep women's suffrage firmly before the public, not only through their militant activities, but also by organising marches and processions, an exhibition, and Christmas bazaars. A notable aspect of the WSPU's publicity was their genius in marketing. Not only did they produce merchandise that could be purchased by the faithful, they also liaised with firms such as Selfridge's and Liberty who stocked clothes and accessories in the WSPU colours: purple for freedom and dignity, white for purity and green for hope. This colour scheme had been developed by Emmeline Pethick-Lawrence, and suffragettes were encouraged to wear "the colours" at all times, especially at public events such as demonstrations (Atkinson, 1992, 15). Firms were quick to focus their advertising and market their products in order to appeal to suffragette consumers, and *Votes for Women* readers were encouraged to patronise those firms which advertised in the newspaper's pages. The WSPU also maintained its own business ventures. The Woman's Press, founded in 1906, published pamphlets and books, tracts, speeches, and lectures at its premises at 156 Charing Cross Road. There, and in many other locations around London, were WSPU shops selling items emblazoned with "the colours" (such as scarves, ribbons, sashes, badges, handkerchiefs, and jewellery), as well as items bearing designs by artist Sylvia Pankhurst including teapots and cups, soap, playing cards, and brooches. Also for sale were "Panko" (a card game), "Suffragettes in and out of Gaol" (a board game and puzzle), and "Pank-a-Squith" (a table game in which a suffragette attempts "to get from her house to the Houses of Parliament. She has to cross fifty sections and meet with all sorts of opposition" [Atkinson, 1992, 30]).

Since the WSPU is important to *Suffragette Sally*, the following two pieces give a sense of how the WSPU were constructing their demand for the vote and how they were explaining their activities to readers of *Votes for Women*.]

1. "Constitution" (of the WSPU), 1908 [*Votes for Women*, 17 December 1908, 200]

Objects:—To secure for women the Parliamentary vote as it is or may be granted to men; to use the power thus obtained to establish equality of rights and opportunities between the sexes; and to promote the social and industrial well-being of the community.

Methods:—The objects of the Union shall be promoted by:—

1. Actions entirely independent of all political parties.

2. Opposition to whatever Government is in power until such time as the franchise is granted.

3. Participation in Parliamentary Elections in opposition to the Government candidate, and independently of all other candidates.

4. Vigorous agitation upon lines justified by the position of outlawry to which women are at present condemned.

5. The organising of women all over the country to enable them to give adequate expression to their desire for political freedom.

6. Education of public opinion by all the usual methods such as public meetings, demonstrations, debates, distribution of literature, newspaper correspondence, and deputations to public representatives.

Membership:—Women of all shades of political opinion who approve the objects and methods of the Union, and who are prepared to act independently of party, are eligible for membership. It must be clearly understood that no member of the Union shall support the candidate of any political party in Parliamentary elections until women have obtained the parliamentary vote. The entrance fee is 1s.

Suffragettes advertising Women's Sunday, from a boat on the Thames. This mass demonstration organised by the Women's Social and Political Union took place in London on 21st June 1908. Ref. No. 1023 © Museum of London.

2. "Some Questions the Electors are Asking"

[Periodically, *Votes for Women* would run explanatory columns, in question and answer format, on issues germane to the cause. The following column is from 7 January 1910.]

1. *Why does the Women's Social and Political Union oppose all Liberal Candidates, even where they declare themselves friendly to woman suffrage?*

The fate of a Bill in the House of Commons does not depend upon the support or opposition of individual private members, but upon the decision of the Cabinet to support or reject it. In the last House of Commons there were 420 members, *or nearly two-thirds majority*, pledged to support a measure for Woman Suffrage. On February 28, 1908, a Woman Suffrage Bill was carried through its second reading in the House of Commons by a majority of 170 (271 to 92), but the Bill did not become law because the Liberal Government blocked its further passage through the House of Commons. Mr. Asquith and the other members of his Cabinet are still in power to-day, and they still refuse to promise to carry a Woman Suffrage Bill. So long, therefore, as they remain the Government they are the obstacle to Votes for Women. Every Liberal candidate is asking electors to send him to Parliament to support this Government. If he is defeated the Government will be weakened in their power to resist the claims of women. Therefore, women are asking the electors to vote against Liberal candidates, and show the Government that they disapprove of the Government's policy towards women.

Constitutional Agitation

2. *Why do women not agitate for the vote along lawful and constitutional lines?*

Women have agitated for many years along quiet and constitutional lines. Numberless petitions and memorials have been signed and have been presented to the House of Commons and to the Government. Between 1866 and 1879 there were over 9,000 Petitions with Three Million Signatures in support of giving votes to women. In 1896 alone an appeal to members of Parliament was signed by over a Quarter of a Million Women.

In 1867 the wording of the Household Franchise Act was supposed by many people to allow of the enrolment of women as voters. A canvass of the women in Manchester was made, and out of 4,215 women who might be qualified 3,924, or 92 per cent., Sent in Claims.

The Court of Appeal, however, decided against the women (Chorlton v. Lings), and compelled them to make their demand again to Parliament.

Fifty Thousand Meetings

Countless public meetings have been held all over the country, which have carried resolutions in favour of VOTES FOR WOMEN. The Women's Social and Political Union alone have held over 50,000 meetings, indoor and out, during the four and a-half years of their existence. Of these, the great Hyde Park demonstration on Sunday, June 21, 1908, when half a million people came together, was admittedly The Largest Political Demonstration in the History of the World. Other great outdoor demonstrations have been held in all the largest towns throughout the country. At some of these demonstrations it was estimated that over 100,000 persons were present. Of indoor meetings the Albert Hall, London; the Free Trade Hall, Manchester; the Sun Hall, Liverpool; the Colston Hall, Bristol; the Town Hall, Birmingham; the St. Andrew's Hall, Glasgow; the Synod Hall, Edinburgh, and all the other great halls in the country have been filled over and over again by audiences who enthusiastically supported the women's demand.

Breakers of the Law

3. *Do women who break the law deserve to have a share in making the laws?*

The best answer to this question was given by the Right Hon. W.E. Gladstone who said in 1884:—

"I am sorry to say that if no instructions had ever been addressed in political crises to the people of this country except to remember to hate violence and love order, and exercise patience, the liberties of this country would never have been attained."

After many years of quiet agitation women have come to realise that it is no use any longer praying and pleading for the vote, but that some further step is necessary in order to obtain it. Put into plain language, the militant policy of the Women's Social and Political Union means that when people ask for a thing which is their right in a proper manner, politely and courteously, and are put off with subterfuge and prevarication, there is nothing left but to take forcible measures deliberately designed to be disagreeable to those who withhold justice.

4. *What right have women to interrupt Cabinet Ministers at their meetings, or to provoke disturbances outside the halls where they are speaking?*

A glance at the Liberal daily papers shows that the Liberal men certainly consider they have the right to interrupt Tory meetings as much as they like. Women have a greater right to interrupt Cabinet Ministers because *while men have an alternative means of voicing their displeasure by the use of their votes, women have no such means.*

But to understand properly why women behave as they do at the meetings of Cabinet Ministers it is necessary to go back to the beginning of the militant methods of the W.S.P.U.

How The Militant Methods Began

Militant methods began in 1905. Sir Edward Grey was addressing a great meeting in the Free Trade Hall, Manchester. Two women, Christabel Pankhurst and Annie Kenney, determined to find out what was going to be the policy of the Liberal Government towards Woman Suffrage if they were returned at the general election. Accordingly, after Sir Edward Grey's speech was over, at *question time* they put a question to him on this point, but, though other questions from the audience were answered, this question was ignored, and as they insisted upon receiving an answer they were taken by the stewards and thrown out of the meeting, and because they held a protest meeting outside the hall, were arrested and thrown into prison.

During the four years that the Liberal Government has been in power Cabinet Ministers have persistently dealt in this way with women at their meetings. Sometimes the questions came at the end of the meeting; at other times, as is the custom with men hecklers, they took the form of interruptions during the speeches of the

Cabinet Ministers. In almost every case the *women were thrown out with violence*, until at last Cabinet Ministers decided to exclude women altogether from their meetings. When women protested against this in the streets outside the hall, great barricades were erected and a large posse of police called out to deal with the crowds that came to support the women. In consequence, many women were arrested and thrown into prison.

How Many Women Will Vote

5. Is the Women's Social and Political Union asking that every woman should have a vote?
No. The W.S.P.U. are not asking that every woman should have a vote. They are asking that *qualified* women should have a vote, that a woman shall not be refused simply because she is a woman; that is to say, they ask that women who are owners, householders, lodgers, or university graduates shall be voters. This would give votes to about 1 1/4 million of women (most of whom would be working women) as compared with 7 1/2 millions of men who have the vote. They are not asking for the vote for every woman, since every man has not got a vote. The Women's Social and Political Union claim that a simple measure giving votes to women on these terms shall be passed before any other franchise reform is considered.

6. Why do women want the vote?
Because no race or class or sex can have its interests properly safeguarded in the Legislature of a country unless it is represented by direct suffrage.
Because women, whose special care is the home, find that questions intimately affecting the home are being settled in Parliament, where they are not represented.
Because politics and economics go hand in hand, and while men voters can get their economic grievances attended to, non-voters are disregarded. Women are thus compelled to sell their labour cheap, and in consequence men are undercut in the labour market.
Because women are taxed without being represented, and taxation without representation is tyranny. They have to obey the laws equally with men, and they ought to have a voice in deciding what those laws shall be.

Because all the wisest men and women realise that decisions based upon the point of view of men and women together are more valuable than those based upon either singly.

Because women, like men, need to have some interests outside the home, and will be better comrades to their husbands, better mothers to their children, and better housekeepers of the home when they get them.

The Hunger Strike

7. Why do Suffragette prisoners adopt the hunger strike instead of serving out their sentences as other prisoners would do?

The Suffragettes are political prisoners and they refuse to be treated as common felons. In 1889 the Right Hon. W.E. Gladstone, referring to the Irish political prisoners, said:—

"I know very well that you cannot attempt a legislative definition of political offences, but what you can do, and what always has been done, is this: you can say that in certain classes of cases the imprisoned person ought not to be treated as if he had been guilty of base and degrading crime."

In spite of this trenchant saying of his father, Mr. Herbert Gladstone had treated the Woman Suffrage prisoners as ordinary criminals, and has denied to them the privileges which in all civilised countries are accorded to those who have gone to prison for a political offence.

For a long while the Woman Suffrage prisoners contented themselves with written and spoken remonstrances against this treatment. But finding this protest of no avail, in June, 1909, Miss Wallace Dunlop, one of the Woman Suffrage prisoners, adopted the hunger strike with the view of calling attention to this disgraceful state of affairs. The Home Secretary refused to order that she should be treated as a political offender; but seeing that she would persist until she died of starvation, and fearing an outbreak of popular indignation against himself, ordered her release, after ninety-one hours' starvation. Many other Woman Suffrage prisoners followed her example, and with heroic endurance went without food for four, five, and six days as a protest against their treatment, but the Home Secretary still denied them justice, and in the end released them from prison. Since that he has subjected them to forcible feeding.

8. *Is not forcible feeding a comparatively painless operation?*

Mrs. Leigh, who suffered it for one month in Birmingham Gaol, says of it: "the sensation is most painful. *The drums of the ears seem to be bursting*; there is a horrible pain in the throat and breast."

Sir Victor Horsley says that, apart from the brutality of the proceeding, it has the following consequences:—

"Pain, congestion of the nose and pharynx, leading, in my own hospital experiences, to ulceration of the nasal mucous membrane, retching, vomiting, and depression."

Mr. Mansell-Moullin, M.D., says:—

"It is absolutely inhuman and unjustifiable."

Mr. Hugh Fenton, M.D., says:—

"It is an absolutely beastly and revolting procedure."

In addition to these doctors over one hundred other medical practitioners have petitioned the Government to abandon this disgraceful procedure. In spite of this terrible medical indictment, however, the Government have still continued to adopt it rather than treat their women political opponents as political offenders are treated in every civilised country in the world.

Tory Gold

9. *Is it not a fact that the funds of the W.S.P.U. are derived from Tory gold?*

The W.S.P.U. is an absolutely non-party organisation, and accepts money from men and women who are in agreement and sympathy with its aims or objects, whether they happen to be Liberals, Tories, or Socialists, or whether they are outside all political associations. It is not subsidised by any party, and would definitely refuse any money given in this way.

As fully audited subscription lists are published every year, anyone who likes can verify these facts [...].

3. Helena Swanwick, "The Hope and the Meaning," *The Common Cause* 1.1 (15 August 1909), 3

[Helena Swanwick (1864–1939) wrote reviews and articles for the *Manchester Guardian*. In her autobiography, *I Have Been Young* (1935) she writes that when she read the news of Christabel Pankhurst and Annie Kenney's protest at the Manchester Free Trade Hall, "[her] heart rose in support of their revolt" (183). She immediately joined the WSPU, but soon realized she could not work with the Pankhursts, and became a member of the North of England Society for Women's Suffrage, as well as a speaker for the NUWSS and editor of their newspaper, *The Common Cause*. She was not, as the piece below indicates, a supporter of militancy. In her autobiography, she writes: "certain of the militants were *Frondeuses*,[1] and they made a policy of martyrdom. This was deeply repugnant to me. If derision, persecution, martyrdom come to one by reason of what conscience compels one to do, or say, one must take them in one's stride. But to say 'the world is vulgar and must have sensation before it will take notice, therefore we must have martyrs, and if authority refuses to make martyrs of us, we will provoke martyrdom'—this strikes me as dishonest and cynical. Dishonest because it is 'faked' martyrdom; cynical because it attempts to base a reform not upon right reason but upon ballyhoo" (188–89).]

A woman speaking at a recent anti-suffrage meeting said that it was not for the unmarried women to "break up the homes" of their more fortunate married sisters by demanding political equality. It is this notion that women's suffrage means the breaking up of the home, the causing of domestic strife, the setting of woman against man that the every name of this paper is intended to deny. We hold that the liberation of women is the cause which good and intelligent men and good and intelligent women have in common, even when they don't recognize it, and this because when you have freed women, you have given them scope to develop themselves and to protect their young, so that the cause of the woman is also the cause of the man and of the child.

This paper is called the organ of the women's movement for reform. It is this urgent need for social reform that has given the tremendous impetus of late years to the woman's movement. Everywhere social conditions have developed so that the individual

---

1 The term *fronde* means "sling," and was the name given to the civil war in France from 1648–53 in reference to the pelting of windows with stones by the Paris mobs. *Frondeur* (m) or *frondeuse* (f) originally meant someone who suggested that the power of the King should be limited, but has passed into normal usage to mean anyone who criticises the current power structure.

is more and more powerless to do what he would and is more and more moulded by conditions outside his power to determine as an individual. The present trend of thought and legislation is the despair of individualists. These frequently say to the women who ask for the vote, that they overrate its power, that all this interference with individual liberty is bad, that you can't make people good by Act of Parliament.

They don't seem to see that even if this be so, and many women think it is, those very women cannot give effect to their conviction; they are compelled to be quiescent, while men, as some of them think, are legislating them out of existence. If Parliament is interfering too much with the lives of the people, this state of things will not be remedied by all the people who object to interference keeping or being compelled to keep out of politics. Yet this is what some politicians of the *laissez-faire* school would urge upon us. Women do not ask for the vote mainly because they want to govern, but because they want not to be misgoverned. Women's homes, their houses and children, their food and drink and work and sickness, the attendance upon them in labour, every minute matter of their daily life, from the registering of their birth to their final old-age pension and death certificate, is bound round, hedged in, prescribed by law, and the laws are not always what the women approve—they are by no means what they would be if the women's voices were heard. Most women who work believe in reform. There are certain social ulcers eating into the very bone of the nation which they want to see cured. But the women's demand for the vote is more than the mere demand to effect reformative legislation, though that is much. It is also the demand that the mother half of humanity should be given its proper place: that the preserver and producer of life, the maker of men, should be as highly honoured as the destroyer of life, the maker of things: that the temperate affectional woman-nature, intent upon the conversation of the home and the race, should have its due representation beside the more extreme and appetitive male nature.

For a long time the process of agitating for liberty took the form of proving that women were in the main very much like men. The old conception seemed to be that women were so different that they did not need the same things at all, and scope, opportunity, training, were masculine prerogatives; also that the capacities of women were so different from and inferior to those of men that it would be sheer waste to expend effort in developing them. But now it seems more necessary to point out the unlikeness; to insist that women have a different point of view, quite as respectable and quite as important as the man's. In the vulgar sense of the word "difference," we see how the old Adam reads into it something hostile—"Me and my husband, we had a difference, so I threw the jug at him"—instead of hailing the difference as a god-sent preventative of dulness and stagnation. These differences are most precious and enlightening, but they can only be so when they are acknowledged and expressed and given their full value. Repression of one sex is bad for both sexes. We have long ago learned what a safety-valve are public discussion and expression, yet these are denied to women, by those who profess to consider public life as degrading to womanhood. This state of things is full of danger. It is well-known that you do not get the best out of people by governing them against their will: a benevolent despotism is a political state which has only a negligible handful of supporters in England; yet, where women are concerned, many Englishmen are still Muscovites or Turks, and would be kind to women only in their own way. And so we have the strange situation that many of the women who are most eager for social reform are resisting with growing bitterness every attempt on the part of men to get on with it. "We can't do anything right for you!" say men with some heat. But is it not easy to see why?—The reason lies just in those two little words, "for you." As a child grows, the first thing he desires is "to do things myself." Women have grown up and desire to do things themselves.

To many men, women appear politically incompetent, for the simple reason that they are not practised in the arts and customs of politics as men have evolved them. We hear of political experience as being a necessity. But the use of the vote is not a function requiring exercise: it is but the expression of an opinion on certain matters and on nearly all these matters women actually have or should have an opinion. As for the arts and customs of politics, some of them, doubtless, women could learn, with their usual quickness and adaptability; but we must confess, here and now, that many of these customs do not result from women's nature as we conceive it, but from men's nature, and we fervently hope that all women will not consider it necessary to imitate them. To most men, for ages, politics have been either sport or war, and they still are. To us it would seem better that they should be neither. We feel that to understand each other should be the first desire of human beings who form part of one society. By recrimination, by attributing ignoble motives, by begging instead of meeting the question, by scoring off people in petty ways, one never arrives at this understanding. Now we start with the assumption that every one has a point of view: the creature we call a criminal does not regard himself with horror; even the anti-suffragist has a point of view, and the better we understand it, the more effective we will be in our efforts to change it. We don't want to score; we don't want to conquer; we want to understand. Therefore this paper is non-party; therefore, believing in the ultimate victory of right, not might, we advocate peaceful penetration and constitutional action. But we advocate this for men as for women. To hear some of the opponents of women's claim to enfranchisement, you would suppose that the law of love was never preached by a Man to men, as well as to women. It is the most difficult of all laws to follow and we shall, like others, fail again and again; but at least we intend to follow it, however often and disastrously we may fail in carrying out our intention. The hope in which we start this paper is that we may yet see men and women understand each other better; the meaning of the common cause is that through liberty and mutual trust, men and women will arrive at a higher development than through doubt and domination.

4. Mary Augusta Ward, "Editorial," *The Anti-Suffrage Review* I (December 1908): I–2

[Mary Augusta Ward, also known as Mrs. Humphry Ward (1851–1920), is probably best known as the author of *Robert Elsmere* (1888). A prolific writer, she was also the author of two anti-suffrage novels, *Diana Mallory* (1908) and *Delia Blanchflower* (1915). Ward was an early opponent of women's suffrage, becoming an executive member of the Women's National Anti-Suffrage League (later the National League for Opposing Women's Suffrage, under the Presidency of Lord Cromer). In *Suffragette Sally*, the anti-suffrage characters, particularly Mr. Bilkes, Mrs. Dallas, Aunt Elinor, and Uncle Beauchamp Leigh, are presented as prissy and extreme, their views arising from a particular moral and class-based perspective on how women should behave. The anti-suffrage speech in the chapter "The Plot that

Failed" is based on one given by Lord Cromer who was, at the time, the President of the Men's League for Opposing Women's Suffrage, and who did indeed say that "his main objection to give the vote to women was because they were not men" (*Times*, 19 May 1908, 8). While many of the anti-suffrage arguments were noxious, not all of the anti-suffragists were as simple-minded as the novel presents them, nor was the anti-suffrage position quite as black and white as it may seem. Brian Harrison, for example, argues that it would be wrong simply to equate anti-suffrage with anti-feminist (56), though there were certainly some "antis" for whom the equation is apt. Ward makes clear that her (and her League's) disagreement with the Parliamentary franchise for women is because it would involve "a kind of activity and responsibility for woman which is not compatible with her nature, and with her proper tasks in the world." This did not necessarily mean, however, that woman should stay out of specific kinds of politics or social activism, even if these were limited to the "domestic" spheres of education, child welfare, or care for the sick and elderly. Nor were the pro- and anti-suffragists completely at odds when it came to woman's nature and her tasks in the world. As Julia Bush points out "women on both sides of the suffrage debate were agreed upon the existence of maternal powers which were beneficial to British society.... Women who disagreed over the specific issue of the franchise might well share similar perspectives on 'natural' gender roles, social class divisions and religious matters as well as on their duties towards nation and Empire" (432, 433). Anti-suffragists worked to promote higher education for women as well as increased activity in local government. Ward and Lord Curzon, for instance, worked to support women's higher education, specifically admission to Oxford, and Ward was active in promoting women's activity in local government (Harrison, 56). Ward founded, and found funding for, the Passmore Edwards Settlement (named for the philanthropist who financed it, now called Mary Ward House) which provided education for children with disabilities.]

The first number of *The Anti-Suffrage Review* seems to demand a fresh though short statement of the aims and hopes of the Women's National Anti-Suffrage League, of which it is to be the organ; a statement brought up to date, and taking account of recent events.

No moment could ever be more favourable for the appearance of our little journal. The recent performances of the Women's Social and Political Union; the attempt to "rush" the House of Commons, with its accompaniment of riot and injury, and its sequel in a mock-heroic trial, and a mock-heroic imprisonment, which could be terminated at any moment by the will of the prisoners; the ludicrous, but nonetheless scandalous, attack by women of the same body on the decency and dignity of the House of Commons itself, have sent a shock of repulsion—a wave of angry laughter—through England, and are bringing recruits from all sides to the Anti-Suffrage League. In the week after the attempted "rush," the offices of the League were besieged by visitors and correspondence; the opposition to the suffrage movement is strengthening throughout the country; branches are being rapidly formed in the provinces; in London whole districts are waking up to the peril at our doors; and in general, as may be seen by the protest at High Wycombe against the Mayoralty of a woman so respected as Miss Dove, and by the defeats of women candidates in the municipal elections, the strong antipathy of our serious, slow-moving middle class has been aroused; and no movement has ever yet been successful in England that had the feeling of our great middle class against it.

But although the omens for our League are good, and the Suffragettes have been rapidly destroying all that generous respect for the cause and the advocates of woman suffrage, which the efforts of Mrs. Fawcett and many others have awakened even among those who could not agree with them, the peril is still great, and the league has its work before it! For in these days of wide publicity, any movement which takes to the streets, and gets something of a hold there—any movement which involves riot and disorder, struggles with the police, and the defiance of the ordinary decencies of life, is sure to obtain momentarily—far more attention from a democracy than it gives to reformers who are law-abiding and self-controlled. Something is gained—temporarily—by headlines, by arrogance and violence, and the defiance of all measure and all authority.

But it is not a gain that lasts. And it is our business as a League to take full advantage of the present reaction visible in all spheres of life, to make our protests heard.

We protest against the Parliamentary franchise for women, because it involves a kind of activity and responsibility for woman which is not compatible with her nature, and with her proper tasks in the world. Men who have built up the State, and whose physical strength protects it, must govern it, through the rough and ready machinery of party-politics. Women are citizens of the State no less than men, but in a more ideal and spiritual sense. The great advance of women during the last half-century, moral and intellectual, has been made without the vote; and the work under their hands, for which the nation calls upon them, work with which the Parliamentary vote and party-politics have nothing to do, is already more than they can accomplish. To plunge women into the strife of parties will only hinder that work, and injure their character. Have not the spectacles of the last few weeks shown conclusively that women are not fit for the ordinary struggle of politics, and are degraded by it? Their nerves are of a different tension from men's. Once admit them to the Parliamentary vote, and we shall see many other attempts to "rush" the House of Commons whenever any strong agitation is at work among the women voters; the violent excitable element in politics will be largely increased; and a sex feeling and sex antagonism will be aroused, rendering the calm and practical discussion of great questions impossible; a feeling and antagonism disastrous to women, disastrous to England.

Meanwhile the members of the new League are no mere advocates of things as they are. They do not deny in the least the existence, both for women and for men, of grievances that should be redressed, of wrongs that should be righted. But they believe that many agencies exist, or could be developed out of those that exist, whereby reform could be obtained without the rash and ruinous experiment of the Parliamentary vote for women. Our columns will always be open to signed advocacy and discussion of the reforms concerning the life and work of women. We shall support their present privileges and powers in local government with all our strength. But we shall do all that in us lies to prevent the spread of a movement, the success of which would weaken our country in the eyes of the civilised world, and fatally diminish those stores of English sanity, of English political wisdom, based on political experience, which have gone—through all vicissitude, failure, and error—to the making of England, and the building up of the Empire.

5. From Sir Almroth E. Wright, M.D., F.R.S., "Suffrage Fallacies," a letter to the editor of *The Times*, 28 March 1912, rpt. as "Letter on Militant Hysteria" in *The Unexpurgated Case Against Woman Suffrage*, London: Constable and Company, 1913, 77–86

[Sir Almroth Wright (1861–1947) was a physician of some note in the early part of the twentieth century, a reputation that comes from his development of anti-typhoid inoculation, the use of preventive vaccines made of bacteria which had been killed (Warboys), and his contribution to the treatment of war casualties (Dunnill, 159). The following extraordinary letter to the *Times*, expanded into a short book in 1913, is an attempt to medicalise militant activity by suggesting that those who persist in it suffer from "physiological emergencies" that lead to hysteria. The letter received considerable publicity, both for and against, and the correspondence columns were busy for the next few weeks (the discussion was halted upon the sinking of the *Titanic*). Michael Dunnill writes that senior members of the medical establishment were quick to dissociate themselves, though more on the grounds of the impropriety of mentioning matters proximate to sexuality than on grounds of pro- or anti-suffrage (150–51). Responses to both Wright's letter and his book are fascinating for the terms of the debate (see Dunnill, 135–60). As controversial as Wright's position was, it brought into focus many publicly unspoken prejudices that may serve to remind us why the suffragettes were militant.[1]]

Sir,— For man the physiological psychology of woman is full of difficulties.

He is not a little mystified when he encounters in her periodically recurring phases of hypersensitiveness, unreasonableness, and loss of the sense of proportion.

He is frankly perplexed when confronted with a complete alteration of character in a woman who is child-bearing.

When he is a witness of the "tendency of woman to morally warp when nervously ill," and of the terrible physical havoc which the pangs of a disappointed love may work, he is appalled.

---

1 Suffragette responses to Wright include the following: Eleanor Rathbone, "What Anti-Suffragist Men Really Think About Women: Sir Almroth Wright and His Critics" (Liverpool: Liverpool Society for Women's Suffrage, 1912); May Sinclair, "Feminism" (London: Women Writers' Suffrage League, 1912); Beatrice Webb, *New Statesman* (1 November 1913).

And it leaves on his mind an eerie feeling when he sees serious and long-continued mental disorders developing in connexion with the approaching extinction of a woman's reproductive faculty [...]

Nonetheless, [...] no doctor can ever lose sight of the fact that the mind of woman is always threatened with danger from the reverberations of her physiological emergencies.

It is with such thoughts that the doctor lets his eyes rest upon the militant suffragist. He cannot shut them to the fact that there is mixed up with the woman's movement much mental disorder; and he cannot conceal from himself the physiological emergencies which lie behind.

The recruiting field for the militant suffragists is the million of our excess female population—that million which had better long ago have gone out to mate with its complement of men beyond the sea.

Among them there are the following different types of women:—(a) First—let us put them first—come a class of women who hold, with minds otherwise unwarped, that they may, whenever it is to their advantage, lawfully resort to physical violence.

The programme, as distinguished from the methods, of these women is not very different from that of the ordinary suffragist woman.

(b) There file past next a class of women who have all their life-long been strangers to joy [...] These are the sexually embittered women in whom everything has turned into gall and bitterness of heart, and hatred of men.

Their legislative programme is licence for themselves, or else restrictions for man.

(c) Next there file past the incomplete. One side of their nature has undergone atrophy, with the result that they have lost touch with their living fellow men and women.

Their programme is to convert the whole world into an epicene institution—an epicene institution in which man and woman shall everywhere work side by side at the selfsame tasks and for the selfsame pay.

These wishes can never by any possibility be realised. Even in animals—I say *even*, because in these at least one of the sexes has periods of complete quiescence—male and female cannot be safely worked side by side, except when they are incomplete.

While in the human species safety can be obtained, it can be obtained only at the price of continual constraint.

And even then woman, though she protests that she does not require it, and that she does not receive it, practically always does receive differential treatment at the hands of man.

[...] when man sets his face against the proposal to bring in an epicene world, he does so because he can do his best work only in surroundings where he is perfectly free from suggestion and from restraint, and from the onus which all differential treatment imposes.

And I may add in connexion with my own profession that when a medical man asks that he should not be the yoke-fellow of a medical woman he does so also because he would wish to keep up as between men and women—even when they are doctors—some of the modesties and reticences upon which our civilisation has been built up.

Now the medical woman is of course never on the side of modesty, or in favour of any reticences. Her desire for knowledge does not allow of these.

(d) Inextricably mixed up with the types which we have been discussing is the type of woman whom Dr. Leonard Williams's recent letter brought so distinctly before our eyes—the woman who is poisoned by her misplaced self-esteem; and who flies out at every man who does not pay homage to her intellect.

She is the woman who is affronted when a man avers that for him the glory of woman lies in her power of attraction, in her capacity for motherhood, and in unswerving allegiance to the ethics which are special to her sex. [...]

The programme of this type of woman is, as a preliminary, to compel man to admit her claim to be his intellectual equal; and, that done, to compel him to divide up everything with her to the last farthing, and so make her also his financial equal.

And her journals exhibit to us the kind of parliamentary representative she desiderates. He humbly, hat in hand, asks for his orders from a knot of washerwomen standing arms a-kimbo.*

---

* I give, in response to a request, the reference: *Votes for Women*, March 18, 1910, p. 381. [Wright refers to the cover page of that week's edition of *Votes for Women* where it was customary to publish a cartoon dealing with some aspect of the campaign. The cartoon here is entitled "The Woman's Charter." The caption reads: "When women's point of view will be listened to. Parliamentary Candidate (after women have the vote): 'As free

(*e*) Following in the wake of these embittered human beings come troops of girls, just grown up. [...]

The programme of these young women is to be married upon their own terms. Man shall—so runs their scheme—work for their support—to that end giving up his freedom, and putting himself under orders, for many hours of the day; but they themselves must not be asked to give up any of their liberty to him, or to subordinate themselves to his interests, or to obey him in anything. [...]

It is not necessary, in connexion with a movement which proceeds on the lines set out above, any further to labour the point that there is in it an element of mental disorder. It is plain that it is there. [...]

Quite as fatuous are the marriage projects of the militant suffragist. [...] [I]f a sufficient number of men should come to the conclusion that it was not worth their while to marry except on the terms of fair give-and-take, the suffragist woman's demands would have to come down.

It is not at all certain that the institution of matrimony—which, after all, is the great instrument in the levelling up of the financial situation of woman—can endure apart from some willing subordination on the part of the wife.

It will have been observed that there is in these programmes, in addition to the element of mental disorder and to the element of the fatuous, which have been animadverted upon, also a very ugly element of dishonesty. In reality the very kernel of the militant suffrage movement is the element of immorality.

There is here not only immorality in the ends which are in view, but also in the methods adopted for the attainment of those ends.

We may restrict ourselves to indicating wherein lies the immorality of the methods.

There is no one who does not discern that woman in her relations to physical force stands in quite a different position to man.

Out of that different relation there must of necessity shape itself a special code of ethics from woman. And to violate that code must be for woman immorality.

---

and independent electors, what do you wish me to undertake on your behalf?'" The cartoon depicts the male candidate, top hat in hand, addressing six women of different ages and from different classes. The central figure is a woman who is wearing a large hat, warming her hands inside a fur muff and is hardly a "washerwoman."]

So far as I have seen, no one in this controversy has laid his finger upon the essential point in the relations of woman to physical violence.

It has been stated—and in the main quite truly stated—that woman in the mass cannot, like man, back up her vote by bringing physical force into play.

But the woman suffragist here counters by insisting that she as an individual may have more physical force than an individual man.

And it is quite certain—and it did not need suffragist raids and window-breaking riots to demonstrate it—that woman in the mass can bring a certain amount of physical force to bear.

The true inwardness of the relation in which woman stands to physical force lies not in the question of her having it at command, but in the fact that she cannot put it forth without placing herself within the jurisdiction of an ethical law.

The law against which she offends when she resorts to physical violence is not an ordinance of man; it is not written in the statutes of any State; it has not been enunciated by any human law-giver. It belongs to those unwritten, and unassailable, and irreversible commandments of religion, [...], which we suddenly and mysteriously become aware of when we see them violated. [...]

We see acknowledgment of it in the fact that even the uneducated man in the street resents it as an outrage to civilisation when he sees a man strike a blow at a woman.

But to the man who is committing the outrage it is a thing simply unaccountable that any one should fly out at him.

In just such a case is the militant suffragist. She cannot understand why any one should think civilisation is outraged when she scuffles in the street mud with a policeman. [...]

Up to the present in the whole civilised world there has ruled a truce of God as between man and woman. That truce is based upon the solemn covenant that within the frontiers of civilisation (outside them of course the rule, lapses) the weapon of physical force may not be applied by man against woman; nor by woman against man. [...]

And it is this solemn covenant, the covenant so faithfully kept by man, which has been violated by the militant suffragist in the interest of her morbid, stupid, ugly, and dishonest programmes.

Is it wonder if men feel that they have had enough of the militant suffragist, and that the State would be well rid of her if she were crushed under the soldiers' shields like the traitor woman at the Tarpeian rock?[1] [...]

The parliamentary vote is an instrument—and a quite astonishingly disappointing instrument it is—for obtaining legislation; that is, for directing that the agents of the State shall in certain defined circumstances bring into application the weapon of physical compulsion.

Further, the vote is an instrument by which we give to this or that group of statesmen authority to supervise and keep in motion the whole machinery of compulsion. [...]

So that the difference between voting and direct resort to force is simply the difference between exerting physical violence in person, and exerting it through the intermediary of an agent of the State.

The thing, therefore, that is withheld from "the noblest woman in England," while it is conceded to the man who is lacking in nobility of character, is in the end only an instrument by which she might bring into application physical force.

When one realises that that same noblest woman of England would shrink from any personal exercise of violence, one would have thought that it would have come home to her that it is not precisely her job to commission a man forcibly to shut up a public-house, or to hang a murderer. [...]

The evils of woman suffrage lie, *first*, in the fact that to give the vote to women is to give it to voters who, as a class, are quite incompetent to adjudicate upon political issues; *secondly*, in the fact that women are a class of voters who cannot effectively back up their votes by force; and, *thirdly*, in the fact that it may seriously embroil man and woman. [...]

If woman suffrage comes in here, it will have come as a surrender to a very violent feminist agitation—an agitation which we have traced back to our excess female population and the associated abnormal physiological conditions. [...]

---

1   According to this legend, the Vestal Virgin Tarpeia, daughter of Spurius Tarpeius, governor of the citadel on the Capitoline Hill, betrayed the Romans by opening the city gates to let in the Sabines in return for the promise of payment of what they bore on their arms. She anticipated receiving their golden bracelets. Instead, the Sabines crushed her to death with their shields, and she was buried on the rock that was later named after her.

A conciliation with hysterical revolt is neither an act of peace; nor will it bring peace. [...]

Peace will come again. It will come when woman ceases to believe and to teach all manner of evil of man despitefully. I will come when she ceases to impute to him as a crime her own natural disabilities, when she ceases to resent the fact that man cannot and does not wish to work side by side with her. And peace will return when every woman for whom there is no room in England seeks "rest" beyond the sea, "each one in the house of her husband," and when the woman who remains in England comes to recognise that she can, without sacrifice of dignity, give a willing subordination to the husband or father, who, when all is said and done, earns and lays up money for her.

Appendix C: Imprisonment, Forcible Feeding, Release

1. From "A Speech by Lady Constance Lytton, Delivered at the Queen's Hall, January 31, 1910," *Votes for Women*, 4 February 1910, 292–93

[The character Lady Geraldine Hill is modeled on Lady Constance Lytton, who became famous for her actions in bringing class-based prison practices to light. In October 1909, Lytton was arrested in Newcastle for having thrown a stone at Sir Walter Runciman's car, in which she believed David Lloyd George to be a passenger. Sent to prison for assault and malicious damage, she adopted the hunger strike; but, before she could be forcibly fed, doctors were called in to test her heart, which had been weak since childhood. They determined that it was too weak to undergo forcible feeding, and Lytton, along with Jane Brailsford, was released after two days. The following January, Lytton was in Liverpool and Manchester where she met with suffragette Mary Gawthorpe. She writes that they had been "distressed beyond words to hear of the sufferings of Leslie Martin and Selina Hall":

> Mary Gawthorpe said, with tears in her eyes, as she threw her arms around me: "Oh, and these women are quite unknown—nobody knows or cares about them except their own friends. They go to prison again and again to be treated like this until it kills them!" That was enough. My mind was made up. The altogether shameless way I had been preferred against the others at Newcastle, except Mrs Brailsford, who shared with me the special treatment, made me determine to try whether they would recognise my need for exceptional favours without my name. (235)

Consequently, in January 1910 Lytton disguised herself as a working-class woman, Jane Warton. She was arrested in Liverpool for exhorting a crowd to protest against forcible feeding, and for dropping stones over the prison governor's hedge. She refused food but, whereas Lady Constance's heart had been thoroughly examined,

Jane Warton's heart was given only a cursory listen, and was pronounced to be "splendid" (275). She was released from prison 23 January 1910, having been forcibly fed since 18 January. She had been losing weight at the rate of two pounds per day, and was released on medical grounds. Shortly after Lytton's arrest, the Press Association contacted her family (from whom she had kept her intentions secret) for confirmation of a rumour that she was imprisoned in Liverpool. A Prison Commissioner at the Home Office, confirmed that there was a prisoner in Walton Gaol "whom they [had] for some days suspected of being other than her declaration" (*Prisons and Prisoners*, 296). After her release, Lytton wrote an article about her experiences for *Votes for Women*, wrote letters to the *Times*, and gave the speech of which the following is an excerpt. Shortly thereafter, she collapsed from heart disease. Her experiences in prison continued to affect her health and, in 1912, she suffered a stroke the results which incapacitated her for the rest of her life. Emmeline Pethick-Lawrence writes that "when her right hand became helpless, she wrote [her memoir] *Prisons and Prisoners*, with her left hand" (247).

Parts of the following speech appear verbatim in *Suffragette Sally*, especially in the chapters "What is in a Name" and "The Valley of Vision."]

[...] At last they came. It is like describing a hospital scene—and much worse. The doctor and four wardresses came into my cell. I decided to save all my resistance for the actual feeding, and when they pointed to my bed on the floor I lay down, and the doctor did not even feel my pulse. Two wardresses held my hands, one my head. Much as I had heard about this thing, it was infinitely more horrible and more painful than I had expected. The doctor put the steel gag in somewhere on my gums and forced open my mouth till it was yawning wide. As he proceeded to force into my mouth and down the throat a large rubber tube, I felt as though I were being killed—absolute suffocation is the feeling. You feel as though it would never stop. You cannot breath, and yet you choke. It irritates the throat, it irritates the mucous membrane as it goes down, every second seems an hour, and you think they will never finish pushing it down. After a while the sensation is relieved, then the food is poured down, and then again you choke, and your whole body resists and writhes under the treatment; you are held down, and the process goes on, and, finally, when the vomiting becomes excessive the tube is removed. I forgot what I was in there for, I forgot women, I forgot everything except my own sufferings, and I was completely overcome by them.

What was even worse to me than the thing itself was the positive terror with which I anticipated its renewal. Very soon I thought to try and appeal to that man as a doctor to perform the operation in a better way, but whatever one said or suggested was treated with most absolute contempt.

There was one even worse thing, and that was the moral poisoning, if one may call it that, of one's whole mind. I always closed my eyes. I tried not to see the beings who came to do this thing. I felt it was all too hideous, and I did not wish it imprinted on my eyes. Nevertheless I got to hate those men and women, I got to hate infinitely more the powers that stood behind them, I got to hate the blindness, the prejudice, in those who turn away and won't look or listen to what is being done under their very eyes. I tried to think of the splendid heroes and heroines since the world began, of all the martyrs, all the magnificent women in this movement, and I felt a tremendous gratitude to them, an admiration which overpowered me. But it was no use to me—it did not help me and it did not strengthen me.

I must go back a little, and tell you that when the chaplain visited me he seemed to have said to himself, "This is a Suffragette; one must mend her ideas of women." So he began speaking in this style: "I can tell you one thing, any woman you see in this prison, you may take it from me, is as bad as bad can be. Everything has been done to help her, but she is absolutely hopeless." These remarks came back to me later, and I thought, Here is this man, the only man in this prison who could strike a different note, who could help the wretched souls, and that is his summing up of all the unhappy people under him—'as bad as bad can be.'"

Two Pictures

Then one evening, as I lay on the bed on the floor of my cell, I looked up. There were three panes of clear glass, and on them as the light fell there came shadows of the moulding that looked like three crosses. It brought to my mind the familiar scene of Calvary with its three crosses, and I though: What did they stand for? One for the

Lord Christ who died for sinners, and one for the sinner who was kind, and one for the sinner who had not yet learnt to be kind, and behind those crosses I saw those hateful faces, the self-righteous, all those hateful institutions of superior goodness and moral blindness of officialdom, of all the injustice done, not only in prison, but in the world outside, and I thought surely it was for these that Christ died and is dying still and will have to die until they begin to see. When I thought that my blind hatred should be standing between these people and their better selves, I felt the hatred and the hell-like surroundings go from me. I was grateful to those panes, and the next day I put the table and the chair together and roused myself to wash the three windows cleaner, and as I looked though the glass, I saw, in the waning evening light, suffused by a pink glow, a scene which was to me more beautiful than the most beautiful picture I had ever seen. Outside was a little exercise yard, into which I had never been. Wandering round and round in the evening light, quite alone, was a slight figure of a woman, and as she turned the corner I saw that in her arms, under her shawl, she had another little prisoner, a baby, and she was happy and talking and singing to it; she seemed the very symbol of what we are fighting for—fighting to restore what has been lost—and I looked at that woman, who seemed so helpless, and I thought of the parson's words, "Bad as bad can be." And I felt as strong as Samson! A strength which no stories of heroic people had been able to give to me came to me.

After each time the hideous process of forcible feeding was repeated it meant a ghastly kind of washing-up. Two of three times I was so absolutely unmanned that I was not able to do it myself, and an ordinary prisoner came in to do it. She was a new hand, and the wardresses said contemptuously in her presence, "Just look at that, look at the way she is doing it." But the woman's face never changed, there was no resentment and no anger. I ventured to say, "At any rate, she is doing the work I ought to do myself, and I am very grateful to her," and from that woman there came to me an immense strength, and I felt I could fight on and live on to the end. As I was taken out to be weighed I passed a little girl, she was not more than a child. She may for aught I know have been taken straight off the streets, but she had at that moment the face of an angel, and she looked down on me with a smile which you can never see out of prison. She gave me that angel's smile, and it positively touched my very soul. When I went out of the prison I felt my resentment and anger were gone. In a way my physical courage was no better than before, but at least I could go on. I knew that I should last out.

Then you come out of prison, and you hear people say: "You have gone in as a practical joke to do the Home Secretary," or "You went in for a piece of hooliganism," and so on. What are these people made of? Is that what we want? No. We want that from those helpless officials who are only blindly doing what they are told to do, there should be removed these hideous orders from high quarters, that it should become impossible for orders of that kind to be carried out on women who can in no sense be compared with ordinary criminals. It must not be left to the magistrates and the law, but in public opinion it must be made impossible.

Even now there are many people to-day who kindly extend their personal sympathy to me. What are those people? Everyone counts immensely. Do not, at any point where you touch this movement, think you are of no account. Do your part and leave the rest. We want your sympathy, and are glad of it. We want your money, and I will tell you a story about that. One woman, a poor working woman, wrote to the Union, and enclosed a postal order for half-a-crown, and she said: "Will you take this and use it in any way Constance Lytton would like best." Another said: "I should have liked to send you flowers, but I thought you would like the money better." With this I mean to start a fund simply for educating this blind world, for trying to take the scales from the eyes of those who do not yet understand. We want your help for that, and we want your money for that, but we want, even more than that, that you should stand by us. Let me tell you one more personal anecdote. When the doctor first came into my cell I said: "Will you shake me by the hand?" And what I had been going to say to him if he had granted me my request was, "I want to shake hands with you for you have taken service on the wrong side. Those who back the Government in this matter are on the wrong side, and when they discover it they will have a very black moment, so let us shake hands over it now." Well the doctor, being a prison official, could probably do nothing else; he did not shake hands. But do not let it come to you—that black moment when you will find you have taken service on the wrong side. This is the most glorious fight that has ever been. Become a member of our Union. It is so easy to do that. Before you leave this hall, say: "I will stand by you whatever the world says, whatever public opinion says, I am for you now, before another minute goes by."

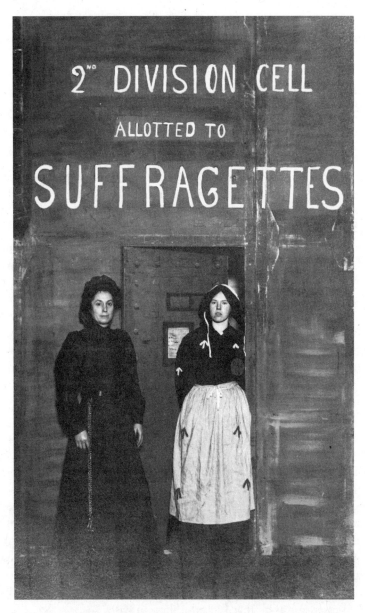

Suffragettes dressed as prisoner and warden at the Prison Cell Exhibit reconstructed for The Women's Exhibition. This fund-raising and propaganda event was held at Princes' Skating Rink in May 1909. Ref. No. 1065 © Museum of London.

2. From Constance Lytton and Jane Warton, Spinster, *Prisons and Prisoners: Some Personal Experiences*, London: William Heinemann, 1914

[The first excerpt below is Lytton's description of her physical transformation into Jane Warton; the second is upon her arrest.]

[...] I accomplished my disguise in Manchester, going to a different shop for every part of it, for safety's sake. I had noticed several times while I was in prison that prisoners of unprepossessing appearance obtained least favour, so I was determined to put ugliness to the test. I had my hair cut short and parted, in early Victorian fashion, in smooth bands down the side of my face. This, combined with the resentful bristles of my newly-cut back hair, produced a curious effect. I wished to bleach my hair as well, but the hairdresser refused point-blank to do this, and the stuff that I bought for the purpose at a chemist's proved quite ineffective. A tweed hat, a long green cloth coat, which I purchased for 8s. 6d., a woollen scarf and woollen gloves, a white silk neck-kerchief, a pair of pince-nez spectacles, a purse, a net-bag to contain some of my papers, and my costume was complete. I had removed my own initials from my underclothing, and bought the ready-made initials "J.W." to sew on in their stead, but to my regret I had not time to achieve this finishing touch.

All this sounds simple enough, but I suppose it was due to my preoccupation of mind that I have never known a day's shopping fraught with such complications and difficulties. At the frowzy little hairdresser's shop, the only one that seemed to me inconspicuous enough for so important a part of disguise, the attendant was busy, and I had to return in an hour's time. I told him that I was going a journey and wanted the hair short, since that would be less trouble. He cut it off. Then I wanted what remained to be worn in a parting, with the hair falling straight on either side. This part of the process was most absurd, for that way of wearing my hair was obviously disfiguring to me. "Ah! now that looks very becoming," said the hairdresser, and with that I left the shop in haste.

The eye-glasses I had first bought made me giddy from the quality of the lens. I had to take them back and have the glasses changed to the weakest possible. At the first place, in spite of my protests, the shopman insisted on elaborately testing my sight, afterwards requiring me to wait for half an hour or so while he fitted up the glasses. So I went to another shop, and in self-defence invented the story that the glasses were for stage purposes, for a friend of mine who had very good sight, and that if she was not to trip up in her part the glasses must be as nearly plain as possible. This time I was more successful with the lens, but the grip of the folders was still galling to the very large bridge of my nose.

When I had finished this errand I was startled to see walking along the street one of my kind hostesses, whom I had parted from early that morning, professedly to return to Liverpool without delay. I took refuge down a side-street until she had passed by. Then I had strayed into the more opulent quarters of Manchester, in my search for another spectacle shop. All the shops were of a high-class order, and Jane Warton could find nothing to her requirements. On inquiry for a "cheap" draper, three different people recommended me to a certain shop named "Lewis." A sale was on there and Jane found that it was the very place for her. So many Miss Wartons were of the same mind that the street was blocked with customers for some distance down; but I was obliged to wait, for no other shop was of the same description. The hat was a special difficulty; every article of millinery was of the fashionable order, warranted to cover half the body as well as the head. This did not suit Jane. Finally she succeeded in getting the right one of stitched cloth, with a plait of cloth round the crown. Before leaving Manchester I realised that my ugly disguise was a success. I was an object of the greatest derision to street-boys, and shop-girls could hardly keep their countenances while serving me (239–41).

[...] Towards about 3 a.m. we were taken out of the cell and ranged along a seat by the wall of a large room; at the other end was a desk with a policeman sitting at it. We went up in turn to give our names, ages, etc., that is, about seven or eight other prisoners, all females, and our three selves. It was the turn of Jane Warton. She walked across to the policeman, one shoulder hitched slightly above the other, her hair sticking out straight behind and worn in slick bandeaus on either side of her face, her hat trailing in a melancholy way on her head. The large, grey woollen gloves were drawn up over the too short sleeves of her coat; on the collar of it were worn portraits of Mrs. Pankhurst, Mrs. Lawrence and Christabel, in small china brooches; her hat had a bit of tape with "Votes for Women" written on it, interlaced with the cloth plait that went round it, and eye-glasses were fixed on her nose. Her standing out in the room was the signal for a convulsed titter from the other prisoners. "It's a shame to laugh at one of your fellow prisoners," said the policeman behind the desk, and the tittering was hushed. It was all I could do not to laugh, and I thought to myself "Is the *Punch*[1] version of a Suffragette overdone?" As I got back to my companions they too were laughing, but I thought it wonderfully kind of the policeman to have spoken on my behalf (249).

3. Mary Leigh, "Forcible Feeding: Statement of Mrs. Mary Leigh to Her Solicitor," *Votes for Women*, 5 October 1909, 34

[Mary Leigh was arrested in September 1909, for throwing slates onto the roof of Bingley Hall, Birmingham while Asquith was making a speech. She was among the first suffragettes to be forcibly fed, but protested that such feeding was an operation and could not, therefore, be performed without a patient's consent. The WSPU took legal action on her behalf against the Home Secretary (Gladstone) as well as the doctor and governor of Winson Green Prison. The Lord Chief Justice who heard the case ruled that it was the duty of the prison medical officer to prevent the prisoner from suicide by starvation (S. Pankhurst, 1931, 318–19).]

On my arrival at Winson Green Gaol on Wednesday afternoon, September 22, I protested against the treatment to which I was subjected and broke the windows in my cell. Accordingly at nine o'clock in the evening I was taken to the punishment cell, a cold room on the ground floor—light only shines on very bright days—with no furniture in it. A plank bed was brought in. I was then

---

1   The satirical magazine, *Punch*, first published in London in 1841, was known particularly for its caustic cartoons and illustrations. Lisa Tickner describes the visual stereotype of the suffragette body portrayed in popular illustrations as thin and angular, with sharp features etched by lines of disappointment: "She wears pretentiously 'arty,' shabby or masculine clothes and probably spectacles. Her appearance is presumed to derive from her indifference to her femininity, her desire to ape men's place in the world, and the hardening effects of public speaking on a woman's countenance and sensibility. She is devoid of feminine attributes, in fact, which explains both her looks and her political sympathies in a way which allows each to reflect the other" (164).

stripped and handcuffed with the hands behind in the day, except at meals, when the palms were placed together in the front with the palms out. On Thursday, food was brought into the cell—potatoes, bread and gruel—but I did not touch it.

On Thursday afternoon the visiting magistrates came, and I was taken before them, handcuffed. After hearing what I had to say they sentenced me to nine days' close confinement, with bread and water, and to lose forty-two days' remission marks, and pay 5s. damage. The handcuffs were removed at midnight on Thursday by the matron's orders. I still refrained from food. About noon on Saturday I was told the matron wished to speak to me, and was taken to the doctor's room, where I saw the matron, eight wardresses and two doctors. There was a sheet on the floor and an armchair on it. The doctor said I was to sit down, and I did.

He then said: "You must listen carefully to what I have to say. I have orders from my superior officers ... that you are not to be released, even on medical grounds. If you still refrain from food I must take other measures to compel you to take it."

I then said: "I refuse, and if you force food on me I want to know how you are going to do it."

He said: "That is a matter for me to decide."

I said he must prove I was insane, that the Lunacy Commissioners would have to be summoned to prove I was insane, and that he could not perform an operation without the patient's consent. The feeding by the mouth I described as an operation and the feeding by the tube as an outrage. I also said: "I shall hold you responsible, and shall take any measure in order to see whether you are justified in doing so."

He merely bowed and said: "Those are my orders."

The Horror of the Process

I was then surrounded and forced back on to the chair, which was tilted backwards. There were about ten persons around me. The doctor then forced my mouth so as to form a pouch, and held me while one of the wardresses poured some liquid from a spoon; it was milk and brandy. After giving me what he thought was sufficient, he sprinkled me with eau de cologne, and wardresses then escorted me to another cell on the first floor, where I remained for two days. On Saturday afternoon the wardresses forced me on to the bed and the two doctors came in with them. While I was held down a nasal tube was inserted. It is two yards long, with a funnel at the end; there is a glass junction in the middle to see if the liquid is passing. The end is put up the right and left nostril on alternate days. Great pain is experienced during the process, both mental and physical. One doctor inserted the end up my nostril while I was held down by the wardresses, during which process they must have seen my pain, for the other doctor interfered (the matron and two of the wardresses were in tears), and they stopped and resorted to feeding me by the spoon as in the morning. More eau de cologne was used. The food was milk. I was then put to bed in the cell, which is a punishment cell on the first floor. The doctor felt my pulse and asked me to take food each time, but I refused [...].

A Padded Cell

On Tuesday afternoon I overheard Miss Edwards, on issuing from the padded cell opposite, call out, "Locked in a padded cell since Sunday." I called out to her. But she was rushed into it. I then applied (Tuesday afternoon) to see the visiting magistrates. I saw them, and wished to know if one of our women was in a padded cell, and, if so, said she must be allowed out. I knew she had a weak heart and was susceptible to excitement, and it would be very bad for her if kept there any longer. I was told no prisoner could interfere on behalf of another; any complaint on my own behalf would be listened to. I then said this protest of mine must be made on behalf of this prisoner, and if they had no authority to intervene on her behalf, it was no use applying to them for anything. After they had gone I made my protest by breaking eleven panes in my hospital cell. I was then fed in the same way by the feeding cup and taken to the padded cell, where I was stripped of all clothing and a nightdress and bed given to me. As they took Miss Edwards out they put me into her bed, which was still warm. The cell is lined with some padded stuff—india-rubber or something. There was no air, and it was suffocating. This was on Tuesday evening.

I remained there until the Wednesday evening, still being fed by force [...]. On Saturday, October 2, about dinner time, I determined on stronger measures by barricading my cell. I piled my bed, table, and chair by jamming them together against the door. They had to bring some men warders to get in with iron staves. I kept them at bay about three hours. They threatened to use the fire hose. They used all sorts of threats of punishment. When they got in the chief warder threatened me, and tried to provoke me to violence. The wardresses were there, and he had no business to enter my cell, much less to use the threatening attitude. I was again placed in the padded cell, where I remained until Saturday evening. I still refused food, and I was allowed to starve until Sunday noon. Food was brought, but not forced during that interval.

Sunday noon, four wardresses and two doctors entered my cell and forcibly fed me by the tube through the nostrils with milk. Sunday evening I was also fed through the nostril. I remained in the padded cell until Monday evening, October 4. Since then I have been fed through the nostril twice a day and by spoon mid-day, the last being meat juice, which does not require a tube, being only a small quantity.

The sensation is most painful—the drums of the ears seem to be bursting and there is a horrible pain in the throat and the breast. The tube is pushed down twenty inches. I have to lie on the bed, pinned down by wardresses, one doctor stands up on a chair, holding the funnel end at arm's length so as to have the funnel end above the level, and then the other doctor, who is behind, forces the other end up the nostrils.

The one holding the funnel end pours the liquid down—about a pint of milk, egg and milk sometimes being used. When the glass junction shows the fluid has gone down a signal is given; a basin of warm water is put under my chin, and the doctor withdraws the tube and plunges the end into the water. Before and after use they test my heart and make a lot of examination. The after effects are a feeling of faintness, a sense of great pain in the diaphragm or breast-bone, in the nose and the ears. The tube must go down below the breast-bone, though I cannot feel it below there.

The Governor told me of the action taken on my behalf on Saturday, October 2, whereupon I expressed a wish to see my solicitor.

I was very sick on the first occasion after the tube was withdrawn. I have also suffered from bad indigestion. I am fed in this way very irregularly.

I have used no violence, though having provocation in being fed by force. I resist and am overcome by weight in numbers. If the

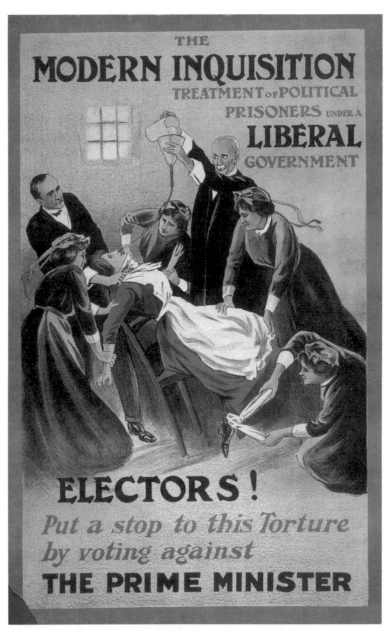

Poster by 'A Patriot' showing a suffragette prisoner being force-fed,
1910. Ref. No. 762 © Museum of London.

doctor does not think the fluid is going down sufficiently swiftly he pinches my nose with the tube in it and my throat, causing me increased pain.

4. Emmeline Pethick Lawrence, "Welcome Christabel Pankhurst!" *Votes for Women*, 17 December 1908, 200

[In October 1908, the WSPU held a meeting in Trafalgar Square at which they distributed a leaflet: "Men and Women—Help the Suffragettes to Rush the House of Commons" (C. Pankhurst, 104). The word "rush" led to an accusation that the suffragettes were inciting the public to behave illegally, and summons were served on Christabel and Emmeline Pankhurst and on Flora Drummond. The famous trial that ensued saw two cabinet ministers, Herbert Gladstone and David Lloyd George, called as witnesses and cross-examined by the accused. Christabel's sentence was ten weeks, her mother and Flora Drummond were given three months.

The following editorial, written by *Votes for Women*'s editor, Emmeline Pethick-Lawrence, anticipates Christabel Pankhurst's release from prison in passionate language. Christabel is likened to the young Siegfried, a character from Norse and Teutonic myth, and the fearless hero of Richard Wagner's *Der Ring des Nibelungen* (1848–76). As Siegfried rescues Brünnhilde from the ring of fire into which she was placed for disobeying her father, so Christabel is destined to awaken "the womanhood that is both human and divine" asleep on the "fire-girt mountain top." Pethick-Lawrence's editorials often reached Wagnerian heights in their language, though this one is particularly notable. Helena Swanwick described her as someone "who has in her a strong vein of poetry and mysticism and who used to attract young women to daring and sacrifice by methods that seemed to me hypnotic" (191). Elevated language and sentiment with reference to the Pankhursts, however, was not uncommon among members of the WSPU. Marion Wallace Dunlop, who had been imprisoned with Emmeline Pankhurst in 1908 said, at the customary breakfast following her release: "I can't tell you what it is like to see her exercising in prison dress and spoken to rudely by a young wardress. If by striking anyone I could have done any good I should certainly have struck someone." On the same occasion, Gertrude Ansell said that the sight of Mrs. Pankhurst in prison dress roused in her not seven devils but 7,000: "her smile was like the smile of one who has had a vision, and who knows that the vision will be realised. She has consecrated her life to the realisation of that vision. It was the smile of one who had dauntless courage and high hope. After I had seen it I ran out to exercise, and I can tell you I did not tread the earth that morning. She holds in the hollow of her hand the hearts of all in the movement" (*Votes for Women*, 26 November 1908, 154).]

Great joy is the predominating note in all our thoughts at the present time, for next Tuesday sees the release, after many weeks of detention in prison, of one of the two deeply revered and beloved founders of the Women's Social and Political Union. In our hearts to-day a welcome is being prepared of infinite gladness and of infinite honour and love.

Christabel Pankhurst! Who can tell what hope, what vision, what possibility, what joy in conflict, what certainty of victory are bound up in the hearts of women to-day with that name?

To women whose backs have been bent under age-long subjection; to women whose hearts have been subdued by age-long sorrow; to women patient with the burden of birth and death, which they have carried since the human race began, there has suddenly come the call to arise and lift up their hearts, and the voice that proclaims deliverance is the voice of the very spirit of dauntless and conquering youth, strong, joyous, and confident, and untouched by the shadow of fear. It is the voice of the very spirit of the dawn, which even as it tells of a coming day brings the light of the rising sun.

Christabel! Christabel! As the dawn to the waiting earth upon whose breast have lain all night the chilling mists of tears, so are you dear to the hearts of women.

Long, long, we waited for your coming. Too well have we learned the lesson of sorrow and of patience. Fear was upon us, and the anguish of womanhood had subdued us and brought us under submission.

Then you came like the young Siegfried in his maiden might. Like him you took the broken pieces of the weapon of destiny, and welded them into "Needful," the magic sword. Like him, utterly without the knowledge of fear, you have gone forth to break the curse of terrible domination.

Child of destiny! Spirit of the dawn! You will emerge undimmed even from the black recesses of a common gaol, for until the appointed time you are immune from the griefs which pierce and wound the hearts of those to whom has not been given at birth your magic armour.

All the wit of your enemy, all their evil machinations and devices are doomed to come to naught. They cannot teach you that one lesson, which life itself has never taught you. They cannot teach you the meaning of hesitation or fear.

Dauntless champion! Herald of the coming day of deliverance, whose story is already written in the book of Fate. We glory in your courage, in your overcoming youth, in the unshadowed morning radiance of your spirit, that has never known eclipse, in your laughing zest for conflict that has never experienced the check of failure or defeat.

You who come to meet us out of the sunlit plains of a future which we know only as a bright dream, we love you differently, but not one whit less than we love your mother, who has walked with women through the valleys of shadow, carrying the burden of all their sorrow, forgetful of her own.

I do not know what you will be to the women who are to come after us. I will not speak of what you are to those in this movement, whose feet are still upon the threshold of life, but to the women who have lived and suffered and wept, you are the living fulfilment of their earliest and brightest hopes. You are the living denial of the bitter lessons of futility and disappointment which precept and the limitations of inheritance and environment have tried to teach them. For them you challenge experience. Striking off its hideous mask you reveal the fair child beneath, who is the promise of the days to be. For them you stand as the messenger of the sun in the heavens, the bulwark against the fears that have haunted the long night.

Maiden warrior! We give you rapturous welcome. Go forth with the fiat of the future, strong in your gladness and youth of your dauntless spirit to smite with your sword of destiny the forces of stupidity and unreasoning prejudice, and blind domination.

Far away upon the fire-girt mountain top sleeps the womanhood that is both human and divine. She will not awake nor give unto the world her lore of wisdom and of love until you and we have accomplished all that has been decreed.

Appendix D: The Conciliation Bill and Black Friday

[The Conciliation Bill was drafted by a committee of fifty-four members of Parliament from all parties, and chaired by Lord Lytton with Henry Noel Brailsford as Secretary. The Bill was introduced in the House of Commons in June 1910, and passed its second reading in July by a vote of 299 to 189 in favour. However, it was referred to a Committee of the Whole: this meant that consideration of the Bill would happen on the floor of the Commons rather than in committee, and this essentially derailed it. Asquith announced on 18 November that Parliament was to be dissolved, and that the Conciliation Bill would not be considered prior to the dissolution. The WSPU had declared a hiatus from militancy during the course of discussion of the Bill; but, at the announcement by government that it would not allow time for further deliberation, WSPU members voted to march on Parliament. Three hundred women, in groups of twelve, headed to Parliament Square where they were met with extraordinary violence on the part of the police. According to Andrew Rosen, the police who were usually called upon to defend the House of Commons had become accustomed to dealing with suffragette demonstrations; however, their ranks were supplemented on this occasion by police brought in from Whitechapel and other East End districts. These men had no previous experience of dealing with this kind of protest (142). The battle lasted six hours, at the end of which 116 women and four men had been arrested.[1] The day became known as Black Friday.

The following Tuesday, November 22, Asquith made the statement that "The Government will, if they are still in power, give facilities in the next Parliament for effectively proceeding with a Bill which is so framed as to admit of free amendment." The emphasis on free amendment seemed to indicate that the Bill would be so broad that it would have little chance of passing the Commons (Rosen, 145). In response to Asquith's statement, Emmeline Pankhurst led a deputation to Downing Street, and another battle ensued between the suffragettes and the police.]

---

1   The numbers vary slightly from account to account. The *Times* article, below, reports that 116 women and three men were arrested. *Votes for Women* reports 116 women and four men (25 November 1910).

1. From H.N. Brailsford, "The 'Conciliation' Bill: An Explanation and Defence," London: Women's Press, 1910, 4, 5–6

A Bill to Extend the Parliamentary Franchise to Women Occupiers (The "Conciliation" Bill).

1. Every woman possessed of a household qualification, or of a ten-pound occupation qualification, within the meaning of the Representation of the People Act 1884, shall be entitled to be registered as a voter, and when registered, to vote for the county or borough in which the qualifying premises are situate.

2. For the purposes of this Act, a woman shall not be disqualified by marriage for being registered as a voter, provided that a husband and wife shall not both be qualified in respect of the same property.

2. Henry Noel Brailsford and Dr. Jessie Murray, "The Treatment of the Women's Deputations by the Police: Copy of evidence collected by Dr. Jessie Murray and Mr. H.N. Brailsford, and forwarded to the Home Office by the Conciliation Committee for Women Suffrage," London: Woman's Press, 1911

Being a copy of a Memorandum* forwarded by the "Parliamentary Conciliation Committee for Woman Suffrage" to the Home Office, accompanying a request for a public enquiry into the conduct of the police.

The facts which gradually came to our knowledge regarding the behaviour of the police towards members of the Women's Social and Political Union on November 18, 22, and 23 have induced us to collect the testimony of women who took part in

---

* The evidence collected by Dr. Jessie Murray and Mr. Brailsford regarding the conduct of the police towards members of the Women's Social and Political Union was laid before the Conciliation Committee on February 2nd. The Committee unanimously decided to transmit the evidence to the Home Office, and to demand a public enquiry into the conduct of the police. This memorandum was accordingly drafted by Mr. Brailsford in collaboration with other members of the Committee and forwarded in the course of the following week to Mr. Churchill. Owing to considerations of space only a few typical statements have been selected from the great mass of evidence before the Committee, and for the purpose of publication in this memorandum it has been thought better to omit the names of the witnesses. [Although this footnote is unattributed in the original it is assumed to be by Brailsford.]

these demonstrations, and of eye-witnesses who have volunteered their evidence. The gravity of the charges which emerge from these statements impels us to lay the evidence before the Home Office, in the belief that it constitutes a *prima facie* case for a public inquiry.

It is necessary by way of preface to comment upon the order under which the police were acting. They were instructed, as we understand the answer given by the Home Secretary to Mr. Chancellor, to refrain as far as possible from making arrests. The usual course would have been, when the women persisted in attempting to force their way towards the House of Commons, to arrest them on a charge of obstruction. We are satisfied that this would have been at once the more humane and the more regular course. Previous experience gave warrant enough for supposing that the efforts of the women to accomplish their purpose would be persistent and determined. The consequence was that for many hours they were engaged in an incessant struggle with the police. They were flung hither and thither amid moving traffic, and into the hands of a crowd permeated by plain clothes detectives, which was sometimes rough and indecent. The police, who are men of exceptional muscular power, may not always have realised the injuries which an incautious use of their strength must inflict upon women. Had their conduct been exemplary, the consequence of this order would still have been deplorable. It is indeed difficult to understand what motive or calculation can have prompted it. The only reason for interfering at all with the women was to prevent an obstruction of the thoroughfare, and to keep open the approaches to the Houses of Parliament. The consequence of ordering the police to engage in a protracted conflict with the women was that for many hours on November 18 the whole of this area was abandoned to a struggle which was by the tactics of the police so prolonged as to cause the maximum of disturbance to traffic.

But there emerges from the evidence before us a much graver charge. We cannot resist the conclusion that the police as a whole were under the impression that their duty was not merely to frustrate the attempts of the women to reach the House, but also to terrorise them in the process. They used in numerous instances excessive violence, which was at once deliberate and aggressive, and was intended to inflict injury and pain. Many of them resorted to certain forms of torture. They frequently handled the women with gross indecency. In some instances they continued to injure and insult them after their arrest.

I.—Unnecessary Violence

Nearly all of the 135 statements communicated to us describe some act or acts of unnecessary violence. It is generally possible to determine from the frank statements of the members of the deputation how far these acts of violence were provoked. In some cases the women merely held their ground near the police cordon. In other cases they tried to push their way through it. In the few instances in which they themselves struck a policeman their statement usually shows that it was to force him to desist from his brutal usage of some other woman.

The first statement to which we would call attention mentions no exceptional violence. It does, however, describe simply and vividly the effect produced by the more violent methods used by the police, particularly on November 18.

> For hours one was beaten about the body, thrown backwards and forwards from one to another, until one felt dazed with the horror of it. [...] Often seized by the coat collar, dragged out of the crowd, only to be pushed helplessly along in front of one's tormentor into a side street, while he beat one up and down one's spine until cramp seized one's legs, when he would then release one with a vicious shove, and with insulting speeches, such as, "I will teach you a lesson. I will teach you not to come back any more. I will punish you, you —, you —." This took place over and over again, as, of course, each time they released one, one returned to the charge. [...] The chest bruises one received while pushing forward were, of course, inevitable, but it was this officious pummeling of the spine when they collated you and held you helpless which wore you out so, and left you so shaken. [...] A favourite trick was pinching the upper part of one's arms, which were black with bruises afterwards. One man began thumb-twisting. I dared him to do it again, and he dropped my arm before serious harm was done, but I have only just lost the feeling of sprain. [...] Once I was thrown with my jaw against a lamp-post with such force that two of my front teeth were loosened. [...] What I complain of

on behalf of us all is the long-drawn-out agony of the delayed arrest, and the continuous beating and pinching. [...]

Four witnesses describe the barbarous usage to which another woman, Miss H—, was subjected. After she had been flung to the ground, shaken, and pushed, and had had her arms and wrists twisted, she exclaimed, "Help me to the railings." While trying to recover breath a policeman seized her head, and rubbed her face against the iron railings. To illustrate the recklessness with which the police seized women (usually by the throat) and flung them backwards on the ground, we would draw attention to two separate cases in which a woman was flung almost under the wheels of a passing motor-car. In one case a wheel went over a woman's dress as she lay on the ground, and in the other grazed her head. In one at least of these cases the attack was absolutely unprovoked, and the lady who was its victim is described as "a woman with grey hair, and whose age ought to have commanded a certain respect."

II.—Methods of Torture

The clearest proof that the aim of the police went beyond the fulfilment of their duty in preventing an obstruction, and included the terrorising of the women, is supplied by the overwhelming evidence that they resorted to various painful and dangerous methods of torture. The more common devices were to bend the thumb backwards, to twist the arm behind the victim's back, and to pinch the arm continually and with evident deliberation. These processes are described by the sufferers in almost identical terms in no less than 45 statements. It will suffice to quote one statement:—

> My left arm was black and discoloured from the back of the hand up to the elbow through being twisted by a policeman. He watched my face as he was doing it, and because I would not scream or cry out he went on, till one more twist would have snapped the bone, and the agony made me wriggle free. [...] They turned back the thumb of my right hand, and it was discoloured all round, not from pressure, but from being turned back, and to this day (February 8) the joint is sensitive.

There is ample proof that in many instances the effects of this treatment were visible for many days after. Nurse H—'s thumb was dislocated. Other women for some days afterwards had to be helped by their friends to dress. Another expedient frequently used was to grip the throat, and force back the head as far as possible. In one instance an inspector forced his finger up the nostril of a woman who was clinging to the railings in Downing Street. The descriptions given by the women of many of these acts of cruelty is detailed enough to make it clear that they were not in most cases incidental to a scrimmage. They were wantonly done in order to inflict pain, and the women who suffered them were already completely in the power of the policemen who held them.

III.—Acts of Indecency

The intention of terrorising and intimidating the women was carried by many of the police beyond mere violence. Twenty-nine of these statements complain of more or less aggravated acts of indecency. Women describe such treatment only with the greatest reluctance, and though the volume of evidence under this head is considerable, there are other instances which we are not permitted to cite. The following experience is one of the worst, but it is not without parallels. The victim is a young woman:—

> Several times constables and plain-clothes men who were in the crowd passed their arms round me from the back and clutched hold of my breasts in as public a manner as possible, and men in the crowd followed their example. I was also pummelled on the chest, and my breast was clutched by one constable from the front. As a consequence, three days later, I had to receive medical attention from Dr. Ede as my breasts were much discoloured and very painful. On the Friday I was also very badly treated by P.C. —. I think that was the number, but I and a witness could identify the men. My skirt was lifted up as high as possible, and the constable attempted to lift me off the ground by raising his knee. This he could not do, so he threw me into the crowd and incited the men to treat me as they wished. Consequently, several men who, I believe, were policemen in plain clothes, also endeavoured to lift my dress.

In another instance a young girl on her way to the police station under arrest was called a "prostitute," and made to walk several yards while the police held her skirts over her head. The action of which the most frequent complaint is made is variously described as twisting round, pinching, screwing, nipping, or wringing the breast. This was often done in the most public way so as to inflict the utmost humiliation. Not only was it an offence against decency; it caused in many cases intense pain, and may well have led to lasting injury. The language used by some of the police while performing this action proves that it was consciously sensual. Another brutal insult which was frequently inflicted is thus described to Dr. Jessie Murray by one of the ladies who endured it:—"The policemen who tried to move me on did so by pushing his knees in between me from behind, with the deliberate intention of attacking my sex."

Women were not free from these indecent brutalities even after arrest. One woman was indecently assaulted by a man in the crowd while she was in the hands of a policeman who was holding her arms behind her. In spite of her complaints, the policeman took no notice and did nothing to protect his prisoner. Such misconduct has naturally produced a degree of resentment and indignation even greater than was caused by the less insulting brutality of blows. [...]

CONCLUSION

Such experiences are not new in the annals of the militant societies, and they have hitherto observed an almost unbroken tradition that it is unsoldierly to complain. Their spirit is entitled to respect, but we as citizens are not content that the police should form a habit of indulging in such excesses. If even a fraction of this testimony, which all of it bears to our minds the stamp of truth, can be established, the police will have been convicted of violating almost every instruction in their Manual which forbids (p. 6) swearing and foul language, prescribes (7) an equable temper, requires that in making an arrest (p. 105), "no more violence should be used than is absolutely necessary," and enjoins that "needless exposure" shall not be inflicted on the person in custody.

We claim that the evidence here collected suffices to justify our demand for a public inquiry into the behaviour of the Metropolitan Police on November 18, November 22, and November 23. The object

A LANCASHIRE LASS IN CLOGS & SHAWL 98
BEING "ESCORTED" THROUGH PALACE YARD.

CHORUS.

Take me back to Palace Yard, Palace Yard, Palace Yard,
That's where I long to be, with the friends so dear to me;
The tall policeman, smiling, bland, to gently take me by the hand,
For "Women's Rights" anything we will dare; Palace Yard, take me there!

PARODY ON "TAKE ME BACK TO LONDON TOWN."

Lancashire mill girl arrested during a suffragette demonstration
at the House of Commons, 20 March 1907.
Ref. No. 557 © Museum of London.

of such an inquiry should be to ascertain, not merely whether the charges of aggressive violence, torture, and indecency here made can be substantiated, but also to ascertain under what orders the police were acting. The order to make no arrests goes some way to explain their conduct, and must in itself have led to much unnecessary and dangerous violence. But it would not explain the frequency of torture and indecency, nor the more obviously unprovoked acts of violence which many of the men committed. A man acting under this order might feel that he was justified in flinging a woman back with some violence when she attempted to pass the cordon. But this order alone would not suggest to him that he should run forward and fell her with a blow on the mouth, or twist her arms, or bend her thumb, or manipulate her breasts. The impression conveyed by this evidence is from first to last that the police believed themselves to be acting under an almost unlimited licence to treat the women as they pleased, and to inflict upon them a degree of humiliation and pain which would deter them or intimidate them. We suggest that the inquiry should seek to determine whether such an impression prevailed among the police, and if so, whether any verbal orders (which may or may not have been correctly understood) were given by any of the men's superiors by way of supplement to the general order. This is not yet the time to make any general comment on a mass of evidence which, we believe, does, on the whole, fairly represent the facts. We are content to observe that such an exhibition of brutality is calculated not to deter women of spirit, but rather to provoke them to less innocent methods of protest, that it must be destructive of discipline in the police and demoralising to the public which witnesses it, and finally that if it were to be tolerated or repeated it would leave an indelible stain upon the manhood and the humanity of our country.

H.N. BRAILSFORD,
Hon. Secretary of the Conciliation Committee.

3. "Mr. Churchill and the Suffragists," *The Times*, 21 November 1910, 11–12

[Although many were arrested in the Black Friday demonstration, only those accused of assault or property damage were charged, and the controversy surrounding Winston Churchill's decision to release the others was widespread. For women who had been witnesses to and victims of the violence, release meant no opportunity for a public hearing. Christabel Pankhurst and others suggested that, in light of the upcoming General Election, the Liberals did not want the publicity a trial would generate (166). The editorial in *Votes for Women* the week after Black Friday argues: "Mr. Churchill realizes that it is bad electioneering tactics to be responsible for the imprisonment of women of good reputation who are merely fighting for their freedom" (22 November 1910, 117).

Further controversy arose from accusations made in *Votes for Women* (25 November 1910, 117), that the police were under orders to delay making arrests. The Brailsford and Murray report, above, concurred that "the police believed themselves to be acting under an almost unlimited licence to treat the women as they pleased, and to inflict upon them a degree of humiliation and pain which would deter them or intimidate them." Christabel Pankhurst accused Churchill of giving the orders that led to this license on the part of the police, and her accusations, lasting as they did well into the new year, led Churchill to consider prosecuting her for libel (Churchill, 1468). Nevertheless, Churchill's various explanations of his orders to the police seem contradictory. In his letter of 22 November 1910 to Sir Edward Harvey, Commissioner of the Metropolitan Police, he writes: "I am hearing from every quarter that my strongly expressed wishes conveyed to you on Wed evening & repeated on Fri morning that the suffragettes were not to be allowed to exhaust themselves, but were to be arrested forthwith upon any defiance of the law, were not observed by the police on Friday last, with the result that very regrettable scenes occurred" (1457). In Parliament on 24 November 1910, however, he responded to Lloyd George's question, "What instructions were issued to the police in connection with the deputation to the Prime Minister on Friday last ..." with the following: "I find on inquiry that the police for the most part acted under the instruction which has been in force for some time, that they should avoid, as far as practicable, making arrests. The result was that some of the ladies who desired to be arrested, made repeated efforts, and no doubt a few of them exhausted themselves and may have required medical treatment."[1]]

---

1   Parliamentary Debates, Commons, Official Reports, 5th Series, 1910, Vol. 20 (15–28 November), 389.

What does the Home Secretary mean? That question will be asked by many who read our report of the proceedings at Bow-street on Saturday against the suffragists arrested for brawling outside the House of Commons and the extraordinary ending to those proceedings. When the first case was called on, Mr. Muskett, who appeared for the prosecution, made the amazing announcement that the Home Secretary had considered the matter, and had come to the conclusion that no public advantage would be gained by continuing the proceedings; and Mr. Muskett asked leave to withdraw the charges, which was of course granted. No evidence having been given, the 116 ladies and three men who had been arrested were released. It is difficult to say what aspect of this incident is strangest. A Home Secretary may advise the exercise of the prerogative of mercy in favour of annulling or reducing a sentence. He may decline to take official action in regard to a merely technical offence, or one as to which there is insufficient evidence; which may have been the case as to some of the charges. It is a novelty, and one not to be welcomed, to intervene in this manner and to stop a prosecution in respect of offences serious and repeated. No public advantage, it is said, was to be derived from proceeding with the prosecution; which, so far as it is true, might be said of every occasion in which the assertion of the law might bring unpopularity, and might with equal force be urged as to the lawless doings in Wales.[1] But is no public harm done by discharging those who are charged with taking part in a carefully planned breach of the peace? Does not this intervention somewhat unsettle ordinary ideas as to punishment?

There was no question of an accidental breach of the peace. The raid on Friday was deliberate and persisted in. It is one of a multitude of similar incidents, and is the outcome of concerted action with a view to bring about a change of the law by systematic disorder. It was not a sudden outburst of passion on the part of poor and ignorant people out of work and in want and with an overpowering sense of physical suffering. The persons charged belonged to the well-to-do classes, and doubtless after assaulting the police they went to comfortable homes or clubs. What extenuating element is there

---

1   In November 1910, 12,000 Welsh miners went on strike after bitter disputes over wages. Riots broke out, and Churchill sent in troops to keep the peace. Miners returned to work in October 1911, but only after they accepted the owners' offers of lower wages.

in these circumstances? Mr. Churchill may indeed say that he does not intend to give the offenders the glory of a cheap martyrdom; that a few days imprisonment spent, it may be, under exceptionally easy conditions, may serve as an advertisement, but will not act as a deterrent; and that the result of past prosecutions has not been very encouraging. He may have in mind the trouble which the suffragist prisoners gave to his predecessor and the officials of the gaols in which they were confined. The fact remains that those charged with brawling on Friday are told that their conduct merits no punishment—an announcement not the less serious and fraught with consequences that it is made on the eve of a General Election, and after repeated threats that, if the suffragists do not have their way, they will make things unpleasant during that election. It is with something like a sense of shame, at all events of incongruity, that one turns from the treatment of these privileged lawbreakers to the report of the prosecution, conviction, and real punishment of some ignorant man or woman who has made a disturbance and come into conflict with the police. A home may be broken up, a breadwinner may be taken away, but there is no interposition in his or her favour. We would put two questions. What does the announcement made at Bow-street mean, if not that the militant suffragists may do with impunity what others may not? What time, in one sense, could be more opportune, in another sense worse chosen, for such an announcement than the eve of an election in which the militant suffragists will not fail to make themselves heard? The same newspaper which states the withdrawal of the prosecutions at Bow-street mentions serious outrages committed by miners or their sympathisers in Wales. It will not be easy to draw a rational and convincing distinction between the militant suffragists and the militant Welsh mobs.

It is not to be forgotten that the Home Secretary the other day intervened to question a conviction by magistrates under the Vagrancy Acts, in circumstances and in a manner which must leave magistrates a little puzzled as to what they may do in regard to a class of offenders not meriting exceptional commiseration. He has not been very vigorous in repressing the violence which has marked the recent strikes in Wales, and he has thrown out, amid some excellent suggestions as to improvements in the administration of the criminal law, some proposals which a correspondent of great experience as a Judge, Sir Alfred Wills, seems not to be able to understand, and which might be understood by the lawless as a promise of immunity. We have no fault to find with measures of leniency all round, measures intended to keep out of prisons people who ought not to be there. There is still plenty of room for discriminating action in this direction, and it is to be hoped that in this direction Mr. Churchill may carry out large measures of reform. The objectionable policy is to single out certain classes of offenders and to say, or seem to say, to them, "You are so many as to be troublesome; you might break up public meetings now about to be held in great numbers; we will try to mollify you for the time by not punishing you in circumstances in which other breakers of the law less persistent would go to prison." That is, of course, an intelligible position to be taken up to-day as to suffragists; perhaps to-morrow to be extended to those concerned with acts of *sabotage*. But consistency requires a further announcement to the effect that no public advantage is to be gained by arresting suffragist brawlers. It is mere foolery to stop short of that.

4. Christabel Pankhurst, "We Revert to a State of War," *Votes for Women*, 25 November 1910, 126

The Government will, if they are still in power, give facilities in the next Parliament for effectively proceeding with a Bill which is so framed as to admit of free amendment.

Prime Minister's statement in the House of Commons, Tuesday, Nov. 22.

At last we have the Government's eagerly awaited statement on Woman Suffrage. The recent declarations made by individual Cabinet Ministers had aroused some expectation that the Government would promise to give full facilities for a Woman Suffrage Bill next year. The Women's Social and Political Union had determined beforehand to accept no declaration from the Government which did not comply with certain conditions. The more important of these were as follows:—The pledge must be to give full facilities for a Woman Suffrage Bill next session. The Bill in question must be no more extended in its scope than the Conciliation Bill introduced by Mr. Shackleton[1] or the Women's Enfranchisement Bill introduced two

---

1   David Shackleton, a Labour MP, introduced the Conciliation Bill.

years ago by Mr. Stanger,[1] a pledge to give facilities to a Bill on a so-called democratic basis being worthless, because such a Bill would have no chance of passing through either House of Parliament.

The statement made by the Prime Minister on Tuesday fulfils neither of these vital conditions and has accordingly been indignantly rejected by the Women's Social and Political Union. In the first place the pledge does not guarantee the enfranchisement of women *next session*. The promise for next *Parliament* is utterly worthless. There is no precise moment when we could call for its fulfilment. Session after session the Prime Minister could reply to our demand for instant enfranchisement that he had undertaken to let the Suffrage Bill be carried not in any particular session but in the existing Parliament. After thus postponing the satisfaction of our demand for a year or two, he could, and his past record teaches us that he would, suddenly cause the life of that Parliament to be brought to an end. With a new Parliament the same farce would begin again. The trick is too obvious to deceive anyone for a single moment.

The Government strongly desires a cessation of the militant movement. Therefore their plan is that during the next Parliament we shall, session after session, be led on in quiet and peaceful courses by hope deferred—hope which it is their intention finally to disappoint. Into so open a trap not the most guileless would fall; and the women of the present day possess a ripe political intelligence and knowledge. It would indeed be strange if they had learned nothing from the history of the past half century, packed as full as it is with instances of treachery and duplicity displayed by politicians in their dealing with the Woman Suffrage Movement. Especially does our experience during the present Parliament prevent us from cherishing any illusion as to the true nature of the Prime Minister's latest "pledge." Let us recall the facts! Before the last General Election Mr. Asquith declared at the Albert Hall that "the question of Woman Suffrage is clearly one on which the new House of Commons ought to be given an opportunity of expressing its view," and on a subsequent occasion he said that the House ought to have an opportunity of effectively dealing with this whole question. The

---

1 In 1908, H.Y. Stanger introduced a Women's Suffrage Bill that passed its second reading in the House of Commons by 271 votes to 92. However, the bill was blocked by the government's referring it to a Committee of the Whole House.

undertaking so expressed Mr. Asquith has deliberately broken, and by terminating the existence of the present Parliament he has now made its fulfilment impossible. It will be seen that the Government's new promise is virtually the same as the promise which they gave before the last General Election, and (unless women can prevent this second breach of faith) they will have as little compunction in breaking their new promise in the next Parliament as they had in breaking the old promise in this Parliament.

Again, the Government's "pledge" does not comply with the second condition above referred to—that is to say, it does not apply exclusively to a moderate and practicable Bill.

To this second grave defect in the Government's statement the Conciliation Committee have already drawn attention in the following words: "Mr. Asquith's promise applies not to our Bill specifically but generally to a Bill so framed as to admit of free amendment. The Conciliation Committee had already undertaken to make its Bill conform to this condition by giving it a general title, but Mr. Asquith's promise would apply to any Suffrage Bill, even to an Adult Suffrage Bill. It would be open to any private Member, without consulting other Suffrage Parties or the Women's Societies, to introduce a Bill which would not receive wide support."

This in itself is a sufficient reason for regarding the Government's pledge as worthless.

At the moment when the Prime Minister was making his statement in the House of Commons a great deputation of women representing the Women's Social and Political Union was assembled in Caxton Hall.

When the news came of the Prime Minister's hostile declaration there was but one thing to be done, and they did it. They went instantly to Downing Street to see the Prime Minister and to protest against his refusal to give an undertaking that the question of women's enfranchisement shall be honestly and finally dealt with in the coming year. The brave, prompt, and determined act of the deputation told the world more clearly than mere words could have done that women are not to be deceived by any illusory promise, and that they are determined to have justice, and to have it now. In a word, the Government having uttered false political coin, the women of this Union nailed that false coin to the counter.

The Prime Minister's statement, constituting as it does a message of defiance to us, means that we revert to a state of war. At the beginning of the present Parliament we declared a truce, which, if the Government had acted in the same spirit of reasonableness and conciliation that we have displayed, would have ended in peace; but the Prime Minister, by his recent statement, so injurious to our right as citizens and so insulting to our intelligence, has put an end to all hope of a peaceful settlement of the issue between us. "Negotiations are over. War is declared."

Appendix E: Contemporary Reviews

1. *The Bookman* 40.237 (June 1911): 144

In *Suffragette Sally* we not only get a vigorous, inspiring story, but a clear outline of the militant movement which is undoubtedly one of the most discussed topics of the present day. To many—those who talk of the militants and "cheap martyrdom" and "self-noto-riety"—the book will be a revelation. A number of the incidents in the story are taken from real life—most of us will remember reading garbled reports of them in the newspapers, when they took place—and some of the characters are also taken from life, and given such thinly disguised names as Mrs. Amherst, Christina Amherst, Annie Carnie, and Lady Henry Hill. Sally is a "general" in the Bilkes household, and between her mistress's scoldings, her master's un-welcome attentions, and the care of the little Bilkeses she drudges through her daily life. Then one day she goes to a meeting, and hears Lady Henry Hill speak—and a new life opens out before her. A good vindication of the militant movement is given by Lady Hill: she likens it to the incoming tide, and the opposition to the rocks on the shore—the rocks that make the breakers, the rocks that the tide is going to overtake. There are many different types of men and women in the story, some of them Suffra*gettes*, some of them Suffra*gists*, and some of them Anti's. Believers in Women Suffrage will read the book with keen interest, and feel deeply grateful to the author for using her able pen to such good purpose and lay-ing before the public so powerful and vivid a story as *Suffragette Sally*. A copy might be placed with advantage in the hands of every broad-minded Anti-Suffragist.

[unsigned]

2. *Votes for Women*, 12 May 1911, 528

Suffragette Sally is a story of the Woman's Movement of today, a story of the militant movement. In it the Suffragette will read and live once more through the exciting scenes which have crowded so quickly one upon the other during the last two years. Deputations, processions, arrests, imprisonment, hunger strike and forcible feeding, are all mirrored within its pages, the whole being deftly woven into a continuous tale.

Sally, the heroine of the book, is a cockney slavey who attends a Suffragette meeting one evening and straightaway becomes attracted to the movement. The book tells of her experiences, of her conversion, of her attempts at speaking, at paper-selling; of her imprisonment and hunger strike, and how she finally paid that greatest of all sacrifices—life itself—for the sake of the cause she held so dear.

Interwoven with the story of Sally are the stories of two other women—Lady Henry Hill, who by her work and sacrifices persuades her husband to turn from an academic supporter to an enthusiastic worker for the cause, and Edith Carstairs, a "constitutional worker" who is gradually led to see that in the militant movement alone can her soul find salvation. [...]

The full story of Edith Carstair's gradual conversion to militancy we must leave our readers to find out for themselves. Suffice to say that she goes through all the stages so well known to those in the movement [...]

The general public will probably say that this book is exaggerated—that such scenes as are depicted could not have happened in civilised England. But the women in this movement know that the incidents are only too real, that the scenes are only too familiar, and knowing, they thank Miss Colmore for what she has done.

M.D.H.

3. The Times Literary Supplement, 4 May 1911, 178

G. Colmore has shown some ability in former novels—here it is devoted to female suffrage; which, so an "author's note" asserts with a generous vagueness, "is already possessed by the women of England's colonies"; and the book is simply a contribution to the campaign literature of the movement, detailing recent events with vigorous partisanship.

[Unsigned]

4. Votes for Women, 28 June 1911, 706

The experience of the past few years has taught Suffragists that the boasted freedom of the Press is not always exercised on behalf of liberty, and that in the case of the women's battle it has been used to retard the coming of reform. But this lesson, which has been one of disillusionment, has been followed by another of a very different kind. Women have learned that by sticking together and working with energy they can overcome every obstacle, including even that of the Press boycott; and this new knowledge has filled them with hope and self-confidence.

Recently I was invited by one of the leading daily papers to review a book by Mr.[1] Colmore—*Suffragette Sally*. Books on various subjects have passed through my hands for the same journal, and in no instance has the Editor altered my reviews. In this case only did he find it necessary to do so. I had written solely from the standpoint of an impartial critic, as my review, which I here quote, will show:—Who will read *Suffragette Sally* without feeling anew that verily the pen is a mightier weapon than the sword? All honour to Mr. Colmore that he uses his in defence of the weak and struggling, waging war on their behalf against the injustice that oppresses them. The theme of this book, as the title implies, is the fight for freedom by the women of England, and as he carries us step by step through one of the greatest movements of modern times, he convinces us that we are witnessing no passing game, but a battle that is being fought in grim earnest *à outrance*. The book is full of incidents with which we are all familiar, but which strike us with fresh significance when described by Mr. Colmore's able pen, and we shrink in horror from the knowledge of what our countrywomen have suffered—"things which done to women in Russia would have aroused in England a blaze of indignation, with admiring plaudits of those who served liberty." We only hope *Suffragette Sally* will be read as widely as its merits deserve, and we strongly advise all to get it, if only to make the acquaintance of the heroine, little Cockney Sally, the household drudge, large of heart and soul, who responds to the call of duty as did the martyrs of old, and gives up her love, her home and life itself, suffering imprisonment and death with the sublime unconsciousness of heroism which is the distinguishing mark of all true heroes.

---

1   Colmore published under the name "G. Colmore," though no other reviewer of *Suffragette Sally* mistook her gender. No retraction or correction appeared in subsequent editions of *Votes for Women*. The cover of her 1919 novel, *The Thunderbolt*, gives the author's name as "George Colmore."

The Editor on reading the above remarked that I had taken rather strong line, and that it was better to avoid partisanship. I understood he might make some slight alteration, but was not prepared to see my notice mutilated so as to become a thoroughly adverse and hostile criticism of the book. Apparently it is not partisanship which matters, but the side on which it is exercised.

Mr. Colmore's books are too well known and appreciated to need any commendation by me, but I hope that Suffragists and others with a sense of fair play will take the opportunity of proving once more that the boycott of the Press can be overcome by those who believe in justice, and that this interesting novel will find a place on their shelves.

M.R.

5. *The Vote*,[1] 1 July 1911, 125

Years hence, when the story of the great movement towards the political emancipation of women comes to be written in the pages of history, the true meaning of militancy in this connection—its inspiration and genesis, its brave stand against the arrayed powers, its sacrifices and its ultimate triumph—will be appreciated and understood by those who will have reaped the harvest of freedom. Meanwhile, education on the *raison d'être* of militancy is sadly needed by many who have been content to look on and to be swayed in their judgement this way and that by the imperfect, untruthful and biased accounts of the campaign which have appeared in the public press.

Suffragette Sally is a novel with a purpose, but it is nevertheless a fascinating story. Sally is a maid-of-all-work in a suburban household, who, by chance, wanders into a hall where a suffrage meeting is being held, and becomes enamoured of the speakers and the cause. How she learns and works and fights and suffers and, in the end, how she makes the supreme sacrifice of life itself, is told in thrilling language, while, interwoven with the story of Sally, is a vivid and stirring account of the various phases of the militant movement. [...]

---

1 The newspaper of The Women's Freedom League.

The author shows fine descriptive powers in her pictures of the deputations, processions and arrests, and in her scenes of prison life. Sometimes the latter seem almost too realistic, and if the reader did not know that they are in every case drawn from actual occurrences, he would be tempted to ask, "Can these things be?" There is no exaggeration, however; only a sympathetic setting down of incidents in one of the greatest struggles for liberty that the world has ever known. [...]

We feel that a debt of gratitude is due to the author for the valuable literary contribution she has made to the cause of women's suffrage, and we earnestly hope that a trend of political events may make possible the appearance of a happy sequel to the story in the near future.

Louisa Thomson-Price

Select Bibliography

1. Works by Gertrude Colmore

"Standards and Ideals of Purity." *Theosophical Ideals and the Immediate Future. Lectures by Mrs. A. Besant, Mr. Laurence Housman, Mr. Baillie Weaver and Mrs. Baillie Weaver.* London: Theosophical Publishing Society, 1914. 78–94.

"The Nun." *Mr. Jones and the Governess.* London: Women's Freedom League, c.1908–1914. 107–11.

A Brother of the Shadow. London: Noel Douglas, 1926.

A Conspiracy of Silence. London: Swan Sonnenschein, 1889.

A Daughter of Music. London: William Heinemann, 1894.

A Ladder of Tears. Westminster: A. Constable, 1904.

A Living Epitaph. London: Longman's, 1890.

A Valley of Shadows. London: Chatto and Windus, 1892.

"Broken." *The Suffragette* 26 September 1913: 862.

Concerning Oliver Knox. Unwin's Novel Series (Vol. 3). 1888.

Love for a Key. London: William Heinemann, 1896.

Mr. Jones and the Governess. London: Women's Freedom League, 1913.

Poems of Love and Life. London: Gay and Bird, 1896.

Points of View and other Poems. London: Gay and Bird, 1898.

Priests of Progress. London: Stanley Paul, 1908.

Suffragette Sally. London: Stanley Paul, 1911.

Suffragettes: A Story of Three Women. London: Pandora, 1984.

The Angel and the Outcast. London: Hutchinson, 1907.

The Crimson Gate. London: Stanley Paul, 1910.

The Guardian. London: T. Fisher Unwin, 1923.

The Guest. London: Edward Arnold, 1917.

The Life of Emily Davison: An Outline. London: Woman's Press, 1913.

The Marble Face. London: Smith, Elder, 1900.

The Strange Story of Hester Wynne Told by Herself with a Prologue. London: Smith, Elder, 1899.

The Thunderbolt. London: T. Fisher Unwin, 1919.

Trades That Transgress. London: Theosophical Order of Service, c.1918.

Whispers. London: Hurst and Blackett, 1914.

—— and Beatrice de Normann. *Ethics of Education*. London: The Theosophical Publishing House, 1918.

2. Secondary Sources

"Mr. Churchill and the Suffragists." *The Times* 21 Nov. 1910: 11–12.

"Suffragettes at Home." *The Vote* 26 March 1910: 261.

Abrams, Fran. *Freedom's Cause: Lives of the Suffragettes*. London: Profile, 2003.

Adickes, Sandra. "Sisters, Not Demons: The Influence of British Suffragists on the American Suffrage Movement." *Women's History Review* 11.4 (2002): 675–90.

Alberti, Johanna. *Beyond Suffrage: Feminists in War and Peace, 1914–28*. New York: St. Martin's, 1989.

Ardis, Ann. "Organizing Women: New Woman Writers, New Woman Readers, and Suffrage Feminism." *Victorian Women Writers and the Woman Question*. Ed. Nicola Diane Thompson. Cambridge: Cambridge UP, 1999.

Asquith, H.H. *The Licensing Bill of 1908: A Speech Delivered in the House of Commons on the Introduction and First Reading, February 27, 1908, Together with a Summary of the Bill*. London: Liberal Publication Department, 1908.

Atkinson, Diane. *Funny Girls: Cartooning For Equality*. London and New York: Penguin, 1997.

——. *The Purple, White & Green: Suffragettes in London, 1906–1914*. London: Museum of London, 1992.

——. *The Suffragettes in Pictures*. Stroud: Sutton, 1996.

——. *Votes for Women*. Cambridge: Cambridge UP, 1988.

Baker, T.F.T. *A History of the County of Middlesex*. Vol. 8: *Islington and Stoke Newington Parishes*. London: Victoria County History, 1985.

Bartley, Paula. *Emmeline Pankhurst*. London and New York: Routledge, 2003.

Beckett, Jane and Deborah Cherry, ed. *The Edwardian Era*. Oxford: Phaidon Press and Barbican Art Gallery, 1987.

Belinki, Karmela. *Women's Suffrage and Fiction in England 1905–1914: Facts and Visions*. Helsinki: U of Helsinki P, 1984.

Betterton, Rosemary. "Women Artists, Modernity and Suffrage Cultures in Britain and Germany 1890–1920." *Women Artists and Modernism.* Ed. Katy Deepwell. Manchester: Manchester UP, 1988.

Blavatsky, H.P. "An Open Letter to the Archbishop of Canterbury." Toronto: H.P.B. Library, 1887.

———. *Studies in Occultism.* Theosophical UP, n.d.

Blease, Walter Lyon. *The Emancipation of English Women.* London: Constable, 1910.

Brailsford, H.N. "The 'Conciliation' Bill: An Explanation and Defence." London: Garden City, 1910.

——— and Dr. Jessie Murray. "The Treatment of the Women's Deputations by the Metropolitan Police. Copy of Evidence Collected by Dr. Jessie Murray and Mr. H.N. Brailsford, and Forwarded to the Home Office by the Conciliation Committee for Women's Suffrage." London: Women's Press, 1911.

Bush, Julia. "British Women's Anti-Suffragism and the Forward Policy." *Women's History Review* 11.3 (2003): 431–54.

Butler, Josephine. *Social Purity.* London: Morgan and Scott, 1879.

Campaign Committee of the National League for Opposing Woman Suffrage. *The Anti-Suffrage Handbook of Facts, Statistics, and Quotations for the Use of Speakers.* London: National Press Agency, 1912.

Carlson, Susan. "Comic Militancy: The Politics of Suffrage Drama." *Women, Theatre and Performance: New Histories, New Historiographies.* Ed. Maggie B. Gale and Viv Gardner. Manchester: Manchester UP, 2000.

Churchill, Randolph S. *Winston S. Churchill, Companion* Vol. 2, Part 3 (1911–1914). London: Heinemann, 1969.

Colvill, Helen Hester. "Power, Direct and Indirect." *The Anti-Suffrage Review* 13 (January 1910): 4–5.

Crawford, Elizabeth. *The Women's Suffrage Movement: A Reference Guide, 1866–1928.* London: University College London P, 1999.

Delap, Lucy. "'Philosophical Vacuity and Political Ineptitude': The Freewoman's Critique of the Suffrage Movement." *Women's History Review* 11.4 (2002): 613–30.

Despard, C[harlotte]. "Theosophy and the Women's Movement." London: Theosophical Publishing Society, 1913.

DeVries, Jacqueline R. "Transforming the Pulpit: Preaching and Prophecy in the British Women's Suffrage Movement." *Women Preachers and Prophets through Two Millennia of Christianity.* Ed.

Beverly Mayne Kienzle and Pamela J. Walker. Berkeley: U of California P, 1998.

DiCenzo, Maria. "Gutter Politics: Women Newsies and the Suffrage Press." *Women's History Review* 12.1 (2003): 15–33.

Dixon, Joy. *The Divine Feminine: Theosophy and Feminism in England.* Baltimore and London: Johns Hopkins UP, 2001.

Dobbie, Beatrice Marion Willmott. *A Nest of Suffragettes in Somerset: Eagle House, Batheaston.* Batheaston: The Society, 1979.

Dow, Bonnie J. "Historical Narratives, Rhetorical Narratives, and Woman Suffrage Scholarship." *Rhetoric and Public Affairs* 2.2 (Summer 1999): 321–40.

Dunnill, Michael. *The Plato of Praed Street: The Life and Times of Almroth Wright.* London: Royal Society of Medicine, 2000.

Ellmann, Maud. *The Hunger Artists: Starving, Writing, and Imprisonment.* Cambridge, MA: Harvard UP, 1993.

Elston, M.A. "Anderson, Elizabeth Garrett (1836–1917)." *Oxford Dictionary of National Biography.* Ed. H.G.C. Matthew and Brian Harrison. Oxford UP, 2004.

Eustance, Claire, Joan Ryan, and Laura Ugolini, ed. *A Suffrage Reader: Charting Directions in British Suffrage History.* London, New York: Leicester UP, 2000.

Faraut, Martine. "Women Resisting the Vote: A Case of Anti-Feminism?" *Women's History Review* 12.4 (2003): 605–21.

Fawcett, Millicent Garrett. "Home and Politics. An Address Delivered at Toynbee Hall and Elsewhere." London: Women's Printing Society, n.d. 1-8.

———. "Men are Men and Women are Women." *The Englishwoman* 1.1 (February 1909). 17-29.

———. *What I Remember.* London: T. Fisher Unwin, 1925.

Fletcher, Ian Christopher, Laura E. Nym Mayhall, and Philippa Levine, ed. *Women's Suffrage in the British Empire: Citizenship, Nation, and Race.* London: Routledge, 2000.

Flint, Kate. *The Woman Reader, 1837–1914.* Oxford: Clarendon, 1993.

Fulford, Roger. *Votes for Women: The Story of a Struggle.* London: Faber, 1957. London: White Lion Publishers, 1976.

Garner, Les. *Stepping Stones to Women's Liberty: Feminist Ideas in the Women's Suffrage Movement, 1900–1918.* London: Heinemann Educational Books, 1984.

Goodman, Lizbeth and Ellen J. Gainor. "Gender and Drama, Text and Performance." *Literature and Gender*. Ed. Lizbeth Goodman. London: Routledge, 1996.

Green, Barbara. "Advertising Feminism: Ornamental Bodies/Docile Bodies and the Discourse of Suffrage." *Marketing Modernisms: Self-Promotion, Canonization, Rereading*. Ed. Kevin J.H. Dettmar and Stephen Watt. Ann Arbor: U of Michigan P, 1996.

———. "From Visible Flâneuse to Spectacular Suffragette? The Prison, the Street, and the Sites of Suffrage." *Discourse: Journal for Theoretical Studies in Media and Culture* 17.2 (Winter 1994–95): 67–97.

———. *Spectacular Confessions: Autobiography, Performative Activism, and the Sites of Suffrage, 1905–1938*. New York: St. Martin's, 1997.

Greenaway, John. *Drink and British Politics since 1830: A Study in Policy-Making*. Basingstoke: Palgrave Macmillan, 2003.

Grewal, Inderpal. *Home and Harem: Nation, Gender, Empire, and the Cultures of Travel*. Durham, NC: Duke UP, 1996.

Griest, Guinevere L. *Mudie's Circulating Library and the Victorian Novel*. Bloomington: Indiana UP, 1970.

Hamilton, Cicely. *Life Errant*. London: J.M. Dent and Sons, 1935.

Hannam, June. *Socialist Women: Britain, 1880s to 1920s*. London and New York: Routledge, 2002.

———, Mitzi Auchterlonie, and Katherine Holden. *International Encyclopedia of Women's Suffrage*. Santa Barbara, CA: ABC-CLIO, 2000.

Harrison, Brian Howard. *Separate Spheres: The Opposition to Woman Suffrage in Britain, 1867–1928*. London: Croom Helm, 1978.

Harrison, Patricia Greenwood. *Connecting Links: The British and American Woman Suffrage Movements, 1900–1914*. Westport: Greenwood, 2000.

Hartman, Kabi. "'What Made Me a Suffragette': The New Woman and the New(?) Conversion Narrative." *Women's History Review* 12.1 (2003): 35–50.

Heaton, William. *The Three Reforms of Parliament: A History, 1830–1885*. London: T. Fisher Unwin, 1885.

Heilmann, Ann, ed. *Words as Deeds: Debates and Narratives on Women's Suffrage*. *Women's History Review* (Special Issue) 12.1 (2003).

———, ed. *Words as Deeds: Literary and Historical Perspectives on Women's Suffrage. Women's History Review* (Special Issue) 11.4 (2002).

Hewitt, Martin and Robert Poole, ed. *The Diaries of Samuel Bamford.* New York: St. Martin's, 2000.

Higgins, Susan. "The Suffragettes in Fiction." *Hecate* 2.2 (1976): 31–47.

Holder, Jean and Katharine Milcoy. *Dare to be Free: How Women Won the Vote.* London: London Guildhall University, 1997.

Holton, Sandra Stanley. "'In Sorrowful Wrath': Suffrage Militancy and the Romantic Feminism of Emmeline Pankhurst." *British Feminism in the Twentieth Century.* Ed. H.L. Smith. Aldershot: E. Elgar, 1990. 7–24.

———. *Feminism and Democracy: Women's Suffrage and Reform Politics in Britain, 1900–1918.* Cambridge: Cambridge UP, 1986.

———. *Suffrage Days: Stories from the Women's Suffrage Movement.* London and New York: Routledge, 1996.

Hostettler, John and Brian P. Block. *Voting in Britain: A History of the Parliamentary Franchise.* Chichester: Barry Rose, 2001.

Housman, Laurence. "What is Womanly?" *Votes for Women* 31 December 1908.

———. *Articles of Faith in the Freedom of Women.* London: A.C. Fifield, 1910.

Howlett, Caroline J. "Writing on the Body? Representation and Resistance in British Suffragette Accounts of Forcible Feeding." *Bodies of Writing: Bodies in Performance.* Ed. Thomas Foster, Carol Siegel, and Ellen E. Berry. New York: New York UP, 1996.

Hume, Leslie Parker. *The National Union of Women's Suffrage Societies, 1897–1914.* New York: Garland, 1982.

Ingram, Angela and Daphne Patai. *Rediscovering Forgotten Radicals: British Women Writers, 1889–1939.* Chapel Hill and London: U of North Carolina P, 1993.

Joannou, Maroula and June Purvis, ed. *The Women's Suffrage Movement: New Feminist Perspectives.* Manchester and New York: Manchester UP; New York: St. Martin's, 1998.

John, Angela V. and Claire Eustance. *The Men's Share?: Masculinities, Male Support, and Women's Suffrage in Britain, 1890–1920.* London: Routledge, 1997.

Jordan, Ulrike and Wolfram Kaiser, ed. *Political Reform in Britain, 1886–1996: Themes, Ideas, Policies.* Bochum, Germany: N. Brockmeyer, 1997.

Jorgensen-Earp, Cheryl R. "'The Waning of the Light': The Forcible-Feeding of Jane Warton, Spinster." *Women's Studies in Communication* 22.2 (Fall 1999): 125–51.

——. *The Transfiguring Sword: The Just War of the Women's Social and Political Union.* Tuscaloosa: U of Alabama P, 1997.

——, ed. *Speeches and Trials of the Militant Suffragettes: The Women's Social and Political Union, 1903–1918.* Madison: Fairleigh Dickinson UP; London: Associated University Presses, 1999.

Kaplan, Joel H. and Sheila Stowell. *Theatre and Fashion: Oscar Wilde to the Suffragettes.* Cambridge: Cambridge UP, 1994.

Kean, Hilda. "Weaver, Gertrude Baillie (1855–1926)." *Oxford Dictionary of National Biography.* Ed. H.G.C. Matthew and Brian Harrison. Oxford: Oxford UP, 2004.

——. *Animal Rights: Political and Social Change in Britain since 1800.* London: Reaktion Books, 1998.

Kent, Susan Kingsley. *Sex and Suffrage in Britain, 1860–1914.* Princeton: Princeton UP, 1987.

Law, Cheryl. *Suffrage and Power: The Women's Movement, 1918–1928.* London and New York: I.B. Tauris; New York: St. Martin's, 1997.

Leigh, Mary. "Forcible Feeding: Statement by Mrs. Mary Leigh to Her Solicitor." *Votes for Women* 15 October 1909: 34.

Leneman, Leah. "The Awakened Instinct: Vegetarianism and the Women's Suffrage Movement in Britain." *Women's History Review* 6.2 (1997): 271–87.

——. *A Guid Cause: The Women's Suffrage Movement in Scotland.* Edinburgh: Mercat, 1995.

Lewis, Jane, ed. *Before the Vote Was Won: Arguments For and Against Women's Suffrage.* New York: Routledge and Kegan Paul, 1987.

Liddington, Jill and Jill Norris. *One Hand Tied Behind Us: The Rise of the Woman's Suffrage Movement.* London and New York: Rivers Oram, 2000.

Linklater, Andro. *An Unhusbanded Life: Charlotte Despard, Suffragette, Socialist and Sinn Feiner.* London: Hutchinson, 1980.

Lutyens, Lady Emily. *Candles in the Sun.* Philadelphia and New York: J.B. Lippincott, 1957.

Lyon, Janet. "Militant Discourse, Strange Bedfellows: Suffragettes and Vorticists Before the War." *Differences* 4.2 (1992): 100–32.

Lytton, Constance. "A Speech by Lady Constance Lytton." *Votes for Women* 4 February 1910: 292–93.

—— and Jane Warton, Spinster. *Prisons and Prisoners, Some Personal Experiences*. London: William Heinemann, 1914.

MacAuslan, Janna. "Protest Songs of the Suffrage Era." *Hot Wire: The Journal of Women's Music and Culture* 7.3 (September 1991): 12–13.

Mackenzie, Midge. *Shoulder to Shoulder: A Documentary*. New York: Knopf, 1975.

Marcus, Jane, ed. *Suffrage and the Pankhursts*. London and New York: Routledge and Kegan Paul, 1987.

Marlow, Joyce, ed. *Votes for Women: The Virago Book of Suffragettes*. London: Virago, 2000.

Mason, Francis M. "The Newer Eve: The Catholic Women's Suffrage Society in England, 1911–1923." *The Catholic Historical Review* 72 (October 1986): 620–38.

Matthew, H.C.G. "Gladstone, William Ewart (1809–1898)." *Oxford Dictionary of National Biography*. Ed. H.G.C. Matthew and Brian Harrison. Oxford: Oxford UP, 2004.

Mayhall, Laura E. Nym. "Defining Militancy: Radical Protest, the Constitutional Idiom, and Women's Suffrage in Britain, 1908–1909." *Journal of British Studies* 39.3 (July 2000): 340–71.

——. *The Militant Suffrage Movement: Citizenship and Resistance in Britain, 1860–1930*. Oxford and New York: Oxford UP, 2003.

Mill, John Stuart. *The Subjection of Women*. Philadelphia: J.B. Lippincott, 1869.

Miller, Jane Eldridge. *Rebel Women: Feminism, Modernism and the Edwardian Novel*. London: Virago, 1994.

Morgan, David. *Suffragists and Liberals: The Politics of Woman Suffrage in England*. Oxford: Blackwell, 1975.

Morley, Ann and Liz Stanley. *The Life and Death of Emily Wilding Davison: A Biographical Detective Story*. London: The Women's Press, 1988.

Morrell, Caroline. *"Black Friday": Violence against Women in the Suffragette Movement*. London: Women's Research and Resources Centre Publications, 1981.

Mulford, Wendy. "Socialist-Feminist Criticism: A Case Study: Suffrage and Literature, 1906–14." *Re-Reading English*. Ed. Peter Widdowson. London: Methuen, 1982.

Mulvey-Roberts, Marie. "Militancy, Masochism or Martyrdom: The Public and Private Prisons of Constance Lytton." *Votes for Women*. Ed. June Purvis and Sandra Stanley Holton. London and New York: Routledge, 2000.

Murray, Simone. "'Deeds and Words': The Women's Press and Politics of Print." *Women* 11.3 (Winter 2000): 197–222.

Nelson, Carolyn Christensen. *Literature of the Women's Suffrage Campaign in England*. Peterborough, ON: Broadview, 2004.

Nessheim, Ragnhild. *British Political Newspapers and Women's Suffrage, 1910–1918*. Oslo: U of Oslo P, 1991.

Norden, Martin. "'A Good Travesty upon the Suffragette Movement': Women's Suffrage Films as Genre." *Journal of Popular Film and Television* 13.3 (Winter 1986): 171–77.

Norquay, Glenda, ed. *Voices and Votes: A Literary Anthology of the Women's Suffrage Campaign*. Manchester: Manchester UP; New York: St. Martin's, 1995.

Pankhurst, Christabel. *Unshackled: The Story of How We Won the Vote*. London: Hutchinson, 1959.

Pankhurst, E. Sylvia. *The Suffragette: The History of the Women's Militant Suffrage Movement, 1905–1910*. New York: Sturgis and Walton, 1911.

———. *The Suffragette Movement: An Intimate Account of Persons and Ideals*. London and New York: Longmans, Green, 1931. New York: Kraus Reprint, 1971.

Pankhurst, Emmeline. "The Importance of the Vote." London: The Women's Press, 1908. *Speeches and Trials of the Militant Suffragettes*. Ed. Cheryl R. Jorgensen-Earp. Madison and London: Associated University Presses, 1999. 31–41.

———. *My Own Story*. London: Eveleigh Nash, 1914.

Park, Jihang. "The British Suffrage Activists of 1913: An Analysis." *Past and Present* 120 (August 1988): 147–62.

Park, Sowon. "The First Professional: The Women's Writer's Suffrage League." *Modern Language Quarterly: A Journal of Literary History* 58.2 (June 1997): 185–200.

———. "Suffrage Fiction: A Political Discourse in the Marketplace." *English Literature in Transition (1880–1920)* 39.4 (1996): 450–61.

Parliamentary Debates (Hansard). House of Commons Official Report. 27 September 1909. London: H.M.S.O., 1909. 923–25.

Peterson, Shirley. "The Politics of a Moral Crusade: Gertrude Colmore's *Suffragette Sally*." *Rediscovering Forgotten Radicals: British Women Writers, 1889–1939*. Ed. Angela Ingram and Daphne Patai. Chapel Hill, NC: U of North Carolina P, 1993. 101–17.

Pethick-Lawrence, Emmeline. "Welcome Christabel Pankhurst!" *Votes for Women* 17 December 1908: 200.

——. *My Part in a Changing World*. London: Victor Gollancz, 1938.

Phillips, Melanie. *The Ascent of Woman: A History of the Suffragette Movement and the Ideas Behind It*. London: Little, Brown, 2003.

Pugh, Martin. "The Limits of Liberalism: Liberals and Women's Suffrage, 1867–1914." *Citizenship and Community: Liberals, Radicals and Collective Identities in the British Isles, 1865–1931*. Ed. Eugenio F. Biagini. New York: Cambridge UP, 1996. 45–65.

——. *The March of the Women: A Revisionist Analysis of the Campaign for Women's Suffrage, 1866–1914*. Oxford: Oxford UP, 2000.

——. *The Pankhursts*. London: Allen Lane, Penguin, 2001.

——. *Women's Suffrage in Britain, 1867–1928*. London: Historical Association, 1980.

Purvis, June. "Daily Life in the WSPU." *Votes for Women*. Ed. June Purvis and Sandra Stanley Holton. London and New York: Routledge, 2000.

——. "'Deeds, Not Words': The Daily Lives of Militant Suffragettes in Edwardian Britain." *Women's Studies International Forum* 18.2 (1995): 91–101.

——. "Emmeline Pankhurst: A Biographical Interpretation." *Women's History Review* 12.1 (2003): 63–102.

——. *Emmeline Pankhurst: A Biography*. London and New York: Routledge, 2002.

——. "A 'Pair of Infernal Queens'? A Reassessment of the Dominant Representations of Emmeline and Christabel Pankhurst, First Wave Feminists in Edwardian Britain." *Women's History Review* 5.2 (1996): 259–80.

——. "The Prison Experiences of the Suffragettes in Edwardian Britain." *Women's History Review* 4.1 (1995): 103–33.

——, ed. *Women's History: Britain, 1850–1945*. London: University College London Press, 1995.

Purvis, June and Sandra Stanley Holton, ed. *Votes for Women*. London and New York: Routledge, 2000.

Raeburn, Antonia. *The Militant Suffragettes*. Newton Abbot: Victorian Book Club, 1974.

———. *The Suffragette View*. New York: St. Martin's, 1976.

Reid, Robert. *The Peterloo Massacre*. London: Heinemann, 1989.

Rendell, Jane, ed. *Equal or Different: Women's Politics, 1800–1914*. Oxford: Basil Blackwell, 1987.

Roberts, Marie and Mizuta Tamae, ed. *The Disenfranchised: The Fight for the Suffrage*. London: Routledge/Thoemmes Press, 1993.

———. *The Exploited: Women and Work*. London: Routledge/Thoemmes Press, 1993.

———. *The Militants: Suffragette Activism*. London: Routledge/Thoemmes Press, 1994.

Rock, Paul. *Reconstructing a Women's Prison: The Holloway Redevelopment Project 1968–88*. Oxford: Clarendon, 1996.

Rolley, Katrina. "Fashion, Femininity and the Fight for the Vote." *Art History* 13.1 (1990): 47–71.

Ronning, Anne Holden. *Hidden and Visible Suffrage*. Berne: Peter Lang, 1995.

Rosen, Andrew. *Rise Up Women! The Militant Campaign of the Women's Social and Political Union 1903–1914*. London: Routledge and Kegan Paul, 1974.

Rover, Constance. *Suffrage and Party Politics in Britain, 1866–1914*. London: Routledge and Kegan Paul, 1967.

———. *Women's Suffrage and Party Politics in Britain, 1866–1914*. London: Routledge and Kegan Paul; Toronto: U of Toronto P, 1967.

Rubinstein, David. *Before the Suffragettes: Women's Emancipation in the 1890s*. Brighton, Sussex: Harvester, 1986.

Searle, G.R. *The Liberal Party: Triumph and Disintegration, 1886–1929*. Houndmills, Basingstoke: Palgrave, 2001.

Sleight, John. *One-way Ticket to Epsom: A Journalist's Enquiry into the Heroic Story of Emily Wilding Davison*. Morpeth: Bridge Studios, 1988.

Smith, Angela K. "'That Silly Suffrage': The Paradox of World War I." *Nineteenth-Century Feminisms* 3 (Fall–Winter 2000): 88–104.

Smith, Harold L., ed. *British Feminism in the Twentieth Century*. Amherst: U of Massachusetts P, 1990.

———. *The British Women's Suffrage Campaign, 1866–1928*. London and New York: Longman, 1998.

Snellgrove, Laurence Ernest. *Suffragettes and Votes for Women*. London: Longmans, 1964.

Stern, Katherine. "The War of the Sexes in British Fantasy Literature of the Suffragette Era." *Critical Matrix* 3 (Spring 1987): 78–109.

Stowell, Sheila. "Suffrage Critics and Political Action: A Feminist Agenda." *The Edwardian Theatre: Essays on Performance and the Stage*. Ed. Michael Booth and Joel H. Kaplan. Cambridge: Cambridge UP, 1996.

Strachey, Ray. *The Cause: A Short History of the Women's Movement in Great Britain*. London: Virago, 1978.

Swanwick, H[elena] M. "The Hope and the Meaning." *The Common Cause* 1.1 (15 August 1909): 3.

———. *I Have Been Young*. London: Victor Gollancz, 1935.

Sypher, Eileen. *Wisps of Violence: Producing Public and Private Politics in the Turn-of-the-Century British Novel*. London and New York: Verso, 1993.

Thane, Patricia. "What Difference Did the Vote Make? Women in Public and Private Life in Britain since 1918." *Historical Research* 76 (May 2003): 268–85.

Thesing, William B. "Mrs. Humphry Ward's Anti-Suffrage Campaign: From Polemics to Art." *Turn-of-the-Century Women* 1.1 (Summer 1984): 22–35.

Thomas, Sue. "Scenes in the Writing of 'Constance Lytton and Jane Warton, Spinster': Contextualising a Cross-Class Dresser." *Women's History Review* 12.1 (2003): 51–71.

Thompson, Nicola Diane, ed. *Victorian Women Writers and the Woman Question*. Cambridge: Cambridge UP, 1999.

Tickner, Lisa. *The Spectacle of Women: Imagery of the Suffrage Campaign, 1907–1914*. Chicago: U of Chicago P, 1988.

Van Wingerden, Sophia A. *The Women's Suffrage Movement in Britain, 1866–1928*. New York: St. Martin's, 1999.

Vicinus, Martha. *Independent Women: Work and Community for Single Women: 1850–1920*. London: Virago, 1985.

Vickery, Amanda, ed. *Women, Privilege and Power: British Politics, 1750 to the Present*. Stanford, CA: Stanford UP, 2001.

Walker, Linda. *The Women's Movement in Britain, 1790–1945*. London and New York: Routledge, 1999.

Walkowitz, Judith R. "The Indian Woman, the Flower Girl, and the Jew: Photojournalism in Edwardian London." *Victorian Studies* 42.1: 3–47.

Warboys, Michael. "Wright, Sir Almroth Edward (1861–1947)." *Oxford Dictionary of National Biography*. Ed. H.G.C. Matthew and Brian Harrison. Oxford: Oxford UP, 2004.

Ward, Mary Augusta. "Editorial." *The Anti-Suffrage Review* 1 (December 1908): 1.

Wilson, Trevor, ed. *The Political Diaries of C.P. Scott, 1911–1928*. London: Collins, 1970.

Wright, Sir Almroth E., MD, FRS. "Suffrage Fallacies." *The Times* 28 March 1912: 7–8. Reprinted as "Letter on Militant Hysteria." *The Unexpurgated Case against Woman Suffrage*. London: Constable and Company, 1913. 77–86.

Yeo, Eileen Janes. "Social Motherhood and the Sexual Communion of Labour in British Social Science, 1850–1950." *Women's History Review* 1.1 (1992): 63–87.